Insider Just

A Marc Kadella Legal Mystery

by

Dennis L. Carstens

Previous Marc Kadella Legal Mysteries

The Key to Justice

Desperate Justice

Media Justice

Certain Justice

Personal Justice

Delayed Justice

Political Justice

Exquisite Justice

ONE

"Do we have to meet with him again?" Dane Cannon asked the two people seated with him at the conference room table.

Dane Cannon was the current CEO of Cannon Brothers Toys. Cannon Brothers was a family owned and operated toy business located a few miles Northwest of Minneapolis in Glover, a suburb. Dane's younger brother, Greg was the company COO. Cannon Brothers was founded by their grandfather, Everett Cannon in 1938. Over the years it had grown to a mid-size, privately owned company with revenue of approximately two hundred million dollars. As a private company, of course, earnings did not have to be reported publicly. Dane and Greg were the third-generation top management of the business.

"Yeah, we do," replied Greg, Dane's forty-four-year-old brother. "He's being insistent."

"What now?" asked Marissa Duggins. Marissa was the executive vice-president. She was also the first high-level corporate officer to come from outside the family.

Over the years, as the number of family members had grown, their interest in running the business dropped in direct proportion to their all-around slothfulness. All of the family members, more than twenty of them now, owned a piece of the company. Profitability, brought on by a reputation for quality toys, kept all of them in a very comfortable lifestyle. Their uninterested attitude toward where and how the money came from suited Dane and Greg just fine. The less interference they had from their kinsmen, the better.

Marissa Duggins, at fifty, a couple of years older than Dane, was brought in ten years ago. She was an accounting wiz and a manager with steel balls and a killer attitude. Plus, although an attractive woman, she was a lesbian in a long-term relationship. This fact kept her relationship with the brothers friendly but professional.

"I don't know," Greg answered Marissa. "Same thing as far as I know."

There was a knock on the door, a man opened it and walked in. His name was Irving Haraldson and he was the chief engineer of the company. Sixty-two years old, mostly bald with scattered, disheveled tufts of gray hair on his head. Irving was Hollywood's idea of a geeky, engineer, tech guy. No coat, a short-sleeve white shirt, polyester blue tie with white stripes and the ever-present plastic pen holder in his shirt pocket.

1

"Hello, Irv," Dane pleasantly said. "Come in and tell us what's on your mind."

Irving went around the conference room table to sit opposite the three executives. Greg and Marissa both stood up, reached across the table and shook hands with him. When they were all seated, Irving opened a manila folder he had placed on the table. In it was a single copy of a multi-page document.

"Sorry," Irving began. "I thought I was meeting with just you," he said looking at Dane. "I didn't bring extra copies of this memo I wrote on the problems with the skateboard."

"What problems?" Dane asked as he took the document from Irving's outstretched hand.

"Well, there are a couple of things," Irving said.

Marissa and Greg were both leaning forward, hands folded, elbows on the table while Dane scanned through the memo. The three of them knew what was coming. It was something their chief engineer had complained about, cryptically, for months.

Cannon Brothers Toys was on the verge of marketing a new product. It was a motorized skateboard designed for a broader, younger market. Most motorized skateboards were marketed to older users, typically, those sixteen and older. Cannon was going to claim that they had designed a much safer version, one that included a speed regulator and an automated braking system. With the usual warnings about wearing safety equipment, Cannon was going to claim their product was safe for users as young as ten years old. With adult supervision, of course.

"Go on," Dane told the older man while placing the memo on the table.

"We've been through this," Irving said looking at Dane. "It is the lithium batteries. We need to replace every one of them with batteries from a more reputable source."

"Wait, wait, hold on," Greg interjected. "We have a half million of these things ready to go. Now you come to us and..."

"Let him finish," Marissa calmly said placing her left hand on Greg's right arm.

"This Chinese manufacturer is not reputable," Irving continued. "We're still getting a failure rate that is too high. The batteries overheat and damage the speed regulator and braking system. Some even explode and start on fire!" The old man was almost yelling and even slapped the table when he said this.

"How many?" Marissa quietly asked.

"It's between one and two percent," Irving answered her.

"I thought we had this fixed?" Dane asked.

2

"Well, okay, we seem to have it down to a little less than one percent," Irving admitted. "But," he quickly continued when he saw Greg start to say something, "we're talking about children's lives here. Kids as young as nine and ten could get seriously injured, even killed."

"Come on, Irv," Greg said. "Killed? Now you're overreacting."

"If the speed regulator and brakes fail while they're going downhill…"

"Their parents have a responsibility," Greg started to protest.

"You're right, Irving," Marissa said interrupting and stopping Greg. "We need to rethink this. How many copies of this memo do you have?"

"That's the only one I printed off from my computer," Irving said.

"Okay," Dane said taking charge. "Irv keep this to yourself for now. Right now, nothing's been done. I think you're right. We will have to pull the batteries on all of them and replace them with more reliable ones."

"Thank God," Irving said, obviously relieved.

"We don't need dead kids on our conscience," Marissa added with a warm smile.

Dane stood up and said, "Thanks, Irv, you may have saved us from a terrible mistake."

Irving, Greg, and Marissa also stood, and Dane reached across the table to shake Irving's hand. Marissa went around the table, took Irving's arm and smiling, led him to the door.

"Keep this to yourself for now," Marissa said. "Tell no one. Your wife, kids, employees. Give us a couple of days to talk to purchasing and manufacturing and figure out how we can fix this. Okay?"

"Yes, sure, that's fine," the engineer said. "I can't tell you how relieved I am. I thought you'd fight me on this."

"Irv, Greg and I have kids, too," Dane said.

"We're really not monsters," Marissa said still smiling. "In fact, take the rest of the week off. You've earned it. We'll get together on Monday or Tuesday with an action plan."

As soon as he was sure Irving was gone, Dane took the fourteen-page memo and angrily flung it at the exterior window. His fists were balled up and pressed to his hips. Dane looked at the ceiling and noisily inhaled.

"Sonofabitch!" Dane angrily let loose.

By now Marissa and Greg were again seated at the table while Dane vented his frustration. He stood next to his chair, deeply inhaling and noisily exhaling until he regained his composure. When he did, he returned to his seat and looked at the other two.

3

"Now what?" Dane asked.

"One percent is nothing," Greg said. "Insurance will cover the losses."

"It would cost us millions to replace all the batteries and fix this," Marissa said. "Not to mention the delay. The PR campaign is about to swing into overdrive. We have every industry publication, website, and skateboard user source ready to sing our praises."

"They should be, we've paid them enough," Greg added.

Dane sat silently thinking over their situation for a minute. He then said, "Obviously we have to go forward. Everything is set, and the timing is locked in."

By this point, while Dane was quietly thinking, Greg had retrieved the memo and placed it back on the table. He returned to his seat before speaking.

"What do we do about this? How do we keep this quiet?"

"Less than one percent. We can claim that was a fluke," Marissa said.

"Or the over-cautious claim of the engineering department. And it is the fault of the Chinese manufacturer," Greg said.

"The lawsuits would come down on us," Dane said. "Try suing a Chinese manufacturer for a products liability claim. It would take ten years. Our own State Department would try to stop you. And even if you did get at them, the Chinese government would shut down the company and reopen it the next day under a different name."

"You need to talk to Cal," Marissa said. She was referring to Calvin Simpson, an investment advisor, venture capitalist, speculator and corporate raider. It was through Cal that Cannon Brothers had obtained a very favorable loan to develop the skateboard.

The motorized skateboard, to be released as four separate models simultaneously, was going to blow its competition away. It was being priced from a low of $499.00 to the supermodel at $999.00. Because it was going to be promoted as safer than any other, it would take over the market. Worldwide estimates projected sales in the first two years exceeding twenty million. Coupled with the company going public with an IPO a month after the product's release, the Cannon family was looking to get rich, then walk away. Calvin Simpson and his friends were also looking to pick up quite a few bucks themselves. Of course, this was all illegal insider-trading. But Cal Simpson had a lot of friends in Washington and New York who were along for the ride. Cal Simpson had become rich the old-fashioned way; by being a well-connected crook.

"I'll talk to Cal. He'll have some ideas about how to handle this," Dane said lightly waving a hand toward the memo. "I'm sure he's run into these kinds of problems before."

TWO

The thirty-five-foot Chris Craft cabin cruiser moved slowly along Lake Minnetonka. The luxury gas-guzzler was barely leaving a wake it was moving so slowly. The two bikini-clad teenagers sunning themselves on the foredeck raised their heads and looked shoreward. A lone man was sitting on shore in a patio chair watching the big boat cruise past. The girls rose to their knees and waved to him as their pilot/father gave him a quick horn salute.

Cal Simpson, enjoying the sight of the girls, raised his drink with his right hand and waved with his left. The girl's mother stepped out on deck also in a bikini, filling it better than the daughters. *Minnesota blondes*, he thought and smiled. Cal continued thinking, *Minnesota, filled with Germans and Scandinavians, grows them like a cash crop.*

The boat passed out of sight, and Cal continued to enjoy the day. He sipped his glass of ice and Pappy Van Winkle's. Real men drink bourbon, the British drink scotch, Cal was fond of saying. He puffed on his Monte Cristo several times to get it going again while watching a two-masted sailboat gliding across the big lake.

Calvin Simpson was born fifty-five years ago in Boston as Martin Kelly, the son of a strong-arm thug who was shot and killed by the police when Cal was four. He grew up a tough, gang kid, a member of an Irish teenage gang loosely affiliated with Whitey Bulger's Winter Hill gang. Mostly they were tough kids who were Winter Hill wannabees. Martin/Cal was one of the smart ones. By the time he was in his late teens he had learned that the big criminal bucks were made through sales and politics, especially if you combined the two. Sales, of course, being a con game of some kind; politics being old-fashioned, corrupt, local politics.

Cal's first real bite at the apple came when he was not even out of his teens. With a change of identity, the first of several, he went to work for a local brokerage firm. It was a penny stocks firm owned and operated by the brother of a local politician. It was the politician/brother who got Cal the job. Cal and his gang buddies had done an excellent job of making sure the city council member's significant constituency was not disenfranchised. With a little cash—euphemistically called "walking around money"—to grease the wheels, homeless people, drunks, junkies, and other assorted derelicts and of course, dead people, were persuaded to vote properly by Cal and his friends.

The councilman saw in Cal an intelligence being wasted on the streets. The brokerage job followed soon after. Within two years, the smooth-talking Cal was the top salesman/con man in the place.

6

Over the next forty years, Cal Simpson had lied, cheated, conned and bribed his way to become almost elitist rich. Along the way, he had incurred three felony convictions all of which were eventually wiped off of the books. A name change, a satchel of cash to the right local pols, a little help from old neighborhood pal and presto, Cal would be back in business barely missing a beat.

Cal had also acquired and discarded three wives but had only one child, a daughter, Samantha, now age twenty-eight. Despite Cal being a totally jaded narcissist, Samantha was the apple of his eye. There was nothing he would not do for her. That should have made her a spoiled, rotten brat but Samantha was actually the sensible rock in Cal's life. She was under no illusions about her father and in fact, Samantha was a shrewd corporate lawyer with only one client: Daddy.

Cal had moved to Minnesota four years ago after Samantha graduated from Yale Law School. At the time he needed to get away from greedy ex-wives and the East Coast. In Minnesota he was treated by most as a rich, successful investor and venture capitalist.

"Hi, Dad," he heard Samantha's voice a few feet behind him.

"Hello, sweetheart," he replied as she bent down and kissed his cheek.

Cal watched her as she pulled up a chair to join him. As usual, he was forever grateful she obtained her mother's physical genes. A beautiful brunette with Cal's brains would have opened a lot of doors for her if she needed it.

Samantha slid her chair across the artificial grass covering the concrete, lakeside patio. She sat down at the table between them, picked up her dad's drink and swallowed half of what was in the glass.

"What time is the guy from the toy company stopping by?" she asked.

Cal looked at his Rolex and said, "He should be here in about fifteen minutes, four o'clock."

"Do you want me to stick around?" she asked.

"No," Cal emphatically replied.

The tone that he used was a clear indication that Cal did not want Samantha to hear what they had to talk about. The two of them had an understanding between them. As long as Samantha was not privy to any conversations that may involve less than legal activities, she was shielded by attorney-client privilege. This privilege was not available when a third-party was present. It would also allow her to advise him as his lawyer.

Of course, Samantha knew exactly what the problem was with the toy company. The two of them had discussed it several times. But without Samantha being present at this meeting she could legally shield

7

herself by claiming privilege and deny any knowledge of the problem. Or the solution.

At precisely 4:00 P.M. one of the household personnel interrupted the father and daughter. With her was Dane Cannon, Cal's four o'clock appointment.

Both Cal and Samantha stood to greet Dane. The six-foot-four Cal always seemed to be about six-foot-ten to the five-eleven Dane. Seeing Samantha there took some of the edge off of the intimidation Dane always felt from Cal.

"Hello, Dane," Samantha pleasantly said. She shook his hand and added, "I'll leave you two to discuss whatever it is you came for."

"You're not staying?" an obviously disappointed Dane Cannon replied. Despite his marital status, Dane Cannon had a barely disguised thing for the beautiful Samantha Simpson.

"No," she replied. "Sorry, but I have to go. Dad," she continued looking at Cal, "I'll talk to you later."

When Samantha was gone, Dane politely tried to decline a drink offered by Cal. Ignoring him, Cal refilled his own glass from the ice bucket and bottle on the table. He then filled a second glass for his guest. Cal handed it to Dane, raised his glass in a silent toast and the two men clicked glasses together and swallowed. Unknown to Dane, Cal always measured a man, at least in part, by how well he handled his bourbon. So far, Dane Cannon passed each test.

"Isn't that the Corwin Mansion a couple places down the road?" Dane asked referring to the estate of one of Minnesota's leading families.

"Yeah, it is," Cal grumbled.

"Have you met her?" Dane asked referring to Vivian Corwin Donahue.

"Couple times. Political events. She strikes me as a stuck up, phony bitch. And why shouldn't she be? She earned her money the old-fashioned way. She inherited it. Why?" Cal said.

"Um, ah, just wondering," Dane said wanting to get off the subject after Cal's display of antipathy.

"Okay," Cal said beginning the discussion, "Tell me what's on your mind."

A few minutes later, Dane had told Cal everything about the problem with the skateboard project.

"A less than one percent failure rate," Cal said, a statement not a question. "And this engineer believes we need to scrap the whole thing and start over?"

"Pretty much," Dane replied, taking another sip of the whiskey.

"What do you think? Have you calculated the cost?"

"Of replacing all of the batteries on the boards we have produced? At least seven million," Dane said.

"What about injuries and lawsuits? It seems to me one percent isn't worth the trouble and expense. Insurance will cover the cost of lawsuits," Cal said.

"Yes," Dane agreed, nodding his head. "But that's not the worst of it. Doing it would throw everything off schedule. The product release, the PR campaign, the IPO, all of it."

"The cost, individually, will be many multiples of seven million. If word gets out before the PR campaign that there's a problem..."

"Everything will swirl down the toilet," Dane said.

"How many copies of this memo are there?" Cal asked.

"Just the one," Dane replied.

"Are you sure?"

"Not positively, no. But I know Irving. If he says he only made one, then I believe him. This guy is such a tech-geek-nonhuman I don't think he's capable of deception," Dane said.

"He's off work for a few days?"

"Until Monday," Dane replied.

"Okay," Cal said after taking twenty or so seconds to think it over. He set his drink on the table and looked squarely at Dane. "Do nothing until Monday. Give me a few days to think about this. But get in the office early and grab this guy's computer first thing tomorrow morning."

Cal went to the trouble of walking Dane through the house to his car. While doing this, he was quite affable and treated Dane as if he were a younger brother. While Dane was driving off, Cal stood silently watching him go. Having been made aware that there might be battery problems before and the engineer would make a stink about them, Cal Simpson had already made plans on how to solve it. Five minutes after Dane had left, Cal made a discreet phone call on a burner phone he had. A cryptic twenty-second conversation with the man who answered the call set the solution in motion.

Irving Haraldson, Cannon Toys' chief engineer, and project whistle-blower had an itch that needed to be scratched. He had been married to the same woman, Catherine, for forty years. Four now grown children had come along and the two of them had built a good life together. Irving was an excellent engineer and made a good living. Catherine had raised the three girls and one son to be solid, productive adults.

9

But Irving had this itch he could not deny. Catherine knew what it was but refused to admit it. By maintaining that attitude, she could pretend, or at least tell herself, it did not exist. Irving's itch was a sexual need for other men. Irving had successfully suppressed it for the first fifty-plus years of his life. Then, on a business trip to a seminar in Chicago, he had a couple of drinks too many and gave in to his yearnings. Since then, for the past ten years or so, he had stopped bothering to pretend they were not real.

The Saturday evening following his meeting with his bosses, Irving was in downtown Minneapolis. Catherine, as usual, had gone to bed early allowing Irving to head out to his favorite hookup bar for middle age men. Even socially awkward men like Irving had little trouble finding a friend for the evening at Pauline's on Fourth.

Irving squeezed onto a bar stool between two men at the bar and waited for the bartender to finish with a customer. The place was crowded for a Saturday night and it took all of ten minutes for Irving to get a ten-dollar glass of bad, trendy, specialty beer that, like almost all of them, tasted like it was strained through someone's gym socks. A minute later the two men to his right moved off. The empty bar stool was quickly filled with a man who looked to be close to Irving's age. Within a few minutes Irving and his new friend, Bud, had made the connection.

"Um, I'm, ah, kind of new to this," Bud claimed. "You, ah, want to get out of here?"

"Sure," Irving replied, the tightness in his lower abdomen increasing. "I know a secluded place we can go. It's down by the river," Irving added thinking of a spot he had been to before.

When they got outside, Irving asked Bud if he was going to tell him his real name. Bud giggled and said maybe later. Five minutes later they were parked among the trees along a street leading down to the Mississippi. Before Irving could get out of his car, Bud, who had parked behind him, was approaching the driver's door where Irving waited.

Irving anxiously pushed the button to open his window. He looked up expecting to see Bud smiling but instead was staring directly into the barrel of a silenced handgun. Three seconds later Bud was calmly walking back to his car. He had popped off three quick shots from a .22 caliber revolver into Irving's head. The hollow point bullets had shredded Irving's brain matter and killed him almost instantly.

The sound suppressor attached to the small caliber pistol had done its job well. Anyone on the street, a hundred yards through the trees, would be hard-pressed to hear the shots. Because it was a revolver, there was no expenditure of gasses which also kept the noise down and no shell casings to recover.

Within fifteen minutes, the disguise and gloves Bud wore along with the gun were in a small burlap bag. He had tossed the bag and its contents into the river and made the call to Cal Simpson.

THREE

Air Force Major General Alex Connors was in a surly mood. Followed by two other senior Air Force officers, General Connors was leaving a briefing room at Nellis Air Force base in Nevada. The three men had just finished conferring with Lt. Colonel Mike Nicoletti, a veteran Air Force test pilot.

The car to take the three officers to observe another test flight was waiting for them. Holding the door was Tech Sergeant Gabriela Torres. She sharply saluted as the three men entered the back seat barely receiving an acknowledgment from any of them. As Sgt. Torres pulled away from the building for the five-mile drive she pressed the button to put the privacy window up so her passengers could talk. Along with General Connors was one-star Brigadier General Stanley Coles and Colonel Gary Kopp.

"The aircraft is coming along. It should be in production in about six months," General Cole said.

"Yeah, another technological wonder that we didn't ask for, don't need and don't want," General Connors grumbled. "What do you think, Gary?" he asked the colonel sitting to his left in the middle of the three men.

"I think I'm a good soldier, sir. I've been given my orders, and I'll do what I'm told," the man said suppressing a grin.

These officers were well known to each other. They were senior members of the Air Force procurement department within the Pentagon assigned to oversee the development of a new aircraft. The aircraft was designated the A-15 Tiger Hawk, and it was being produced to replace the A-10 Thunderbolt, affectionately nicknamed the Warthog.

The Warthog is a close air support aircraft whose primary mission is attacking ground targets, especially enemy tanks. It had been in service since the mid-1970's and had been an enormously effective aircraft. It is a tank killer that can fly at altitudes as low as one hundred feet with armaments, bombs, missiles and machine gun fire that can devastate enemy soldiers in close proximity to U.S. forces.

Members of Congress, in their never-ending quest for re-election, decided the A-10 should be replaced. The A-15, a faster, lighter and far more expensive aircraft was forced on the Air Force. Despite the insistence of the Pentagon that the A-10 was capable of meeting the military's mission requirements for at least another twenty years, Congress decided they knew best, and the A-15 project was born.

"Jobs, Alex," General Coles reminded him. "This isn't about the military's mission. It's a jobs program for eight states, a dozen congressional districts and multiple billions of dollars of re-election pork."

"I know," Connors replied. "It's just aggravating. We're short on spare parts for the aircraft we have, and they're throwing ten to fifteen billion dollars at this."

"But it's always the military who is wasting the taxpayer's money," Coles sarcastically said referring to the media and their constant stories about Pentagon waste.

"And the Army is short on bullets," Colonel Kopp interjected. "Although, it is an exceptional aircraft," he added.

"We'll see," Connors grumbled. "Morton Aviation is not my first choice to build anything."

Sgt. Torres stopped near the door to the eight-story observation tower. She held her salute as the three men exited the car. The July Nevada heat was over one hundred degrees and the officers hurried to get into the air-conditioned building.

Lt. Colonel Mike Nicoletti was a graduate of the Air Force Academy and a twenty-year veteran pilot. He had flown the A-10 in combat in both Afghanistan and Iraq and was one of its most ardent supporters. Married with three children, the oldest heading for high school in the fall, Mike had been a test pilot for two years working primarily on the A-15 program. It was an excellent aircraft, but in his opinion, was only a minimal improvement over his beloved Warthog. Faster because of the thinner skin from new, stronger, bullet resistant covering helped keep the weight down. Other than that, Mike could find no significant advantage to be gained for the Air Force's mission.

Today would be his fourth test flight. The first three went smoothly enough. The one today would be the first time he would go down to one hundred feet to simulate an attack run. He carried no armament on this flight. The purpose was to check out the aircraft at the slower speed and lower altitude. Something in the back of Mike's mind nagged at him a bit. A feeling he could not shake that all was not quite right.

The A-15, like its predecessor the A-10, was a fixed-wing, twin-engine aircraft with only the pilot in the cockpit. Before today's flight Mike had meticulously gone over the pre-flight checklist and found everything in order. Today's flight was scheduled to last two hours, and he was to put the bird through its most rigorous, most thorough test flight so far.

Following a smooth takeoff, he quickly rose to a cruising altitude of fifteen thousand feet. Mike leveled off, all the while talking to the ground control and engineers at Nellis, then punched the G.E. engines to their maximum. The bird responded beautifully. It jumped forward, smoother, quicker and with more ease than the A-10 ever did. *But*, Mike thought, *not necessarily an advantage for a close air support aircraft.*

For the next hour, he put it through its high-altitude paces and was very impressed. Especially with the speed and turning maneuverability.

Lt. Colonel Nicoletti was also a veteran of the Air Force fighter planes and, while the A-15 was not in that class, it was a very smooth, responsive aircraft. However, the Tiger Hawk was not a fighter plane. The real test would come during the second hour of the flight. That was when he would put it through its paces in a simulated ground attack.

Directly in front of the observation tower where the brass and Morton Aviation engineers were watching was a mock target range. No firing would be done today, but Mike was scheduled to make low-altitude runs at various speeds over the targets. Having logged over one hundred actual combat sorties in the A-10, flying over dummy targets should be about as worrisome as driving a car to the grocery store.

As he wheeled the bird around to make his first run from West to East, the nagging little tick in the back of his head came back. Being a professional with thousands of hours of flight time logged, Mike Nicoletti knew better than to ignore it. The aircraft was running smooth-as-silk giving him no indication that anything was wrong. But the little tick was still there. He lined up for the runway from three miles out, dropped the nose and went into a simulated attack.

The first run over the target was at a standard 300 mph at an altitude of 100 feet. Nicoletti went through the motions of firing the 30mm nose gun, blew past the observation tower and target area and quickly rose to cruising altitude. The bird had handled the run flawlessly. If anything, it was the smoothest attack run Mike had ever been through.

The next two runs, one at 400 mph at 200 feet and the last at 350 mph at barely fifty feet off the deck went almost as well. The only glitch, if you could even call it that, was a tiny, almost imperceptible shudder at the lowest altitude. By the time he was back at cruising altitude, Mike Nicoletti was falling in love. Although even he admitted the Air Force did not need to replace the A-10, if Congress was going to force them to do it, this was going to be an outstanding aircraft to replace it with.

While Mike Nicoletti flew back to land the A-15, after relaying to the tower how smoothly the test went, there was a minor celebration among the observers. Mostly among the aircraft's engineers and executives and handshakes from the Air Force brass. Despite the earlier, negative grumblings from the three officers, there was a real sense of relief among them. Their careers were on the line, especially General

Connors, the military's head of the project. If he wanted that third star, as he certainly did, this was the aircraft that would get it for him.

Everyone in the tower hurried down to get to the briefing. By the time Nicoletti had put the A-15 to bed, a small crowd was waiting for him. They were in the same briefing room he had met General Connors in before the flight. Included with the Morton Aviation executives was a very fetching woman in her late-thirties. Her name was Anna Evans and she was from the PR firm hired by Morton Aviation to promote their latest product.

A little over an hour after it started, the pilot debriefing and its Q & A were winding down. Anna went up to Nicoletti and had him read a press release she was preparing.

Nicoletti, sitting on a folding table facing the crowd took a couple of minutes to read it over. When he finished it, he handed it back to Anna.

"Is that a fair statement, Colonel?" Anna asked.

"Yes, a little more hyperbole than I would use, but accurate," he answered wearing a hotshot pilot's smile for a pretty woman.

"You don't mind if I quote you? I won't use your name," she asked ignoring the 'come on' look she was getting.

"No, not at all," he replied.

"Good, thanks," Anna said then turned to show what she had prepared to the Morton execs.

The next edition of *Aviation Week* featured a cover photo of the A-15. Inside was a glowing article about the aircraft and the coup that Morton Aviation had pulled off in its development. The Air Force, or so the magazine article claimed, was going to order seven hundred and fifty of them to be delivered over the next five years. At the cost of twenty-six million each, Morton Aviation, after an absence of more than a decade, was back in the military hardware business.

Over the next two weeks, Morton Aviation stock took off. It rose over thirty–eight percent before dropping a bit and leveling off at seventy-eight dollars per share.

FOUR

Lynn McDaniel was not sure whether to be angry, scared or both. Lynn had spent the entire day—it was now after 9:00 P.M.—in one of the firm's conference rooms. She was a senior associate with Everson, Reed, a one-hundred lawyer firm headquartered in downtown Minneapolis. She had spent the day poring over discovery documents. Even with two full-time junior associates to assist her, it was a slow and tedious process. In this room alone, there were over fifty boxes to go through and at least that many more to come.

Lynn had sent her two assistants home ten minutes ago. They had billed twelve hours each today anyway. She was seated in the middle of the long rectangle conference room table. In front of her was a document she had found and was now staring at, regretting that her fingerprints were on it. The boxes of documents they were going over were corporate records from Cannon Brothers Toys. Cannon Brothers was the client and Everson, Reed was defending the company in a class-action lawsuit. The document Lynn was staring at was pure poison to their client's case.

She had a document box on the table next to her, the one in which she had found the memo she did not want to read. Lynn stood up, placed the box on top of the memo and then exited the conference room. She used her key to lock the door and then went to her office. Lynn had a phone call to make and wanted to use her personal phone, so the firm would not have a record of it. The firm made a record of everything, including phone calls, to make sure you billed everything you did to a case file. While at her desk, she retrieved a pack of cigarettes and a lighter and took them with her to the elevator.

Once outside on the sidewalk, she lit up a smoke and began pacing up and down. The occasional cigarette was a guilty pleasure she enjoyed when happy, drinking or stressed. Lynn lied to herself that it was no big deal; she could quit anytime, and she wasn't really addicted to them.

She finished the first one and tossed it into the street. Calmer now, she looked around and realized she had not been outside since arriving at the office this morning at 6:45. It was a beautiful, late-June, early-summer evening. And once again, Lynn found herself wondering why she was doing this. Why was she working ninety hours a week? Especially on a case she hated. In fact, Lynn wished she was working for the plaintiffs. They had a better case and were actually helping people, not covering up corporate malfeasance.

Lynn lit another cigarette then scrolled through her phone to find the number she wanted. She pressed the dial and listened while the call went through. While waiting for her boss to answer it, Lynn again tried to recall exactly when it was that she sold her soul.

16

It took six rings before her call was answered. When it was, it was the one person on the planet Lynn did not want to hear on the other end.

"Hello, Samantha," Lynn said as cheerfully as possible. "Is Zach available?" she asked immediately regretting her choice of words.

"Just a moment," Lynn heard the woman say barely concealing her annoyance.

Once again, the thought, *she knows* went through Lynn's head. And once again she found herself also thinking, *too bad, I don't care.*

A moment later she heard the familiar voice of her boss, Zach Evans.

"What's up?" he asked.

"We have a problem," Lynn answered him. "I came across something tonight you had better look at."

"Can't it wait till morning? If I leave now, especially after Samantha answered my phone, it will cause problems," Zach replied. "Where are you?"

"Um, outside," Lynn said.

"Smoking?" Zach asked, disapproval in his voice.

"Screw you. You have no business…"

"Sorry," he interrupted her. "Can it wait?"

"Yeah, I guess. Besides, I'm going home. I've had enough for today," Lynn said irritated with the results of the phone call.

"Give me a hint. What did you find?" he asked.

"Not on the phone," Lynn told him. "I'll see you in the morning."

Lynn ended the call, took a last drag on the illicit cigarette then flipped the remains in the street. Clearly annoyed now, mostly with herself for calling him, she went back into the building.

Lynn McDaniel was a cum laude graduate of Michigan Law School with a thirtieth birthday rapidly approaching. She was also a one-time, first runner-up Miss Ohio contestant. During college at Notre Dame and law school, she had been a card-carrying, idealistic, progressive liberal. In fact, she had gone to law school with the intention of becoming an environmental, save-the-planet lawyer.

Upon graduation, she had jumped at the chance to join Everson, Reed. There had been assurances that environmental law was going to become a serious interest of the firm. In fact, it had, but not for starry-eyed tree huggers. Everson, Reed had scored representation of several blatant, Midwest polluters and Lynn had been on the team to protect and defend them and help them avoid cleaning up the messes they made.

Zach Evans had saved her from that, and she was now part of the corporate litigation department. Five years with the firm and she had yet to meet a single client by herself let alone handle a case on her own. A three-hundred-thousand-dollar income helped assuage the guilt, but there were still times when she wondered if it was worth it.

Lynn's two-year-old Mercedes C-class purred along the freeway toward her luxury condo. As she cruised toward home, once again she became determined to straighten out her life. Especially her affair with Zach Evans. Tomorrow morning that discussion, her ultimatum, was going to be delivered in no uncertain terms.

Someone tried the handle on the conference room door only to find it locked. Whoever it was, and Lynn believed she knew who it was, rattled the door handle then knocked on the glass.

The room was glass-enclosed from floor to ceiling. Because of the serious nature of the case being handled inside the windows were covered with dark paper. No one could see in or out.

Before Zach could use his key to unlock the door, Lynn was opening it from the inside.

"Hi," she said as she stepped aside to let him in.

Zach Evans was a firm partner and the number two lawyer in the corporate litigation department. He was also Lynn McDaniel's immediate supervisor.

Forty-two years old, Zach had been with Everson, Reed since graduating from law school. An average student at a local private school, William Mitchell in St. Paul, Zach had come to the attention of a partner by winning the moot court competition between William Mitchell, St. Thomas College of Law and the law school at the University of Minnesota.

Normally a student with the mediocre G.P.A. accumulated by Zach in law school would not even merit an interview with Everson, Reed. But the partner who had spotted him, Evan Carpenter, had insisted on hiring him. Carpenter, who is one of the best known corporate and insurance company lawyers in the Upper Midwest, got his way and Zach was given a chance. Carpenter was and still is Zach's boss and the head of corporate litigation. Unknown to the other partners and a significant plus for Zach, Evan Carpenter's mistress of twenty years was Zach's aunt.

"Okay," Zach said as he placed his briefcase on the table, "what's so urgent?"

Lynn lifted the box on the table covering the document she had discovered the night before. While Zach took a seat at the table, Lynn slid it to him and simply said, "This."

Lynn took the chair next to Zach and sat silently while he read. It took him twenty minutes to first skim through it, then read it slowly and in its entirety. When he finished, he placed it back on the table the way he found it and stared at it while thinking about what it was.

"Well," he finally began, "you're right. It's damaging to our case, but there's nothing on it to indicate anyone saw it. And..."

"Constructive knowledge," Lynn said. "It's an internal memo."

"And," Zach continued more forcefully, "who is this guy, Irving Haraldson, who allegedly wrote it?"

"He was the company's senior or chief engineer," Lynn answered.

"Was?" Zach asked.

"He's dead. In fact, about three years ago, he was picked up in a gay bar a few blocks from here. He was found murdered in his car on a road by the U along the river."

"Murdered? No kidding," Zach said obviously surprised. "How do you know this?"

"I picked it up during the course of our representation," Lynn said.

"Well, that helps us. No proof this memo was ever circulated or seen by anyone and the author is dead. He can't authenticate it."

"Zach," Lynn began with an exasperated expression as if speaking to a child. "It is constructive proof the company knew about the skateboard's defects. For God's sake, we have twenty-four dead kids here and at least another five hundred injured. Many of whom will never walk again!"

"Lynn," Zach quietly said leaning forward, so his nose was only inches from hers. "This memo will never see the light of day. Our job is not to worry about injured kids. To be blunt about it, I don't give a shit. And you'd better not either. Do I make myself clear?"

"Yes," Lynn meekly replied.

"We have ethics, sort of. We do not have morals. Our job is to win this lawsuit and make this go away. To zealously represent our clients."

"Within the bounds of the law," Lynn replied citing the canon of zealous representation more fully to remind Zach.

"Are there any more copies of this?" Zach asked ignoring her comment and pointing at the memo.

"Not that I'm aware of," Lynn said.

"Good, I'll take this one," Zach said as he picked up the document. He opened his briefcase and slipped it under two case files he had inside it.

"We need to talk about us," Lynn abruptly said.

"Okay," Zach replied swiveling his chair around to face her.

Over the years he had been with the firm, he had bedded an even dozen associates and secretaries. Zach's good looks and charm not only worked wonders on jurors. Young impressionable women were easily smitten by him as well. Of course, they all had starry-eyed thoughts of

19

his money and position with the firm. Zach had become quite adept at brushing them off and avoiding harassment claims.

Two years ago, Zach had finally walked down the aisle. He had captured, or so he believed, one of the most significant women in the cities. Samantha Simpson, the daughter of Calvin Simpson. Best of all, Samantha had no interest in having children or the whole family thing. At least not right now. She had also made it clear that Zach's roving eye days were over. In Zach's ego-driven world this only meant he needed to be more careful; which he believed he had been with Lynn McDaniel.

Looking at Lynn now, he knew exactly what she was about to say. Lynn was going to utter the words most men fear more than anything with the possible exception of, "I'm late." Zach was about to hear, "Where is this relationship going?"

After Lynn said those very words, Zach lied by telling her, "I've been thinking about it. I'm not happy with Samantha; you know that. But the Fourth of July is coming up. Cal throws a big party at their lake place up North."

"I know, I got an invitation," Lynn said.

"I can't do anything until after that," he practically pleaded. "Besides, this will have to be handled delicately. You know Cal, he's a huge client."

Zach leaned forward and kissed her on the cheek.

"I have to go," Zach said. "I have a meeting with Evan on another case, and we have court on a discovery motion at nine. Try to find out if there are any more copies of this memo."

During Zach's quick "see you later" effort to flee, Lynn said nothing. She knew the excuse about the Fourth of July was Zach's way of putting her off. She also knew she was about to get dumped. Other women in the firm had warned her about Zach Evans. Like most women, Lynn convinced herself that he would change for her.

"Now what do I do?" she whispered to herself.

FIVE

"Your son's on the phone," Marc Kadella heard Carolyn yell at him through the open door of his office. He stood up and walked around his desk to the door. Marc had a feeling he knew why Eric was calling and did not want to share the conversation with his officemates.

Marc Kadella was a lawyer in private practice and as a sole-practitioner rented space in a suite of offices shared by other lawyers. His landlord, Connie Mickelson, a loveable, crusty, older woman working on her sixth marriage, did mostly family law and personal injury work. Another lawyer renting space was Barry Cline, a man about Marc's age, who was becoming modestly successful at criminal defense and business litigation. The fourth and final lawyer was Chris Grafton, a small business corporate lawyer with a thriving practice who was a few years older than Marc and Barry.

Marc was sandy-haired, blue-eyed of Scandinavian and Welsh ancestry. He was a little over six feet tall, in his mid-forties and the divorced father of two mostly grown children; his son, Eric, age twenty and a daughter, Jessica, age eighteen.

"Thanks, Mom," he said to Carolyn as he closed the door.

"Hey, what's up?" Marc said into his phone after returning to his chair.

"Hey, Dad. How are you doing?"

"Good, how's your mother?"

"Okay. You know, she's Mom," Eric replied. "Um, ah, Dad, I ah figured I'd give you a heads up. I registered for fall classes already…"

"It's barely July," Marc commented.

"I know, but I knew what I wanted to take, so I went ahead and signed up."

"How much?" Marc asked cutting to the chase.

"I'll need around six grand to start the first semester," Eric said.

"How much for the entire semester?"

"Eighty-five-hundred," Eric replied. "But you don't have to pay it all at once…"

"Is your mother gonna chip in?" Marc asked.

"Have you talked to Jessie?" Eric asked referring to his younger sister, Jessica.

"A few days ago, why?"

"Mom's gonna pay for hers," Eric said.

"She's going to nursing school. It's half the money…" Marc blurted out then stopped himself. He should not have said that to his son, and he immediately regretted it.

"I know, but…"

"Hey, sorry, no problem," Marc cut him off. "Forget I said that. It's okay. If she takes care of Jessie I'll take care of you," Marc finished while thinking his ex-wife's husband, Tom, makes a half a million-dollars a year.

"I could take out a loan," Eric said.

"No, don't do that. I'm just glad you're at the U and going to the business school and not some liberal arts factory on socialism," Marc said.

"That reminds me," Eric said. "I'm taking a class entitled the purity of Marxist-Leninist economics. Sounds really interesting."

"Throw my phone number away," Marc said while his son was laughing.

"Hey, what are you doing for the Fourth?" Eric asked.

"Margaret and I rented a cabin up by Bemidji for a couple of days," Marc replied.

"Mom's having a party. I'm trying to think of an excuse not to go."

"Good luck with that," Marc said.

"Oh, hey! I almost forgot I have some good news. I got a job," Eric said.

"Oh, where, doing what?" Marc asked.

"Stanton, Webster," Eric said referring to a well-known, highly respected brokerage firm in downtown Minneapolis. "You've heard of them, haven't you?"

"Sure, of course. What are you...?"

"It's an entry-level kind of thing. Pretty much an intern sort of deal. But they're paying me twelve bucks an hour, and if I work out, they'll keep me on during the school year. It's full-time for the next couple of months then part-time with flexible hours during school. They asked if I was related to you. They knew your name from a couple of your trials."

"And they hired you anyway? I'm amazed."

"No, they were impressed. Said you must be a really good lawyer. How about that, Dad?"

"It's flattering," Marc admitted.

There was a light knock on Marc's door and Sandy Compton, one of the staff, opened it and poked her head in.

"Your appointment's here," she quietly said. "Say hi to Eric and tell him I still wish he was a little older," she added winking at Marc.

"I gotta go, son," Marc said while smiling at Sandy and pointing at the door to indicate she needed to leave.

Two minutes later, now with his suit coat on, Marc took his seat behind his desk. The man Sandy referred to sat in one of the client chairs.

Marc glanced over the man's intake form, looked at him and said, "Have we met? You look familiar."

"Uh, yeah," he said. "I was here about, oh, maybe eighteen months ago. I talked to you about handling my divorce."

Marc looked at the intake form again, read the man's name, Norman Gale, looked back at him and said, "Sorry, I don't remember it."

"Oh, it's okay," Norman said lightly waving a hand at him. "I didn't expect you too. We only met the one time for a what-do-you-call-it, a consultation."

"Okay," Marc smiled. He put the folder down, leaned forward and placed his arms on the desk. "What brings you back, Mr. Gale?"

Gale hesitated for a moment, looked down at his shoes, inhaled and looked across the desk at Marc.

"I kind of feel like an idiot," he started to say.

"Relax," Marc said. "We've all been there."

"Yeah," Gale nodded. "Anyway, when I was here before, you were straight with me. You told me up front what you could do and how the divorce would go. Except, I didn't want to hear that. I guess, looking back on it, I wanted you to tell me a bunch of BS. So, I left and found a lawyer who did that. Now, a year and a half and fifteen grand in attorney fees later, we're right where you said we'd be."

Marc leaned back in his executive chair, crossed his arms over his midsection and listened. Norman Gale's was a story he had heard many times before. Most honest and up-front lawyers have.

Gale continued for another ten minutes explaining to Marc how his lawyer and his wife's lawyer had turned what should have been a relatively easy divorce into an acrimonious nightmare. Between the two lawyers, they had racked up over thirty thousand dollars in fees. And it had taken a private meeting that his wife had instigated between Gale and her without the lawyers to settle it.

"What can I do for you, Norman?" Marc quietly asked when he finished.

Gale pulled a document out of a large manila envelope he had sitting in his lap. He held it across the desk and handed it to Marc.

"We got this settlement agreement written up, and I was wondering if you could go through it and tell me what you think?"

Marc placed the document on his desk, looked at Gale and sadly shook his head.

"I can't do that, Norman. Or, I guess more precisely, I won't. It's not that I don't want to help you," he quickly added holding up a hand when Gale started to protest. "It's not because you hired somebody else or anything like that. You didn't hurt my feelings. It's because there has been too much that's gone on that I don't know about. Plus, I don't know what property you have, or kids or anything like that. I haven't been involved and I don't know anything about it."

"I figured you'd say that," Gale sadly said.

"Let me ask you this. Are you okay with it?"

"Yeah, I guess so."

"Is your wife okay with it?"

"Yeah," he nodded.

"Do you have children?"

"Three," he replied.

"Are they taken care of? Are they going to have both parents in their lives?"

"Yes, absolutely. We won't fight over the kids. They'll live with their mother, and I can see them whenever I want. They're all teenagers and the two older ones have cars so that won't be a problem. The child support is set. It won't be easy, but I'll pay it."

"Then the deal is probably okay," Marc said.

Norman picked up the agreement and slid it back into its envelope. He stood and said, "What do I owe you?"

Marc also stood and said, "Nothing. Don't worry about it. I didn't do anything for you to get paid, so I won't add to your problem with attorney fees. Here," he continued handing the man his card. "Take this and if you or anyone you know needs a lawyer, give me a call. For anything. Even if I can't help them, someone in the office can."

"I'll do that, thanks," Gale said.

"Always appreciate a referral," Marc said smiling as he shook the man's hand.

"What was that about?" Connie Mickelson asked Marc.

Marc had walked Norman Gale to the exit door in front of Connie's office. He was standing in her doorway leaning against the door frame.

"He was here a while back for a divorce. I wouldn't lie to him about what to expect so he left and found someone who would," Marc replied.

"And now he owes twenty grand in attorney fees and he's kicking himself in the ass for not listening to you," Connie said.

"Pretty much. He wanted me to look over the settlement. I politely declined."

Connie rolled her chair back to the window behind her desk and opened it. The Reardon Building, an inheritance of Connie's from her father, had the old-style windows that could open from the inside.

Knowing what she was up to, Marc stepped into her office, closed the door and sat down.

Connie lit a cigarette blew the smoke through the open window and asked, "What are you and the judge doing over the Fourth?"

The judge Connie referred to was Hennepin County District Court Judge Margaret Tennant. Marc had been in a relationship with her, off and on, for several years.

"We're going to Bemidji. We got a cabin rented on Lake Bemidji. They have boats and jet skis, stuff like that. We'll have a good time," Marc said with a lot more enthusiasm than he felt.

"Wow, great, sounds just like you. You gonna go fishing too? Too bad it's not January, you could sit out on the lake freezing your ass off ice fishing. Have a good time," Connie replied with a touch of sarcasm.

"I have friends from high school who go ice fishing and they don't sit on a lake freezing their ass off. They sit in a nice, warm, comfortable ice house mostly to get away from their wives and drink for two or three days."

"Yeah, I know that. I'm pretty sure that's what husband number two was doing. Or was it number three? I can't always keep track myself," Connie replied.

"I got invited to a party at a rich guy's lake place, Calvin Simpson," Marc said. "You know him?"

"I know of him," Connie said. She finished her cigarette and tossed the butt out the window onto Charles Avenue. She closed the window while saying, "I hear he's a pretty shady Wall Street kind of guy."

"A shady Wall Street guy," Marc said feigning surprise. "Who would've guessed? A little redundant don't you think?"

"How'd you get an invitation?"

"His son-in-law, Zach Evans, is a friend from law school. We get together for lunch once in a while. He's with Everson, Reed doing corporate litigation. He invited me. Catered affair with free booze and fireworks," Marc said with a look of disappointment on his face.

"Margaret still hinting about marriage?"

"Not so much. Especially since I casually mentioned I was thinking about buying a townhouse. That was a frosty night," Marc said.

"You're gonna get your walking papers from her pretty soon," Connie said.

"Maybe. I have serious feelings for her, but I'm not ready for marriage. In fact, I'm not sure I'll ever be. It wasn't the nicest experience for me."

"I know," Connie said. She knew Marc's ex-wife and how unhappy she made Marc. "You do what you think is best for you. If you get pressured into marriage, you'll both live to regret it."

Marc thought about what Connie said for several seconds then said, "I know, you're right. Thanks, Mom. I have work to do."

SIX

The driver of the twenty-five-foot SeaRay throttled back the 300hp Mercruiser inboard to drift up to the dock. The pilot had two VIP passengers on board that he was delivering to the Fourth of July party. The luxury craft's owner, Congressman Del Peterson from Minnesota's Fourth District, was bringing two friends to Cal Simpson's party.

Cal had seen the boat a quarter of a mile out coming across Lake Patwin. He was standing next to a good friend, U.S. Senator Albert Fisher, as the boat approached.

"Beautiful day," Fisher said for at least the sixth time.

It was a beautiful day. Minnesota is known as the nation's icebox, an image the natives encourage. "Keeps out the riffraff" is the usual adage. There is, of course, some truth to it. And being referred to as flyover country is taken as a compliment.

Minnesota's summers were typically what makes living there worth dealing with January and February. Senator Fisher, coming from the Deep South, knew what uncomfortable summers were all about.

"Sonofabitch," Cal grumbled. "I can't stand this old hypocrite. Socialist my ass," he said referring to the seventy-two-year-old Senator from Maine. "This phony old bastard has visions of himself standing on Lenin's Mausoleum while the May Day parade passes in review."

"We need him," Fisher reminded him. "And the price for his support is pretty cheap."

"He's gotta be the only multi-millionaire communist on the planet," Cal replied.

"Socialism for the little people," Fisher said with a laugh. "He never said he was a socialist for himself."

"Well," Cal said after swallowing the last of his drink, "let's go greet our illustrious guests."

Cal placed his empty glass on the tray of a young waitress who walked by. He then watched her walk away admiring her backside as she did so.

"You probably have shoes older than her," Fisher admonished his friend.

"Doesn't mean I can't enjoy the view," Cal replied as the two of them started to walk down to the dock.

Extending out from Cal's property was a one-hundred-foot-long portable dock. There were a half a dozen expensive boats already tied to it, but Cal had made sure there was plenty of space still available for Del Peterson and his guests. By the time Cal and Al Fisher reached the boat one of Cal's security men was tying up the boat as another one helped the senator from Maine and Congresswoman Elaine Krohn from

California disembark. When Cal saw Senator Roger Manion, he had to suppress a laugh. Manion was wearing cargo shorts from which extended two of the skinniest, hairless, whitest legs he had ever seen.

"Hello, Senator, Congresswoman," Cal said shaking hands with them. "Welcome to Minnesota."

"Let's make this quick," the self-proclaimed senator of the little people growled. "I don't want to be here all day."

"Lighten up, Roger," Al Fisher said. "What are you worried about? Afraid you might get some sun on those legs?"

This elicited a hearty laugh from Elaine Krohn.

"Go to hell," Manion snarled at Fisher who returned the statement with an irreverent smile.

"Didn't have your prune juice yet today?" Krohn asked.

Elaine Krohn was the exact opposite of Roger Manion. A Republican from a conservative California district, she was attractive, affable, pleasant and practical. She was also chairman of a very important subcommittee of the House Armed Services Committee. Military procurements of any significance had to literally come across her desk and went nowhere without her approval.

"Let's go up to the house," Cal said to the four of them, including Del Peterson who had joined them after securing his boat.

As Cal led the small group across the manicured lawn toward the house, the hundred or so guests turned to watch them. The most recognizable one in the group was the grizzled-looking senator with the disheveled white hair from Maine. He had recently run for the Democratic Party's presidential nomination. With the promise of more free goodies than Santa Claus, Manion had made quite a name for himself. He had also created a significant following, mostly among younger people who didn't realize someday it would be their turn to pay for all of the "free" things Manion promised.

"Too goddamn many people here. I do not like to be seen like this," Manion grumbled.

"Relax, Roger," Fisher replied. "You can claim you're trying to convert us by promising us seats on the Politburo."

Cal lightly bit his cheek to avoid laughing, but Fisher, Krohn and Del Peterson laughed at the old socialist's discomfort.

"Go to hell, Albert," Manion said again.

"I thought all of you good commies didn't believe in heaven and hell," Fisher replied needling the man again.

"Okay, then kiss my ass," Manion said.

Cal led them through the house and down the stairs to the meeting room. Waiting for them were fifteen people; nine men and six women. All of them were representing themselves and others. None were here on behalf of "The People." Six were members of the Congressional House and four were U.S. Senators. The rest were from private industry including three retired generals.

The new arrivals, except for Manion, went around the room introducing themselves. The socialist senator stood in a corner by himself fuming at the number of people in attendance. He had been led to believe, or so he thought, that there would only be three or four people involved.

Cal started off the meeting by introducing one of the retired generals. He was a former USAF three-star who sat on the board of a half-dozen companies involved in the military aviation industry. His name was Floyd Madison.

For the next hour, Madison, after giving the group a quick update, conducted a Q & A roundtable discussion. While this went on, Cal circulated among his guests acting as the genial host refilling drinks. Most of the questions were answered by General Madison or a woman and a man from a large investment firm from Chicago. When the last of the questions had been answered, Senator Manion stood and went to the door.

"Simpson," he said, in a demanding voice, "get us back to the boat. I've heard all I need to hear. The rest of you," he continued pointing a bony index finger and waving it around the room, "wait here until I'm gone. I don't want to be seen with any of you."

He looked at Cal and said, "And don't invite me to any more of these meetings. Fisher can bring me up to date on anything I need to know."

Manion turned, opened the door and started up the stairs. Five minutes later he was back on board Del Peterson's boat without Elaine Krohn, who had decided to stay for the party.

"What the hell's the matter with him?" Krohn asked Al Fisher. The two of them were standing on Cal's lawn looking out over the lake watching the boat with Manion aboard pulling away from the dock. Cal Simpson was walking quickly toward them having seen Manion off.

"You want a complete list or just the highlights?" Fisher asked. Without waiting for a reply, he said, "He truly believes his own bullshit. He believes the rich should turn over all of their money to the government so he, Manion himself, can redistribute it for the greater good. Of course, like most socialists, the party elites will live like royalty while everybody else lives like peasants. He and his political allies won't be subject to all of this confiscation for the greater good."

"Leave it alone," Cal said. He had heard the last part of what Fisher said to the congresswoman when he joined them. "We need him. He'll get us a few bipartisan votes in the Senate," Cal said.

"For how much?" Krohn asked.

"A million bucks for him and another million or so to be spread out to his pals on Armed Services," Fisher answered her.

"Cheap," she said.

"Cheap," Cal agreed. "I should attend to my guests," he continued.

"Is your wife here?" Krohn asked.

"Somewhere," Cal replied as the three of them turned to head back toward the party. Unnoticed by anyone, Elaine Krohn slyly pressed a hotel room card into Cal's hand. The married congresswoman was staying across the lake in a twelve-hundred-dollar a night suite at the Remington Lodge, paid for by her host.

SEVEN

"Do you know if Lynn is coming?" Evan Carpenter asked Zach Evans. Zach was standing next to his father-in-law, Cal Simpson answering questions about the toy company lawsuit. Most of the inquiries Cal was making were out of bounds and none of his business; details about the suit that Zach should not be disclosing. Cal Simpson, Zach had learned a long time ago, was not to be put off by trivialities such as attorney-client privilege. Zach had been doing his best to be ambiguous, but Cal pressed him until he got what he wanted.

"I thought so," Zach answered his boss, relieved to be interrupted. "The last time I talked to her she was."

"Have you met her, Cal?" Carpenter asked.

"Not sure," Cal replied.

"You'd remember her," Carpenter said with a wink. "Being the horndog you are. Good looking girl. In fact, I'm gonna see if I can't fit into those pants myself."

To this very sexist remark, Zach smiled slightly, Cal chuckled, and Carpenter energetically laughed. He held up his glass to tap Cal's then took a healthy swallow.

Evan Carpenter was one of twenty members of the firm in attendance. Cal Simpson was a seven-figure per year client who merited significant ass kissing by firm partners. It was Zach's landing of Cal as a client, due to his marriage to Samantha, that had put Zach on the partner's list.

"Maybe you should introduce me to her," Cal said while slyly looking for a reaction from his son-in-law.

"Sure," Zach said after an obvious hesitation. "If she comes."

"Be sure to mention Everson, Reed's policy about keeping fat cat clients happy," Cal added while still watching Zach.

"I'm not your pimp, Cal," Zach said staring back at the man. Zach had learned before his wedding to Samantha that standing up to Cal would raise you up in his eyes and these little encounters were becoming more frequent.

Carpenter's eyes widened, and he cleared his throat. A signal to Zach to not insult their host.

"You kiss his ass, Evan," an annoyed Zach told his boss. "I'm going to circulate for a while."

As Zach stomped off, Carpenter started to sputter an apology. Instead, Cal laughed and cut him off.

"Relax, Evan. I like to push him once in a while. Poke him a little to see how much he'll take. He's tougher than he acts sometimes. I like that."

While she was being made the object of lewd comments, Lynn McDaniel was at the Everson, Reed offices. Two days before, Lynn and Zach had a blow-up argument over their client's case. Lynn had cornered Zach in the conference room where she had discovered the chief engineer's memo about the skateboard problems. Lynn was determined to find out what Zach had done with the memo and what he was going to do. Zach hemmed, hawed and stammered around the issue and tried to shut down the discussion.

Getting nowhere with that, Lynn then hit him again with the question: "Where is our relationship going"? This elicited anger and frustration and then what were obvious lies. Once again, he tried to put her off with promises to leave Samantha as soon as the time was right. Every cheating husband had used that excuse to string along a mistress since the beginning of time. Lynn McDaniel finally awakened and read the writing on the wall.

Today she had been in the office sorting through documents since eight this morning. It was now almost 6:00 P.M. Having decided not to attend Cal Simpson's party at his lake place and with nothing else planned, Lynn spent the day at work. Except the more she thought about what she was doing and why, the angrier she became.

"If I go home now, eat, shower, change and head out, I should be there shortly after ten," she quietly said to herself. Lynn thought it over for a minute, then decided to go after all.

Zach was standing in a small group of people chatting about innocuous nonsense. Zach was adding nothing to the conversation. In fact, he was not even listening. All he could think about was how stupid he had been to tell Cal about the engineer's memo.

He knew Cal owned stock in the toy company. Or at least, he thought Cal did. At one time, when Everson, Reed was hired to defend Cannon Brothers Toys in the skateboard case, Zach had asked Samantha about her dad's ownership interest. Her response was to vaguely admit he had purchased some stock during or shortly after the IPO. But she did not know if he still owned it.

Zach knew she was lying. Samantha was intimately involved in all of Cal's holdings. She knew everything about what Cal was doing. Samantha's ambiguous answer was her way of telling Zach it was none of his business. It was also her way to avoid admitting Cal had made a fortune from the IPO and it was not strictly legal. Likely an insider trading arrangement. A hot tip from a company executive.

When Zach told Cal about the memo, Cal's eyes lit up for a brief second. Zach had played enough poker with his father-in-law to spot

Cal's tell. That tiny movement of eye sparkle was hard to spot, but when he saw it, Zach knew Cal was holding. In this case, the information about the memo made an idea flash through Cal's brain.

The conversation about the memo had taken place earlier that morning. Cal tried to act casual about it, but Zach knew him well enough to know he was scheming up something. Cal wanted to know a little too much detail about the memo, especially who else knew what was in it and what Zach planned to do with it. When Zach told him only Lynn McDaniel knew about it, Cal adamantly made him promise not to tell anyone else and avoid disclosing it as long as possible.

Zach's phone buzzed in his pocket, and he retrieved it. "God, I hate carrying this damn thing," he said as he looked at the screen. "Excuse me," he said to his friends then walked away to read the text.

It was a message from Lynn, and it read, "I changed my mind. I'm coming. See you soon."

"You okay?" Zach heard a voice ask. He looked up and saw Evan Carpenter looking over his shoulder at his phone.

"A text from Lynn?" he asked reading the screen. "She's coming?"

"Uh, yeah, um, she is," Zach said as he tried to calmly delete the text before Evan saw what she had written.

"Good," Carpenter said. "Look, some of us are going out on Cal's pontoon and cruise around for a while. You want to come along?"

"Ah, no, I don't think so, Evan. Have fun," Zach replied with a weak smile.

All Zach could think about was having Lynn and Samantha in the same place at the same time. This had occurred a couple of times at other social events with uncomfortable results. After the second one, Samantha had turned to ice. A clear indication she knew, or at least believed, something was up between Zach and Lynn.

"Are you going out on the pontoon?" Zach heard Cal ask Evan. Cal had walked up unseen by either man.

"Yeah, you coming? I just found out that hot chick we were talking about, Lynn McDaniel, is coming after all," Carpenter replied.

"Oh, really? How did you find that out?" Cal asked.

"I got a text. Technically she works for me. I guess that's why she sent it to me," Zach replied.

Cal looked at his son-in-law for a moment then said, "I just remembered, I need to talk to someone." He handed the pontoon keys to Carpenter and said, "You take her out, Evan. Nothing to it. Be back by dark for the fireworks."

Every year Cal hired an ordinance company to put on a fireworks display. They had a raft set up about a hundred feet from the dock and would blow up about fifty-thousand-dollars-worth of fireworks. It was quite a show for his guests.

The Simpson lake home was a million-five-hundred-thousand-dollars of buildings and lakeshore property on Lake Patwin. It is in Foster County approximately two and a half hours north of Minneapolis. The house, set back two hundred feet from the lake, is a two-story, four-bedroom, four-bath luxury home. The exterior's lower half is covered in cut granite, and the upper half has the look of an expensive log cabin.

The side facing the lake has a floor to ceiling window running the entire side of the building. It looks out on a magnificent hardwood deck, large enough and strong enough to hold a hundred people. All of this overlooks a beautiful view of the fifteen-square mile lake. Nice living if you can afford a one-and-a-half-million-dollar part-time residence.

Cal walked up the exterior stairs leading to the deck. He had asked around the crowd looking for his daughter then saw her with a U.S. Senator on the deck. Knowing the senator well, Cal hurried up before the man's handprints were all over Samantha.

Cal strolled as quickly as possible while stopping to chat with several guests seated at tables on the deck. A couple of minutes after finding her, he managed to get to Samantha and Senator Grab-ass.

"Hello, Galen," Cal said when he reached them. "Having a good time, Senator?"

"Hey, Cal," the senator replied with a slightly alcohol-induced slur. "Happy Fourth of July," he said and raised his glass in a toast.

"You, too, Senator," Cal replied. "Can I borrow my daughter?"

"Of course," the senator replied. He turned to Samantha, bowed slightly at the waist then said, "Ms. Simpson, charming as ever."

"I saw Valerie down by the dock talking to a young man," Cal said to the senator, referring to his wife.

"Well, I suppose I should go and rescue the poor lad before Valerie drags him off into the woods," he replied.

When Senator Carroll had stumbled off, Cal took Samantha by an elbow and led her to an empty corner of the deck.

"Lynn McDaniel is on her way," Cal quietly told her.

"Nervy bitch," Samantha snarled. "What are we going to do about her?"

"I think we'll kill two birds with one stone," Cal replied.

"Did you find out where the engineer's memo is?" Samantha asked.

"Zach has it. It's in his briefcase at your home."

"Are you sure?"

"Yes. He told me about it this morning while we were at the range with the rifles," Cal replied referring to a target shooting range he had set up on the property.

"Good," Samantha said with a twinkle in her eye.

EIGHT

Lynn McDaniel was stopped at the corner of Walnut and Main Street in Foster, Minnesota impatiently waiting for the red light to change. She was heading west on Main to get to Lake Drive for the final few miles to the Simpson party. To her right, across Walnut, was the Foster County Courthouse. To her left, directly across Main Street was the jail and the offices of both the county sheriff and the city police department.

Lynn had been here one other time. The year before for the same Fourth of July celebration. This was before the start of the affair with Zach. For Lynn, in the beginning, it was nothing more than a sexual dalliance. She had no intention to let a fling with a married man become anything more than that.

The light turned green while she reminisced at her stupidity. A few seconds later the car behind her politely beeped and she quickly drove on.

Two miles past the courthouse and the downtown business district, Main Street merged with Lake Drive. Lynn checked her dashboard clock which read 9:33 P.M. As she had previously calculated, she would arrive at the Simpson lake home just about 10:00, about the time when the fireworks all around the lake would go off.

Only seven or eight miles to go. Lake Patwin was an elongated lake, the farthest point nine miles from the city of Foster. Lynn was still uncertain what she would do. Should she confront Zach and Samantha? If she did that, she would likely be looking for a job tomorrow. Part of her, a large part, relished the idea. Why not go out in a blaze of glory? Finding a job could be a problem, but the idea of leaving the Everson, Reed slave ship had enormous appeal. Plus, an affair with a partner, even Zach Evans, would probably doom her career with them anyway. Who knows, maybe she could get Zach fired. Cal was a whale for the firm and his idiot son-in-law cheating on darling Samantha might do it.

Lynn pressed down on the accelerator, and the Benz jumped in response. Why not air some dirty laundry in public? The whole thing might be the most fun she had in years.

"What time do you think your little cupcake will get here?" Samantha asked her husband.

She had maneuvered him away from several guests he had been chatting with. They were off by themselves on the lakeside lawn. Zach had backed up against a large oak tree while Samantha looked at him. Her head was slightly cocked to the left; she wore a sly I-dare-you-to-lie-to-me smile while waiting for him to reply.

"I don't know…." he started to say.

"Stop it! Don't insult my intelligence by lying to my face," Samantha quietly snarled. "I know she's coming here tonight, and I am royally pissed at your stupidity. Now," she continued while Zach stood there unable to look her in the eye, "what are you going to do about her?"

"I'll take care of her," Zach told her.

"Samantha," they heard a female voice say in the darkness, "I'm sorry to intrude, but your dad is looking for you."

The voice belonged to Maggie Shepherd, one of the several executive assistants who worked for Cal. She had stepped up to the two of them unnoticed by either.

"I'll be right there, Maggie. Thanks. Tell my dad I'll be along in a minute. Where is he?" Samantha replied.

"On the deck. The fireworks are going to start in a little while," Maggie answered her then turned and walked off.

When Maggie was out of earshot, Samantha turned back to the sullen, whipped Zach.

"You'd better. Tonight. Oh, and by the way," she continued leaning in to whisper into Zach's ear, "just so you know, I had a nice get-even-fling with one of your country club pals. I won't tell you which one. You can wonder who it is every time you see them."

"You bitch," a steaming mad Zach said.

"Yeah, asshole. I had him bend me over and ride me like a stallion. It was the best piece of ass I've ever had. You happy now?"

Of course, Samantha was lying. She would never stoop to such a stunt and certainly not with any of Zach's country club buddies. She considered all of them to be barely adults and was never more than courteously polite to them. Samantha put that bug in Zach's ear just to give him something to think about.

Lynn found the turn, no thanks to the car's GPS, leading to the Simpson place. It was a forty-five-degree angle between two large oak trees. After making the turn, the road gradually went down through the dark forest toward the lake. She remembered it from the year before and reduced her speed to barely twenty mph.

Except for the starlight, which was spectacular, the road was pitch black. Lynn turned on the car's high beams which helped considerably in the darkness. Even so, she kept the car at the much slower pace.

Lynn tried to recall how many houses she had to pass. She knew it was at least two miles to the campground and then another right turn. She went by three more lake homes, all with parties taking place, then saw campfires straight ahead.

Lynn found the road to the Simpson home which was on a peninsula, about a half a mile ahead. It jutted into the lake to her right just past the campground to her left which appeared to be almost full. Knowing she was almost there, Lynn took a deep breath and relaxed.

Samantha had left a thoroughly chastened Zach standing by the tree feeling like a complete fool. He realized what was at stake. If Cal Simpson snapped his fingers, the firm's senior partners would jettison Zach in a heartbeat. He was a competent enough trial lawyer but Everson, Reed could replace him quicker than they could replace a client with Cal's money.

Zach finished his drink then tossed the plastic cup onto the lawn. He needed some time to think and decide the best way to handle this. Zach walked off toward the house ignoring the guests. He wanted to get out front and stop Lynn before she joined the party and caused a scene.

"Hey, Zach, aren't you staying for the fireworks? Where are you going?" Zach heard a voice say a few feet from the door he was walking toward.

"Oh, ah, hey, Rudy," Zach said to the man he had almost run into. The man's name was Rudy Caine, and he was an Everson, Reed partner a couple of years older than Zach.

"I thought you were gonna run me down," Rudy said. "Where are you going?"

"Sorry. I, ah, I have a problem to take care of. I, ah, I gotta take care of something," Zach said as he hurried away.

Lynn could see the party lights at the Simpson house on her right at the end of the peninsula. Through the trees along the lakeshore next to the road, the yard leading down to the lake was lit up. She also remembered that her turn was coming up almost where the campground on her left ended.

The Benz went up a slight incline on the dirt road for about a hundred feet. When she started down the other side, her foot reflexively slammed on the brake pedal. Standing fifty feet ahead of her, in the middle of the road was a man with a flashlight waving it back and forth.

Lynn skidded to a stop less than twenty feet from him. She had an excellent view of him in the wash of her headlights. He was dressed in tan camo made up of a short-sleeve cotton shirt, cargo pants, and baseball cap. He wore a stern expression and held something along his left leg.

"Please get out of the car," he politely but firmly said shining the heavy-duty flashlight on her.

Lynn put her window down, stuck her head out and said, "What?"

"Get out of the car," the man repeated.

"Why?" Lynn said, a puzzled look on her face. She opened her door, got out and standing behind the car's door asked, "Who are you and what are you doing?"

Being a strong, intelligent, capable woman, Lynn McDaniel was used to being in control. Standing behind her car door, questioning this strange man, she had no idea the danger she was in.

"Step away from the car and close the door, please," the man said.

Annoyed now, Lynn replied, "Who the hell are you and why should I do what you say? In fact, get out of my..."

At that moment the man held up and pointed the object he was holding in his left hand at her. It was a short rifle.

"I said, get away from the car."

Terrified now, Lynn put up her hands and stepped to the middle of the road.

"Take the car, please. I won't even report it," she stammered.

"Run," the man quietly said.

"What?" a confused Lynn Mc Daniel replied. "I don't..."

"Run," he said again only this time more forcefully.

Lynn was wearing a light cotton blouse, shorts, and sneakers. Good running clothes. She turned away from the man and began sprinting down the road. She went ten feet then realized her best chance was to get in the trees.

There was a shallow, six-foot-wide ditch along the road. Lynn went through that and just before she reached the trees, three copper-jacketed .223 caliber bullets hit her squarely in the back. The force of them propelled her face first into a tall poplar tree which snapped her head back and broke her neck.

Lynn's killer found the brass from the bullets in the light of the headlights and retrieved them. He then calmly walked over to her. With no more feeling than if he had shot a rabid dog, he grabbed her by her collar. Ignoring the noise from the fireworks that were exploding along the lake and from the campground, he dragged her body fifty feet through the trees. His orders were to leave her in a place where she would be found, but not for a day or two.

He had dragged her most of the way through the trees almost to the opening leading to the campgrounds. He knelt and looked through the trees and saw several occupied campsites about two hundred feet away. Because of the sound suppressor he used on the gun and the fireworks' explosions, no one had heard the shots.

Twenty minutes later, having hidden his victim's car where it would be found shortly after the body, he was in his car heading for the cities. He had also left the rifle where instructed, so it could be put back where it came from.

NINE

Warren Goode parked his cruiser and got out on the road at what was obviously the crime scene. Goode was the Foster County sheriff. He had received the call a few minutes before 11:00 P.M. as he was getting ready for bed. He listened carefully to the office dispatcher while his wife of twenty years sat up against the headboard listening. A call this late at night, especially during the summer tourist season, was never good news.

Foster County was a resort area with more than thirty lakes, and no one knew how many resorts were on those lakes. The county itself had a permanent population of just over eighteen thousand. During the summer, because of its easy access to the Twin Cities, the population could swell to almost forty thousand people. On a Fourth of July weekend that could easily rise to fifty thousand.

Sheriff Goode's office had a total of sixteen deputies to handle those fifty thousand summertime residents. Mostly what they did was handle speeders and drunks. A late-night call invariably meant a dead body. Probably an accident. A traffic or boating accident, even one causing the occasional death, would merit a call to the sheriff himself. A rare homicide certainly would.

"Okay," Goode said into the phone. "Has Chris been called?" he asked referring to Chris Newkirk, the sheriff's lead investigator.

"How about Abby?" he added asking about Abby Bliss, a fourteen-year veteran deputy. Abby was Newkirk's assistant.

"Okay," he said after being told they had been called. "I'll be along as soon as I can."

"What?" his wife asked.

"A woman's body was found by campers. Looks like she was shot. Go back to sleep."

Sheriff Goode, dressed in jeans, a pullover shirt and blue windbreaker with Foster County Sheriff on the back, began walking toward the crowd. He was also wearing his black baseball cap with the word Sheriff stitched into it. Including his cruiser, there were five patrol cars and Chris Newkirk's Tahoe parked on the road, all with lights flashing.

"Hey, Earl," Goode quietly said, greeting the senior deputy on the scene. There were four deputies all together, and each muttered a greeting to their boss.

"Chris and Abby are in there now," Earl said, nodding his head toward the trees. "The BCA crime lab people are on their way from St.

Paul. Even with lights and sirens, it will be another hour before they get here."

Chris was Chris Newkirk, a retired detective formerly with the Duluth P.D. He had put in twenty-five years with Duluth then retired to Foster County. His idea was to draw a pension, sit in a boat fishing and make enough from the county to cover his alimony payments. Except, being the only experienced investigator, he was busier than he had been in Duluth.

Abby was Abby Bliss, a thirty-six-year-old, divorced mother of two, with fourteen years with the sheriff's department. She had been pregnant and married to the high school football star at age eighteen. Her second son came when she was twenty. At age twenty-two, she woke up one day to find a note on the table that the football star had run off with a thirty-five-year-old married woman. It had taken Abby about two minutes to get over the shock and realize what a break her worthless husband had given her. One less mouth to feed and a drunken, abusive bully on top of it. Her boys were now teenagers, and she was being groomed, with Warren Goode's help, to be sheriff in a few years.

"Tell me what happened," Goode said.

"A couple of teenage kids from the campground found her. They were probably sneaking off to fool around, maybe smoke a little weed," Earl replied.

"They called it in, and I was here in about five minutes. I was on my way to cruise the lake anyway. I found the two kids, they're over in my squad," he said pointing to his car. "Scared shitless. The boy showed me the body. Looks like three bullet holes in her back. Not much bleeding. She was still pretty warm."

"No car?" Goode asked.

"No," Earl said shaking his head. "I was about to send Ronnie and Mike up the road to see if they could find one," he continued referring to two deputies, a woman and a man standing in the road.

Goode looked at the two of them and said, "Good idea. But walk it. Take flashlights and check the ditch for any signs of a car going in."

"How far do you want us to go?" the woman, Ronnie asked.

"I don't know," Goode shrugged. "Go a couple of miles. Put your vests on and stay together. We might have a nut with a rifle out here."

"Yes, sir," Ronnie replied.

"Anybody go over there?" Goode asked Earl, looking toward the Simpson property. The sheriff's office knew there was a party going on. There were plenty of wealthy people with homes on the lake. The sheriff and his people were abundantly clear who all of them were, especially the politicians.

"I was waiting for you," Earl replied. "I thought you should have the pleasure."

"Thanks," Goode sarcastically told him.

They heard a noise coming from the trees and turned to see the investigators come out. They joined the sheriff on the road.

Goode shook hands with Chris Newkirk, smiled and said hello to Abby then asked, "What do we have?"

"Woman, blonde, probably five-foot-seven, one-twenty to one-thirty. Good looking. Three bullet holes in her back. I didn't check for exit wounds on the body, but there was no blood on the front of her blouse. Here comes Gayle," Newkirk said looking down the road toward a coroner's office vehicle coming toward them. Gayle Parker was one of four doctors in the county who took turns doing six-month tours as the medical examiner.

"It looks like she was dragged through the trees. Her neck appears to be broken, too," Newkirk added.

"Why would he break her neck after shooting her in the back?" Goode asked.

"She could've done it when she went down," Abby interjected. "We'll probably find the place where she went down in the morning when it's lighter."

"Did you get a picture of her?"

"No. We didn't want to disturb the scene any more than we had to."

They waited for the fifty-year-old Dr. Parker to join them. Newkirk gave her a quick rundown of the scene while Goode talked to Earl.

"These kids' parents know where they are?" Goode asked.

"Yeah. They're camped right over there. They've called three times."

"Take them back but get a promise from their parents to bring them in tomorrow for a formal statement."

"Will do, Boss," Earl replied.

Goode turned back to the doctor and his investigators and said, "Abby, you go with Doc Parker. Chris, you come with me. We'll go over to the Simpson place and see if anyone is missing or if anyone heard or saw anything."

"With all the fireworks going off…" Newkirk started to say.

"Yeah, I know." Goode nodded. "Let's take the Tahoe. No point in scaring his guests unless we have to."

While Sheriff Goode and his people were having their discussion, Cal Simpson was watching from his front yard. In the driveway, along the road coming in and parked on the grass were over fifty cars, some quite expensive. Cal casually looked them over while sipping his drink and puffing on his Cuban.

Cal had come out front a little while ago, after the fireworks show, to get away from his guests and find a little quiet solitude. Instead, he saw the flashing emergency lights through the trees on the main road leading in. Cal knew it wouldn't be long before the sheriff would come driving up his driveway for a little chat. Unperturbed, he took a seat on the front deck and calmly waited for him. About a half-hour after coming out the front, Cal saw headlights coming down his quarter-mile-long driveway. There were no emergency lights flashing on the vehicle, but he assumed it was the sheriff. Instead of waiting where he was for the car to drive up to him, Cal started walking toward it.

"Good evening, Sheriff," Cal said as Sheriff Goode walked toward him.

Cal had met the Tahoe about a hundred yards from the house. Recognizing the wealthy resident standing in their headlights, Newkirk had stopped before him.

"Good evening, Mr. Simpson," Goode said as the two men shook hands. Goode introduced Newkirk to Simpson.

"What's all the fuss about up on the road?" Cal asked.

"Well, sir, I'm afraid there's been a homicide," Goode said.

"What? How, what, are you serious? Sorry, of course you are," a startled Cal Simpson replied.

"A young woman," Goode continued. "Shot in the back then dragged into the trees. A couple of kids from the campgrounds found her."

"My God, that's horrible. How did this…"

"We're not sure," Goode said. "She hasn't been dead long. We stopped to see if you or any of your guests saw or heard anything?"

"Or if anyone is missing," Newkirk interjected.

Cal stood still, silently thinking about the question before saying, "No, not a thing. And if someone saw anything out of the ordinary, I'm sure they would have come to me with it. Several of the guests have left. Mostly by boat."

"I'd like to ask around if you don't mind," Goode said.

"No, I don't think I want you doing that. Sorry, but well, just between us, there are some very important people here. A couple of U.S. Senators and four or five members of Congress. There must be at least a dozen lawyers here. You know what a pain-in-the-ass they can be."

"That's true," the sheriff said.

"Plus, as I said, a lot of them have already left. They stayed for the fireworks then took boats across the lake to their rooms.

42

"I'll tell you what," Cal said, "let me check around. If I find out anything, I'll let you know."

Newkirk's phone rang. He checked the ID, saw it was Abby, excused himself and walked several steps away to take the call.

"I guess that will be okay, for now. Tell your guests to be careful. We may have a lunatic with a gun on the loose. Do you have security on the premises?"

"Yes, I do. I'll be sure to talk to them. Can my guests leave? Do you have the road blocked?"

"We'll set up, so they can get out," Goode answered.

Newkirk came back and said, "That was Abby. Ronnie and Mike found the car about a mile up the road. It was driven into the trees. A woman's purse was on the front seat with the victim's ID A Lynn McDaniel. Do you recognize the name, Mr. Simpson?"

Cal slowly shook his head as if thinking about it, trying to place the name. "No, it doesn't sound familiar," he said.

Newkirk was staring at Cal's eyes watching his reaction. Goode stuck out his hand which Cal took.

"Okay, maybe ask your guests. And be sure to tell them to be careful."

"Sure, of course. A murder, this is horrible," Cal replied. "Call me anytime Sheriff. If I find out anything at all, I'll let you know right away."

"All right, sir," Goode replied. "Good night and again, be careful."

While Newkirk was turning the Tahoe around to drive back to the crime scene, Goode asked him for his impression.

"He's lying," Newkirk said. "He knows her or at least recognized her name."

Newkirk, after over thirty years as a cop, detective and investigator had a reputation as a walking lie detector. Most cops with his experience are able to spot a lie. That was why, before they arrived, the two men had agreed to let the sheriff do the talking while Newkirk observed.

"You sure?"

"Yeah," Newkirk said as he drove back down the driveway. "In fact, I'd like to play poker with him. He's got a tell. Very slight around the eyes, but it's there. The question is why?"

"Maybe he didn't want us bothering his guests," Goode replied.

"Yeah, well, he just guaranteed that we have to."

TEN

Sheriff Goode heard a sharp rap on the glass window of his office door. He looked up from his desk as Chris Newkirk, coffee cup in hand, came in followed by Abby Bliss.

"What do you have?" Goode asked.

The sheriff had waited at the scene until the crime scene unit from the BCA arrived. It was well past midnight by then. After hearing the news, Cal Simpson's guests had all left and with Newkirk on the scene with Abby, there wasn't much more for him to do. Chris and Abby had both stayed until the crime scenes where both the body and car were found had been analyzed as much as possible by floodlight. The areas had been taped off and Newkirk had two of the mid-watch patrol deputies stay there to keep the scenes as clean as possible. A few hours of sleep and they were back in the office.

"Just got off the phone with Gayle Parker," Newkirk said as the two of them took seats in front of the sheriff's desk. "She recovered all three bullets. 223 caliber copper-jacketed still in pretty good shape. If we find the gun, we should be able to get a match. One went through the victim's heart. Parker says that was the killer. She also had a broken neck. Doc says she found particles of tree bark in her face. She's guessing a bit, but it looks like McDaniel was running away and took three shots in rapid order in the back. She went down and smashed her face into a tree and that's what snapped her neck."

"But she's sure about the bullet hitting the heart is what killed her?"

"Yeah," Newkirk said after swallowing some coffee. "Probably dead by the time she fell into the tree."

"We're gonna run out there now," Abby added. "The crime scene people are about done. They found the spot where she went down."

"The bullet killed her," Goode quietly said speaking to himself. "Good. I don't want some asshole lawyer trying to claim the fall killed her and not the bullets."

"Why is that important?" Abby asked.

"Could be the difference between murder and manslaughter," Newkirk said.

"That's ridiculous," Abby said. "That's like pushing someone off a twenty-story building then claiming you didn't mean to kill the guy. You only meant to push him off the roof. It was the sudden stop that killed him, not me."

"Stranger things have happened," Newkirk said.

Newkirk turned to the sheriff and asked, "Didn't Simpson say there were a dozen lawyers at his party?"

"Yeah," Goode replied. "So?"

"McDaniel was a lawyer. We found her ID's in her purse along with a few business cards. She was with a firm, Everson, Reed, in Minneapolis. I pulled them up online and guess what I found? Simpson's son-in-law, Zach Evans, is a partner with Everson, Reed."

"Oh, that's interesting," Goode said.

"We're gonna need a list of the guests at that party," Abby said.

"Yes, we are," Goode agreed. "Shit," he added. "Politically, this could be a problem."

"Warren, we can't worry about that..." Newkirk started to say.

"Yes, we do have to worry about it," Goode said cutting him off. "This is a small town, and Cal Simpson is a big fish. A couple of U.S. Senators..." Goode said letting the word trail off.

"We'll be gentle," Abby said with a cynical smile.

"Okay," Goode said standing up. "I'll go talk to Simpson. You two check with the crime scene people."

Having already told Samantha about Lynn McDaniel the night before, Cal decided to wait until morning to tell Zach. Because of this, Samantha had decided to drive back to the Cities early. Sleeping in a separate room from her husband, she was able to get up and slip out shortly after 7:00 A.M.

It was now 10:00 and Cal was on the deck watching the catering crew cleanup after the party. He was seated at the main table waiting for Zach. He was sipping his third cup of the strong Columbian coffee he preferred when he heard the patio door slide open. A moment later Zach, with a cup of coffee and a carafe greeted his father-in-law.

"Where's Samantha?" Zach asked after taking a chair.

"She went back to the Cities," Cal replied. "Zach, I have to tell you something."

"Okay," Zach said as he sat down. What flashed through his mind was the word divorce from which he inferred all sorts of issues, all of them negative for him.

"Lynn McDaniel was murdered last night," Cal calmly told him while intently looking for a reaction.

"What? How, what? No, that can't be," Zach stammered with a genuinely shocked look on his face, "No," he continued shaking his head. "No, she was..."

"It happened around ten," Cal interrupted him. "Right out on the main road. It looks like a random thing. A maniac with a gun."

Zach turned his head away from Cal and remained silent for thirty to forty seconds staring out past the lawn to the lake. He turned back to Cal and sadly asked, "Are they sure? Do they know…?"

"They found her car up the road with her purse in it. Her license and IDs were in the purse."

"They're going to need someone to identify the body," Zach sadly said. "When she didn't show up I assumed she had changed her mind about coming."

"Are you sure you want to get involved?" Cal asked.

The patio door opened again, and one of the housekeepers came through it.

"Excuse me, Mr. Simpson, the sheriff is here, and he would like to talk to you," she said.

"Fine. Take him into the den, and I'll be right there. Thank you, Lois," he added.

Cal turned to Zach and said, "You wait here. We'll talk about this later."

"Bullshit, Cal. I'm not one of your servants. Lynn was a good friend…"

"A little too good," Cal said.

"And she has no family here," Zach continued ignoring Cal's snide remark, "and they'll need an ID And don't talk to me like that. You're a fine one to be talking."

Cal's face grew red as his anger rose. His eyes narrowed, and he quietly said, "Your ass is dependent on my goodwill. That's my daughter you're married to and your job is hanging by a thread."

"A woman I cared about is dead, Cal. Right now, I'm not sure I care about your good graces. Besides, you have no idea what it's like being married to your Ice Queen daughter."

Zach stood up and said, "I'm going to talk to the sheriff."

He walked off, and before he reached the patio door, Cal caught him and gently took his arm.

"You're right. I'm sorry. You must be hurting. That was thoughtless of me," Cal sincerely said. "Let's go talk to the sheriff."

"Morning, Sheriff," Cal said as he and Zach entered the room. Dark paneling, firearms, trophy heads and leather loudly stated this was a man's room. Cal introduced Zach to Sheriff Goode then Zach told Goode he knew Lynn McDaniel from work and offered to ID the body for them.

Interesting, Goode thought while he said, "Thank you, I'd appreciate that. So, you knew her from work?"

"That's right. We work for the same law firm," Zach replied.

"Was she here? At your party?" Goode asked looking back and forth between the two men.

"She was on the way," Zach replied while Cal remained silent. Zach was barefoot and dressed in basketball shorts and a white T-shirt. He said, "Let me go clean up and change, and I'll drive into town to the coroner's office. Where is it located?"

"It's on the north side of the jail. It's on Main across…."

"I know where it is," Zach said. "I'll find it."

When Zach left, Cal, who had taken his chair behind a large oak desk, a position of power, asked, "How's the investigation going?"

"Well, sir," Goode began. He was standing to Cal's desk right next to a large, expensive, locked, glass-enclosed gun case with at least twenty rifles and shotguns on display. "It's barely started. That's why I'm here. Since Ms. McDaniel was on her way here, I'm going to need a list of all of your guests. Right now, we're assuming this was some type of random nut job killing. But I'll tell you, Mr. Simpson, I sure as hell hope not."

"Why?" Cal asked.

"Because if that's true, then we have a problem. These guys don't just do one person. If it is some psycho, we have more victims to come."

"And if it isn't?" Cal asked.

"Then we need to start looking for a motive. And we need to start with your guests."

"I see what you mean," Cal said with a frown. "How about I decide who to put on the list?"

"No, sir, that won't be acceptable. I understand you had a lot of VIPs here. My people are professionals. They'll be discreet."

"And if I refuse?"

"I can easily get a warrant. And I'll make you sign an affidavit attesting to the accuracy of the list. You'll be under penalty of perjury. I'd rather not do that."

"Relax, Sheriff. I was just messing with you," Cal said with a smile. "Of course, I'll have the list for you. Give me a couple of days."

"Sir, there is something else," Goode said nodding toward the gun case. "I see you have a Browning semi-automatic that looks to be a .223 caliber. I'd like to take it in and have a ballistics comparison done. If nothing else, to eliminate it."

"Sure, no problem," Cal said. He reached into the middle desk drawer and removed a key. As he walked to the gun case, unlocked it and opened it for the sheriff, Cal asked, "She was shot with a .223?"

"Yes, she was. Any other .223's around the house?"

"No, uh-uh," Cal replied.

Goode put a surgical glove on each hand and removed the rifle from its case. He held it up by the shoulder strap and thanked Cal for his cooperation. Cal escorted the sheriff to the front door and out to his cruiser. Goode placed the rifle in his trunk and thanked Cal again.

"I'll have the rifle back in a few days," Goode assured him.

"Take all the time you need," Cal said. "I'll have the list for you tomorrow or the next day. I would appreciate your people's discretion when dealing with my guests."

"Absolutely, sir."

Cal stood in the driveway and watched while Goode turned his car around to leave. The men gave each other a brief wave as Goode drove off.

Cal turned to go back inside just as Zach came through the front door.

"After I do this," Zach said. "I'm going back to the Cities."

"All right," Cal said. "We'll talk soon."

As Cal watched Zach's car drive toward the main road, his phone went off. He pulled it out of his pocket and checked the caller. Pleased to see who was calling, he put the phone to his ear.

"Did you find it?" Cal asked without a greeting.

"No, Dad," Samantha replied. "I've looked everywhere. I even went to the bank and checked our safe deposit box. Not there. It must be at his office."

"Can you go there and look for it?"

"Yes, but he'd find out. Someone would tell him."

"Okay. I know someone else who can check for it," Cal said.

"It could be in the trunk of his car," Samantha said. "He's the only one with a key."

"Damn," Cal quietly said. "We should have thought of that before."

"Sorry," Samantha replied.

"It's all right, darling," Cal said. "We'll get it. I have to make a call. I'll talk to you later."

Cal reviewed his phone number directory, found the one he wanted and pressed the dial button.

"Brody Knutson," he heard a voice on the other end answer his call.

"Brody, it's Cal Simpson," Cal said.

Brody Knutson was the managing partner of Everson, Reed. A mediocre lawyer, Brody was a shrewd office politician. At sixty-four years old, he had been managing partner for nine years. It was Brody who held the keys to the Kingdom. Partner pay, and bonuses came from Brody's office. Of course, the management committee could overrule

48

him, but the committee members were all selected by Brody. Brody Knutson was without peer, the first among equals at Everson, Reed.

"Cal, always a pleasure. What can I do for you?" Brody said.

"You remember that thing we talked about yesterday, just the two of us?"

"Certainly," Brody answered.

"I think it's in his office. Can you check on it?"

"Of course. I'll see to it right away."

"He just left, and he has to make a stop in Foster. Then he'll be back. You have no more than maybe two and a half hours."

"No problem. I'll call back right away. A thin, tan, hard shell Louis Vuitton with locking clasps?" Brody asked.

"That's it," Cal answered. "Call me as soon as you know something."

Two hours later Cal's phone rang. He checked the caller ID and answered the call.

"Did you find it?"

"Sorry, Cal, no. I went in while the staff was at lunch. I checked everywhere, even his desk which was not locked. I have the combination to his safe, and it wasn't there either."

"Don't worry, we'll get it. Thanks," Cal said then ended the call.

ELEVEN

Within twenty-four hours, every county within a hundred-mile radius of Foster, which overlapped into Wisconsin, was on high alert. Every sheriff's office and police department authorized overtime for additional patrols. In addition, the word had spread throughout the civilian population. Carry permit requests and approvals took a dramatic spike. Gun stores reported a significant jump in sales, especially for ammunition. Rural Minnesota was filled with hunters; people who are quite comfortable with firearms. If a stranger was caught wandering around with a rifle, he could be in serious trouble.

The news had been picked up by the media, state, local and even some national news because of the presence of several prominent politicians at Cal's party. It barely lasted 48 hours before a silly political squabble broke out in Washington. With this occurrence and nothing much happening in the investigation, or at least nothing being leaked, now that the story was a week old, even the media in the Cities started to ignore Lynn McDaniel's murder.

The investigation itself was moving along, albeit slowly. True to his word, Cal Simpson had provided the sheriff's office with a guest list. At least a partial guest list. He made it clear he was going to call the more prominent invitees and give them a heads up. Sheriff Goode was infuriated by this, but he let it slide. Cal gave him his word he would only tell them to expect a phone call. He would have no substantive discussion with anyone about the case. Goode was forced to accept that.

"Thanks for your time," Abby Bliss said into her phone. "I appreciate your cooperation. If you think of anything else, please call the sheriff's office."

Chris Newkirk and Abby Bliss had been working on Cal's guest list for a couple of days. With so many names and only the two of them, it was decided they would call everyone first and do a phone interview. Any who might merit a personal visit would be seen later.

"All right," Abby said to Newkirk. "That's the third one. Another lawyer from that firm who says rumor has it that Zach Evans was involved with the victim."

"Apparently, it's time we had a little chat with Cal Simpson's son-in-law," Newkirk replied.

Newkirk's direct line rang on his office phone. He looked at the caller ID and said, "The BCA. Let's hear what they have to say."

Newkirk picked up the phone, identified himself and then silently listened for almost a minute.

"What? Say that again, please," Newkirk urgently said. "Are you sure?" he asked.

"What?" Abby said, her curiosity piqued.

"Well, that's damn interesting," Newkirk said while holding up his right index finger to Abby.

He listened some more than said, "That would be great. Thanks, Sherry. Hey, you did good, kid. I owe you."

Newkirk hung up the phone, turned to Abby and sat silently for ten seconds thinking about their next step.

"What!?" Abby practically yelled.

"That was Sherry Watkins at the BCA. She says Cal Simpson's .223 varmint gun is a match. No doubt about it."

Abby sat up straight, wide-eyed taking in the news, and quietly said, "No shit?"

"That's not all. The prints they got off of it belong to a certain Zachary Evans. Several good quality prints and only his. His prints are in the database from a while back, probably college. Busted for a little dope possession. The BCA is going to messenger all of the evidence up to us today including the rifle. We'll have an email with the formal report in an hour or so."

Newkirk picked up his phone and dialed an intraoffice number. "We need to see you, right away."

A minute later Newkirk and Abby were seated in front of Sheriff Goode's desk. Newkirk quickly brought him up-to-date.

Without responding Goode dialed a number he knew by heart and waited.

"Demarcus, its Warren Goode. I'm fine. Yourself? Great. Listen, I'm sending Newkirk and Bliss across the street to see you."

"Is it about the McDaniel case?" Goode heard Demarcus Tice ask.

"Yeah, it is. Listen, I'll let them tell you what we've got, but in my opinion, I think it's enough for an arrest."

"No, not yet," Newkirk jumped in.

"Hang on," Goode said into the phone. "Why?" he asked Newkirk.

"I want to talk to him, first," said Newkirk. "See if we can't get him to admit to the affair. So far, all we have for motive is rumors."

Goode nodded his head in agreement then said okay to Newkirk's proposal.

"But I still want the two of you to go see Demarcus and bring him up to date."

"Okay," both investigators said.

"Did you hear that?" Goode said into the phone.

"Yeah, I did," the Foster County Attorney said. "Send them over now."

A short while later while sitting in the office of Demarcus Tice, Newkirk made a phone call to Minneapolis. It was answered by a receptionist with a sultry British accent, and less than a minute later Zach Evans was on the phone.

"Mr. Evans, this is Detective Newkirk of Foster County. I'm investigating the death of Lynn McDaniel."

"Okay, what can I do for you, Detective?"

"Well, sir, my partner and I are in the Cities right now," he lied, "and I'd like to drop by and get your statement. We're interviewing everyone who was at the Simpson party that night."

"Oh? I'd heard you were doing the interviews by phone."

"We've been told that Ms. McDaniel worked for you, so we'd like to meet with you in person. Could you find time this afternoon?"

"Let me check my schedule," Zach said. A moment later he was back and said, "How about 1:30? I could give you fifteen or twenty minutes."

"That should be fine, sir. We'll see you then."

Newkirk ended the call and looked at Tice.

"Nail down the affair. He probably won't admit it but get your impression," Tice said.

"We'll also get the names of every secretary who works anywhere near him. If anyone knows what's going on in that office..." Abby started to say.

"They will," Tice finished for her.

Zach Evans realized it was decision time. He had been hiding the Cannon Brothers' engineer's memo for almost three weeks and he needed to do something with it. Zach knew Cal Simpson, and by extension Samantha, must have a serious stake in Cannon Brothers Toys. Cal had asked him about the memo and its contents at least a half a dozen times. Samantha had also inquired. And when he got home after the party at the lake he had checked his den at home and knew it had been searched. As had his office at work.

Without bothering to put on his suit coat, Zach left his office. Passing his personal assistant, Marjorie Griebler, without looking at her he muttered, "I'll be right back."

Zach returned in less than ten minutes carrying his expensive tan briefcase. Marjorie silently watched him go into his office with the small piece of luggage. Apparently, he had gone down to the parking garage and retrieved the briefcase. As soon as he closed his door, Marjorie made a call to another office in the firm.

"Yes?" she heard a man say.

"It's Marjorie, Mr. Knutson. He's in his office with the briefcase."

The managing partner of Everson, Reed silently thought about what he had just been told. He was silent long enough for Marjorie to ask if he was still there.

"Yes, of course," Knutson said. "Okay, let me know if he leaves with the briefcase. If he mails anything, be sure to bring it to me. Thank you, Marjorie. I won't forget this."

"Thank you, sir," the woman said into an empty phone. Knutson did not wait for anyone.

At 1:15 that same afternoon, Marjorie's desk phone rang. It was Christine, the British tart receptionist that Marjorie loathed but was also secretly jealous of. Every man in the place, including the janitors, was totally smitten by her.

"Marjorie, there are two police detectives here. They say they have an appointment with Mr. Evans."

"I don't see anything on his schedule," Marjorie icily replied. "I'll check with him."

She went to Zach's door, softly knocked then opened it. She could see through the floor to ceiling window alongside the door that he was at his desk working.

"Mr. Evans? There are two police detectives here to see you."

"Oh, yeah. Um, bring them back, will you please?"

"Yes, sir, Mr. Evans."

As she left, Zach once again shook his head wondering why she refused to call him Zach. He gathered up the paperwork on his desk, placed them in a folder and put it in a drawer. A minute later there was a knock on his door and Marjorie opened it for Newkirk and Abby Bliss.

After introductions, Newkirk took the lead. Both detectives took notes. Most of the questions, at least initially, were about the party. What was Zach doing? Did he notice anything out of the ordinary? Where was he at the approximate time of death?

Gradually Newkirk moved into Zach's professional relationship with McDaniel. A few minutes of this then some softball questions about any personal relationship.

The entire time, as the two of them had previously decided, Abby Bliss remained silent, letting Newkirk, the older man, do the interview. Then seemingly out of nowhere with no warning whatever, Abby interrupted.

"Does your wife know you were having an affair with Lynn McDaniel?" she blurted out.

This had also been set up. They had decided to hit him with this question when he least expected it. The detectives wanted to get an unprepared response.

"What? What are you talking about? I, ah, I, um, have no idea… How dare you? Where did you get this?"

While Zach effectively admitted it by stammering around, Newkirk and Abby simply watched.

Getting control of himself and remembering he was a lawyer, he finally defiantly said, "That's it. This interview is over. We're done. Get out."

Without a word, the two cops stood and casually walked out. As they walked down the hallway toward the exit sign, Abby quietly muttered, "He's our guy."

"Oh, yeah," Newkirk just as quietly replied.

Marjorie heard Zach yell at the detectives to get out. She waited a few minutes for the dust to settle after they walked past her then placed another in-house call to Brody Knutson.

Five minutes later, a still shaken Zach Evans emerged from his office. He was wearing his suit coat, carrying his briefcase in one hand and had a large mailing envelope in the other.

"Marjorie, I need you to see to it this gets mailed today," Zach said as he handed her the envelope.

"Yes, sir," she said. "Are you leaving? Will you be back?"

"Yes, I'm going to get some lunch. I'll be back in half an hour," Zach said as he walked off.

Marjorie waited ten minutes to be sure Zach was gone then called Knutson again.

"He gave me an envelope to mail," Marjorie told Knutson.

"To whom?" Knutson asked.

"A lawyer, a Marc Kadella."

"Does he have a case that Kadella is involved with?"

"No, sir. Not that I know of. I've heard of Kadella. He's a criminal lawyer," Marjorie said.

"Yes, I know. I've heard of him, too. Bring it up right away," Knutson ordered.

"Yes, sir."

TWELVE

Newkirk was second in line to exit the parking ramp of Zach's building in Minneapolis. He watched the driver in front of him as she used a credit card to pay the cost of parking. When he saw this, he began frantically searching himself for his wallet.

"Oh, shit," he grumbled. Newkirk looked at Abby and started to say, "Um, I, ah, misplaced my wallet…"

"Here," she said giving him a disapproving look as she handed him a credit card. "Use this, but now you owe me lunch."

"Deal. Wait a minute," he continued as he pulled up to the automated payment kiosk, "you'll get reimbursed."

Abby laughed and said, "Yeah, around this time next year."

Newkirk handed her the card and receipt, then sheepishly smiled as he pulled out onto Seventh Street for the trip north.

"Call Warren and Demarcus," Newkirk said a few minutes later. "Tell them about the interview and our impression."

"We have no proof of the affair," Abby replied.

"Doesn't matter. We have witness statements, and besides, the ballistics report and his prints on the rifle will be enough for an arrest and search warrant."

"Should be," Abby agreed.

"We can go through his credit cards and probably find evidence of the affair. Hotel and motel receipts, things like that. We'll find it."

For the next half-hour, while Newkirk drove, Abby was on the phone. She had called Sheriff Goode first who had conferenced in Demarcus Tice. By the time the conversation was finished, it was agreed to get warrants and arrest Zach Evans for the murder of Lynn McDaniel.

By the time the two detectives arrived back in Foster, Tice had the supporting affidavit prepared and ready for Newkirk to sign. He also had the arrest and search and seizure warrants prepared and already signed by Judge William Anderson.

As soon as Tice had all of the documents typed and ready for the judge, Tice himself took them to Anderson's courtroom. Technically, the supporting affidavit should have been signed first. Technically.

Judge Anderson, a fishing and hunting buddy of both Demarcus Tice and Warren Goode had barely skimmed the documents. Before he took them to the judge for signing, Tice, on the phone, had already told his friend what was in them and assured the judge that Newkirk would sign the affidavit.

"Okay," Anderson said. As he signed the warrants he told Tice the originals had better be in the court's file before they were executed.

"When are you going to serve them?" Anderson asked.

"Today, yet," Tice replied. "We're gonna turn Newkirk and Abby Bliss around and with a couple sheriff's deputies send them down to the Cities to get this guy. Warren has a BCA crime scene unit standing by to search his home and office. They'll impound his car and go through it. Warren also has Minneapolis in on it. They'll meet at his home and office and seal the places."

"This firm is gonna have a shit fit," Anderson said. "Are you sure about this guy? A firm that size can raise a lot of hell."

"The firearm evidence and the affair are enough. We'll keep digging. Chris Newkirk's a very good investigator and Warren tells me Abby Bliss has learned a lot."

"She'll make a great sheriff someday," Anderson replied. "Good luck."

Newkirk and Abby were back in Foster just long enough to grab a burger, sign the affidavit then head back with the two deputies. This time, on the way back to Minneapolis, they went in separate vehicles.

With lights flashing, they cut almost a full hour off of the driving time. It had been decided Abby would meet the local cops at Zach's house in Edina and Newkirk would head downtown to arrest him. That was when the fun started.

Newkirk and the two sheriff's deputies met a pair of Minneapolis detectives in the building's lobby. With the usual amount of bad attitude toward lawyers that cops have, all five men were delighted to crash a law firm. A few minutes before 5:00 they rode up to the seventeenth floor together then hurried down the hall to the firm's entrance. Since Newkirk had been there and knew the way, he led the parade.

"I need to know if Mr. Zachary Evans is in his office," Newkirk politely said to the British receptionist.

Staring at the MPD detective's shield, she quickly dialed the phone. Receiving an affirmative answer, she started to say some gentlemen were here to see him. Before she finished, Newkirk was through the interior door with the others on his heels. While they hurried through the inner office, Newkirk and the detectives held up their shields. The two uniformed deputies were obviously recognized for what they were.

Marjorie was standing in the walkway with a stern look trying to block their passage.

"You can't go in there," Marjorie said. "He's with a client."

"Get out of the way, ma'am, or I'll put you in handcuffs," Newkirk replied as he gently pushed her aside.

Marjorie rushed back to her desk, and by the time Newkirk was opening Zach's door without knocking, she was on the phone.

"Zachary Evans," Newkirk said as they burst into Zach's office.

Zach stood up and angrily said, "Get the hell out of here or I'll have all of your asses hanging on my trophy wall!"

Newkirk went behind his desk and continued. "You are under arrest for the murder of Lynn McDaniel."

Zach tried to pull his arm away as Newkirk was putting on the handcuffs. Zach stuttered, "What the hell, goddamnit, who do you people think you are?"

"Please don't resist or I'll have to use force," Newkirk quietly said.

"Who are you, sir?" one of the MPD detectives asked Zach's client, who by now was standing with an astonished look on his face.

"I'm, ah, I'm, ah," he started to say as he looked back and forth at his lawyer and the cops. "I'm, ah, just leaving. I don't know anything about this."

Newkirk had the cuffs on Zach now and said to one of the deputies, "Paul, get his name, address and phone number then kick him loose," referring to the client.

By this point, all hell was breaking loose outside Zach's office. Within seconds, an average looking bald man with a fringe of gray hair, gold-rimmed glasses, and an expensive three-piece suit came in. The crowd at the door had parted like the Red Sea for him which told the cops this guy was a big shot in the firm.

"I am Brody Knutson, the managing partner of this firm and you men are in a lot of trouble."

"Are you Mr. Evans' lawyer?" Newkirk asked him.

"For these purposes, yes, I am and just what the hell do you think you're doing?" a steaming Knutson asked glaring at the calm Newkirk.

Newkirk pushed Zach back into his chair and told him to shut up. He then walked up to Knutson and handed him a copy of the arrest and search warrant to allow them to search Zach's office and confiscate his computer.

Knutson skimmed over the warrants then shook them in Newkirk's face. "I'll have your ass for this you…"

"Sir, if you interfere, I'll put handcuffs on you and drag you through your firm like a common criminal," Newkirk whispered in his ear.

Knutson, having never been spoken to like that in his entire life, straightened up and clamped his lips together.

Newkirk gave him his best mischievous little boy smile then turned back to Zach. While looking at Knutson, Newkirk pulled a card from his shirt pocket and loudly read Zach his rights.

"Okay you two," Newkirk said to the Foster County deputies, "take him down and put him in your squad car. Don't talk to him, don't ask him anything and," he turned to Knutson and continued, "arrest anyone that gets in your way or tries to interfere. I'm going to wait for crime scene to show up. You guys want to stick around?" Newkirk said to the MPD guys.

"Sure, we got nothing better to do."

"Most fun we've had on the job for quite a while. Should arrest a lawyer at least once a week. Never realized how good it would feel," his partner said.

"You idiots are through," Knutson said.

"You have to leave now, sir," Newkirk told him. "This office is about to be sealed off."

With that, Knutson turned and stomped off.

Newkirk turned around to find the MPD guys barely able to suppress a laugh. That's when Newkirk saw it. On the credenza behind Zach's desk was his laptop. A piece of evidence he and Abby had talked about earlier on the ride back to Foster, and he had almost overlooked. Everson, Reed was going to claim privileged information in it and try to keep it out of the authorities' hands.

"Watch the door, please," Newkirk said to the larger of the two detectives. "Give me a hand," he told the other one.

The two men moved the credenza away from the wall and unplugged the computers power cord. Newkirk wrapped the cord around the laptop. He took out his phone and called downstairs to the deputies. He told them to wait for him then shoved the laptop under his suit coat to carry it out.

"Come with me. Run interference for me so I can get this out before anyone tries to stop me," Newkirk told the detective who helped move the credenza.

"Is that covered by the warrant?" the man asked.

"Yeah, but I don't know for how long. We have to get it out of here. They'll be heading for a judge to stop us as soon as they think of it."

"You wait here, please," Newkirk told the one at the door. "Let's go."

It took over five minutes to get through the crowd, out the exit door, and onto an elevator. During the trip, they were stopped three times by lawyers telling them they could not take the computer. Each time the MPD detective held up his handcuffs and threatened to put them on the lawyer and bring him along to jail. That did the trick.

With Zach strapped into the backseat, the deputies were waiting at the curb in front of the building. Newkirk placed the laptop in the trunk and told them to leave. At that moment an MPD patrol officer pulled up, put down the car's passenger window and talked to the MPD detective.

Newkirk had an idea and joined the conversation. He asked the patrol cop if he could guide the deputies to Zach's home. They agreed, so Newkirk made a call to Abby.

He told her to get any and all computers in the house ready for transport. He gave the address to the MPD patrolman and a half-hour later the sheriff's deputies were being guided back to the freeway with both home and work laptops in the trunk.

When Brody Knutson steamed away from Zach's office after the threat from the impertinent, redneck cop from Podunk, Minnesota, he went right back to his office. A couple of deep breaths then he dialed Cal Simpson's private line.

Cal answered, and Brody gave him a quick rundown of the arrest. Cal quietly listened then told Brody to assign his best criminal defense lawyers.

"We don't have any," Brody confessed. "We don't sully ourselves with…"

"Find a couple of lawyers to go up to Foster and make sure my son-in-law knows enough to at least keep his mouth shut."

"Sure, will do," Brody said. "Holy shit! I just realized."

"What."

"I left Zach's firm computer in his office. The cops will try to take it," Brody said as he stood to leave.

"You better get down there and try to stop them."

"I'm on my way."

By the time Brody got back to Zach's office, most of the crowd had dissipated. He saw Newkirk coming back down the hallway followed by two crime scene techs from the State Bureau of Criminal Apprehension. A firm lawyer stopped him and told him about the laptop.

"Why the hell didn't you stop him?" a furious Brody Knutson yelled. "What the hell…"

"Because they threatened to arrest anyone who tried," the lawyer said.

Newkirk was there by now and Brody turned his wrath on him.

"You get that goddamn laptop back here right now. That's firm property with privileged information on it."

Newkirk barely slowed down as he continued toward Zach's door. "We'll be sure not to look at that stuff," he said in reply.

"I'm going to have your ass. Who do you think you are?" Brody screamed.

Newkirk turned around to look at him and calmly said, "Any interference of any kind and I'll show you who I am. I'll be the guy that puts your ass in jail."

"I'll have your ass," Brody screamed again.

"Get in line," Newkirk said then turned to go back in the office.

THIRTEEN

Demarcus Tice was the only African-American county attorney in Minnesota outside the Twin Cities metro area. While in law school at the University of Minnesota, a white friend had invited the then single Demarcus for a week at his home in Foster. Three days into the vacation, Demarcus realized this was where he wanted to be.

He graduated fifth in his class and was wooed by any number of downtown firms in both Minneapolis and St. Paul. Instead Demarcus, on his way to marriage, convinced his bride-to-be to follow him 'Up North' to Foster.

A retirement had created an opening in the Foster County Attorney's office. Shocked, surprised and delighted, the county attorney at the time, one William Anderson, now Judge Anderson, had snapped up the newly minted lawyer. Now twenty-two years, three kids and a peaceful existence later, Demarcus was waiting for an opening on the bench which would be his for the asking.

"Come on in," Demarcus loudly said to the knock on his door.

He was in his spacious, walnut-paneled corner office on the fourth floor of the Foster County Courthouse. Seated in front of him were four lawyers, including Brody Knutson. Despite his position with a large, downtown law firm, Brody was eyeing over Demarcus' office almost green with envy.

The office door opened, and Sheriff Goode and Chris Newkirk entered.

"Come in and find a seat," Demarcus told them. "Mr. Knutson here, and company, are bringing an emergency hearing for a temporary restraining order. They want to stop your use of any Everson, Reed material in your investigation. Especially the computers of Zachary Evans."

"There is proprietary, privileged information…"

"Please, Mr. Knutson," Demarcus said raising a hand to stop him. "We're not in court."

Demarcus turned to Goode and Newkirk and asked, "What do you think? Do you need these things?"

"Absolutely," Newkirk jumped in and answered.

"Any way we can reach a compromise?" Demarcus asked.

"No," Brody said. "We must not allow the police to go on a fishing expedition into firm business."

Goode sensed that Newkirk was about to lose it and blast the arrogant lawyer. Instead, Goode gently placed his left hand on Newkirk's right arm.

"Mr. Knutson, no one's going fishing. We are conducting an investigation into what appears to be a lying-in-wait, first-degree murder. There is nothing your firm does that is more important than that."

"That's debatable," said one of the two lawyers that Brody had sent to Foster the day before to represent Zach Evans.

"We can be careful and not compromise anything we come across that does not pertain to our investigation," Newkirk said.

"No, no," Brody said shaking his head.

For the next minute, there was an awkward silence in the room while each side looked over the other. Finally, Brody stood up to leave.

"I guess we'll go to court," Brody said.

"Okay," Demarcus said with a big, charming smile. He walked around to the front of his desk and went to the door. He held it open and shook each man's hand as they filed out.

"Nice office," Knutson, the last one to leave, said as they shook hands.

"The taxpayers of Foster County thank you for the compliment," Demarcus replied.

As Demarcus was closing the door, Abby Bliss came through it carrying a small stack of papers.

"Wait, wait," she said to stop Demarcus.

"Hey, Abby," Demarcus said. "Come in."

"What do you have?" Goode asked her.

"Kelly got through all of the emails on both computers," Abby said referring to their tech wiz, Kelly Thomas. "I don't know what we're gonna do when she goes to college next year," Abby added.

The sheriff and his top investigator had been sitting on a leather couch. When the lawyers were leaving, they moved and took the chairs in front of the desk. Abby joined them as Demarcus returned to his chair.

"Kelly found almost a hundred emails between our two love-birds, Evans and Lynn McDaniel," Abby said as she handed the papers to Newkirk. "Some of them are pretty sexually explicit."

"That's not the best news," she continued. "I was making more phone calls to people on the party guest list. I talked to two people," she said opening her notebook. "Margaret Shepherd. She's one of Cal Simpson's executive assistants. The night of the party Cal asked her to find his daughter Samantha. This was shortly after 9:30. She remembers it because she looked at her watch thinking of the fireworks that would start soon. Anyway, she found Samantha and her husband, Zach, talking quietly, her words, by a tree. As she came up to them, she says she heard Zach say, quote, 'I'll take care of her.'"

Abby flipped a page in her notebook then continued. "A few minutes later, a lawyer with Everson, Reed, Rudy Caine, saw Zach with a stern look on his face, again his words, walking quickly toward the house.

"He stopped Zach to chat with him and asked Zach if he was going to watch the fireworks. He then said Zach abruptly, again his words, said he had something to take care of. This was just before ten. Just before the time of death."

"I'm surprised they talked to you," Demarcus said.

"I got a sense from the way they were acting on the phone that they had something to say. I threatened to subpoena them before the grand jury."

"Now we have to hang onto the computers for chain-of-evidence," Newkirk said.

"Abby, we have a hearing at 2:00 for a TRO on the computers," Demarcus said.

"Yes, sir. I've heard," Abby replied.

"I'll need you and Kelly Thomas available to testify to all of this. About the emails, not about the witness statements," Demarcus said. "You and you," he said looking at Abby and pointing at Newkirk, "will have to visit these two and get their statements nailed down."

"The lawyer won't cooperate," Goode said.

"Then we'll subpoena him before a grand jury," Demarcus replied.

Abby's phone went off and she looked at the ID. "Kelly," she said before answering.

"Hey, Kelly, what's up?" Abby said.

"I found something I thought you'd want to know about," Kelly told her. "I'm going through the perp's phone and I found a text from the vic to him the night of the crime. She sent him a message to let him know she was coming and would be there about ten."

Abby had cringed a bit at Kelly's use of the TV cop terms, perp and vic. Then said, "That's great. Good job. Keep digging."

Abby told Kelly about the hearing at 2:00, ended the call and told the others what she had found.

"Another nail," Newkirk said.

"Okay," Demarcus said. "Anything else?"

When no one responded, he said. "I'll see everyone at 2:00. Don't be late. Bill Anderson's courtroom."

"Don't you need to file a bunch of paperwork?" Goode asked.

"Yeah, I'll have some," he said. "What I ought to do is stand up and ask the judge, 'So, Bill, are we going fishing this weekend?' That would give these big city guys something to think about."

When the laughter died down Demarcus said, "Abby, one more thing. I want you to re-interview the wife face-to-face. If the two of them were discussing killing Lynn McDaniel when the woman overheard them, we might have a conspiracy case. I want your impression of her when you tell her your other witness overheard them."

"You got it," Abby said.

"Before I hear the petitioner's motion," Judge Anderson began looking at Demarcus Tice, "why aren't we conducting the rule 5 appearance today at this time? Mr. Tice?"

"We're not ready, your Honor," Demarcus stood and replied. "We understand Mr. Evans is considering his options for counsel."

"Very well," the judge replied. "Mr. Knutson, before you proceed, you should know I've read your pleadings and supportive affidavits. I would appreciate it if you would restrict yourself to giving me only things not contained in these documents."

Brody Knutson stood at his table and said, "Well, your Honor, we don't really have anything new..."

"Good," Anderson said. "Let's move on then."

"Except, your Honor, we would like to strongly stress the significance of maintaining attorney-client privilege by getting back the computers before they have been compromised."

"I understand that," Judge Anderson said with a touch of annoyance as if to remind Brody he was not an idiot. "Mr. Tice."

Demarcus stood and said, "Your Honor, as you know we have had possession of the computers since yesterday afternoon. We obtained them via a legal search warrant and have already found additional evidence of the accused's guilt."

Brody stood up and angrily interrupted Demarcus. "You've already been in them?"

"Be quiet, Mr. Knutson, you'll get a chance to rebut. Don't interrupt again," the judge quietly told him.

"Of course, we've been in them," Demarcus said. "We had no reason to wait. At this time, we would like to call two witnesses, your Honor."

"Who you got?" Anderson asked.

"Officer Abby Bliss and our technical expert, Kelly Thomas."

"Any objections?" Anderson asked Knutson.

"Of course, your Honor," Brody replied. "We have not had occasion to interview these witnesses. We have no idea what they will say. We have no idea who they are or what their expertise is."

Anderson sat silently as if he was thinking over the objection. He had made up his mind right away but wanted to appear as if he was giving Brody's objection due consideration.

"Well, I'll tell you, Mr. Knutson. Abby Bliss is an investigator with the sheriff's office, and Kelly Thomas is a young woman who is a computer genius. She has testified several times and I have found her to be extremely credible. So, I'll overrule the objection and we'll see what they have to say."

For the next hour, first Kelly and then Abby testified about what they had done and found in the computers. Except, neither of them discussed the substance of anything they had obtained.

While Abby was on the stand, a man in a business suit carrying a soft leather briefcase, entered the courtroom and quietly took a seat in the fourth row. Obviously a lawyer, he sat and silently observed the proceedings.

When they finished, Judge Anderson allowed both sides to make one final argument. Brody Knutson tried to argue since they found what they wanted, the computers should be returned. Demarcus made the argument that the prosecution needed to hold onto them to establish chain-of-evidence.

"Okay," Anderson began when the lawyers were finished.

"I find that the petitioner has failed to show sufficient harm to warrant a return of the two laptop computers. They were obtained with a valid search warrant and I am satisfied the state's case in the murder of Lynn McDaniel will be harmed without the evidence found in them. Further, there is no privilege extending to an attorney for his own possible criminal conduct.

"I'll issue an order that the state will retain custody of the computers. Any information found, even of a criminal nature, will be held in strict confidence if it does not directly pertain to the prosecution of Zachary Evans and only Zachary Evans."

He then looked at Demarcus and added, "By that I mean if you find any evidence implicating anyone else in this crime, you cannot use it against that person. Clear?"

"Yes, your Honor," Demarcus said.

"Kelly," Anderson said addressing Kelly Thomas who was seated behind the rail in the front row. She stood, and Judge Anderson continued. "Can you make a copy or whatever you call it of everything on the computers for Mr. Knutson, so no data will be lost? So, they can use whatever is on there for cases their firm is handling?"

"Yes, your Honor," the pretty blonde teenager answered. "Give me an hour and I'll have it ready."

"Great, we're adjourned."

FOURTEEN

That same day during the morning when all of the parties were meeting in Demarcus Tice's office, Marc Kadella was getting back from an early court appearance. He placed his briefcase and suit coat in his office and was getting a cup of coffee when Carolyn Lucas spoke to him.

"That's something about Zach Evans, isn't it?"

Marc turned and looked at Carolyn with a puzzled expression. Everyone in the office knew Marc and Zach were friends going back to law school. By now, all of the people in the office, including the lawyers, were in the common area watching Marc.

"What are you talking about? What about Zach?" Marc asked.

"Don't you ever pay attention to the news?" Carolyn asked.

"No," Marc answered. "Have you ever really watched this junk? It's painful. And the newspapers are worse."

"How do you know what's going on?" Carolyn asked.

"I do what they do. I make it up myself. Now, what's up with Zach?"

By this time, Connie Mickelson was handing Marc the A section of the Star Tribune. Below the fold on the front page was a picture of Zach and the story of his arrest.

Marc read the first three or four paragraphs then looked around the room.

"I don't buy this for a minute," he said. "The Zach I know is a hound, but he doesn't have the balls to do something like this."

"Speak of the devil," Sandy Compton, another staffer said. She had answered the phone while Marc was reading, put the caller on hold and was pointing the phone at Marc.

"Zach?" Marc asked.

"Yep," Sandy replied.

"I'll take it in my office."

Less than five minutes later, Marc was out the door putting on his suit coat. "Anybody know where Foster, Minnesota is?"

"Yeah," Barry Cline, Marc's friend and officemate lawyer replied. He gave Marc simple to follow directions then Marc was out the door.

"Don't you want to know if I did it?" Zach asked Marc. It was now past 2:00 P.M. and after waiting almost an hour, Marc and Zach were meeting in a secure conference room in the jail.

"No," Marc said. "I don't want to know…"

"Well, I didn't," Zach told him anyway.

66

"Great, now that we have that out of the way, don't bring it up again," Marc said.

"You should know," Zach said, "they are all over at the courthouse, across the street, arguing about my office and home laptops. The firm is trying to get them back. I decided to wait here for you."

"I should go over there and see what's going on. Here, sign this," Marc said as he handed Zach a retainer agreement.

Zach glanced it over and said, "Thirty grand! You want…"

"This isn't a parking ticket. You'll be lucky if we can keep this under one fifty. Now, you want me, sign."

"I thought we were friends," Zach grumbled while he signed.

"That's why it's only thirty," Marc replied. "Besides, because we are friends I shouldn't be doing this. I'm going over to see what's going on. I'll come back afterward."

A few minutes later, Marc walked up the front sidewalk of the one hundred and twenty-five-year-old recently modernized courthouse. As he walked toward the front doors, he paused for a moment next to the fifteen-foot cast iron statue of Jacob Foster. The statue was a Union soldier kneeling, his head down holding an American flag on the second day of Gettysburg. Marc read the inscription for the Congressional Medal of Honor awarded to the twenty-year-old Corporal Foster. He was found after the second day of the battle with thirteen bullet holes in him but still holding the flag. When he finished, he reminisced about the story.

On the second day of the battle, the Confederates were attacking up and down the Union line. A Union general made a significant mistake causing a hole to open near the center along Cemetery Ridge. The only available Northern unit to plug the hole was the First Minnesota Volunteer Regiment.

Union General Winfield Scott Hancock saw fifteen hundred Rebels from Alabama heading toward the gap in the line. There was another five thousand close behind them. He also saw the Union losing the battle, and possibly the war, if something did not stop them.

Hancock did not hesitate. He ordered the only Union outfit available, the First Minnesota, fewer than three hundred soldiers, to charge into the gap. Despite knowing it was likely an order to commit suicide, the men from Minnesota did not hesitate. They crashed into the Alabamians and held the line just long enough to allow Hancock to bring forward reinforcements. When the fighting was over, the regiment had suffered over eighty percent casualties, but not a single man was missing.

"Insane courage," Marc muttered to himself. "And today we are raising a generation of rose petals, cupcakes, and snowflakes. They need safe spaces with puppies, kittens, balloons and Teddy Bears if they hear a word that might be offensive. Let's hope they never figure out how to procreate."

Marc found the courtroom where the hearing was taking place. He quietly slipped in and sat down on the hard, wooden bench in the fourth row to watch the proceedings. There was a woman on the stand testifying about emails they had recovered from Zach's computers. Marc took out a tablet of paper from his briefcase and made a note to get copies and the use of the computers for an expert to examine.

When the witness finished testifying the lawyers made a final argument then the judge ruled from the bench. This made Marc smile a bit. Normally when a judge is this decisive it is usually because his mind was made up before the hearing. Marc was not at all surprised when Judge Anderson ruled against the law firm.

"Great, we're adjourned," the judge said.

While the lawyers started packing up to leave, Judge Anderson looked at Marc and asked, "Are you here to see me?"

"Yes, your Honor. If I may approach," Marc replied.

As he walked up to the bench, he continued by saying, "I'm also here to see Mr. Tice, your Honor," as he turned his head to look at Demarcus Tice.

"Demarcus, come on up," Anderson said.

"Mr. Knutson should hear this too," Marc said.

Anderson waved Knutson forward, and Marc handed out copies of a document he had.

"My Notice of Representation, your Honor. I've been retained by Zach Evans to represent him."

"Welcome to Foster," Anderson pleasantly said. "You're a little late for this hearing."

"I understand, your Honor. If I could get a copy of your order…"

"No problem," Anderson said while Demarcus and Marc shook hands.

"The name 'Kadella' sounds familiar," Demarcus said with a warm grin. "You've handled a couple of high-profile cases."

"Trust me, the publicity isn't what it's cracked up to be," Marc said. "When is he scheduled for a first appearance?"

"Tomorrow at 1:00," Demarcus replied.

"In front of you, judge?" Marc asked Anderson.

"Yeah, it will be here. Is there anything else? Anything you need from me?" Anderson asked.

"No thank you, your Honor. I just wanted to let you and Mr. Tice know I've been retained."

Anderson stood up and extended his right hand over the bench to Marc. As they shook, Anderson said, "Well, again, welcome to Foster. Get one of my cards from Jeanelle and leave one of yours," he said pointing at his clerk seated next to him. "If you need anything, don't hesitate to call."

Marc had brief, separate conferences with both Demarcus Tice and Brody Knutson. Demarcus made it clear he was going to ask for remand or at least a very high bail. Of course, Marc expected that.

Brody Knutson, all smiles and charm, wanted Marc to know the resources of Everson, Reed were at his disposal as long as Marc kept them up to date on the defense. He even offered to assign one or two lawyers to assist him. Marc smelled that rat as soon as Knutson said it. Marc politely let him know he would think about it, without any intention of doing so. The last thing he needed was Brody Knutson looking over his shoulder through a couple of spies.

Marc followed the Everson, Reed lawyers out of the courtroom and found Demarcus, Sheriff Goode, Newkirk and Abby waiting in the hall for him. Demarcus introduced him to the sheriff and his investigators who greeted him warmly, professionally and genuinely friendly.

"What's wrong? Why are you guys being so nice? Even in Minnesota cops aren't this nice to defense lawyers. What's going on?" Marc half-jokingly said.

Sheriff Goode laughed and replied by saying, "There's nothing going on. We just thought we'd introduce ourselves."

"And measure you for a cell," Newkirk added.

"I knew you were up to something," Marc said as the others laughed.

"Are you going back across the street?" Goode asked referring to the jail.

Marc said he was, and Goode invited him to walk along with them.

While they waited for the street light to change on the corner, Goode said, "You're pretty well known in law enforcement circles."

"Oh, oh," Marc said. "Here it comes."

"No, no," Goode smiled. "Believe it or not we really respect defense lawyers. We have a couple of pretty good ones who wanted this case. You see," he continued as they started across the street, "this our first homicide in four years. Pretty big deal."

"Yeah, okay, I see that," Marc said. "Believe it or not, it's not quite Chicago level mayhem in the Cities."

When they got inside, Goode told Marc, "Look, I'll leave notice here at the front desk. You can see your client anytime, day or night, without any hassle. Anyone gives you any shit about it, I want to know.

"Abby, would you take Mr. Kadella back to his client?"

"Sure," Abby said.

"He has a visitor, Sheriff," the counter deputy said.

"Oh?" Marc said.

"His wife," the deputy told him.

Abby knocked on the conference room door's window then opened it for Marc. He walked in and found Zach and Samantha seated at a small table. Marc took a quick look around at the bleak room. Big city, small town, it didn't matter. These rooms were all the same. Designed to remind the people using them where they were: jail.

"Hey," Zach said to him.

"Marc! Thank God!" Samantha practically wailed. She jumped up and threw her arms around his neck and said, "I'm so happy and relieved you agreed to take Zach's case."

Marc, a puzzled look on his face, barely returned her embrace. When she let go, she stepped back, looked at him, and said, "Thank you. I feel much better knowing you're going to help him."

"Really? I have to tell you, Samantha, I thought you didn't like me," Marc said. He glanced at Zach who had covered his mouth with his hand to stifle a laugh.

"Why wouldn't I like you? Of course, I like you. I don't know how you got that impression," she said.

"Okay," Marc shrugged. "My bad, I guess. Sit down, and I'll tell you where we are."

When he finished telling them about the hearing, Zach asked about bail.

"Don't know. I talked to Tice and he said he would oppose it. I don't know this judge. They're gonna impanel a grand jury for a first-degree murder indictment, and they'll get it. If we get bail, it will be high," Marc said.

"Bail is no problem," Samantha said. "My father will make bail for him. Please get him bail."

Samantha stood up and announced she had to leave. She kissed her husband and rapped on the door for a deputy. After she was gone, Marc looked at Zach and silently smiled.

"What?" Zach asked.

"I was just thinking, now that I know she really does like me, maybe I should throw your case and then take a shot at her. Good looking, rich dad. What the hell?" Marc said.

Zach started laughing and said, "That's not funny, you asshole."

"Then why are you laughing?" Marc asked.

"At the thought of you and Samantha. She would neuter you," Zach laughed.

"Probably," Marc said with a grimace.

The two men talked for another half hour then Marc had to go. He would see his client the next day before court.

Samantha Evans was hurrying toward the jail's front exit when she was met by Abby Bliss.

"Excuse me, Mrs. Evans," Abby said. "Might I have a word with you?" she politely asked.

"I'm in a bit of a hurry," Samantha replied. Not being a criminal defense lawyer, Samantha didn't realize she could simply refuse. Like most people, when a cop asks to talk to you, people almost always feel obligated.

"It won't take but a minute. Please, in the conference room right here," Abby said with a smile pointing to a door.

They went in, sat down and Abby started asking a few bland, innocuous questions to get Samantha to relax. After a couple of minutes of this, she hit her with the big one.

"Did you know your husband was having an affair with the victim, Lynn McDaniel?"

Samantha noticeably froze for a full three seconds. Long enough for Abby to read her face and reaction. The answer was obviously yes.

"How dare you…"

"By your reaction, it's pretty clear you did," Abby calmly said waiting for another reaction.

Samantha hesitated again trying to think of something to say to refute the sheriff's deputy. It took three or four more seconds then she grabbed her purse, stood and abruptly announced she was leaving.

Samantha stomped off, angry with herself for allowing this nobody cop to sucker her like that. As Samantha walked off without closing the door, Abby quietly watched with a knowing smirk on her face.

FIFTEEN

Marc was waiting in the same barren conference room of the jail for a deputy to bring Zach to him. He had picked up a modest, tasteful suit and set of clothes for Zach to change into for the first appearance in court. Marc looked at his watch for the fourth time and noted it was less than two minutes since the last time he checked it.

Marc heard a rattling at the door and looked over to see Zach entering the room. The appearance was scheduled for 1:00 and it was already past noon.

"Take those off of him," Marc said referring to the handcuffs and chain around his waist. Zach was wearing an orange jumpsuit, white socks, and flip-flop rubber shower clogs. He had showered but had not shaved since being arrested.

"Sorry, the bracelets stay on," the deputy said.

Marc stood up, narrowed his eyes, icily glared at the deputy and said, "Not only are you going to take those off, so he can put on some decent clothes, but you're going to take him to the men's room and let him shave."

The deputy started to protest, but Marc cut him off.

"Either do it, or we go have a little chat with Judge Anderson with Sheriff Goode standing next to you."

Without another word, the deputy took the shackles off of Zach. Marc handed the deputy a cheap, plastic razor and a small can of shaving cream. Less than five minutes later, they were back. While Marc talked, Zach changed clothes.

"This is the first appearance. The judge will ask if you understand your rights and ask if we want the charges read. I'll decline. Then we'll make application for bail."

"What do you think?" Zach asked the question every defendant asks.

"I don't know," Marc replied. "I don't know this judge or this county. If he does set bail, it will be high."

"Samantha was here this morning. She'll be in court. She assures me her dad will wire whatever they want today," Zach said as he finished tying his tie. "Feels good to have real clothes on again," he said.

"I almost forgot," Zach said in a whisper as he sat down at the table next to Marc. "I mailed something to you a couple of days ago. What with everything that's happened, I forgot about it. Did you get it?"

"No," Marc said. "I haven't gotten anything from you. What was it?"

Zach took a few minutes to give Marc a brief rundown of the Cannon Brother's products liability class action lawsuit he was

72

defending. He then told Marc about the engineer's memo that showed that the company knew about the skateboard problems and chose to ignore them.

"Lynn knew about it, too," Zach said.

"Who else knew?" Marc asked.

"Dear old dad, Cal Simpson. And I'm pretty sure he told Samantha. I have no idea who else they might have told. I know Cal had a lot of stock in the company. At least he did at one time."

"You realize, of course, keeping that memo from going to the plaintiffs could be a motive for murder," Marc said.

"I know," Zach whispered back to him. "Keeping that thing quiet would be in everyone's best interest."

Marc sat back in the cheap, plastic, molded chair and stared at the blank wall for a moment.

"Did you make any copies before you sent it to me?"

"No," Zach said shaking his head. "I figured the fewer that were out there, the better. Didn't you get it? It shouldn't take more than a couple of days."

"No," Marc said. He took his phone out, dialed the office and put it to his ear.

"Carolyn, its Marc. Did the mail come today?"

"Yeah," he heard Carolyn reply. "A few things for you."

"Have you opened them? Anything from Zach Evans?"

"Yes and no," Carolyn replied. "Yes, Sandy opened it and no, nothing from Zach."

"Thanks, see you later," Marc said. He looked at Zach and said, "Nothing today, either. Are you sure it…"?

"That bitch," Zach said realizing who must have stopped it.

"Who?"

"My secretary, Marjorie. I'll bet she intercepted it. I don't know who would have it, but…"

"We'll find out," Marc said. He looked at his watch and announced it was time to go. Marc summoned the deputy who told them to leave Zach's jail clothes in the room.

"I'll meet you over there," Marc said.

The crowd was moving slowly out of the courtroom as the deputies put handcuffs on Zach. A woman was reaching across the railing and tugging on Marc's sleeve. Her name was Gabriella Shriqui. She was the host of an afternoon news show on a local TV station in the Cities. Gabriella had silky black hair six inches below her shoulders, light caramel skin that looked like a perpetual tan and dark, almost black, slightly almond shaped eyes. She was also Marc's investigator's best friend and a good friend of Marc.

"Gabriella! Stop it!" Marc said feigning annoyance with her. "Go out in the hall and I'll be out in a few minutes. You'll get you your interview."

Gabriella turned her mouth down, stuck out her lower lip and cast her eyes down into a fake pout. Marc laughed then said, "Yeah, that'll work."

Gabriella flashed a big smile at him and said, "Hurry up. I haven't got all day."

"You know her?" Zach whispered after she left. "Could you introduce me?"

"Aren't you in enough trouble?" Marc replied.

"Yeah, you're right. I sometimes forget myself."

"Besides, Samantha is in the hall waiting for me. We'll get the million dollars sent in and get you out of here. Keep your mouth shut."

The hearing itself had been short and sweet. Judge Anderson came out at 1:00 on the button and started right away. He knew exactly what he wanted and how to conduct a court appearance.

The first thing he did was take a moment to look over the crowd. Half of Foster was trying to get in to see the show. The clerk's office had received almost a dozen requests for reserved seats from the media. All of them were accommodated but without allowing recording devices. And no one would be allowed to stand.

The judge took a minute to address the crowd and sternly warned them about court decorum. Any nonsense and the person or persons involved would find out what the inside of a jail cell looked like.

He then got down to business. Marc waived reading of the charges. Zach entered a not guilty plea, and the argument over bail began.

Demarcus Tice was arguing for the state. The county attorney himself handling a first appearance was unusual in the extreme. Of course, he argued that given the defendant's resources, he was certainly a flight risk. Also, the severity of the crime demanded that the defendant be held without bail.

Apparently, Judge Anderson did not believe that an officer of the court with a sterling reputation would skip out. He set bail at a million dollars, ordered Zach to surrender his passport, and the whole thing was over by 1:20.

"Were you surprised that the judge allowed bail?" Gabriella asked Marc while Kyle Bronson, her cameraman, filmed.

"A little, yeah, to be honest. It's a small town, the judge and prosecutor are elected officials, and the easy thing to do would be to remand him into custody. I think Judge Anderson was correct when he said that keeping him in jail with his lawyer two hours away would be detrimental to his defense. That's why he set bail."

Gabriella tossed him a few more questions about the case digging for facts and evidence she could use. Marc knew better than to bite on it and the interview ended.

"What are you doing here anyway?" Marc asked as Kyle put away their equipment.

"I'm on vacation," she replied. "I went home for a few days, back in Michigan. I love my parents but staying in that house with them about drove me nuts."

"Mom still reminding you about the ticking biological clock?" Marc asked with a smile.

"Never ends," Gabriella said. She tilted her head backward, looked Marc over then said, "You know, maybe I should have you help me with that."

Marc looked at his watch then said, "Wow! Look at the time. I better get going."

"Feet don't fail me now?" Gabriella asked. "Don't worry," she laughed. "I don't want to risk the kid getting lawyer genes."

"Seriously, how long before he gets out?" she asked.

"His wife is working on it now. Shouldn't be more than a couple of hours," Marc replied.

"I'm gonna stick around and get some film of him leaving the jail," she said.

Marc leaned down and whispered in her ear, "He's being held in a holding cell downstairs here in the courthouse. I'll walk him out the front door for you. Be nice and give us a little space."

"Okay. Do you want to get coffee? There's a place up the street," Gabriella asked.

Marc could see Samantha walking toward him, probably with news about bail.

"Um, yeah, sure. Give me a minute. I need to talk to someone."

Marc walked off and met Samantha. She gave him the paperwork for the bail and told him her dad would wire it in shortly. She then said she was leaving, which Marc knew. He had already agreed to wait for Zach and drive him home.

Marc went first to check on Zach and tell him what was going on. He then left his cell phone number with the court clerk's office and asked to be notified when the wire was received.

At 3:45, Marc and Zach walked out the front door of the courthouse. Marc had warned him about Gabriella and her cameraman. The two of them walked down the sidewalk, past the monument of a dead Jacob Foster still holding the flag at Gettysburg, then turned left to go to the corner of Walnut and Main. All the while, Gabriella was filming them.

They waited at the corner for the light to change so they could cross Main to where Marc's car was parked. The light changed, and they started out. When they were almost half-way across, a nondescript, plain-looking, older brown van began racing down the street. Hearing the engine, Kyle turned toward it and began filming it as it raced toward the corner. Barely a second before it happened, both Marc and Zach turned toward the vehicle. Zach froze a step behind Marc who started to move just as the van hit them both.

Gabriella looked on in wide-eyed horror while Kyle remained calm and professional and filmed it all. At the moment of impact, Gabriella's view of her friend and his client was blocked by the van. Still filming, the two of them saw the van race through the intersection, through a red light almost hitting another car. The entire hit and run occurred directly in front of the sheriff's office and the Foster PD department.

SIXTEEN

The bell for the elevator dinged then the doors started to move. Before they finished opening, all five passengers were out and quickly, almost trotting, walked down the third-floor hallway. They were in the Foster County Medical Center.

Maddy Rivers was in front leading the way with her arm around the shoulders of Jessica Kadella. With them were Tony Carvelli, Connie Mickelson, and Eric Kadella.

While the paramedics worked on Marc while he was lying in the street, Gabriella had stepped away to make a phone call. Maddy had answered on the third ring and within five minutes was on her way to pick up Eric and Jessica. While she drove, she called Carvelli who then called Connie Mickelson. Maddy called Judge Tennant, Marc's ex-girlfriend. She told the judge what happened who in return told Maddy she could not leave yet but to keep her informed.

Maddy picked up the kids, then met Carvelli and Connie at the law office. They drove up in two cars and walked into the Medical Center before 7:00 P.M.

In the hallway, in front of the room Marc was in, were Maddy's best friend, Gabriella, and her cameraman, Kyle Bronson. Also standing around were two uniformed Foster cops along with Chris Newkirk and Abby Bliss.

"How is he?" Maddy asked Gabriella.

Gabriella, who was well acquainted with both of Marc's kids, was hugging a wet-eyed Jessica who was fighting back the tears.

"No word lately. Nothing new that I didn't tell you on the phone," a red-eyed Gabriella said.

While the others continued to huddle around Gabriella, Tony Carvelli walked over to Chris Newkirk. He had been leaning against the wall opposite Marc's room watching the new arrivals.

"Tony Carvelli," he said to Newkirk with an extended right hand. "I'm retired off the job from Minneapolis," he continued as the two of them shook hands. "I'm a private investigator now and a good friend of Kadella's. What can you tell me?"

Newkirk introduced Tony to Abby then said, "Looks like a hit and run. The other guy, Zach Evans, got the worst of it. He was DOA at the scene. Sorry to tell you but your guy took a pretty hard hit too. He was thrown a good twenty feet. I don't know. His condition is critical."

Tony squeezed his eyes shut in a moment of pain for his friend. He then asked, "What about the accident? Any witnesses?"

"Oh, yeah," Newkirk said with a touch of sarcasm. "Your media pals there," he continued, nodding at Kyle Bronson seated along the opposite wall, "They got the whole thing on film but won't let us see it. We're working on getting a court order," Newkirk said with a shrug.

Tony turned and glared at Kyle Bronson. Kyle knew Tony and why he was looking at him the way he was. He mouthed the word sorry at Tony, held his hands out, palms up and shrugged.

"Let me see what I can do," Tony told Newkirk.

He started to walk back toward his friends when a doctor came out of Marc's room. Everyone waiting in the hallway, except Kyle Bronson and the uniformed cops, gathered around her. Gabriella introduced Eric and Jessica and the doctor spoke to them.

"I'm not going to soft-pedal this. Your dad's in bad shape. He's critical but stable," the doctor said.

"That sounds not terrible," Eric said looking for a little good news.

"Yes, it's not terrible," she agreed. "He's still unconscious, but he needs surgery. There is probably internal bleeding and he needs a surgical trauma center that we are not equipped for.

"I've been in touch with Regions in St. Paul. In about an hour, if he is still as stable as he is now, we're going to helicopter him there. You two will be able to fly up with your dad. Is your mom here?"

"They're not married, but I need to call her and let her know what's going on. She knows about the accident," Eric told her.

"The rest of you," she continued looking at the worried faces, "look, he's doing okay for what he's been through. Regions is terrific, and they will have a surgical team standing by. Although if he is stable enough, they may wait until morning."

"Can I see him?" Jessica asked.

"That's probably not a good idea, sweetheart."

"I don't care. I want to see my dad," she insisted.

"Okay, I'll let you two go in for a minute. He's not able to talk and be advised, he looks bad."

"We need to talk," Tony said to Gabriella while the doctor went in with the two kids.

"No, we don't," Gabriella replied. She had seen him talking to Newkirk and knew what he wanted. "I can't do it, Tony. Not without a court order."

"Bullshit," Carvelli said. "This is Marc we're talking about."

"I understand, and it breaks my heart, but I gotta do what I gotta do. Sorry."

"What?" a confused Maddy said.

"She filmed the accident and won't let the cops see it," Carvelli told her. "Every minute counts!"

"Gabriella," Maddy pleaded, "show them the tape. Call Hunter and tell him," she continued referring to Gabriella's boss.

"I did. He told me I'm fired if I give it to them," Gabriella said. "They're arguing to the judge now. The station's lawyer is appearing by Skype. We'll get a decision soon."

By this time, Newkirk and Abby had joined them. Newkirk interrupted the argument by saying, "It's okay. There will be a court order here in ten minutes. I just got a call."

"Good," a greatly relieved Gabriella said. "Kyle," she continued, "can you make a copy for them in the truck?"

"On the way," he replied as he started to hurry off.

Carvelli almost ran after Kyle and grabbed him by the arm. As they walked down the hallway toward the elevators, Carvelli whispered, "I need a copy of it too."

"Tony, I don't think I can do…" Kyle started to say.

"Five hundred," Tony said.

"You got it," Kyle nodded then hurried off.

Maddy, Carvelli, and Connie Mickelson stood in the parking lot and silently watched the helicopter turn south. They waited until its lights could no longer be seen then Carvelli looked at the two women. Both had tears trickling down their cheeks.

"Hey, c 'mere," he softly said to both of them. He put his arms around them, and they maintained a group hug for a minute. "He's going to be okay," Carvelli said. "You'll see."

Maddy pulled away, brushed the tears off with her hand and said, "We need to see that tape. I'm not waiting for the local cops on this."

Carvelli reached in the right-hand pocket of his sport coat and held up a plastic case with a disk in it.

"Got it," he said with a smile. "Kyle burned a copy for me. Keep that to yourself. He could get fired for it."

"Why, you sneaky sonofabitch," Connie said playfully punching him in the shoulder.

"Let's go. I want to watch this right away. Something stinks. These things don't happen by coincidence," Carvelli said.

As they walked toward their cars, Carvelli's phone went off. He answered it and listened for a minute.

"Where was it?" he finally asked.

He listened some more then said, "Yeah, okay. I understand. Thanks, Chris."

"What?" Maddy asked as Carvelli replaced the phone in his pocket.

"That was one of the investigators, Chris Newkirk. They found the van. It was torched, and the license plates were gone," Carvelli said. They got the VIN, and they'll run that but don't hold your breath that it will lead anywhere other than it was stolen."

"This was no accident," Connie said.

"Can we see the van?" Maddy asked.

"No, he told me it's a crime scene, and he wouldn't tell me specifically where it was. He just said it was about ten miles from here on a side road in the woods. He also told me we are not to interfere in his investigation," Carvelli said.

"Tough shit!" Maddy said. "Let's go. I want to see that disk."

It was past midnight, and the three of them were sitting in Carvelli's living room. They were in the middle of the third viewing of the DVD and Carvelli had frozen the image on the screen. It was a clear shot of the van's driver.

"What?" Maddy asked looking at Carvelli.

"Look at him," Carvelli said. "Look at his face. Assume that he's not a drunk driving down the street."

"He's not," Maddy said. "That's pretty obvious."

"Right," Carvelli agreed. "He's driving down the street right at his target or targets. There is a guy with a camera pointed right at him. He had to see Kyle standing there filming. He couldn't miss him. Now, look at his face."

"He doesn't bother to cover it at all. He's wearing a disguise and doesn't care if somebody takes his picture," Maddy said.

"Exactly," Carvelli replied. "He's about as average looking as anyone could be. Medium length brown hair, mustache, and goatee. No visible markings of any kind. The guy could be a ghost."

"A professional," Maddy said.

"I would bet on it," Carvelli said.

He shut off the TV and said, "That's enough for tonight. I'll take this to my computer guy tomorrow…" Carvelli paused and looked at his watch. "Maybe yet tonight. I'll call and see if he's up. These guys don't keep normal hours like the rest of us. Why don't you two go home and get…"

"I'm going to the hospital," Maddy said.

"Want some company?" Connie asked.

"Sure. You need a ride anyway," Maddy said.

"I can always Uber a ride," Connie replied. "What else can I do to help?"

Taking turns, they had all called Marc's son, Eric, at Regions to keep informed. They were putting off surgery until morning. Marc was still listed as critical but stable. The kids were going to spend the night.

"There's nothing you can do there," Carvelli said. "Get some sleep."

"I'll call when we get there," Maddy said ignoring his very sound advice.

Before they got to the door to leave, Connie turned to Carvelli and again asked, "What else can I do to help?"

Carvelli thought about the question for a moment then said, "Try to think of some way, some legal grounds for getting the Fuller sheriff's office to give us copies of their case file."

"It's an ongoing investigation," Connie said. "At least that's what they will claim."

"What about if you're acting as Marc's lawyer?"

"Maybe," Connie replied.

"Are you sure we want to do that?" Maddy asked. "Won't we be waving a flag at them letting them know we're involved?"

"We're not doing anything, yet," Carvelli replied. "We'll see."

SEVENTEEN

At 3:00 A.M. Maddy drove into the parking lot of Connie's building. The two women had spent a fruitless two hours hanging around the ICU waiting room. Eric and Jessica were asleep in an empty room and Marc was still unconscious but still stable. He was scheduled for surgery at 7:00 A.M. to stop the internal bleeding. His broken and fractured bones, of which there were many, would have to wait.

Around 2:30 they had sneaked a peek into Marc's room. What they saw brought another round of tears. He looked awful. Bruised, battered and quite beaten with tubes in various places and a huge bandage wrapped around his head. They quietly left and decided to go home.

Connie's car was still parked behind the office. Maddy dropped her off and headed for home herself. The long day was catching up with her and without noticing it, she blew through a red light on 26th and Lyndale. Just her luck, an MPD patrol car was right behind her. Thinking he had a drunk, his rooftop light bar went on when he was almost at Maddy's bumper.

"Damn," she whispered. "What is this?"

She immediately pulled over and when the patrolman got to her window, Maddy flashed him a big smile.

Madeline Rivers was an ex-cop from the Chicago Police department in her early thirties. In her three-inch suede half-boots she liked to wear she was over six feet tall. She had a full head of thick dark hair with auburn highlights that fell over her shoulders, a model-gorgeous face and a body worthy of Playboy. In fact, foolishly posing for that magazine was what led her to quit the Chicago P.D.

Maddy, as she was called by her friends, had moved to Minneapolis after quitting the Chicago cops following her Playboy pose. At the same time, she went through an ugly breakup when she found out the doctor she had fallen for was married. After arriving in Minnesota, she obtained a private investigator's license. Maddy was befriended by Tony Carvelli and she was now doing quite well for herself.

The cop used his flashlight and shined it directly into her face. When he saw that smile, he froze for several seconds, unable to speak.

"I'm sorry, officer," Maddy said. "I'm not sure what I did."

"Um, ah, you, ah, went through a red light, ma'am," the young man managed to say.

Great, she thought, *they're calling me ma'am.*

"God, I'm sorry," she said.

"Have you been drinking, ma'am?"

Please stop calling me ma'am, she thought.

"No, no, officer. Not at all. It's, well, been a long day. A good friend was in a bad accident, and I'm heading home. I was at the hospital until now."

"Is she going to be okay, your friend?"

"He," Maddy corrected him. "We're not sure yet."

By now he had lowered his flashlight and was still staring. "Would you like an escort home? I'd be glad to do it."

"No, I'll be fine," Maddy said while thinking, *please don't ask for my phone number.*

"All right, ma'am. You take it easy."

"I will and thank you, officer," Maddy replied noticing the subject of a ticket for the red light never came up.

While Madeline was avoiding a traffic ticket, Tony Carvelli was at the home of an off-the-books tech guy he knew.

Tony Carvelli was in his fifties and due to his years on the streets of Minneapolis, looked it, but could still make most women check him out. He had a touch of the bad boy image they couldn't resist plus a flat stomach and a full head of thick hair touched with gray highlights; a genetic bequest from his Italian father.

Carvelli was an ex-Minneapolis detective and had the reputation of being a street predator which was well deserved. He looked and acted the part as well. Dressed as he normally was today, he could easily pass for a Mafia wiseguy. Growing up in Chicago, he knew a few of them and could have become one himself and very likely a successful one at that. Instead, after his family moved to Minnesota, he became a cop.

Carvelli had retired as a detective with over twenty years on the job with the MPD, the last three years in the department's intelligence unit. As a result of his time in intelligence, Carvelli knew just about everything and everyone there was to know in the seedy underside of the entire metro area. When he retired from the police, despite several lucrative corporate security job offers, he decided to go into business for himself. The thought of wearing a suit and tie every day and playing ass-kissing office politics in the corporate world had no appeal whatsoever. Over the years, he was able to build a successful business doing mostly corporate security investigations.

Paul Baker was the name of the man Carvelli was seeing at 1:00 A.M. Christened Pavel Bykowski by his devout Roman Catholic mother, Paul was a world-class hacker. Whatever there was to know about someone, Paul could dig it out of the internet.

Baker's office was the entire second floor of his South Minneapolis mortgage-free home; mortgage-free because Paul had hacked the lender and wiped the debt clean. There were two bedrooms upstairs and the wall separating them was gone, creating sufficient space for his setup. Tony knew of at least two FBI agents, four and maybe five or six MPD cops who also used him. He suspected the man had another dozen or more cash clients as well. It was enough to keep Paul Baker supplied with the latest equipment, at least three or four luxury vacations each year and all the best weed he desired.

"This is a disguise?" Baker asked.

"Yeah, I'm pretty sure it is. The guy didn't even try to cover up and he had to see the camera filming him," Carvelli replied.

The two of them were in Paul's living room watching the DVD on his large HD TV. Carvelli had paused it at the spot where the driver was closest to the camera. There was a clear picture of him. Medium length brown hair, black-framed glasses, and a mustache and goatee; a man you could see a hundred times on the streets of any major city and never notice.

"From the way he's seated in relation to the steering wheel I'd say he's about six feet tall. Maybe an inch or two less but no more," Paul said.

"Good guess. Probably about one-seventy to one-eighty," Carvelli added.

"This will take some time," Paul said. "I'll have to go through a lot of different looks."

"See his nose," Carvelli said. He had moved right up to the front of the screen, kneeled and was using a finger to go over the driver's nose. "It's a little too wide. See it?"

"Yeah. Probably some putty to make it bigger. I'll find this guy for you, Tony. Once I remove the glasses, I'll get a good look at his eyes. You can do a lot to reshape your face and even color the eyes with contacts. But there's not much you can do with the shape of the eyes without surgery.

"I'll find him. I'll have to run through a lot of different looks, but I'll find him. Anyone that would do this is in someone's database somewhere."

"True," Carvelli said. "Okay, Paul. Get at it. This is a priority..."

"I know," the hacker acknowledged. "Go home and get some sleep."

At 8:15 that morning, at least an hour before the night owl Carvelli habitually got out of bed, he stepped off the elevator at Regions Hospital. With him was a very well dressed, elegant looking woman. They were on the floor of the ICU walking toward Marc's room. Oddly there was no one in the hall.

Carvelli and his lady friend stopped at the nurse's station and inquired. They were told Marc was in surgery and everyone with him was downstairs. They got directions and a few minutes later walked into a surgical center waiting room.

The woman with Carvelli smiled at the small crowd then hurried to Eric and Jessica and sat down with them. They were sitting side-by-side along a wall, and she sat next to Jessica and took her hand.

"Hi," she softly said. "You don't know me, officially. I'm Vivian Donahue…"

"I know who you are," Eric said.

"I've known your dad for a while and consider him a friend," Vivian said.

By now Maddy had sat down next to Eric.

"I just want you to know that anything he needs, he'll get. He's going to be okay. I can't tell you how sorry I am, but I'll do anything I can for him."

Jessica wiped a few tears from her eyes, looked at the older woman and softly thanked her. Eric also did.

Vivian looked Jessica in the eyes and said, "I could really use a hug from you."

After they embraced, Vivian looked at Maddy, whom Vivian would like to adopt and asked, "Any word?"

Maddy shook her head and said, "No, nothing yet." She looked at the clock on the wall and added, "He's only been in there about an hour. We'll see."

By now the others had sat down in chairs around them. Vivian had that innate ability to draw people around her. She smiled at Connie Mickelson and Carolyn Lucas, both of whom she knew well.

Vivian Corwin Donahue was the current matriarch of a very well-known family that was one of the most socially prominent, politically connected and old-money wealthy in Minnesota. The lineage could be traced directly back to the 1840's when the family patriarch, Edward Corwin, immigrated to the mostly empty prairie that was Minnesota at that time, started farming and began building an agricultural empire that was worth billions today. The family itself was no longer involved in Corwin Agricultural but Vivian, as the current head of the family, could still move political mountains and when she called a governor, senator, congressman or mayor, that person had better sit up and pay attention.

Maddy stood up and took a couple of steps to where Carvelli was sitting. She bent down and whispered in his ear, "In the hall."

She walked to the door with Carvelli following and said to the others, "We'll be right back."

The two private investigators strolled down the hall toward the exit stairway door. Maddy started by saying, "I've been thinking. We both agree this was no accident and the target was Marc's client..."

"Zach," Carvelli agreed.

They had reached the end of the hallway and were standing in front of a window facing each other.

"...and Marc was collateral damage. The sheriff's office found the van later that day. Tell me, how did the driver leave the van and get away?"

"Had a car there," Carvelli said. Then the light in his head turned on, and he added, "How did the car get there? It was ten miles away out in the woods. He couldn't drive both the car and the van himself. He had help. Someone was waiting for him."

"Which adds up to a conspiracy," Maddy added.

"Who, what and why?" Carvelli said.

"And do you believe it is a coincidence that they killed the guy accused of murdering the woman, Lynn McDaniel?"

"No," Carvelli agreed. "And the nice thing about a conspiracy is the more people involved, the less likely it will hold up."

"It's likely the two guys driving the cars are not the ones behind the whole thing," Maddy said. "Probably hired help."

Carvelli stood silently thinking about what his P.I. friend had come up with. He tapped her on the end of her nose with an index finger and said, "You're a smart cookie, you know? What we need now is a motive."

"Who stands to gain," Maddy agreed.

Almost two hours later a young doctor came into the waiting room. He addressed Marc's son and daughter and said, "He's out of danger. We stopped all of the internal bleeding. In fact, it wasn't as bad as we feared. There doesn't appear to be any serious damage to any internal organs."

With this news, Jessica burst into tears while Vivian held her.

"We still have fractured bones to repair. We'll give it a couple of days before we do that."

"The worst of it is over?" Carvelli asked.

"I'd say yes. We're pretty sure he has a concussion but no fractures to the skull. His right leg is broken in a couple places. He has a fractured hip and wrist. A couple of fractured ribs and pretty badly bruised and beaten. I don't see anything permanent. I understand the man he was with wasn't so lucky," the doctor added.

"DOA at the scene," Carvelli told him.

"We won't know anything about recovery time or when he can go home for a few days. For now, he's basically out of the woods and resting comfortably. Unless complications arise. He's still out of it and in recovery. Probably best to let him rest for a couple of hours before you go in to see him."

"Will he be conscious?" Carvelli asked.

"Sure," the doctor said with a puzzled look.

"Oh, god, I forgot to tell you," Maddy said. "He regained consciousness during the night. Eric and Jessica even got to talk to him."

"Good," Carvelli said.

When the doctor left, Vivian stood up and said, "Well, that's good news. I don't know about the rest of you but all of a sudden, I'm famished. How about I take everyone out to grab a bite?"

EIGHTEEN

Tony Carvelli impatiently rang the doorbell for the third time. It was 9:00 A.M., two days after he had dropped off the DVD of the hit and run scene. Between the trips to the hospital and Foster, Minnesota, Carvelli's sleep was a mess. His nerves were a little frayed and it was already eighty-five degrees and humid which didn't improve his disposition. Standing on the stoop, waiting for his hacker pal was getting annoying. He was reaching for the doorbell again when the door came open.

"Hey, dude, come on in," Paul said as he stepped back holding the door open.

"Where the hell..., ah, never mind," a grumpy Carvelli started to ask. He looked at the rumpled, disheveled hacker and asked, "When was the last time you slept?"

"Ah, what day is it?"

"Forget I asked," Carvelli said walking past him into the living room. "What do you have?"

"I have worked my ass off on this. I had to go through hundreds of different looks for this guy and..." Paul started to explain.

"Stop! Don't try padding your bill," Carvelli said from the couch.

"Come on, dude, that's insulting."

"Right," Carvelli sarcastically replied. "Show me what you have."

Paul took a seat in a chair next to his TV. He had prepared a video show to explain how he found what he did. For the next half hour, while Carvelli grew more and more impatient, the hacker took him through a tour of the internet and facial recognition software.

Carvelli finally tilted his head onto the back of the couch to stare at the ceiling to show his frustration. At that point, Paul pressed a couple keys on his laptop and got to the end.

"I came up with five solid possibles," he said as the image of the first one appeared on the screen.

Carvelli was intently looking at the screen, a police mugshot of the first one.

"I got a paper report of each one for you," Paul continued as he retrieved five manila folders from the floor next to himself. He handed them to Carvelli and said, "They're in order. The guy on the screen is the folder on top."

The two men spent ten to fifteen minutes on each reviewing the first three. Paul would explain each one while Carvelli went through the material in the folders following along.

"The photos of the first three are close, but I'm not convinced. Plus, what I'm looking at in their background reports doesn't strike me as people sophisticated enough for this," Carvelli said. "These guys were paid by someone to do this and the first three don't strike me as hitmen with high placed connections. They're more lowlife scumbags."

"That's kind of what I thought, too. You said somebody else must have been involved. There must have been two people to pull this off. That's why I saved these last two for last," Paul said.

He clicked a couple more keys and a new face appeared. Like the others, it was a police mugshot.

Carvelli sat forward on the couch and stared at the man's face for almost a minute. "That's the best one yet," he finally said.

Paul clicked another keystroke and the photo of the van's driver appeared next to the subject.

"I think so, too," Paul said.

Carvelli picked up the folder and began reading out loud.

"Ryan Tierney, age forty-seven. Height five-eleven, weight one seventy-five. Born Boston, Mass," he said. He flipped a page and continued silently reading the man's criminal history.

When he finished, he said, "Quite an illustrious career. He certainly fits the bill."

"And you wanted known associates," Paul said. "Check out number five."

He hit a couple more keys and a new face appeared, very similar to the previous one.

"He could be the guy's brother," Carvelli said.

"There's a good reason for that. He *is* the guy's brother. Michael Tierney, five-foot-ten, one-ninety. A real leg breaker. Check out his bio. Looks like big brother Ryan is the brains and Little Mikey, a nickname, is the muscle,"

"In fact, he looks more like the driver than the other guy, number four," Tony said.

"He probably was the driver," Paul said. "If it was these two. As I said, Ryan is the brains; Little Mikey is the muscle."

Tony picked up the last manila folder and silently paged through it. It took almost ten minutes to go through it and when he finished, he placed it on the coffee table.

"This guy's a real asshole," Carvelli said. "Suspected of at least a dozen homicides. Both of the brothers affiliated with a Boston Irish gang but also known to do freelance."

"I checked something else on all of them," Paul said. "I checked for each traveling lately under all the names they are known by. I came up with this."

On the screen was security camera filming from the Minneapolis/St. Paul airport. It was of two men walking through the airport a week before the murders of Lynn McDaniel and Zach Evans.

Carvelli got up and knelt in front of the screen. Paul had stopped the film at a place with the best shot of the men. Tony stared at them for almost thirty seconds then stood up.

"It's a little fuzzy, but it could be our guys. Have you found any film of them leaving?"

"No, not yet. They could've split any number of ways," Paul said with a shrug, "Or they could still be here. I'll keep looking."

"Anything from hotels, motels?"

"I haven't had a chance yet. That's a pretty big job. You want me to try, I will," Paul said.

"I don't know," Carvelli said. "I don't think these guys would stay at a place with cameras hooked up to their computer system. What do I owe you?"

"I don't know," Paul shrugged. "A couple of grand?" he said as a question.

"Normally I'd complain," Carvelli said. "But you did good. I'll get it for you by the end of the week."

With Vivian Donahue backing the investigation and as fond of Marc as she was, money would not be an issue.

Maddy Rivers stepped off the elevator and checked the signs on the opposite wall. Now that Marc was off the critical list and doing better, he had been moved out of ICU. Maddy had his new room number and after checking the wall signs, turned right to go to his new room and see him.

Halfway there, she went past a nurse's station on her left and saw a woman she knew coming out of a room.

"Hi, Margaret," Maddy said smiling at Margaret Tennant, Marc's girlfriend.

"Hi, Maddy," Margaret pleasantly replied.

"How is he?" Maddy asked.

"In good spirits. Pretty beat up but he seems to be taking it all well," she replied. "I really have to get going," Margaret continued. "I have a trial on hold this morning while I came here." Margaret was a Hennepin County trial judge.

"Oh, okay," Maddy said. "Well, nice to see you again."

"You too," Margaret said. She took a couple of steps then turned back and said, "Maddy, take care of him. Okay?"

"Of course," Maddy replied with an uncertain look on her face.

Margaret wiped a tear from her cheek, turned and hurried off.

A few seconds later Maddy strolled into Marc's room. He was in a semi-private room. The bed nearest the door was nicely made up and the space appeared to be unoccupied. Marc's bed was by the window with a view of the back of the Minnesota State Capitol Building.

Marc still looked pretty bad and beat up. The surgeries needed to repair the fractures in his left arm, the one he had landed on, right leg and hip were done. He probably had enough pins in various bones to set off an airport alarm. Because of his age and general good health, the doctors were confident he would heal up and be as good as new.

Maddy pushed the curtain back that separated the two spaces. She dropped her purse in a chair and stepped up to him.

"Hey," she said as she bent down to kiss his cheek. She stood up and gently placed a hand on his shoulder. "How are you feeling?"

"Great, never better. I have more drugs in me than a street junkie. This is why I never got into drugs. I was always afraid I'd like them too much."

Maddy sat down with her back to the window. "I saw Margaret in the hall just now. What's up with that?"

Marc took a moment to think through the fuzziness in his head then replied, "I think that's done."

"That's too bad," Maddy said. "I liked you guys together. She's a terrific lady."

"These things happen," Marc replied.

"What happened?"

"She wants marriage. I'm not ready. It's that simple. I guess it just ran its course," Marc said. He paused for several seconds then added, "I think she's got someone on the back burner. We kind of had it out over the Fourth. I don't blame her. She wants what she wants for herself. She's entitled to that, but so am I."

"Tony's on the way," Maddy said changing the subject. "He called while I was coming here. He says his hacker guy may have found the driver and his accomplice." She looked at her watch and said, "He should be here pretty soon.

"You look a little better," she continued. "Not so pale. Have Eric and Jessica been up today?"

"They both called. They'll be by later on. Eric has a job."

"Really? Where?" Maddy asked.

Slowly, Marc told her about his son's job at a local investment firm. Maddy knew the firm well and even had money with them. As he was finishing, the door opened, and Tony Carvelli came in.

Carvelli and Marc went through the "how are you feeling" routine. When they finished, Carvelli said he thought he saw Margaret Tennant driving out of the hospital's parking ramp as he drove up to it.

When Marc and Maddy finished telling Carvelli about the breakup, Carvelli the smartass decided to rub it in a bit.

"So, Margaret Tennant's on the loose. She's a pretty good-looking woman. I just might take a shot at her."

"Nice friend," Maddy admonished him.

"What's friendship got to do with it?" Carvelli asked.

Marc was trying not to laugh. He finally chimed in, "You couldn't handle her. At your age, she'd kill you."

"Might be worth it," Carvelli said then both he and Marc laughed.

"Men. Delusions of grandeur," Maddy said rolling her eyes at the ceiling.

"Maddy says your guy may have found something," Marc said getting down to business.

Carvelli stood and moved Marc's portable tray table to the end of the bed. Maddy shifted her chair next to the bed so she could see what Carvelli had to show them.

He laid the two manila folders on the tray. Before he started, Carvelli looked at the bandage wrapped around Marc's skull and sincerely asked, "How's the head feeling?"

"I'm so drugged up, Tony, I don't even know. They tell me it's a fairly severe concussion, whatever that means."

"Still no recollection of the accident?"

"No, I don't even remember going up there. Talking to Zach, the court appearance, any of it. His wife was there too and has been by to see me. I guess I talked to her too, but I got nothing. The doctors think some of it will come back, maybe."

With that, Carvelli told them about what the hacker had come up with. As he did this, he passed photos and documents from the two files to Maddy. She looked them over and held them up for Marc.

When Tony finished, Maddy asked Marc, "How much of that did you get?"

"I don't know. Maybe half. Tony thinks we may have found the guys who did this," Marc replied.

Marc looked at Tony and said, "Now what?"

"We try to find the guys. Or a connection to who ordered this. These two didn't drop out of the sky on their own. They are out of Boston. Unless we can find a direct connection between them and either you or Zach, they were hired to do this."

"I have no idea who they are. If you want to go through my files looking for leads, go ahead. I trust you two to keep things confidential. You've worked for me enough."

"It's a thought," Carvelli said. "My guy is looking for known associates and known associates of known associates."

"You're confusing me," Marc said.

"Sorry. We're looking for them. We'll find something."

NINETEEN

"Tell your people to relax," Cal Simpson said into his private phone. "Everything is on schedule."

Cal was on the phone with Senator Albert Fisher who was calling from Washington on a burner cell phone.

"It's that damn Manion," the senator said. "He's so worried about his senator-for-the-little-people bullshit image. I swear the old fool must say President Roger Manion into the mirror a dozen times a day."

"God help America if that happens. I'd move to Cuba just to be able to hang onto some of my money," Cal replied.

He heard a soft knock on his door and covered the phone with his hand. Before he could respond to the knock, Samantha came in.

"Don't tell anyone else about the engineer's memo. I have it. We're good to go. The stock price has recovered. Even increased a bit."

"When is the press release about the weakness of the plaintiff's case going to be released?"

"I talked to Brody Knutson about it at Zach's funeral. They have an entire PR media blitz planned for the next month. We'll get the stock price pushed up even further."

The two of them made a little more small-talk then Cal ended the call.

"Hi, sweetheart," Cal said to Samantha.

They were seated in Cal's office in the mansion on Lake Minnetonka. It was two days after Zach's funeral and things seemed to be settling down. With Zach's death, the investigation into the murder of Lynn McDaniel appeared to be stalled. In fact, from what they were told by the Foster County Sheriff's office the cops seemed satisfied Zach was guilty. The focus was now on Zach's death. The sheriff of Foster County was investigating Zach's death as a hit and run vehicular accident and not necessarily a deliberate act. At least that is what Cal and Samantha were told.

"Did you know as a firm partner they had a two-million-dollar insurance policy on Zach? It's to buy me out and release any claim to his interest in the firm," Samantha said.

"Yes, I did," Cal replied while nodding his head. "Brody Knutson mentioned it the other day. I'm sorry, I forgot about it. What the hell," he continued, "there's a nice bonus for you.

"How's the lawyer doing? Kadella?" Cal asked. "Heard anything?"

"He's still at Regions," Samantha said. "I guess he's going to be okay."

"I'm sorry that happened," Cal said while pouring more coffee from the carafe on his desk. He held it up at Samantha who shook her head at the offer.

Cal took a swallow from his cup, set it on the desk blotter and said, "I've been thinking about Zach. Maybe we can steer the investigation in a new direction."

"Oh, how?" Samantha asked.

"This lawyer, Kadella, he's done a lot of criminal defense work over the years, hasn't he?"

"Yes, I guess so. He's pretty good, too," Samantha said.

"Isn't he the one who represented that Muslim, the one accused of treason?"

"Yes, he was," Samantha agreed. "Oh, I see where you're going. Who says it wasn't him who was the target of the hit and run and Zach was the collateral damage?"

"Exactly. There are plenty of kooks out there who are probably still pissed at him for getting the Muslim out of jail. And he likely has plenty of disgruntled clients."

"Maybe I should make a call to that investigator, Newkirk. Find out if he has thought of this," Samantha said. "Just ask him if he has thought about Kadella being the target."

"That would be a reasonable idea coming from you," Cal agreed.

"That's an interesting theory, Mrs. Evans," Chris Newkirk replied. "We have thought of it and aren't ruling it out. So far, we haven't seen any indication of that, but we are looking at all possible angles, just in case."

"Oh, um, yes, of course, you have," Samantha replied. "I don't mean to imply you aren't doing your job. It's just something I thought about. Please don't take offense."

"Oh, not at all, Mrs. Evans," Newkirk said. "In fact, if you think of anything else, please don't hesitate to call. Or if you have any questions, call anytime."

"Thank you, Detective," Samantha said.

"My pleasure, ma'am."

Newkirk hung up the phone on his desk and looked across his desk and Abby's. She was staring at him with an expectant look on her face.

"Well?" she asked.

"The P.I. was right," Newkirk said. "Carvelli predicted she would call and try to steer us toward Kadella as the victim."

"To deflect us away from her husband," Abby said. "Why? Why would the widow want us to look in a different direction?" Abby rhetorically asked while Newkirk was dialing his phone from a number he read off a card.

"You were right," Newkirk said when Tony Carvelli answered the call. "The grieving widow just called with suggestions as to why your friend might be the target."

"Well, now we know," Carvelli said.

"She could be right," Newkirk said.

"Sure. It's possible. But why would she be the one to bring it up?"

"That's the question, of course," Newkirk said. "How's your guy doing?"

"Okay. It's been what, ten days since the accident? He's still having memory problems. I'm on my way to the hospital now. I'll let you know how he's doing and if he starts to remember anything."

Carvelli entered Marc's room and said hello to the elderly patient who was Marc's new roommate. The man was in for a knee replacement and had been whining like a child about the pain. Every time the physical therapist tried to get him moving, the man almost screamed about how much it hurt.

Carvelli pushed the curtain aside and found Marc and Maddy idly chatting. He said hello to Maddy, sat down and looked at Marc.

"The bruising is pretty much gone," Carvelli remarked. "When are you getting out?"

"Probably tomorrow. They shaved my head," Marc glumly added.

"Well, yeah," Carvelli replied. "They had to bandage it up."

"They just told me this morning."

"Bummer, dude," Carvelli joked. "It will grow back."

"What if it doesn't?" Marc asked almost pouting.

"Bald guys are sexy," Maddy said.

"You really think so?" Marc asked perking up with her comment.

"No," Maddy said. "I just said that to be nice."

"It'll grow back," Carvelli repeated and laughed.

"Samantha called the sheriff's office in Foster," Carvelli whispered to them. He whispered because he did not want Clarence, the elderly whiner in the next bed to eavesdrop. "Just like we thought, she tried to steer them away from Zach being the target to look at our boy Marc as the target."

"No kidding," Maddy quietly said. "Now what?"

"If we suspect her, then the question is still the same; motive. Who stands to gain?" Carvelli said.

"The firm, Everson, Reed, would have an insurance policy on him. As a partner, they would want that to use the proceeds to buy out the widow," Marc told them.

"How much?" Maddy asked.

"I don't know. A firm of that size? A couple million at least," Marc said.

"There's your motive," Carvelli said.

"Not so fast," Marc said. "They're already wealthy. The old man has tons of money. I don't think another two million is going to get them excited."

"How about that he was cheating on her?" Maddy asked. "People have been known to murder for that."

Marc and Tony looked at each other, both frowning in thought. Tony shrugged and said, "Maybe. But I'm not too crazy about it. She knew about it for a while, didn't she?" he asked looking at Marc.

"I think so," Marc said.

"Knock, knock," the three of them heard a woman's voice say.

They all turned their heads to find a familiar looking woman standing there watching them. The three of them all froze for two or three seconds staring at the intruder. It was Maddy who was the first to recognize her.

"Paxton? My god! It is you," Maddy said. She jumped up and stepped quickly to the woman, arms extended.

"Yep, it's me," the woman said with a big smile. Maddy and Paxton O'Rourke exchanged a brief hug as Marc and Carvelli looked on.

TWENTY

A floor nurse brought a wheelchair into Marc's room and the four of them adjourned to a more private setting. They were in a visitors' room; Maddy, Carvelli, and Paxton in separate chairs, Marc in the wheelchair.

Paxton was formerly Major Paxton O'Rourke of the U.S. Army's Judge Advocate General's Corp. Marc and company met her on a case he had tried. It was the court-martial of a soldier Marc knew who had been falsely accused of treason. Paxton had led the Army's prosecution team.

The trial was won by Paxton with a finding of guilt of Marc's client. Eventually, the man's innocence came to light and he was exonerated.

"It's nice to see you again," Marc said to her, "but we're all a little baffled by your presence. What?"

"Well, I'm not with the Army anymore. After the fiasco of Samir Kamel, the Army needed a scapegoat and I was it," Paxton began.

"What did you do?" Maddy practically yelled. "You did your job! How can they blame you?"

"Because they're the Army and they can do what they want," Marc said. "I'm not at all surprised."

"The good news is," Paxton continued, "they got a job for me with the DOJ. I'm an Assistant U.S. Attorney out of Chicago now."

"So, you landed on your feet," Carvelli said.

"I landed on my feet," Paxton agreed, smiling at Carvelli. She turned her head to look at Marc, the smile went away and with a sad look asked, "Are you okay?" She was close enough to reach his right hand and give it an affectionate squeeze.

"They cut off all of his hair," Maddy said.

"And it's not going to grow back," Carvelli added.

"Don't say that! You said it would!" Marc almost shrieked.

"Bald, older men are sexy anyway," Paxton said.

"Really? You're not just saying that?" Marc hopefully asked. "Wait a minute. What's this 'older men' business? I'm barely older than you, I think."

By now Maddy and Paxton were laughing hysterically.

"It will grow back! Calm down," Maddy assured Marc.

"Probably," Carvelli tossed in just to annoy Marc.

"What are you doing at Justice?" Marc asked Paxton, wanting to change the subject.

"White collar crimes are about all I can tell you," she answered.

"Why are you here? Not that we're not happy to see you again but you didn't just happen to be in the neighborhood and dropped by to say hello," Maddy asked.

"I can't tell you why but Marc's accident or hit and run, whatever you want to call it, came across my desk. I managed to finagle a legitimate business reason to come here for a couple of days. So, I wanted to stop and see how he was and say hi to you guys. Especially the Italian Stallion sitting there," Paxton said with a wink at Maddy.

"Don't call him that, there'll be no living with him," Maddy said.

Carvelli looked at Marc and said, "So much for the bald, older-men theory. It's all about the hair."

"It'll grow back," Marc said.

"Probably," Carvelli teased him again.

"You seem to be in good spirits," Paxton said to Marc. "Nothing permanent?"

"My memory of that day is a problem," Marc said.

"Concussion?" Paxton asked.

"Yeah, but they tell me it could come back," Marc answered.

"Any news on the investigation?" Paxton asked looking first at Carvelli then Maddy.

Maddy looked at Carvelli and asked, "Should we tell her? Show her what we have? She has resources."

"And if she misuses them she could end up in jail," Carvelli said.

The room went silent while they all pondered the exchange between Maddy and Carvelli. Finally, after more than a minute, Paxton broke the silence.

"Okay, I'll tell you this…"

Carvelli quickly leaned forward and interrupted her by asking "Why did a hit and run in northern Minnesota come across an AUSA's desk in Chicago?"

"Okay," Paxton continued, "I have more than a curious interest in what happened here. For now, that's all I can tell you, and I have to ask you to keep that confidential. I showed you mine, now show me yours."

"You didn't show us anything," Carvelli said.

"Tony! We can trust her," Maddy said. She looked at Paxton and said, "We can, can't we?"

"Not entirely, no. I can look into what you have, but I may or may not be able to offer you anything I might find. I will if I can."

"At least she's being honest," Marc interjected. "And we'd be no worse off than we are now."

Carvelli thought about it for a moment then said, "We think we've identified the driver and his accomplice. We have pictures and biographies, don't ask me how we got them. What we need is a motive and to find these guys. Your office has an interest in this?"

"Maybe, probably," Paxton replied. "Get me what you have, and I'll see what I can find out."

"Do not bring the FBI into this," Carvelli said. "At least not yet."

"Why? They have enormous resources," Paxton said.

"I got a sheriff up North who is on my ass now to stay out of it. He has a small-town department with pretty good people but no resources or jurisdiction outside of his county. This is a conspiracy of some kind and it's outside of the scope of their authority. Only part of this took place in Foster, Minnesota. We'll show you film of the accident. You'll see, it was no accident and the two guys we found did not do this on their own," Tony said.

"That's why you need the FBI," Paxton replied.

"No," Tony said emphatically shaking his head. "If they get involved alarm bells will be going off all over the place."

"We think it had something to do with Zach Evans' father-in-law. A guy by the name of Calvin Simpson," Maddy said.

When Maddy said Simpson's name, Carvelli and Marc were both watching Paxton's expression. But she gave no indication at all that she knew who he was.

"And he's rich and has a lot of political clout," Maddy finished.

"Okay, I'll check him out," Paxton said. She turned to Marc and asked, "How are you holding up?"

"I'm getting a little tired," he admitted. "Maybe I should go back and lie down."

"I'm glad you're going to be okay," Paxton smiled and squeezed his hand again. "The hair will grow back."

"I know," Marc answered her.

After getting Marc back to his room and into bed, the three of them drove to Carvelli's South Minneapolis home. When they arrived, Carvelli showed his copy of the investigation documents, including photos of the Tierney brothers, to Paxton. While Paxton paged through the files, Carvelli loaded the DVD of the hit and run into his DVD player.

The three of them watched the crash twice with Paxton handling the remote. She used it to run the disk in slow motion in places where she wanted a closer look. One, in particular, was the best shot of the driver of the van.

"You think this is him?" Paxton asked. The image was frozen on the TV, as she held up the mugshot photo of Michael Tierney.

"Yeah, we think since he made no effort to hide his face from the camera, that must be a disguise," Maddy replied.

"My tech guy, who shall remain anonymous…" Carvelli began to say.

"Because he's a criminal hacker who should be in prison and you want to protect him," Paxton interrupted.

Tony rolled his eyes up at the ceiling and as innocently as possible said, "You have a very suspicious mind. I don't know what you're talking about."

"Uh huh," Paxton said. "Just remember there's no such thing as a private investigator slash internet hacker confidentiality privilege."

"Then don't ask me questions I don't want to answer," Carvelli told her.

Paxton laughed, looked at Maddy and asked, "You know his hacker pal?"

"No, I really don't," Maddy replied. "I'll say this, though. From what Tony has told me and what I have seen, he or she has been extremely helpful to law enforcement."

"Including some FBI guys, I know," Carvelli quickly added.

"Well then, I suppose we'll leave him alone. Some of these guys do a lot of damage and need some serious prison time."

"That's not his thing," Carvelli said confirming that the hacker was a man. "He's a capitalist and makes a lot of money. In fact, he's helped the feds catch a couple of other hackers. The ones who like to mess with serious stuff just for the fun of it.

"Anyway," Carvelli continued, "he put a lot of work into this, running different facial recognition profiles with various looks of the driver. We're pretty certain he's the guy."

"So am I," Paxton said. "But for a different reason, which I can't discuss yet," she added. "Would it be worthwhile to go to…where is it? Where is the sheriff?"

"Foster, Minnesota. It's a nice resort area city and county a couple of hours north of here," Carvelli said.

"Should we run up there?" Paxton asked.

Carvelli looked at Maddy and shrugged his shoulders before saying, "What do you think?"

"What are you looking for?" Maddy asked Paxton.

"Whatever they have," she replied.

"Why are you interested in this? Is this personal or business?" Carvelli asked.

"I told you, it came across my desk for a reason I can't get into yet. We'll see when and if. Until then, I'm asking you to trust me."

"In that case, you should probably call the sheriff in your official capacity. If you show up with us, he'll blow a gasket. He'll think we're messing around with their investigation…"

"Which we are," Maddy said.

"...and he won't take it well," Carvelli said.

"Send a couple of FBI guys up there," Maddy said with a knowing grin.

"Yeah, that will go over big. Just what every small-town sheriff wants. The FBI stomping around in his garden," Paxton sarcastically added. She turned to Tony and said, "I think you're right. I'll call from my office when I get back."

"You'll have to go through Sheriff Goode. He's an okay guy but protective of his turf. The guy you'll want to talk to is Chris Newkirk. He's their lead investigator," Carvelli told her.

"Can I keep your file?" Paxton asked.

"Nice try," Carvelli said. "There's a Kinkos not too far from here. They can copy the DVD for you, too."

"When are you leaving?" Maddy asked.

"Tomorrow morning. I have a Delta flight at 6:50. I should be in the office by 9:00. I've only been here once. I'd like to check out the Mall of America. Do a little shopping."

"I'll take you," Maddy said. "Carvelli can tag along and buy us lunch."

"Yeah, that's what I want to do today. Go to that monstrosity," Carvelli said.

Paxton looked at Maddy and said, "Should we let him off the hook?"

Maddy looked at Carvelli who looked back with a look on his face that made him appear to be begging.

"I suppose," Maddy replied. "But you're going to Kinkos to get the copies made then take us to dinner."

"Deal," he said with understandable relief.

TWENTY-ONE

Paxton O'Rourke reached under the seat in front of her and retrieved her laptop bag. In it was her personal laptop, not the one the government had provided for her. She was on her early morning flight back to Chicago. Paxton had been blessed with a little luck in her seat assignment.

Deciding that an upgrade to first class for one-hundred-forty-dollars was a bit much for a one-hour flight, she followed the herd into what Paxton referred to as the "cattle car" section, coach. Fortunately, the young woman sitting next to her was a petite little thing who didn't seem interested in telling Paxton her life story.

Paxton opened her laptop and placed it on the food tray. She opened a Word document and began typing. She made a complete record of her trip, the one she would keep to herself. The one she would submit to her boss would be a sanitized version. The official report would be truthful, just not entirely truthful.

Her report to herself took up almost four pages of the Word doc. Paxton had concentrated so intently on the proofreading that she missed the final approach announcement. She was typing a couple of additions when she was slightly shaken by the landing gear descending. Twenty minutes later she was hurrying up the concourse, her laptop bag in her left-hand, her purse over her shoulder, and the carry-on bag with wheels trailing behind.

While Paxton was making the final approach to O'Hare, Carvelli knocked lightly on Marc's hospital door. He opened it and peeked in to find Marc's roommate absent, then held it open for the woman with him.

"Thank you, Anthony," Vivian Donahue said as she entered the hospital room.

Vivian stuck her head around the curtain separating the room to find Marc sitting up along with Maddy and Marc's daughter, Jessica.

"Good morning," Vivian said while Carvelli looked over her shoulder.

"Hi!" Maddy yelped as she jumped up. The two women embraced while Carvelli pulled back the curtain.

"Where's the whiner?" Carvelli asked, referring to Marc's roommate. "Hi, sweetheart," Carvelli said to Jessica.

"He's in therapy," Marc said. "And he's doing a lot better. Not as much pain." He looked at Vivian and asked, "To what do we owe the honor?"

"I've decided you're coming home with me," Vivian announced.

"Do I get a vote?" Marc asked.

"No," Maddy and Vivian said together.

"I think it's a great idea," Jessica chimed in.

Marc turned his head to her and said, "A minute ago you were all set to move in with me and take care of me."

"Well, ah, yeah, but, um, this will be better for you," Jessica stammered around.

"I was looking forward to losing some weight trying to eat your cooking," Marc said.

"Very funny, Mr. Smartass," Jessica replied. "I can cook," she added.

Marc looked at Carvelli and asked, "What do you have to say about this?"

"I didn't get a vote either. My advice? Take her up on it. She'll spoil the hell out of you. Do it for a couple of weeks. At least until you get your strength back."

Marc looked at Maddy and Vivian, both of whom were now seated and said, "I surrender. Besides, you're probably right."

"Nice digs," Maddy said referring to the Corwin Family Mansion on Lake Minnetonka.

"Are you sure you want a criminal defense lawyer living in your house? What will the neighbors think? I mean, a corporate lawyer or even an insurance defense lawyer would be almost okay. But a criminal lawyer? Scandalous," Carvelli said to Vivian.

"I lie awake nights worrying about what the neighbors think," Vivian sarcastically replied. "Besides, a little scandal might be fun."

"What are we waiting for?" Carvelli asked.

"The doctor to check me out," Marc replied.

They waited for the doctor and made desultory small talk until Maddy mentioned how nice it had been to see Paxton O'Rourke again.

"Yeah, it was," Marc eagerly agreed.

Maddy tilted her head at him and with a sly smirk and raised eyebrows said, "She's kind of hot for you, you know."

"Stop it," Marc laughed.

"Who is Paxton?" Jessica asked in a teasing manner. "Come on, Dad, let's have it."

"Maddy's just being cute," Marc said.

"She's a lawyer with the government," Maddy told Jessica. "She prosecuted Samir Kamel, and I am not kidding. I could see it in Washington."

"Stop it," Marc said again while they all watched him with amusement. "Seriously? You think so?"

"Can't you tell?" Maddy asked.

"No," Marc said.

"No," Carvelli agreed when Maddy looked at him.

"Men are so simple-minded," Vivian told Maddy. She looked at Jessica and added, "Remember that, dear. We almost have to hit them over the head just to get their attention."

"I've noticed," Jessica said.

"What?" Marc said looking at his daughter. "What have I told you about boys? They're stupid, smell-bad and most of them are barely toilet trained. Stay away from them until you're forty."

Maddy said again, "You really didn't notice? What do you need, a billboard?"

"That would be helpful," Marc said. "Look, there are basically three kinds of men. Those that think every woman is after them. Those that couldn't score in a cat house with a fistful of fifty-dollar bills…"

"Dad!"

"…and those that don't have the slightest idea what's going on with women. Which is about ninety-nine percent of us."

Vivian looked at Carvelli, with whom she had a "friends with benefits" type relationship. "Anthony?"

"Ah, yeah, I think that's pretty accurate," he agreed.

The room went silent for a moment then Maddy said to Marc, "Well, now you know. Paxton is interested."

Marc looked at his left arm in a cast and a sling, his right hip and leg immobilized and said, "Fine, time to find out."

"Chris Newkirk," Paxton O'Rourke heard the man say through her office phone.

It was 8:50 A.M. and Paxton had arrived at the office fifteen minutes ago. Waiting for her was a message on her phone and in her email. Both were from Kamar Haddad, the executive assistant of Paxton's boss. Both messages were the same. Paxton was to report to the boss and both were marked urgent. Paxton decided to ignore them for the time being. She wasn't ready for what she knew was coming.

Paxton identified herself to Newkirk. She then asked him if he would please give her as much information as possible about the homicides of Lynn McDaniel and Zachary Evans.

"How do I know you're who you say you are?" Newkirk asked.

"Well, I guess you could go online, find the number for the Chicago U.S. Attorney's office, call back and ask for me," Paxton replied.

There was silence for a moment between them then Newkirk said, "Okay, I guess I'll leave it at that. What I don't understand is why a U.S. Attorney in Chicago cares about a case in upstate Minnesota."

"I knew you'd ask that and about all I can tell you is it might be peripheral to a case I'm pursuing. I can't go into detail right now," Paxton said.

Again, there was a pregnant pause until Newkirk said, "Okay, here's what we have."

A few minutes later he finished, and Paxton asked, "That's it?"

"Afraid so," Newkirk replied. In his years with the Duluth PD, he had dealt with the Feds, FBI and U.S. Attorneys many times. Newkirk knew what to give them and what not to.

"So, you think the hit and run was not an accident? That it was intentional?"

"Yes, that seems pretty clear," Newkirk replied.

"It was made to look like an accident?" Paxton asked.

"I guess so, but he did a poor job of it," Newkirk said. "What more do you have?"

"Nothing. I have less than you. But if I come across anything, I'll let you know right away."

"I appreciate that, Ms. O'Rourke," Newkirk said while at the same time thinking, *bullshit*.

"Could I get a copy of the file?" Paxton asked.

"I'll have to check with my boss, but I think that will be okay. Give me an email address."

Three minutes before 9:00 Paxton rapped on the opaque glass door with her boss' name embossed in gold on it. She waited for a response and when she heard it, opened the door. Norah McCabe, the U.S. Attorney, had her phone to her ear and motioned to Paxton to take a seat,

"I'll keep that in mind, Senator," McCabe said to her caller. She listened for a moment then said, "Yes, sir. Thank you, sir," and ended the call.

McCabe swiveled around to face Paxton and curtly asked, "Well?"

"I sent you an email with my report," Paxton said. The report she had emailed was little more than a vague summary of the detailed one she had typed on the plane.

"What's in it?"

"Not much," Paxton conceded. "Except, in my opinion, I believe that the hit and run death of Zachary Evans was done by professionals."

"Oh? Your vast years of experience in crime outside of the military led you to that conclusion did it?" McCabe sarcastically asked.

Knowing this was McCabe's way of treating not only subordinates but inferiors, Paxton did not let it bother her. Instead, she looked at her boss and as impassively as possible said, "No, that is the opinion of the lead investigator who has almost thirty years' experience, including over twenty with the Duluth PD."

McCabe waved the statement off with a flick of her left hand and said, "Local cops couldn't find their dicks with a map and a flashlight."

McCabe sighed, folded her hands and placed them on her desk blotter. She smiled slightly and as softly as she could say said, "Paxton, I think you're an exceptional lawyer. Your years with the JAG Corps and the reputation you bring certainly suggests that."

Here it comes, Paxton thought.

"But I don't see a case here. You've been looking into Calvin Simpson for months, and you don't have squat. So, the man is rich and politically connected. Hundreds, if not thousands, of people are. Are they all criminals?"

"Probably," Paxton said.

McCabe fixed her with a serious glare before continuing. "You have other cases…"

"I am absolutely on top of every one of them," Paxton said.

"…and if you need more work I can see you get it. Bring me something or wrap this thing up."

"Yes, ma'am," Paxton quietly said.

"Paxton," McCabe said more softly again, "I admire your ambition. We could use a little more of that around here."

TWENTY-TWO

Paxton removed an inexpensive flip-phone from her briefcase. She was back in the tiny office she shared with Prakesh Kumar. Prakesh was a second-generation Pakistani graduate of Michigan Law. If Paxton had to have an officemate, she was delighted it was him. He was hardworking, eager to learn and doing his best to hide the fact he was struggling with being gay. This morning Prakesh was in court acting as the second chair for a drug prosecution.

Paxton flipped open the phone, but before making the call thought about it for a moment. Word around the office, or at least rumors among staff and attorneys, was that the Dragon Lady in the big, corner office, had spies everywhere. There were also those who believed the place was wired. That one, Paxton did not believe. Still, she was careful what she said, even around Prakesh. She decided to make the call but be short and say as little as possible.

"Hi, Sean," she said when a man answered her call. "Are you going to be home this evening?"

"Yes, sweetheart," the older man replied.

"Can you have your friend there?"

"Probably," he answered. "I'll give him a call, and if he can't make it, I'll call you back."

"Don't bother," Paxton told him. "I'll come either way. Is 7:00-7:30 okay?"

"Sure, anytime," Sean replied.

"Great, see you then."

Sean was Sean O'Rourke, Paxton's uncle and her dad's brother; a sixty-two-year-old, twice-divorced, retired FBI agent. He had started out as a cop with the Chicago police at age twenty-two. A tenacious investigator, the FBI had enticed him away from the CPD by age thirty. Two years ago, Sean had called it quits and retired after five years as a Deputy Executive Assistant for Intelligence. Sean had loved the job and the people. It was the political ass-kissing that finally drove him out.

Sean had a three-bedroom brick mini-colonial house in Schaumberg that he shared with a lady friend, Helen Gregg. Helen was also retired from the Bureau and had a couple of not-so-successful marriages under her belt. Both vowed to never walk down the aisle again, even at the point of a gun.

They were both originally from the Midwest and leaving the East Coast, especially Washington, was not a tough decision. Schaumberg is a suburb slightly northwest of Chicago with a median income of eighty-five-thousand-dollars. Perfect for a two-income government pension couple and basically, home for both.

The friend Paxton briefly referred to was the exact opposite of Paxton's favorite uncle. His name was Lester Snelling. Since around age eleven or twelve, Lester had been in and out of one scrape after another with the law, until eight years ago.

It was the day Lester walked out of the federal prison at Lewisburg, Pennsylvania. Like almost every con that gets kicked loose, the first thing Lester did was to look up at the big, blue sky. While he did this, he filled his lungs with a deep, satisfying, delicious amount of free air for the first time in ten years. Lester started walking toward the bus to take him into town when he saw him. Across the street, leaning on his personal tan Chevy Tahoe was the unmistakable looking Sean Patrick O'Rourke, the man who had put him in Lewisburg. He was also the man who, today, Lester credited for saving his life. If Sean had not been standing there, Lester had no doubt he would either be in another prison somewhere or a lonely, forgotten grave.

Lester Snelling had been a member of a Northern New Jersey gang whose specialty was bank robberies. There were four members. All in their forties, all professional criminals. Over a four-year period, they had robbed over twenty banks in the New Jersey, New York, and Pennsylvania tri-state area. Not once did the cops or the FBI get so much as a whiff of who they were because they were thorough, professional and careful. They did their research and practiced each job to get it under two minutes, the response time for police. And best of all, no one was ever injured any worse than a face slap to get cooperation from a bank manager.

It all ended when they went to the Allentown People's Bank and Trust in Allentown, Pennsylvania. Everything was perfect. The job went exactly the way it was planned. In and out in a minute and forty-five seconds with almost eighty-thousand-dollars. Except for this time, there were forty local, state and FBI agents waiting outside with guns drawn.

The gang members each had their own lawyer who made the best deal they could. Three of them, including Lester, kept their mouths shut. One turned witness for the prosecution. The one who turned got six years at a medium-security prison in California. The leader, not Lester, got fifteen and Lester and the fourth man each ten. No parole.

The man who turned against them and got six years also got a six-inch shiv through his ribs and into his heart. No one was ever charged. The gang's leader, a sociopath with a talent for robbery, died in prison from lung cancer; a three-pack a day cigarette habit, the likely culprit. Lester lost track of the fourth man.

What brought Sean O'Rourke to Lewisburg was a problem that had puzzled him for years. Sean was the special agent in charge, SAIC, of the Philadelphia office. The bank robberies of this particular gang had been giving Sean heartburn trying to track them down. Not a whisper from a snitch or a single decent lead had arisen. Then, one day totally out of the blue, he got a call from the U.S. Attorney himself for the Eastern District of PA. A man by the name of Mason Hooper, who had a tip for Sean. A personal informant of Hooper's, or so he claimed, told Hooper about Lester's gang and Hooper was passing it on. Of course, Hooper would make sure he was in front of the cameras after the arrest.

Sean put the gang under surveillance and that was how they were caught. Of course, after the arrest, Mason Hooper was front and center at the press conference to make sure his office and himself personally received the lion's share of the credit. In fact, Hooper's nickname at the DOJ and FBI was Press Conference Hooper.

Later, rumor around the U.S. Attorney's office and the Philadelphia FBI had it that Mason Hooper's snitch was a criminal of huge significance who had made Hooper's career. This snitch was also alleged to be far worse than any of the bones he tossed to Hooper to get Hooper's protection.

Sean had done a little quiet digging into this story and came up with enough information to believe it was true. He even came up with a name: Walter Kirk. Following that lead got him nowhere. Frustrated, he went to Lewisburg to get together with Lester. Fortunately, Lester Snelling knew exactly who Walter Kirk was. A big-time crook that Lester knew back when he was a kid in Boston. Unfortunately, after doing a little checking for Sean, Lester came to the conclusion that Walter Kirk was dead. A number of sources Lester had known for years confirmed it.

Because Lester had at least provided Sean with solid information about Walter, Sean got Lester employment in Chicago as a limo driver. Over the years of driving limos, he had accrued a steady list of clients. Lester had also remained clean. Then last fall, Lester had delivered a wealthy client to a Democratic fundraiser. As he held the door for the couple in his car, he saw a ghost with a much younger woman also being dropped off. The late and not so lamented Walter Kirk in the flesh.

"Hi, Uncle Sean," Paxton said when he opened the front door for her.

Paxton followed him into the room and found Helen and Lester already waiting. After hellos and a hug from Helen, they all settled down for the news. While Sean took the accident DVD from Paxton and put it in the player, she gave a quick summary of her trip.

"Do you recognize those guys?" Paxton asked while handing two photos to Lester.

"Sure," he replied. "That's the Tierney brothers. This is the smart one, Ryan, although smart is open to debate. He's called the smart one because of his younger brother, Little Mikey, here," Lester continued passing both mugshots to Sean, "Mikey is a real moron and certified psycho. Did they do the hit and run on your friend?"

"We think so," Paxton replied. She handed the file to her uncle. While Helen looked over his shoulder and read along, the two of them skimmed through it.

"How do you know the Tierneys?" Paxton asked Lester.

"From my Boston days," Lester said. "In fact, I've known these two mutts for close to forty years. A couple of serious gangsters. If Walter Kirk, your Cal Simpson, is involved with this, it makes sense these two would be in on it."

When Sean and Helen finished reading the file, he placed it on the coffee table. He picked up the TV remote and hit the power button.

"Do you know these Tierney guys, Sean?" Paxton asked.

"No, I don't," Sean answered. "Do you?" he asked Helen.

"No, never heard of them."

"Neither one of us was ever assigned to Boston. They look to be mostly muscle for Irish gangs. Would you agree, Les?"

"Yeah, that's them. But don't underestimate them."

"Let's watch the movie," Sean said.

A half hour later, having watched it several times at regular speed, slow and super slow motion, Sean shut it off.

"Pretty grim to watch," Helen said.

"What do you think, Les?" Sean asked.

"The size of the driver and the shape of the head, even with the glasses and a ball cap on, it sure looks like Little Mikey," Lester replied. "And the two guys walking through the airport together look like them."

"You're sure?" Paxton asked.

Lester shrugged and said, "I haven't seen them for, I don't know, twenty, twenty-five years. But I'd bet a paycheck it's them."

"Any forensics from the hit and run?" Helen asked looking at Paxton.

"No, nothing. From what my friends in Minnesota said, the van was thoroughly torched. The interior was completely burned out. The local cops traced the van and it came up as stolen from a suburb of Minneapolis a few days before."

"Assuming this was deliberate, they got lucky," Sean said,

"How?" Helen asked,

111

"They couldn't be sure Zach Evans—and we believe he was the target—would get bail. First-degree murder, bail would not likely be given since they had the weapon and motive," Paxton answered her.

"They didn't have much choice. They had to try it," Sean said. "Now we need to find them. Les, you have any contacts back in Boston you can check with?"

"Yeah, I think so. Give me a couple of days to see what I can find out," Lester replied.

"We have another problem," Paxton said. "Or more precisely, I have another problem. Norah McCabe wants me to drop this. She said I have enough other things to do."

"What do you want to do?" Sean asked.

"They almost killed a man I like and respect. I'm not going to just walk away from that. Besides, I told them I'd find these Tierney brothers. We'll just have to work on our time."

Two nights later, while Paxton was standing over her kitchen sink eating a chicken breast from a local deli, her phone rang. She looked at the ID then quickly wiped off her hands and mouth with paper towels.

"Hi, Uncle," she said when she answered.

"Hey, kid," Sean said. "I think I have bad news. Lester called. He's heard from several sources that the Tierneys are gone."

"What do you mean, gone?" Paxton asked,

"Gone as in maybe not coming back because they are no longer breathing."

"Shit," Paxton muttered.

"We'll keep looking. I found a couple of guys I know that are now in Boston. I talked to one just before I called you. He knows the Tierneys and he said he'd heard the rumors too. He'll check into it and get back to me."

"Is he FBI?"

"Yeah, but he said it would be unofficial and discreet. He's a good guy. I trust him."

"Okay, Sean. Thanks," Paxton said.

The subjects of their interest were, indeed, gone and not coming back. They had taken up permanent residence, Ryan on top of Little Mikey, in a hole in a New Hampshire forest, resting comfortably twenty miles north of the Massachusetts state line.

112

TWENTY-THREE

"So, where does that leave us?" Maddy asked into her phone.

Maddy, Marc, and Tony were in the library of the Corwin Mansion barely a quarter of a mile from Cal Simpson. With them was the home's owner, Vivian Donahue. They were on a call with Paxton who had just given them the news about the Tierneys.

"Have you confirmed this?" Carvelli asked into Maddy's phone speaker before Paxton could answer Maddy.

"Yes," Paxton replied to Tony. "At least as best as we can without the bodies. My guy—who I'll tell you about some other time—has good contacts in Boston. Word on the street is, they crossed someone and now they're gone. The Boston PD is convinced. So is the Boston FBI office. Funny thing though, they can't find out who did it."

"How hard are they trying?" Carvelli asked. While Paxton answered him, Carvelli stole a glance at Marc who seemed a bit lost in his own thoughts.

"As in good riddance to a couple of gangster-thugs," Maddy said. "But, I repeat, where does that leave us?"

"I need to tell you guys something," Paxton said. "For reasons I can't go into right now, especially over the phone, I need to tell you a little story."

Paxton then told them, without using any names, about her uncle's ex-con, semi-snitch, Lester Snelling. She told them about Lester seeing a man he had known from his criminal days; a man who was well-known as a politically connected crook but was supposedly dead.

"And you think this guy is Calvin Simpson?" Carvelli asked. "This guy who was known to your snitch as Walter Kirk…"

"And at least three other names," Paxton interjected.

"…and you believe it?"

"Yeah, he is absolutely positive. My…" Paxton caught herself before she used the word "uncle", "…my, um, other guy got a bunch of photos of Simpson. They're sure. If I had access to the FBI's facial recognition software, I could verify it."

"Why can't you take it to them?" Maddy asked. "You're a U.S. Attorney."

"It's not that easy," Paxton replied. "With the government it never is. There's a whole big deal with doing something like that. Plus, my boss is trying to kill my investigation. In fact, as far as she is concerned, she has."

"Tell her, Tony," Maddy said.

113

"I was wondering if maybe you could help with that," Paxton said before Carvelli could answer Maddy.

"Ah, well, it's your lucky day, Ms. O'Rourke. I think maybe I could get that anonymous friend of mine to take a look at your photos and see what he can come up with."

"Great," Paxton said. "In fact, I'm in my car in front of a FedEx Store right now. You'll have them tomorrow.

"I've been thinking," she continued. "I'm pretty much stuck on stupid on my end. I have no official case going and my boss will have my ass if she finds out I'm still at this."

"Why?" Maddy asked.

"She says we have enough other things to do," Paxton answered. "What I was thinking is what we need is somebody on the inside. Somebody close to Cal Simpson to find out what he's up to.

"That sheriff's investigator, Newkirk, he sent me copies of his case. Nice guy," Paxton added. "In it was a list of the people who attended Simpson's Fourth of July party. You know, the night that woman lawyer..."

"Lynn McDaniel," Maddy said.

"Yeah, her, was murdered. There are quite a few politicians on it. Senators and Representatives. Something smells about this..."

"So how do we get to somebody on the inside?" Carvelli asked. "We don't know who to go after."

"Well, I was thinking," Paxton replied, "um, this is a little difficult. Anyway, the word is that this Simpson guy likes women and is a well-known um..."

"Womanizer," Vivian said, "and I hate that word."

"Yeah, right," Paxton said. "Anyway, I was thinking that maybe if you know, we could, ah, find someone with the balls and ability to, um, you know..."

Carvelli looked at Maddy and said loud enough for the phone to pick up,

"Madeline Elizabeth Rivers might be just who we're looking for."

"Wait a minute!" a startled Maddy said. "Ah, let's talk about this."

Carvelli turned back to the phone sitting on the table they were seated around, and said, "Go into FedEx and mail the photos. Call back when you're done." He gave her Vivian's address to send the photos to since someone was always there to receive them.

"Give us a few minutes," Carvelli said then pressed the end button on Maddy's phone.

"You don't have to do this," Vivian said.

"Yeah, I do," Maddy sighed and quietly said. "It's the obvious choice. Who else are we going to get? You're too well known," Maddy continued looking at Vivian.

"That's very kind, sweetheart, but I still don't think..." Vivian said.

Maddy turned to Marc seated to her right. She placed her hand gently on the back of his neck and asked, "Are you okay? You look like something's bothering you."

"Something is," he answered her. "I've got a memory trying to break through. It's very foggy, and I can't quite get at it, but I can almost see it. I think it has something to do with Cal Simpson. It's right there just below the surface. I'm trying to see it but..."

"Don't," Maddy said. "Don't force it. Relax, when it is ready it will come out."

"Are you having any other flashbacks or memories return?" Carvelli asked.

"I get little bits and pieces. I vaguely remember leaving the courthouse and walking past the statue of the Civil War soldier. Little things like that."

"You're not going to change the subject," Vivian icily said to Maddy. "This could be dangerous."

"Dangerous is my middle name," Maddy jokingly said.

"It is not. It's Elizabeth. Even I remember that," Marc said making a little joke out of it. He looked at her and added, "You don't have to do this. Give us time. We can find another way."

"No, we can't. Besides, I can handle myself." She turned to Tony and said, "We should get some of your guys on this."

"I was thinking the same thing. For you, I can only get maybe twenty-five or thirty right away. But if I need to, I could probably get a couple hundred more from the MPD," he joked.

"I think four or five will be enough," Maddy said. She looked across at Vivian and said, "We'll be careful. We'll research and plan it. I agree with Paxton. Calvin Simpson is involved in the death of at least two people and what happened to Marc."

"And if he's not involved, if he is a legitimate guy, we'll find that out, too," Carvelli said.

"All right," Vivian reluctantly agreed. She then said to Tony, "Anthony, I'm going to trust you to make sure nothing happens to my girl. If it does, you will be singing soprano."

"Yes, ma'am," Carvelli replied in a falsetto voice which broke the tension and brought some well-needed laughter.

"Conrad Hilton," Carvelli said when the laughter stopped. "Remember him?" he asked Maddy.

"Yeah, that creepy little dude with the grabby hands," Maddy said. "Is he still around?"

"Yeah, I've heard he's back in town," Carvelli said. "He's the guy that bugged your office that time, remember?"

"Yeah, I remember him," Marc said. "We could use him."

"Yeah," Carvelli agreed. "Best electronic surveillance guy in the business."

Carvelli parked the Camaro two doors down from his destination. He was on Hennepin Avenue a half mile north of the river and downtown Minneapolis. His destination was a familiar one: Jake's Limousine Service. It was owned and operated by an ex-MPD cop, Jake Waschke. Jake had run afoul of the law a few years back. In an attempt to protect his younger brother, Jake, an MPD homicide detective lieutenant, had tried to frame someone for a series of murders. Ironically, the guy he framed was, in fact, guilty. Jake had been dismissed from the MPD and did a couple of years in prison. It was Marc Kadella, with Maddy Rivers' help, that had nailed Jake for what he did.

Waschke had been out of prison now for a while and was running a very successful limo service. It helped to have the connections he did, and the no-hard-feelings attitude he maintained. With eight cars and plenty of business, he provided good paying, easy, part-time employment for quite a few ex-cops and those still on the job, and a place for them to hang out. Mostly to get away from their wives.

Carvelli walked through the open garage door. There were two Cadillac limos and four Lincoln Town Cars inside which meant the other two Lincolns were on the street. The office was to his left. Carvelli walked to it, rapped on the office door's glass and went in. Waschke was at his desk doing some paperwork and three men were seated around a coffee table watching Sports Center and arguing about baseball.

"Hey, look what the cat dragged in," Jake said when he saw Carvelli. The three men watching TV, Dan Sorenson, Franklin Washington and Tommy Craven, all stood to greet him. After a couple minutes of handshakes and good-natured, if somewhat foul-mouthed insults, the five of them got down to business.

"What brings your sorry-ass dragging in here?" Sorenson asked.

"Okay, smartass," Carvelli said looking at Sorenson. "Apparently you don't need any extra money, so I'll scratch your name off the list."

"Hey, hey," Sorenson replied. "I didn't mean that. Besides," he continued as he put his arm around Carvelli's shoulders, "you were always my favorite cop."

"Get out of here, you degenerate," Carvelli said with a light elbow to his friend's ribs.

116

They all pulled up chairs around Jake's desk and Carvelli began.

"I need some help, and there will be some surveillance money in it." Carvelli looked at Jake and asked, "You ever hear of a guy named Calvin Simpson?"

"Sure," Waschke replied. "He's a good customer. He uses us at least a couple times a week."

"Seriously? This might be easier than I thought," Carvelli replied.

Leaving out Paxton O'Rourke and her interest in the case, Carvelli filled his four friends in on what he wanted. When he got to the part about Maddy going undercover and needing them to cover her back, all four men spontaneously said they were in, even if they did not get paid.

"If our girl needs help, we're in," Tommy said.

"She's not ever gonna sleep with you, ya know," Franklin Washington, the lone black man of the group, kidded Craven.

"That's insulting," Craven said. "Besides, I'm not too old to dream."

"Do you know if he uses other car services?" Carvelli asked Waschke.

"Don't know, but I'll call around and find out," he replied. Jake snapped his fingers as if remembering something and said, "Wait a minute. Let me check…" he quietly said while he turned to his computer. He typed in Simpson's name and came up with what he remembered.

"We got him this weekend. Saturday night. There's a Republican fundraiser at the Leamington. He seems to be a big contributor. We take him to a lot of these things."

"He's pretty bipartisan, too," Dan Sorenson interjected. "Goes to both the Dems and Republicans."

"That doesn't surprise me," Carvelli said. "Okay, we'll shoot for Saturday night. We'll get Maddy dolled up…"

"Can I drive her?" all three ex-cop drivers said at once.

"…and get her in to meet our mark, Cal Simpson."

"Maddy dolled up," Waschke said. "Since I get to decide who drives her," he continued, smiling at the others, "I guess this one's on me. I'll do it."

"What do you mean, you can't find any photos of him?" Carvelli said into his phone. He was still at Jake's limo business and had taken the call there.

"I found a shitload of pictures of him, but they're all of him, Calvin Simpson," Paul Baker, Tony's hacker said, "and they're all from newspapers. All photos from various events. His daughter's wedding, political events, even one with the owner of the Vikings at a football game. But none that go back more than a few years. And none from any law enforcement agency or police department."

Baker had received the photos of Simpson from Paxton and had run a comparison to find more information on him.

"Did you try the name 'Walter Kirk'?"

"Sure. Nationwide there's quite a few of them but none that fit our parameters for age, height, or place of birth. I checked Boston PD computers. Not a single photo or any reference to him."

"He's been wiped clean," Carvelli quietly said. "Who is this guy?"

"I don't know," Paul said. "I've seen this a couple of times before, but it's usually CIA or some other spook shit."

"I don't think that's him. Too much money and too much visibility," Carvelli said. "Sit tight. Let me think about this. Thanks, Paul."

TWENTY-FOUR

The surveillance of Cal Simpson by Carvelli's little band of ex-cops started immediately. Sorenson, Washington, and Craven took turns doing a stakeout of Simpson's home on Lake Minnetonka. Using equipment Carvelli had for his P.I. business, they took good, clear, high-resolution photos of everyone coming and going. These would then be immediately emailed to Carvelli who would send them to his hacker, Paul Baker.

They got shots of Samantha Evans, Cal's daughter, coming and going at least two or three times a day. Other than that, there was little activity. Deliveries, mail, and household staff were mostly all that happened. Then, on the second day during the evening shift, Dan Sorenson scored an interesting hit.

Two middle-aged men, both white and one very familiar looking, paid a call on Cal. Sorenson got good shots of the car, a late-model Cadillac DTS, then license plates and the men. Fifteen minutes later another car slowed to turn onto the grounds of Simpson's home. This time there were also two people in it, a man driving and a woman passenger. Again, Sorenson obtained an excellent set of photos of the people, the car, and the plates.

The next day Carvelli's hacker had the identifications. The men in the first car, the Cadillac, were Dane and Greg Cannon of Cannon Brothers Toys. The man and woman in the second car were Congressman Del Peterson of Minnesota and Elaine Krohn from California. Obviously, there was a meeting taking place at Cal's home. A rational guess would be that it had something to do with Cannon Brothers Toys.

"Are you going back to work on Monday?" Maddy asked Marc.

The two of them were in the living room of Marc's apartment. Having spent a week with Vivian, Marc felt foolish and had insisted on going home.

It was the Friday evening before the fundraiser Maddy was to attend to meet Cal Simpson. The surveillance team had been in place for a few days. Carvelli and Jake Waschke were on their way for a strategy session to be sure everything was set for tomorrow night.

"Connie or Carolyn have been dropping off work for me every day. Then one of them stops by to pick up the files when I'm done with them. I need to get back in the office. Carolyn tells me I have four or five appointments every day next week. Plus, I'm going a little stir-crazy sitting inside so much."

119

The front doorbell rang, and Maddy went to answer it. A few seconds later she returned followed by Carvelli and Waschke.

It was Marc's investigation that caused Jake Waschke to be dismissed from the MPD and sent to prison. Despite that, Waschke felt no ill will toward the lawyer. He accepted his responsibility—almost unimaginable these days—did his time and moved on.

Marc was sitting in his recliner, his broken leg still immobilized and extended. Waschke walked over to him reached down and they shook hands. The bandage around his head had been removed and Jake tried to avoid looking at his scarred, hairless head.

"Hi, Jake. Thanks for coming."

"How are you doing?" Jake sincerely asked.

"Better," Marc said.

Maddy took a chair near Marc and the two men sat on the sofa.

"Where are we?" Marc asked, looking at Tony Carvelli.

"We've got a little bit. He's had a few interesting visitors," Tony began.

He gave them all a quick briefing on the surveillance. There was not much to tell. In the few days that they had been on him, Cal Simpson had not left the house even once.

"He's more boring than me," Marc commented.

"That's hard to even imagine," Maddy replied then laughed as she reached over and squeezed his arm.

"Does he have an office somewhere?" Marc asked.

"Not that we know of. He seems to work out of his home," Carvelli replied. "We need to get inside. We need to plant some bugs."

The three men looked at Maddy who nodded her head and said, "And that's where I come in."

"Afraid so, sweetheart," Carvelli said. "Sorry."

"No, it's okay," she said. "I figured we'd have to do this."

"What about your hacker?" Marc asked. "If we, I mean she, could get his phone number or numbers, could your guy monitor them?"

"Good question," Carvelli said. "I don't know."

"Ask Conrad about it," Waschke said. "He might know."

"We'll certainly look into it. Now, tomorrow night," Carvelli said looking at Maddy. "You ready? You need to get your hair done and…"

"Oh, jeez, Carvelli," Marc said while cringing. "You never mention hair, weight or age to a woman. Don't you know that?"

While Marc was saying this, Waschke visibly moved a little farther away from Carvelli on the couch. Maddy was glaring at him with a look that could kill.

Carvelli threw up his hands and with a panicky look said, "I'm sorry, I'm sorry. Your hair looks great. Please pretend I didn't say that."

"I'll be ready," Maddy quietly said.

"You could go the way you are right now," Carvelli said.

"Tony, stop digging trying to get out of the hole you're in," Waschke said. "Maddy, I'll pick up you and the idiot here," Jake continued referring to Tony, "at your place at 7:30. The shindig starts at 7:00 so let's make an entrance. Is that okay?"

"That should work," Maddy said slyly smiling at Carvelli. "Did you get the tickets from Vivian?" she asked Tony. "And a tux?"

"Yes, ma'am."

"Don't forget the tickets. Are Dan and the others all set?" Maddy asked Jake.

"Yeah," Jake answered. "We all know the guy heading security, retired MPD, so we got them on the security detail. You're covered."

"Any problems, you bail out and we'll find another way to go at him," Tony reminded her for at least the tenth time.

"It's okay, Tony. I can handle this guy," Maddy said with a smile.

"Hey, Connie told me a good lawyer joke today," Marc said.

An attorney was sitting in his office late one night when Satan appeared before him. The Devil told the lawyer: 'I have a proposition for you. You can win every case you try for the rest of your life. Your clients will adore you, your colleagues will stand in awe of you, and you will make embarrassing sums of money. All I want in exchange is your soul, your wife's soul, your children's souls, the souls of your parents and grandparents, and parents-in-law, and the souls of all your friends and law partners.' The lawyer thought about this for a moment, then asked. 'So, what's the catch?'"

Maddy's condo was less than a mile from their destination. With Saturday night downtown traffic in the way, Maddy and Carvelli could have walked there more quickly than Jake was able to drive it. Except, Tony in a tux—even Maddy had to admit he cleaned up well—and Maddy in a gown and heels would have drawn a bit too much attention.

Jake pulled the Lincoln into line on Third Avenue. They were the fourth car back from the hotel's entrance. While waiting in line, Waschke looked over his shoulder and said, "I always wanted to get in here and see where the Beatles stayed. Isn't that a little silly?"

"The Beatles stayed here?" Maddy excitedly asked.

"You weren't even born then," Carvelli said. "Come to think of it, neither was I. Did you know Vivian snuck out to see them?"

"Really?"

"Yeah, she was grounded for a month. Her dad hated them. She says it was the best sneak ever," Carvelli said.

"Here we go kids," Waschke said as the car ahead began to pull away. "Now you kids behave. No making out in the back, no smoking dope and…"

"Shut up, Jake," Carvelli said while Maddy laughed.

Being fashionably late had been a good idea. As the two of them made their way to their table in the ballroom, virtually every man in attendance was watching. And most of the women. Maddy in four-inch heels and a clingy yet stylish black gown could attract attention.

Tony held the chair for her and when they were seated, whispered to her that he had spotted Cal Simpson. Within a minute a waiter brought two flutes of champagne. Between the two of them, it took less than another minute to find their ex-cop friends doing security. Tony casually looked around as if checking out the crowd and saw Cal still staring at Maddy despite his sitting next to her.

"Is he looking?" Maddy asked.

"Yeah, he sure is. After the first speaker," Tony said. "I'll go to the men's room; you go to the bar."

"I know, I remember. I'm going to check out the crowd the way you did. Where is he?"

"Two aisles over and one table closer to the front. He's seated facing us," Tony said.

While Maddy did this, two more couples, older and obviously very well-to-do by the jewelry they wore, sat down. Tony stood and introduced themselves while Maddy spotted Simpson. She then took a moment to greet their tablemates.

Carvelli leaned into her and whispered, "Get him?"

"Yes, I did," she replied. "I'll walk right past him. He's practically leering at us."

"I think it's you, probably not me."

A few minutes later the program started. The emcee was the head of the Republican Party in Minnesota. He went through the usual blather of thanking everyone and making a couple of bad jokes. He introduced the first speaker, a U.S. Senator who was rumored to be a potential presidential candidate. Senator Cristian Howell of Pennsylvania was a descendant of East Coast old money. Tony also recognized his name as being on the guest list of Cal's Fourth of July bash.

When the Senator finished, Tony was instantly on his feet. He left for the exit to find a bathroom. As casually as she could, Maddy excused herself from the table and went to the bar. As she strolled past Cal, she could practically feel his eyes undressing her. Coming from him, it made her shiver slightly. Despite that, she deliberately made eye contact with him and politely smiled.

The next speaker was being introduced while she stood in line. Maddy had barely arrived there when she heard a voice from behind.

"Your boyfriend must be a fool to leave you alone," Cal said.

Maddy turned and replied, "How do you know he's not my husband?"

"A woman like you, and I mean this as a compliment, would wear a ring."

"Very good," Maddy said and flashed him a bright smile. As she did, she moved a little closer to the bar. At the same time, out of the corner of her eye, she noticed movement to her left. She looked and saw the large frame of Franklin Washington watching the crowd, barely ten feet from her.

They introduced themselves, Maddy gave her first name only, then Cal said, "I don't think I've ever seen you at one of these political gatherings before and I would have noticed."

"Well," Maddy said, "I don't usually hang out with such lowlife crowds as politicians. I prefer a classier bunch, like biker gangs."

Cal got a hearty laugh from this and Maddy looked over his shoulder to see Mrs. Simpson glaring at them.

By the time they reached the bar, Cal was already asking her to dinner. They ordered drinks, white wine for Maddy, a scotch and soda for Tony.

"I'll tell you what," Maddy said as they slowly walked away toward their tables, "you give me your number and let me think about it. I'll admit, I find you to be one of those handsome, older-men types and interesting. Will your wife be joining us?"

Cal handed his drink to a nearby Franklin Washington and wrote out his private number for Maddy. He gave it to her, thanked Franklin who could barely contain his laughter and said, "My wife is just about out the door."

"Does she know that?" Maddy laughed.

"Well, I'm sure she suspects it. Call me..." he said. "It's just dinner. You do eat, don't you?"

"Just about every day," she replied.

Across the ballroom, standing in the entrance, Carvelli and Dan Sorenson were watching Maddy's play.

"She's reeling him in like a mackerel," Sorenson said. "Kind of amusing to watch."

"Yeah, but let's not forget, this guy is a long-time gangster who has had people killed. Maybe even done the deed himself," Carvelli solemnly said.

TWENTY-FIVE

Cal Simpson had just finished reading the article on page three of *The Wall Street Journal.* He folded the paper and placed it on the table. Cal watched one of the household staff, a poorly paid undocumented from Mexico, walk away with his breakfast dishes. Cal smiled as he sipped his coffee then decided to go onto the patio. The news in the *Journal* deserved a celebratory cigar.

While he lit the cigar, the same housekeeper brought a fresh pot and filled his cup. He thanked her, and she again walked off. It was a warm, sunny, beautiful late July morning and Lake Minnetonka was already filling up with leisure craft. A gorgeous, sunny day was impending. While he watched the boats cruise by, he reminisced about the news story.

For the past two weeks, a PR campaign had been waged on behalf of Cannon Brothers Toys. Stories had been planted through the financial world that Cannon Brothers was about to resolve the class action suit it was fighting. After almost three years the discovery phase was complete. Everson, Reed, the lawyers defending Cannon Brothers, had brought a motion for summary judgment in court the day before. They were trying to convince the judge that the plaintiffs had failed to provide any evidence of Cannon Brothers' liability.

Of course, this was nonsense. Cannon Brothers manufactured and sold motorized skateboards that had a defect. Even though Cannon Brothers did not manufacture the defective part, the batteries, they could not completely escape liability.

What they were really after was a ruling by the judge that there was no evidence Cannon Brothers knew or could have known about the problems with the batteries. If she ruled that, then Cannon Brothers would not be hit with punitive damages. If they had no knowledge, there was no reason to punish them and punitive damages were where the big bucks were in a case like this. Good luck to the plaintiffs collecting them from a Chinese company.

Cal had received a phone call from Brody Knutson, the managing partner at Everson, Reed. The word was already out that Judge Susan Holcomb appeared to be on Cannon Brothers' side. She had flat-out said that the plaintiffs had failed to find actual or constructive knowledge Cannon Brothers knew about the defective batteries. With that news alone, Cannon Brothers stock had opened a full four points higher this morning. It was now barely 10:00 A.M. and the stock was still rising.

Cal took a large hit on the Monte Cristo, blew the smoke out and quietly said, "Things are coming along quite nicely."

Without bothering with a calculator, he knew he had made many millions today. Given his personal wealth, more money than he could possibly spend, more money wasn't his aphrodisiac. More money wasn't what turned Cal Simpson's crank. What Cal was truly after, as it is with almost all of the ego-driven rich, was more power. What really made him smile was the thought of his friends and partners. There were going to be a lot of very happy people this morning due to Calvin Simpson's manipulations. Along with that would come their gratitude. At least for a while until Cal's real plan came to fruition.

While puffing his cigar, he thought back to the fundraiser of the previous Saturday evening and the woman he met. There was something different about this one. Cal Simpson had bedded his share of beautiful women. Almost all of whom were in it for his money. A little bell in the back of his head was very lightly sounding telling him this one was not motivated by that. The realization, if it was true, made her all the more interesting and he hoped she would call soon.

Cal thought of a question he forgot to ask Brody Knutson. He picked up his phone, scrolled through the numbers and dialed it. Brody answered on the first ring.

"I meant to ask," Cal said. "When do you think the judge will rule?"

"She has thirty days. Most of them are procrastinators..."

"Because they're ex-lawyers," Cal interjected.

"...and she'll probably take most of it," Brody said ignoring the comment.

"Let me ask you this: if she rules for us, can she change her mind?"

"Up to a certain point, yes. I'm not sure when that would be. Sometime before trial. But, yeah, she can rescind her own order. Plus, we or the other side can bring an appeal. The appeals court could overturn it and tell her what she has to do to fix it."

"How likely is that?" Cal asked.

"Hard to say. Usually not very. Judges are normally given a lot of discretion. But an appeals court could say the judge overstepped her authority, that punitive damages are a matter for a jury to decide. Relax. I don't think it will happen."

"Why?"

"This would be a finding of fact, not a matter of law. If the judge finds there is no factual basis for punitive damages and then applies the law correctly, we'll be okay. What about the others and the big one?" Brody asked.

"Coming along," Cal said then ended the call.

Two weeks from when that conversation took place, Cannon Brothers Toys, as prearranged, would release preliminary revenue and

126

profit statements for the third quarter. By then the initial jump in the stock price resulting from the court hearing, and the PR campaign that followed it, had cooled off. The stock price needed another boost before the judge ruled in their favor to disallow punitive damages.

While the class action suit hung over Cannon Brothers, investors were not overly thrilled with the company's stock. A year ago, fueled by rumors of significant losses coming from the lawsuit, the share price had dropped from a historic high of sixty-eight and a quarter to twenty-four. That was the point when Cal had bought in.

He quietly acquired a twenty percent stake. To avoid even the insignificant and minimal oversight of the SEC, Cal had used a long list of cutouts for the purchases. Small holding companies and unknown individuals were used to avoid scrutiny. He was able to increase his holdings to two and a half million of the twelve and a half million shares at an excellent price. Of course, it was a price he manipulated with a lot of rumors reporting doom and gloom for Cannon Brothers.

At the same time, he knew Cannon Brothers had weathered the worst of the storm. Last September, the price began to gradually climb. The share price now was almost back to its high-water mark. Before the court hearing, the shares were trading at forty-eight and a quarter. Over the past two weeks, they had jumped up ten points.

Cal's shares and the shares he held for various political friends had gone from a value of sixty million to over one-hundred-forty-five million in barely a year. When the revenue and earnings report was leaked out, the share price would jump another seven and a half points to sixty-five and three-quarters, not far from the company's historic high.

At sixty-five and three-quarters Cal's pals, even the cranky communist of the U.S. Senate, would be smiling. And they wouldn't be done yet.

Following that, over the course of the next three weeks, Cal would quietly, without bringing attention to himself or anyone else, sell off all of it.

TWENTY-SIX

The man in the windowless, brown, older Ford E-Series van was enjoying himself immensely. He was parked in an apartment complex lot on a hill overlooking three other apartment buildings. He was seated on a small, uncomfortable padded stool with no back support. He didn't mind the discomfort. A fan was blowing over him keeping him cool and jobs like this one not only paid the bills but were a source of voyeuristic amusement.

Along the left-hand wall in the cargo area was almost twenty thousand dollars' worth of sophisticated equipment. The man sitting on the stool, leaning forward between the front seats, was an electronic surveillance wiz.

Plugged into his sound equipment were the Bose headphones he was listening through. He used his left hand to occasionally fine-tune the 500mm lens attached to the camera recording the action. In his right-hand was a six-inch ham and salami sub he munched on while he watched through the camera's lens. A 500mm lens at this distance put him right inside the bedroom. It helped that the young woman intentionally left her drapes open.

His assignment was dirt gathering on a cheating husband. His employer, a sleaze-ball, feminist, woman divorce lawyer, was preparing the wife's divorce pleadings. Normally, a cheating spouse would not matter much in a no-fault divorce state. This one was different for a couple of reasons. One, he was an up and coming Republican politician with money and ambition. The other, they lived in Hennepin County. Under the best of circumstances, judges in Hennepin County always blamed the husband and made him pay. Bouncing around on a bed with a twenty-year-old stripper would not help the husband's position politically or judicially.

The wayward politician, in his forties, was losing his hair and growing a spare tire. The girl was why the man watched. Smoking-hot with an outstanding boob job. Why this idiot thought she was attracted to him was anyone's guess. Politician's ego. Even after he was told, the fool would not believe the stripper was a honey-trap in the employ of the same sleaze-ball, feminist lawyer.

The man in the van finished his sandwich then leaned forward into the camera to watch. Three seconds later the door on the right crashed open and a man jumped in. Scared out of his wits, the van's occupant jumped four inches off of his chair and slammed backward into the metal rack that held his equipment.

While the intruder slid the door close, the man recovered his composure, placed a hand on his chest and said, "Jesus Christ, Carvelli, you just took ten years off my life. Sonofobitch..."

"How are you, Conrad?" Tony Carvelli asked.

He duck-walked a couple of steps and found a folding chair in the back of the van. Tony opened it and sat down while Conrad straightened himself out.

Conrad's full name was Conrad Hilton. After losing employment with several police departments for extra-curricular surveillance activities—fired from both Minneapolis, St. Paul and the FBI—Conrad had gone freelance. Financially, it had worked out even better for him. And he was still employed by quite a few law enforcement types who, on occasion, needed some off-the-books, extralegal work done. Despite the intentions of no-fault divorce advocates, there was still plenty of work done in that area as well. Conrad was professional, capable and discreet.

A few years back, while working with Carvelli, Conrad had run afoul of a local gangster. A man Conrad didn't want to cross. Conrad took the sensible way out. He ran. The gangster disappeared, but Conrad stayed away for a couple of years just to be on the safe side.

"What do you want, Carvelli?"

"I've been meaning to stop by and welcome you back. I heard where you were and so...." Tony said with a smile.

"Great, fine, thanks. Hello and goodbye," Conrad said.

"Conrad," Tony continued feigning hurt feelings, "is that any way to greet an old pal."

"Old pal! The last time I saw you Leo Balkus swore he'd cut my balls off and feed them to me!"

"Leo is, well," Tony quietly said, "let's just say he's gone on to a better place. Or, in his case, maybe not better.

"Stop your whining," Tony said turning serious. He gently pushed Conrad aside, leaned forward and looked into the camera while asking, "What do you have here?"

While he continued to watch the scene in the bedroom, Tony said, "Conrad, I'm ashamed of you. Looking at such private, intimate behavior. I think they're done. The chubby guy is getting dressed. You ought to check this out, though. The chick is lying buck-ass naked on the bed. I can see why you were watching."

"Let me look," Conrad said.

"Ah, sorry. She got up and put on a robe. Nice ass on her," Carvelli said as he sat back.

"Thanks..." Conrad sullenly said.

"You can watch the movie till your heart's content. You should have enough film for the Castration Queen of divorce lawyers, Lizzie Boyer. That's who this is for isn't it?"

"How did you know?"

"I've been around a while," Carvelli said. "What were you listening to? Do you have her bedroom wired? You do, don't you? Shame on you."

"Hey, gumshoe, it's a living."

"I have work for you. Serious work," Carvelli told him.

"Not interested. Go away."

"Yes, you are," Tony said.

"No! I'm not, now go…"

Tony leaned forward, and Conrad leaned back. Tony said with authority, "Yes, you are." He leaned back then softly said, "Maddy's involved."

"She is?" a now interested Conrad asked.

"Yes, and she misses you," Tony said.

"Really?" Conrad hopefully asked.

"Well, I wouldn't say she necessarily misses you. It's more like, she's willing to put up with you. As long as you keep your hands to yourself. You can look but don't touch and no pictures."

"Okay, I'm in. Who's paying?"

"Don't worry about it. You'll get paid. Give me your address and phone number and I'll call in a couple of days."

"I've never done anything like that," Paul Baker said to Tony Carvelli.

The two of them were in Paul's living room. Carvelli had stopped by to discuss a project he had in mind for the hacker. He told Baker what he wanted, and Baker was not sure he could do it.

"I'm not NSA," Baker continued. "Tapping into someone's phone call isn't like the old days. Before satellites and cell phones, you could put a physical tap on someone's physical phone line. To do what you want, I'd have to be able to hack NSA's satellite system and listen in."

"Well, if it's too hard for you," Carvelli said trying to prick his ego.

"I'm not going there, Carvelli," Baker replied. "Even if I could hack into NSA, and I probably could, they would have to be listening in on your guy's calls, too. Are they?"

"I don't know," Carvelli said. "Who knows what they're up to? But I do see the problem."

"Maybe I could do it through his service provider. Do you know who that is?"

"No," Carvelli said. "I have the phone number for the phone he uses. At least one of them."

"I could find the provider with that. And I could tap them and get his metadata..." Paul said almost absentmindedly.

"What's that?" Carvelli asked.

"The phone numbers he's calling. With that we could find out who he is talking to and the time."

Carvelli thought about this for a minute then said, "You know, that could be useful. Especially if we could get a bug in his house to record his end of the conversation."

"You got that number? Let me have it and I'll get started," Baker said.

Carvelli removed a folded slip of paper from his shirt pocket and handed it to him.

"Here it is. Go ahead and start gathering whatever you said..."

"Metadata," Baker said.

"...and I'll be in touch. I'm sure he has more phones."

"Get me as many numbers as you can."

"Will do. Thanks, Paul. I'll be in touch."

Jake Waschke looked in his mirror one last time to be sure the van was behind him. He flicked on the turn signal to make the left-turn into the restaurant parking lot. As he did this, the van, with Conrad Hilton driving, Carvelli hanging on in back and Paxton O'Rourke in the passenger seat, drove past. Conrad would park in the lot of the marina next to the restaurant. A nondescript van sitting in that lot would be unnoticed yet close enough to monitor Jake's passenger.

Jake parked a space before the valet parking sign. One of the attendants, a young, darkly handsome Latino, rushed over to open the car's door. Before he did, Jake turned and looked at the lady in the back.

"You okay? Good to go?" he asked Maddy.

"Yes, Dad, I'll be fine," she said with a smile. "No kissing on a first date. I remember."

"Especially with a married man," Jake laughed. "You look fabulous. Reel him in."

The valet attendant opened the back door, and Maddy stepped out. The young man's eyes widened then narrowed into what he believed was a seductive look. Maddy saw this and had to restrain a laugh so as not to embarrass the kid. A minute later, the maître d' of Lesley's on the Lake was leading the striking, tall woman to Mr. Simpson's table.

Lesley's was a fine dining restaurant overlooking Lake Minnetonka. Five nights each week, weather permitting, there was a five-piece jazz band with a female singer on the second-floor deck overlooking the lake. Cal Simpson had a table set above the main level in a semi-private alcove hanging out over the water. A truly terrific way to impress a woman if she was willing to be impressed.

While she was following the maître d' Maddy casually looked over the patrons seated on the patio deck. She stopped looking when she saw Carvelli's ex-cop friend, Dan Sorenson, sitting nearby with his wife at one of the tables.

Cal stood up for her and politely took her hand. He held her chair for her as she sat down. The maître d' poured an excellent white wine and Cal raised his glass to her.

"To a beautiful lady on a lovely summer evening."

"Thank you, Cal," Maddy said. She took a sip of the wine, set her glass down, smiled politely and said, "Now get rid of the thugs."

"What?" Cal asked.

"The two men at the table by themselves. It's insulting to have them hovering over me while we have dinner. Get rid of them."

Cal chuckled then signaled for the two men to leave. "They're not thugs. They're security."

In the van, in the parking lot next door, the three of them clearly heard every word. The bug in Maddy's necklace was working perfectly.

"That chick has brass balls," Paxton said after hearing her tell Cal to get rid of the bodyguards.

"Sometimes a little too brassy," Marc grumbled.

"Ssssh," Conrad said. "I think I'm in love."

For the next two hours, Maddy would later admit, she had an excellent meal and a pleasant conversation. Despite his upbringing and early years as a street hood, Cal Simpson had turned himself around. He could be a very charming, well-spoken and informed gentleman. Unlike most men in his position, he did not talk about himself. Most of what they talked about was Maddy. And most of what she told him were lies. Before anything else, the gang had put together a simple, easy to remember legend for her to use.

When Maddy decided to call it a night, she used her phone to call Waschke. Cal walked her out, followed discreetly by Dan and Marge Sorenson. Cal escorted her to the Lincoln Town Car and opened the door for her.

Maddy held out her hand which Cal took and thanked him for a lovely evening.

"Not even a little kiss?" Cal asked.

Without replying, Maddy slyly smiled and slipped into the back seat.

Before closing the door, Cal poked his head in and said, "I would love to see you again."

"Let me think about it," Maddy replied.

While the car pulled away, Cal stood on the sidewalk and watched it go. The massive ego on the man kicked in and made him even more determined to have that woman.

TWENTY-SEVEN

The Sunday morning after Maddy's first "date" with Cal Simpson, the crew met at Jake's Limousine Service. Waschke had coffee and pastry set out for everyone. Maddy and Paxton, having picked up Marc, were the last ones to arrive. When Maddy entered the customer area where they were meeting, the cynical ex-cops all stood and applauded.

"What's that for?" she asked.

"A fine performance," Carvelli said.

"Screw you, Carvelli," she said forcing back a smile.

"Hey, Paxton was it not a great performance?" Carvelli asked.

"Well, yeah, but leave me out of this," Paxton replied.

Maddy saw the silent little man sitting by himself and said, "Well, hello, Conrad. How've you been?"

"Ah, good, fine, Ms. Rivers," he replied.

"Stay at least an arm's length away from him," Maddy told Paxton. "He can be a little grabby."

Paxton looked at Conrad, sighed and said, "I don't know. It's been so long I might not mind."

Amid the laughter, Maddy said to Conrad, "She's kidding."

"I know that," he said. "Besides, you came after me, remember?"

Maddy narrowed her eyes then snarled, "This conversation is over."

"What were your impressions of Cal Simpson?" Waschke asked. Being a homicide lieutenant, Jake was used to being in charge. He would get the meeting on track.

"Thanks," Maddy said as Tommy Craven handed her and Paxton cups of coffee. "I liked him. He's pleasant company. Nice place, a nice meal and all-around nice evening. And you bunch of slugs could take some lessons from him on how to act like a gentleman."

"Now that hurts," Carvelli said to Marc.

"No kidding. I'll remember it," Marc replied.

"How did Marge like the place?" Maddy asked Sorenson.

"We had a nice time," Sorenson said.

"Did she know you were on the job?" Maddy asked.

"No, I said we needed a night out."

"Did you get lucky?" Tommy asked.

"I knew one of you guys would ask him that question," Maddy said chastising them as a group.

"They're pigs," Paxton added.

"At best," Maddy said. She turned to Sorenson and asked, "Well, did you?"

This brought a healthy round of laughter.

134

"Okay, Conrad," Waschke said. "You're up. What do you have for us?"

"I have four bugs and it would be best if we could get them all placed," he said getting serious. "I'm going to have to leave it with you where to place them. Since I don't have a drawing of the house…"

"Did you try the city?" Carvelli asked.

"Yeah, they told me to go pound sand. They wouldn't let me have it."

"We could get it with a court order," Marc said. "But we might as well knock on the door and ask this guy if we can come in and look around. He'd find out in about a minute."

"I can check the place out and get locations," Maddy said.

"Do you have another date, yet?" Waschke asked.

"Not yet," Maddy replied. "He wants to take me out on the lake. Cruise around and go to lunch or dinner."

"That's probably a bad idea," Carvelli said. "It will cause us problems covering you on a lake of that size."

"I'm not worried about it," Maddy said. "He'll behave. I figure the third date I'll ask him to show me his house. Then I'll scout for the bugs."

"That's going to be risky," Paxton said. "On the third date, he'll expect you to sleep with him."

"No chance," Maddy replied. "I have the perfect excuse. No married men."

"Are you comfortable with that?" Marc asked Carvelli.

"Not one bit," he replied. "On the other hand, she can take care of herself," Carvelli shrugged. "We'll play it by ear. What else do you want to tell us, Conrad?"

"The range on these little devils we'll be planting is, at most, a half a mile. And that's if there's nothing in the way."

"We could set up at Vivian's," Carvelli said. "That's about a quarter mile."

"There are a couple of houses and a lot of trees in the way," Maddy reminded him.

"Conrad?"

"Maybe, but no interference would be best," he said. "These things don't bounce off satellites. Are these houses both on the lake?"

"Yeah," Carvelli said.

"Does Vivian have a boathouse?"

"Yes, she does," Maddy replied. "Could you set it up in there? There are still trees in the way."

"I could find a spot near his house to set up a signal boost. Somewhere along the shore. Maybe in a tree. Have it pick up the signal then boost it to the boathouse. I'm pretty sure that would work. I can set up the receivers and recorders in the boathouse out of the weather and have a separate recorder for each bug. I'll make them frequency activated. As soon as the signal comes in, the recorder starts up."

"What if someone else is on that frequency?" Waschke asked.

"A chance we'll have to take if you want to do this," Conrad said. "I'll make it a very high frequency with a very short range. That should keep the odds down to a minimum."

"Any questions?" Waschke asked. "Okay. We'll get this set up this week."

"I'll call him tomorrow and set up the boat ride," Maddy said. "Wednesday okay?"

When no one objected, they decided on the upcoming Wednesday.

"We're going to need a couple of guys out fishing to cruise along and keep an eye on things," Carvelli said.

"And it can't be any of us," Waschke added.

"I'll get two guys," Sorenson said. "I know who to get."

"Someone he hasn't seen or has not driven for him," Waschke said.

"No problem," Sorenson said.

"When are you going back to Chicago?" Maddy asked Paxton.

"My flight's at 4:10," she replied. "I didn't want to take off any more time so that the Queen Bee won't get on my ass about it."

"Who's paying for these trips?" Carvelli asked.

"Well, me," Paxton replied.

"Keep track of your expenses and I'll get you reimbursed. The rest of you get me an invoice for your time."

"Is she okay with this?" Maddy asked referring to Vivian Donahue.

"Are you kidding? She loves this stuff. She's mad at me because we had this meeting here and not at the mansion. When she says money's no object and spend whatever you have to…" Carvelli said.

"She means it," Maddy finished for him.

"Okay, Conrad," Waschke said. "What next?"

"First, we need to set up the recording station," Conrad answered.

"That's the easy part," Carvelli replied. "I'll call Vivian, and we can do that today if you have the equipment ready."

"I do," Conrad said. "As I said, if Maddy can plant four bugs, we'll have voice-activated equipment for each one."

"Have you thought about how you're going to get in the house?" Marc asked Maddy.

"I can get in," she answered. "All I have to do is ask and he'll be delighted to show me around. Getting out could be the problem. I'm not worried about it.

"I'll call him tomorrow and set up the boat ride. While we're cruising around the lake, I'll casually mention I would like to see his home. He'll jump at the chance. Show me the bugs, Conrad, and how to plant them."

It took him less than a minute to show them to her—he had them in separate small plastic containers in a plastic bag—and how to plant them.

"Where do you suggest?" Maddy asked the group.

"In an office, if he has one," Carvelli said. "Pretty certain he does."

"Kitchen," Conrad added. "People do a lot in the kitchen while on the phone. Remember, they can't hear through doors. They can pick up clear as a bell, sounds up to about twenty feet. After that, the quality drops off."

"I'll find a couple more places," Maddy assured them.

"All set?" Carvelli asked.

Conrad and Tommy Craven were walking across Vivian's manicured lawn toward Carvelli. The two of them had exited the boathouse after spending two hours setting up the recording equipment.

Carvelli and Vivian Donahue were in padded lawn chairs under a tall shade tree waiting for them.

"All set," Conrad said, "and good to go. We tested them, and they're all working."

Carvelli looked at Tommy then raised his eyebrows as if to question what Conrad said.

"Looks good to me," Tommy said with a shrug.

Conrad and Tommy took the two empty chairs at the table. Being the good host that she always is, Vivian poured them each a glass of lemonade.

"Now what?" Vivian asked.

"You do understand how illegal this is, don't you, Mrs. Donahue?" Tommy asked.

"Vivian," she replied. "Of course, that's why it's so much fun. Now what?" she repeated.

"We want to use one of your boats," Carvelli told her. "We need to cruise around by Simpson's place and pick out a tree to plant the other thing."

"The power booster," Conrad said. "Um, ah, about me climbing a tree," Conrad somewhat nervously said. "I've been thinking; it's not really necessary. Tommy could do it…"

"No," Carvelli said. "We're only going to get one shot at this. You're going up the tree and set this thing up."

"I'm not any happier about it than you are, Conrad," Tommy said. "That's why I quit deer hunting. Don't worry; it will be fine."

"I want to ride along in the boat," Vivian said.

"No," Carvelli said. "He might be home and he might recognize you."

"It's my boat," she said. "If he recognizes it, won't it make sense that I am in it?"

"Vivian…"

"My boat," she said again.

Carvelli leaned toward her with a stern look on his face. "It's a bad idea…"

"My boat," Vivian silently mouthed the words at him while smiling.

Carvelli looked at both Tommy and Conrad for a little help, but all he got was a shrug from Tommy and Conrad saying, "Her boat."

"Fine," said as he finally caved in.

Two nights later, a cloudy, moonless night, Tommy, Carvelli, and Conrad found the tree they had selected. It was 3:00 A.M. and as quiet as a church.

The three of them, dressed completely in black, had made their way from Vivian's, down the shore to Simpson's home. Carvelli would stay on the ground with the equipment while Tommy and Conrad climbed as high as they dared to plant the power booster. Once they reached the spot, Carvelli, having attached a rope to the bag holding the equipment, would climb up with it. His job was to make sure it did not snag on any branches. The tree itself was a huge, eighty-year-old maple with easy climbing branches. All went well until the equipment reached Conrad.

Carvelli had climbed about twenty feet up, guiding the bag. The last ten feet or so, the bag went up without a glitch. Conrad, barely able to breathe thirty feet up in a tree, managed to maneuver to where Tommy was casually standing on a small branch. By this point, Carvelli, no fear of heights himself, was back on the ground.

Conrad placed his right foot on the branch Tommy was on, but the extra weight was too much. Tommy started to say no when it snapped. At almost the same moment, a powerful yard light went on in the backyard of the house next door.

Conrad was the lucky one. His left foot was on a sturdy branch and both hands were gripping a branch above his head. Tommy was not so fortunate. When the branch snapped, he lost his balance and went down.

Almost miraculously, ten feet below him was an eight-inch branch strong enough to catch and hold him. Somehow, he managed to hold onto the bag with the equipment. Tommy landed on his stomach draped over the branch. The wind was knocked out of him and his abdomen hurt like hell, but he kept his wits. Conrad was standing on the branch that had

138

held him up. Only now, terrified, he had both arms wrapped around the tree trunk and was hanging on for dear life.

On the ground, Carvelli heard the branch snap, Tommy crashing downward and then saw the light come on next door. Seconds later, the noise from Tommy falling stopped, and a door to the house opened. When it did, the biggest Rottweiler Carvelli had ever seen, or so he thought, came flying across the grass straight toward them.

Carvelli, for a man in his fifties, moved like a flash. As he scrambled to get back up in the tree, he whispered several times, "Be quiet," hoping his companions would hear him.

Fortunately, two miracles occurred. After letting the dog loose, the homeowner had gone back inside. Then, the giant dog—Carvelli would later swear he could put a saddle on the beast—stopped in his tracks fifteen feet away.

It took Carvelli a few seconds to realize that the dog had hit an electronic fence at the property line.

For the next two minutes, everyone, including the dog, was silently frozen in place. Carvelli, now ten-feet up in the tree, held on, stared at the monster and held his breath. The Rottweiler sat on his haunches and stared back. Conrad held onto the tree's trunk while Tommy fought to breathe again.

Apparently satisfied that the men in the tree were not a threat, the big dog moved off to do his business. When he finished, he came back and again sat staring at Carvelli. Five minutes later, a man appeared at the door and the dog silently trotted off to go back inside.

When the yard light went off, Carvelli asked, "Everybody still alive?"

"Yes," both men replied.

"You okay, Tommy?" Carvelli asked looking up at the man draped over a branch just above him.

"I think so," Tommy replied.

"Conrad?" Carvelli asked.

"Yes, I guess," a shaky voice came back.

"Tommy, can you get back up to him?" Carvelli quietly asked.

"Yeah, give me a minute. We'll get this done, then get the hell out of here."

"Before that thing comes back looking for breakfast," Carvelli said.

A few minutes later the excitement was over, the power booster was in place, and the three of them started back to Vivian's. Leading the way, Carvelli waded three feet into the lake to throw off any scent. The other two followed him. Fortunately, the lake bottom here was sandy and the walking was easy. The only obstacle was the neighbor's dock, which they went under. They made it to the far side property line away from Cal's when a powerful light came on in Cal's yard.

The three men had just enough time to scramble behind a large oak tree when they saw another four-legged bullet fly across Cal's yard straight to the tree they had climbed. This time, the man who had let the dog out went with him. Using a heavy-duty flashlight to lead him, the man hurried after the dog. When he caught up with him, they could clearly see the unmistakable silhouette of a large Doberman Pinscher. He scurried around the area of the tree sniffing and obviously quite agitated. At one point he got up on his haunches and used his front paws to lean on the tree to look up into it. Stretched out like he was, the Doberman looked to be taller than the man. He dropped back to the ground and dashed about, then abruptly stopped at the water's edge.

While the dog was doing this, the man used the flashlight to slowly look over the ground for anything that might show why the dog was acting up. He even looked up into the tree with it while the dog leaned on it. Satisfied, unseen by Carvelli or the other two, the man slipped the silenced Beretta .40 caliber handgun back into its holster.

"Come on, Zeus. Probably a deer or some kids," he said.

Tony, Tommy, and Conrad would never know how lucky they were. The man's name was Aidan Walsh, and he was the head of Cal's security and a sociopath thug Cal had known back to his Boston days. He was also the man who had confronted Lynn McDaniel on the road by Cal's cabin the evening of the Fourth of July. After which he had dragged her body into the bush.

140

TWENTY-EIGHT

"Zeus got himself in a bit of an anxious state last night," Aidan Walsh said to Cal.

"Oh?" Cal casually inquired as he set down the newspaper he was reading.

Walsh sat down at the white wrought iron patio table across from Cal. He poured a cup of coffee for himself, lit a cigarette, blew out a long stream of smoke, and continued.

"Shortly after three, we went out to check the grounds. He took off like a shot down to the shoreline at the property's corner," he said pointing across the yard to the spot.

"He ran around sniffing for a bit, looked back and forth along the shore, then settled down."

"You see anything?" Cal asked.

"No, sir. I used the flashlight to look over the grounds, the trees, and the lake. Didn't find anything. Could've been anything. A deer, raccoon, some kids, who knows."

Cal thought about this for a minute or so. He didn't like unusual events to mysteriously pop up when he was about to do a deal. Cal Simpson was not a big believer in coincidence.

"Okay, for the next several days, I want Zeus out on the grounds all night. And I want someone with him at all times. It was probably nothing, but we'll take no chances."

"Yes, sir," Aidan replied. "I'll see to it. Are we sending the package today?"

"We are," Cal answered. Looked at his Rolex and said, "In fact, I'm going in now to get it ready. Come on."

The two men went into the house and then to Cal's office. Cal took the chair behind the desk and Aidan in front.

The first thing Cal did was pull on a pair of heavy surgical gloves. He lifted up a FedEx mailing envelope and showed it to Aidan.

"It's clean," Cal said. "Be careful with it."

Cal then took out a multi-page document already folded into thirds. He removed a self-sealing letter-size envelope from the middle desk drawer. On it were a name and address neatly typed. Cal took a yellow post-it note, scribbled a few words on it, and attached it to the envelope. He placed the document in the small envelope along with a brief note explaining what the document was and that it should be checked for fingerprints. Cal then peeled the cellophane off of the adhesive and sealed it. He placed it in the FedEx mailer, sealed it and laid it on the desk.

"It's already addressed," Cal said referring to the FedEx mailer. "Just take it in, pay the fee in cash and let them have it. Be careful..."

"Not to touch it," Aidan said finishing Cal's sentence. Coming from anyone else, finishing a sentence for him would have elicited a sharp rebuke. Aidan drew a smile instead.

"We can't be too careful," Cal said.

"I'll take it to Hudson," Aidan said referring to Hudson, Wisconsin, a small city just across the St. Croix River border. "There's a FedEx there. I'll hold it with a cloth between two fingers."

"Wear a hat and sunglasses," Cal reminded him. "And I want this place swept for bugs, today. It's been a while. Call and take care of that before you leave."

"Are you seeing Maddy today?" Aidan asked. He knew Mrs. Simpson was at her sister's for a few days and hoped to get a look at his boss' latest arm candy, the lovely Maddy Shore.

"We're going out on the boat. She'll be here around five. She wants to see the house first," Cal said.

"Good, I'll get to see her again," Aidan said with a smile. "She's easy on the eyes."

"Yes, she is," Cal agreed. "But there's something about her. She's a little too cool, a little too confident. Like she's been able to wrap men around her little finger since she was a kid. I do like her company. She's smart, interesting and up on current events."

"So, when you gonna get in her pants?" Aidan almost laughed.

"There's the challenge, isn't it?" Cal agreed.

Cruising in his year-old Cadillac, Aidan made the drive to Wisconsin in under an hour. As he passed over the I-94 bridge, he looked at the river, mildly surprised at the number of sailboats and expensive cruisers he could see. There must have been two hundred on each side of the bridge. He shook his head at the thought of so many people not at work on a weekday. With Labor Day barely two weeks away, a lot of people were grabbing every minute of summer that they could.

Aidan Walsh was born fifty-two years ago as Aidan O'Keefe. His father, Connor O'Keefe was a one-time associate of one James 'Whitey' Bulger. Connor O'Keefe, among others, had helped Whitey wrest away control of the Winter Hill Gang in 1979. Aidan, to the displeasure of his father, was an up and coming teenage gangster himself. Whenever the two of them argued about it, which was frequent, Aidan would remind dear old dad it was either the cops or the crooks for the Southie boys. The argument ended when Aidan was fourteen.

Responding to an anonymous tip, the cops were waiting for Connor and two others outside a small bank. A brief shootout occurred and although Connor had not fired his gun, he took a bullet squarely in the forehead.

It was shortly after Connor's death that Aidan met a semi-legitimate gangster named Marty Kelly. With the blessing of Whitey Bulger—Whitey received tribute from Kelly—Aidan was accepted into a street gang associated with Kelly. Almost forty years later, Aidan was still with the man who had made him a millionaire many times over.

Aidan turned off I-94 at the second exit on the Wisconsin side. He drove north about a quarter mile and saw the FedEx store. He parked the Caddy two doors down from FedEx and put on a black, logo-free, baseball cap. He checked himself in the mirror and satisfied, got out of the car.

Aidan carefully held the mailer using a handkerchief and went inside. He hurried to the counter and quickly dropped the envelope on the counter so as to not be noticed.

Less than two minutes later, after being helped by a cheerful, pretty teenager, Aidan was back outside. As he backed his car out of its space, he muttered to himself, "What the hell is wrong with these people. It ain't normal for everybody to be this nice all the time."

He took one last, quick glance at the FedEx store, shook his head while thinking about the girl then drove off.

The next day Darren Benedict was in his cluttered office; lived in he would normally describe it. He was about half-finished with his column for the next day's business section when he heard a soft knock on his door. It opened, and a mailroom clerk came in. He was holding a FedEx envelope addressed to Darren personally.

"How are you, Paulie?" the affable newsman asked the clerk.

"Fine, Mr. Benedict," the young man replied holding the envelope out to Darren.

"What have we here?" Darren asked.

Receiving letters and FedEx packages was quite routine for any major metropolitan newsroom. Darren Benedict had been with Minnesota's main newspaper, *The Minneapolis Star Tribune*, for over forty years. The past twenty he had been the number one columnist in the business section. Darren wrote three columns each week on almost any business-related subject he wanted.

By the time he had removed the letter-size envelope, the mailroom clerk was quietly closing the door. Darren read the message on the post-it note with a puzzled expression. Whoever sent it had warned him to be careful about leaving fingerprints.

Using a Kleenex to hold the envelope while he sliced it open, Darren carefully removed the document inside. He placed it on his desk blotter, carefully unfolded it using the tissue and read the typewritten note attached to it.

"Holy shit," he said quite loudly to himself when he realized what it was. "What the hell…" he said much more quietly.

It took him the better part of an hour to carefully read the memo. When he finished, he leaned back in his chair thinking through what he should do.

"Aaron, I need you to come to my office," Darren said. He was on his phone talking to his boss, Aaron Towns, a gruff, no-nonsense black man who was the business section's editor.

"I'm busy. You come here," he replied.

"I can't, Aaron. Please, trust me on this. I've got a front-page, Sunday column sitting on my desk. Please."

The phone went silent for a moment while Towns thought about this. He had known Darren Benedict and been his boss for years. His respect for Benedict was well-earned.

"Okay, I'll be right there."

A moment later, Darren saw his boss exit his own office and work his way through the floor toward him.

"Okay, what?" Towns said as he closed the door.

Without going into detail, Darren explained what he had been sent.

"You think it's legitimate?" Towns asked.

Using the eraser end of a pencil, Darren pushed the note that was inside the envelope, so Towns could read.

The note read: There are fingerprints from two lawyers of Everson, Reed who buried this report on it.

He looked at Darren who said, "I was in court the day the lawyers for Everson, Reed swore that Cannon Brothers' had no knowledge of any defect in their skateboard batteries. That they had been duped by their Chinese supplier," Darren answered.

"So, you believe this is genuine?"

"I don't know," Darren replied. "I don't know any more than you do. Except, I know two of the Everson, Reed lawyers who were working this case were murdered around the Fourth of July…"

"I remember that," Towns said. "You think it's their prints on this thing?"

"Aaron, I don't know anything. If they are their prints," he continued looking at his boss, "then this thing will explode. Murder, conspiracy, fraud, you name it."

"You realize Everson, Reed is one of the biggest firms in this state. They'll sue our asses off if we're wrong," Towns said.

"Or, we win a Pulitzer and bring down the mighty if we're not."

Towns thought it over for a moment then said, "Okay. Here's what we'll do. We'll write it up for tomorrow morning."

"Why not Sunday? It will make a bigger splash."

"Don't worry, once this hits the fan there will be plenty of follow-up for Sunday. But write it up as factually accurate as possible. A package was delivered to you with a note claiming this document to be etc...."

"Okay."

"I'm heading upstairs to talk to the higher-ups, including legal. Find out who the head honcho is at Everson, Reed. We'll call him just before five o'clock for a comment."

"So, he doesn't have time to run to court," Darren said.

"Exactly," Towns replied.

TWENTY-NINE

"He'll have an office. Probably a large den with a big ass desk in it," Conrad said. "Put one under the center drawer of the desk. Right where he'll be sitting."

Maddy, Carvelli, Conrad, Dan Sorenson and Vivian were in Vivian's library. Maddy was about to go on another date with Cal. Dan Sorenson was to deliver her to Cal's and pick her up later. Before they went cruising on the lake to go to dinner, Maddy would have Cal show her his house. The discussion was about where to place the bugs.

The devices themselves were state of the art. Half the size of a fingernail, they could pick up sounds up to twenty feet. Tuned into the signal booster in the tree on Cal's property, they would send a clear and easily heard signal to Vivian's boathouse. On the back of each was a small strip of adhesive that would stick to most surfaces. The micro battery would last for at least a couple of months.

"Where else?" Maddy asked.

"The kitchen's always a good place," Conrad said.

"And a living room area," Carvelli said.

"If you can find a conference room and get a chance, that would be great," Conrad added.

"That could be touchy getting in and out of there. He'll most likely do conferences with other people in his office or living room," Carvelli said.

Before Maddy could reply Dan asked, "You ready to go?"

"Yes," Maddy answered.

"We'll follow in the van," Carvelli said.

"We have a couple guys on the lake," Dan told her. "Different boat this time."

"Be careful," Vivian sternly told her.

Dan turned left onto Cal's property and as they drove through the trees they saw activity in Cal's driveway.

"Who are these guys?" Dan rhetorically asked.

"Don't know," Maddy replied from the backseat. Speaking so her friends in Conrad's van could pick her up, she said, "There's a plain, white Dodge van in Cal's driveway. It has no markings or business logo on it." She read off the license plate number as Dan pulled up and stopped.

Before Dan could get out to open her door, a tough-looking man with short-cropped mostly gray hair and hard shoulders opened it for her. While Maddy stepped out, he smiled and held out his hand to help her.

"Hello," he pleasantly said. "We haven't met. My name is Aidan Walsh. I'm Mr. Simpson's head of security."

"Nice to meet you," Maddy said.

She looked toward the house and saw Cal hurrying toward them. When he reached her, they exchanged a brief cheek kiss.

"Escort Ms. Shore inside please, Aidan," Cal said while indicating to Dan Sorenson to wait a moment.

While Maddy was being led to the house, Cal walked around to Dan's side of the car. Cal peeled a hundred-dollar bill from a roll of money, pressed it into Dan's hand and quietly said, "She won't be needing you tonight."

As he said this, what felt like a stone sank into Dan's stomach. Cal's implication was obvious; he expected Maddy to spend the night.

"Very good, sir. Thank you, sir," Dan managed to mutter. He re-entered the Town Car and drove off. By the time he got to the end of Cal's driveway, Dan was on the phone to Carvelli. He told Tony about being dismissed for the night and what they could infer from that.

"He expects her to spend the night," Carvelli said.

"Yeah, now what?" Sorenson asked.

"Now we wait and play it by ear. We knew this was going to happen sooner or later. She'll be okay."

While Aidan was walking Maddy to the front door, the two men loading the van paused for a moment to watch them.

"What?" one of the men asked.

"She looks familiar," his partner replied.

"Yeah, in your dreams."

A few feet from the front door, Maddy said to Aidan, "That's odd-looking equipment."

Although she knew exactly what it was having seen Conrad Hilton use the same devices, she wanted Aidan's answer.

"Mr. Simpson is a careful man," he replied. "As head of his security, I have the house checked for bugs."

"Bugs?" Maddy asked stopping at the door so Aidan could open it for her. "Like spiders and ants and..."

"No," Aidan said with a laugh. "Listening devices."

"Oh, sure. Sorry," Maddy said tossing her head back and forth and rolling her eyes upward. "I can be such a ditz sometimes."

Aidan opened the door, gave her a serious look and said, "I don't believe that for an instant."

He led her into a spacious living room with comfortable furniture. Aidan politely exited which gave Maddy maybe a minute before Cal

147

appeared. She casually walked around as if checking the room then planted the first bug under an antique, French-style, rotary telephone. It was on an end table two feet from what Maddy assumed to be Cal's chair in this room.

Five seconds later she heard, "Well, hello again."

"Hi," she replied.

He came forward, lightly held her shoulders and kissed her cheek. "So, let me show you around."

It took him a half-hour to guide her through the five-bedroom, three-story, and fourteen room mini-mansion. For most normal people it was magnificent. But Maddy had spent too much time with Vivian in the Corwin Mansion to be awed by this. She did an excellent job of acting and even threw herself on a king-size bed in one of the guest rooms. Maddy gave Cal a very brief come-hither look just to distract him.

When they went back downstairs, he showed her his massive corner office.

Maddy looked around at the leather furniture, dark paneling, and large mahogany desk and asked, "No animal heads?"

"Those aren't the trophy's I like to collect," Cal coyly said. "Why, are you an anti-gun and anti-hunting person?"

"No, not really," Maddy casually replied. She moved behind his desk intentionally ignoring his comment about trophy collecting and sat down in his chair.

"This is nice. Maybe a touch too masculine, but it suits you."

Maddy looked around and noticed a multi-line phone, a large computer screen, and printer and other signs of a working office.

"Do you work at home? I mean, do you have a traditional office that you go to?" she asked.

"Mostly I work here," he acknowledged.

"You live very well. I can see where a girl could get used to this," she said while sliding her hands over his desk. As she did this, she attached bug number 2 to the underside of the desk's middle drawer.

Cal looked at his gold Rolex and said, "I'm getting a little hungry. Let's say we finish the tour and head out."

Next, he took her through the dining room. The centerpiece was a long dining table with twelve matching, armchairs around it.

"This is beautiful," Maddy said looking around. "Let me guess," she continued, "your chair is the one closest to the door," she said pointing to it.

"How did you know?" he laughed.

"Simple, you're a busy man. If you use this room for entertaining, you could get called to the phone at any time," Maddy answered. She had slowly moved around to the end of the table where Cal's chair was and sat down on it.

"Very nice," she said.

"I must confess," Cal said. "Wife number two did this room. And most of the others."

"Wife number two?" Maddy asked. "How many have there been?"

"I'm on number three," he reluctantly admitted. "Come on, I'll show you everyone's favorite room."

"Ah, the kitchen," Maddy said.

"Yep, the kitchen," he agreed.

Maddy could see why. It was almost the size of her apartment. If she were someone who enjoyed cooking, she would be standing in Nirvana.

"It's magnificent," she said.

"Do you like to cook?" Cal asked.

"Oh, of course, I get it from my dad," she lied.

Aidan walked in and whispered in Cal's ear. Cal nodded at him and turned to Maddy.

"Excuse me, one moment, please. I have a call I must take," he said.

"Sure, no problem. Take all the time you need," she answered.

Aidan followed his boss out leaving Maddy alone. She quickly looked around trying to find the best place to plant the last bug. Conrad had suggested somewhere near the refrigerator.

Maddy bent down next to the refrigerator's handle and quickly attached the bug to a cupboard door. The opposite wall in the kitchen was at least twenty feet away, almost too far for the bug to pick up.

Sensing more than hearing, somehow, she knew someone was coming. Maddy stood up and went right to a cupboard next to the sink. She opened the door just in time to hear a voice behind her.

"Can I help you find something?" Aidan asked, a touch of suspicion in his voice.

"Oh!" Maddy yelped as she whirled around. Holding her heart, she said, "You startled me. Um, I, ah, was looking for a glass to get a drink of water."

"Other side of the sink," Aidan pointed with a smile. "There are ice cubes in the freezer and you can get clean water from the refrigerator door."

Maddy took a glass and filled it from the door. For the next three or four minutes, she tried to make a little small talk, but he wasn't interested. Finally, Cal came back and rescued her.

"I hate to do this to you, but I'm going to have to cancel tonight. Something has come up," Cal said.

"It's not the end of the world. I'll be okay," Maddy said.

149

"Do you need a ride? I can get one of the staff to take you," Cal asked.

"What about Aidan? Can he give me a lift?" she asked.

"I'm afraid not. He goes with me. I'm really sorry," Cal sincerely said.

"It's okay," Maddy said.

"You get ready," Aidan said to Cal. "I'll take care of her. I'll get Hal to take her home."

Thirty minutes later, Maddy was dropped off at a downtown high-rise three blocks from her own. When the driver left, another thug like Aidan, she called Carvelli and Dan was sent to get her. The phone call Cal received, although one-sided, had provided their first piece of intel.

THIRTY

An hour after leaving Cal's home, Dan Sorenson and Maddy were back at Vivian's. From the driveway, they had seen Carvelli, Tommy, Franklin Washington and Vivian outside the boathouse. Dan parked the Town Car and the two of them hurried through the house and down to the lake.

"Hello, everyone," Maddy said as they watched her arrive.

"You okay?" Carvelli asked.

"Hello, dear," Vivian stood, hugged her lightly and kissed her cheek.

"Any problems?" Carvelli asked before Maddy could answer him.

"I'm good," Maddy said then added, "No, no problems. Thanks," she said to Dan who handed her a cold beer.

They all took seats, and Maddy explained how she planted the bugs. When she finished, Conrad came out of the boathouse.

"Hi," he said to Maddy. "The bugs are working fine. You did good."

"Thanks, Conrad," she sincerely replied.

"He made another call," Conrad said looking at Carvelli. "I got the dialing recorded. Your guy should be able to get us a number."

"Did you send it to him?" Carvelli asked. They were referring to Carvelli's hacker.

"Yeah. I sent it all. So far, he's talked to three people, all men. A guy named Floyd was the first call. He called Cal. They spoke for less than two minutes. Something about another test today went perfectly.

"Thirteen minutes later he called this Al guy. Not sure why it took him so long."

"What time was the call?" Maddy asked.

"Four forty-eight," Conrad replied.

"He was getting me out the door," Maddy said. "I was there when he took the first call. Did you record him from number two?"

"Yeah, I did."

"That's the office bug. Number one is the living room, three is the dining room and four is the kitchen. He left me in the kitchen to take the call. His head of security almost caught me planting number four."

"You get it okay?" Carvelli asked.

"Yeah. It was close, but I got it. This guy, his head of security, he's a scary thug. Name's Aidan Walsh. Probably a phony. I need to get it to Paxton and see if her guys can find out who he is. Anyway, sorry, Conrad, please finish."

151

"He spoke to Al for almost seven minutes, Cal told him about the test Cal said Floyd referred to. Al was very pleased. So was Cal. Then they talked about something they referred to as 'the short'. I have no idea what that could be. And a little about hearings, a funding bill, and a contract. Again, no idea what they meant."

Carvelli looked around at the small group and asked, "Any idea?"

It was Vivian who spoke up. "The hearings and bill could be something coming from Congress. Something tied to this test. There are things like that going on all the time. Especially for the Pentagon. It would be difficult to find out what. But I know some people, a lobbyist or two, who might be able to get me some information on any big spending bills coming out in the next few weeks. Anything that might be tied to a test of some kind."

"Good," Carvelli said. "Do that. In the meantime, we'll try to find out who Al and Floyd are."

"The third call was to a guy named Dan. Again, I got that number and sent it to Tony's guy," Conrad continued. "It was very short. Less than thirty seconds. Cal identified himself then told Dan he could, quote, tell everyone everything is going according to plan. That was it."

"Okay," Carvelli said. "We'll track down who these people are."

When no one said anything further, Vivian said, "Why don't we have a little dinner. Then we can all listen to the recordings together."

"By then there might be others, too," Maddy said.

An hour later, they were seated in Vivian's library listening to all of the phone calls, at least Cal's side of them. There was another call that Cal had made while they ate. He had called Floyd back to tell him he had spoken to Al.

With only Cal's side of each call, no one was able to make an educated guess as to what the calls were about.

"It must be something fairly important," Carvelli said. "Otherwise, why hustle Maddy out the door?"

There was a moment of silence, then Maddy said, "We need to look over the guest list from Cal's Fourth of July party. Look for these names."

"Where is it?" Vivian asked.

"I have it," Carvelli answered her. "I'll check it when I get home. In the meantime, that's about it for tonight."

"Everyone is welcome back tomorrow to monitor his calls. I'm not sure what but I do believe he and these other people are up to something," Vivian told them.

"Hey, it's Maddy," Maddy was saying into her phone. "I got a name for you to run down. It's Aidan Walsh, and I think he's from Boston."

"How do you know that?" she heard Paxton ask.

"He's got a slight accent. That and he's a thug and Cal Simpson's head of security."

"You got a picture? A picture would be helpful."

"No, I don't, but I'll try to get one for you."

"Not that I want to know if you've done anything illegal, but did you get the, um, devices in place?"

"Yep, all set."

"Let me know if you find anything interesting," Paxton said.

"Will do. Are you coming up this weekend?"

"No, can't get away. Probably next weekend, Labor Day."

"Great, see you then," Maddy said.

"Hey, you. Be careful. We've all grown quite fond of you."

"I will, thanks," Maddy softly said.

Maddy ended the call and said, "I just remembered something. There was a white van in front when we got there…"

"My not-so-worthy-competitors," Conrad said. "We ran the license plate. They must have been there to sweep for bugs."

"They were," Maddy replied. "I got it out of his security guy. He didn't tell me how often, but he has it done, and sooner or later they'll find our stuff. And, I hate to say this, but one of the guys with the van, there were two of them, was staring at me."

"A man staring at you is not exactly novel," Carvelli said.

"It wasn't that. I know that look. No, he was watching me as if he knew me."

"I'll have MPD check them out," Dan Sorenson said.

"They're brothers," Conrad said. "Rob and Willie Hanson. They're semi-legit. The cops will know them."

Senator Roger Manion, the U.S. Senate's only admitted socialist, entered the men's room across from his office. He stepped up to one of the urinals and stood waiting for his uncooperative, elderly prostate to allow him to relieve himself. While he did this, two more senators entered the luxury bathroom.

"Roger," Albert Fisher greeted him while Manion faced the wall.

"Albert," the crabby senator from Maine replied.

"When are you going to see a doctor about that prostate?" Fisher asked.

"None of your goddamn business," Manion growled.

While this exchange took place, the third man, Senator Galen Carroll of Delaware searched the restroom. Satisfied the three of them were the only ones there, he let Fisher know that.

Fisher stood next to Manion and quietly said, "I heard from our friend in Minnesota. He heard from Nevada. The final test flight went off without a hitch. Time for the funding Bill to go through."

"It's about goddamn time," Manion replied.

"Are you talking about the Bill or your uncooperative dick?" Fisher asked.

"Both," Manion said. "I've been sitting on the Bill for a month. Have you told your pal, Howell?" Manion asked referring to Senator Christian Howell. Howell was the chairman of the subcommittee that must okay the Bill they were talking about. He would schedule a hearing for a week or so from now. A couple of Air Force generals would testify that the A-1's Tiger Hawk was fully tested and ready for funding. Once that was done, the Bill would pass out of committee and go through the formality of a floor vote.

"Yes, he knows. He will schedule the hearing for the next Tuesday. If it fits your schedule," Fisher replied.

Manion finally finished, flushed the urinal, stepped back and while zipping up his pants, thought about his schedule for next week.

"Tuesday should be fine," he said. He stepped to the sink to wash his hands and continued, "Tell him to hold it in the morning and let this be the only piece of business we conduct, in case something else comes up.

"How's the other thing?" Manion asked while wiping his hands dry.

"Another week to ten days," Fisher said.

"Good," Manion said. "I'm looking forward to the Labor Day break."

"Me, too," Fisher said. "These three to four-day work weeks are a killer."

While the three senators were holding their clandestine men's room meeting, another meeting was taking place in Minneapolis. That morning, the story about the concealed engineer's report had been printed on that day's front page.

The meeting was taking place in a conference room attached to the managing editor's office. His name was John Coyle, and he was joined by the reporter Darren Benedict and Darren's boss Aaron Towns. Lead counsel for the paper, Gwen Charter, was also there on behalf of the paper.

The government sent a local Assistant U.S. Attorney Megan Wilson. With her were two large, intimidating FBI agents. Megan had a federal subpoena demanding the original of the engineer's report.

Finally, the one making the most noise was Brody Knutson, managing partner of Everson, Reed. Brody had brought along an impressive set of serious-looking Everson, Reed lawyers to remind everyone of Brody's importance.

The first thing Brody did was hand out copies of pleadings for a motion he had scheduled in state court. It was set for 1:00 P.M. that day. In it, he was demanding the return of what he claimed was the stolen engineer's report.

"You're not going to win this ass-covering motion, Brody," John Coyle told him. "It was mailed to us anonymously and we are under no obligation to give it back to you. What we will do is give you a copy," he said as he slid a document across the table to a furious Brody Knutson.

"Megan, we've conferred on your request..." Gwen Charter started to say.

"I have a federal subpoena, Gwen," Megan Wilson said.

"As I said," Charter continued, "we have conferred on your request. And, although I think we could beat you in court," Charter quickly held up a hand to stop the government's lawyer from interrupting, "we see no reason not to comply with your request and let you have the original. We have reason to believe you'll find incriminating fingerprints that belong to no one we have an obligation to protect."

"However," Coyle said leaning forward and looking directly at Megan Wilson.

"We'll call you as soon as we know something," Wilson told him. She turned to the cadre of Everson, Reed lawyers and said, "Your screw up..."

"If there was one," Knutson hotly said.

"Fine," Wilson said. "Your potential screw up is not my concern."

"You have no jurisdiction here," one of Knutson's toadies spoke up.

"It's an ongoing investigation. We're not at liberty to discuss," Wilson replied using the government's catch-all excuse for covering up whatever they wanted.

"Are you going through with your motion this afternoon?" Gwen Charter asked Brody. "I need to know. If you are, we will fight you."

"We will too," Wilson added.

"No, I guess not," Knutson replied. "You will let us know what you find?"

"Probably," Wilson said. "No, promises."

"What?" Knutson almost yelled.

"Depends on what we find. As I said, it's an ongoing investigation."

Before the day was over, the FBI had verified that the fingerprints of Zachary Evans and Lynn McDaniel were on the engineer's report. Concerned about the effect this news would have on Cannon Brothers shares, it was decided to keep this quiet for now. Unfortunately, the news leaked out and within a week, Cannon Brothers stock was in free fall.

First, the Plaintiff's lawyers in the class action suit issued a press release that they were going to reopen the issue of punitive damages. There followed other reports that, because of the gross violation of discovery rules, Cannon Brothers and their lawyers would be lucky to survive the fallout. By the end of the first week, Cannon Brothers shares had fallen almost sixty percent.

The Chicago office of the Securities and Exchange Commission issued a statement that they were going to investigate possible stock manipulation.

THIRTY-ONE

At exactly 5:17 A.M. Marc Kadella's eyes snapped open. He lay still staring at his bedroom ceiling for several seconds. He then sat up, looked at his alarm clock, and noted the precise time. For the next two-plus minutes, he stayed this way, staring in the dark at his bedroom wall with a blank expression. He was trying to decide if he was dreaming an unreal event or remembering it. The longer he thought it over, the more vivid it became. As the images became more and more clear, he became convinced that this was not a dream. A memory suppressed by the concussion was breaking through.

For the first time since he came awake, Marc blinked his eyes several times trying to decide what to do. He tossed his covers aside, got out of bed, and went into the bathroom. When he finished in there, he slipped on a pair of basketball shorts and headed for the kitchen

While he waited for the coffee to brew, he found a tablet of paper and a pen. Sitting at his small dining room table, he began to write down everything he remembered. When he finished, he sipped his coffee and read what he wrote. After adding a couple of details, he could wait no longer. It was a few minutes after six, and he was desperate to tell someone.

"What time is it?" Carvelli groggily asked.

"Don't ask," Marc said.

"My clock says 6:10, but that can't be right. No one in their right mind would be up at six on a Saturday morning. I must be having a bad dream. I'm going back to sleep now…"

"Shut up and listen to me!" Marc yelled into the phone. "I had a memory come back, and I think it's important."

"Marc, that's terrific. I mean that, too," Carvelli said. "It couldn't wait a couple of hours?"

"No, I needed to tell someone. You know that story in the paper? The one about Cannon Brothers Toys and Zach Evans and Lynn McDaniel?"

"Hold on," Carvelli mumbled. "Let me get up."

There was a silence for several seconds while Carvelli got out of bed. As he headed toward the kitchen, he put the phone up to his ear.

"Okay, I'm up. Yeah, I remember it, what?"

"The engineer's memo that was sent to that reporter…"

"What memo?"

"There was an internal Cannon Brothers memo from the chief engineer that showed Cannon Brothers knew about the defective batteries," Marc continued.

"So?"

Frustrated with Carvelli's ignorance, Marc said, "If you were a lawyer you'd understand."

"Do I hang up now, so you don't insult me again?"

"Sorry. Listen, Cannon Brothers is being sued for a defective product that killed and injured a bunch of kids."

"Yeah, I know," Carvelli said.

"They claimed the defect was hidden from them by the Chinese manufacturer. It was the batteries. Anyway, Zach found a memo from Cannon Brothers that..."

"Okay, I remember. That was what the paper had. So?"

"Zach told me at the jail in Foster that he had sent the memo to me. But I never got it. Someone in his office, he believed it was his secretary, intercepted it. She probably gave it to someone else at the firm. That's how it got leaked to the paper."

Carvelli thought about this for a moment before saying, "Why would someone at the firm leak a document that would sink their own case?"

"I don't know," Marc sighed. "That's the part I can't figure out. But the more I think about it, the more I think that might have been what got Lynn and Zach killed."

"A lawsuit? Come on..."

"No, the money. There are enormous amounts of money involved in all of this. Zach also told me the firm put on a big PR campaign to make Cannon Brothers look innocent. He said it was to push up the stock price. Then this memo hits the papers and the stock goes in the tank. Cannon Brothers is on the verge of bankruptcy. I've had an eye on it because it's been in the papers so much lately."

"We need to have a little come to Jesus chat with this secretary if we can figure out who it is," Carvelli said.

"Margaret or Marge or Marjorie something is all I can remember. An uncommon last name," Marc said.

"That's something," Carvelli said. "But again, why would..."

"I don't know," Marc said. "We find out who did it and maybe why, it may lead us to who had Zach and Lynn killed."

"Yeah, you're right. We're having a meeting at Vivian's this afternoon. Maddy's going to a party at Cal's and..."

"I know, I'll be there. Hey, I'm having lunch with Eric and Jessie today. Noon at Artie's. They'd love to see you. Bring Maddy, too. I'll buy."

"A meal on you? I'll be there. I'll call Maddy and see if she can make it. Later," Carvelli said then ended the call.

Marc, his kids, and Maddy were already there when Carvelli strolled in. He found them seated in an alcove in the back at a large, round table. Carvelli took the empty chair between Eric and Jessica.

The waitress appeared, and she knew Carvelli. She began a good-natured round of back and forth barbs with him.

"Marc was telling us about his memory coming back about that memo the Star Tribune was sent," Maddy said.

"Yeah, I heard all about it bright and early this morning. Thanks for the call," Carvelli said sarcastically. "Next time, call her," he continued nodding at Maddy.

"I wrote it all down," Marc said. "Before I called you. I wanted to get it on paper in case I forgot it again."

"Good idea," Carvelli said. "Can I see it?"

Marc handed the folded papers across the table to him. While Carvelli read through it, Maddy ran her hand across Marc's scalp.

"I told you it would grow back," she said referring to the short bristles of hair.

"You weren't sincere," Marc said.

"What do you think, Jessie? Should he leave it like that?" Maddy asked.

"No! That is not a good look for middle-aged white guys," Jessica replied.

Eric leaned forward and stared at Marc's hairline. He said, "You're starting to recede a bit, Dad."

"I am not! Really?" Marc replied. He then said with a resigned shrug, "Whatever. Take what life gives. Besides, smartass, it gives you something to look forward to."

"It skips a generation," Eric replied.

"Grandpa Charlie," Marc said referring to his ex-wife's father.

"Oh, I hadn't thought of him," Eric said with a distressed look.

"Is he bald?" Maddy asked.

Carvelli placed Marc's notes on the table and interrupted by asking Marc, "You sure about this?"

"As far as I can remember."

"Could the secretary he referred to be Marjorie Griebler?" Carvelli asked.

"Yes! That's it," Marc said. "How did you..."

"Went on their website and checked out the staff," Carvelli said. "I still don't get it. Why would someone in the firm leak it to the press? It would kill their defense of the lawsuit, wouldn't it?"

"You're assuming it was someone in the firm that leaked it to the media," Eric said.

"Who stands to gain?" Maddy added. "Why would someone leak it to the media? To collapse the stock of a company?"

"Short sell," Eric said."

"What is that?" Marc asked looking at Carvelli.

"I'm not exactly sure how it works, but I'm studying it in school and at work," Eric said.

"Sometimes I wonder about you two," Maddy said. "How did you get through law school?"

"Barely," Marc joked.

"Short selling is betting that the price of a stock is too high. You believe it is about to fall," Maddy began explaining. "Let's say ABC Company is selling at eighty bucks a share and you think it is about to go down. You borrow a thousand shares through a broker. You promise to return a thousand shares at a later date.

"You immediately sell the thousand shares and get eighty thousand dollars. If you are right and the shares are overpriced, and it does go down, you buy a thousand shares when you need to return them at the lower price and keep the difference."

Maddy paused at this point and saw puzzled expressions on Marc and Carvelli's faces. Eric nodded and said he understood.

"Why do I feel like I should use crayons and paper to draw stick figures with arrows and circles to explain this stuff to you two," Maddy said.

Marc looked at his son and daughter and said, "Don't you dare laugh."

Of course, this caused them both to lose it and bust out laughing.

"You borrow the shares and sell for eighty thousand. A month later the time is up, and you have to replace the shares you borrowed. But, lucky you, the price is now seventy bucks a share. You buy a thousand shares for seventy grand. You sold them for eighty. You made ten thousand dollars. Got it?"

"Yeah," both Marc and Carvelli said.

"What happens if the price is ninety bucks a share?" Carvelli asked.

"Then you guessed wrong, and you lose ten grand," Maddy said.

"How do you know this stuff?" Marc asked.

"You mean the ditzy chick?" Maddy asked with obvious displeasure.

"I didn't say that!" Marc tried to protest and backpedal.

"Oh boy, here we go," Carvelli said, then turned his head away from Maddy and looked up at the ceiling.

"Not by reading Cosmo or Sports Illustrated," Maddy replied.

Marc looked at Carvelli and said, "I don't read Sports Illustrated. Do you?"

"Not since I renewed my subscription to Cosmo. I only read the swimsuit edition," Carvelli answered.

"This stuff goes on all the time," Maddy said ignoring the two men. "Stock manipulation by speculators."

"Isn't it illegal?" Carvelli asked.

"Very," Maddy said. "But our government representatives get a lot of campaign money from these Wall Street guys. Both political parties are in it up to their ears.

"Eric," she continued looking at Marc's son, "you want a research project?"

"Sure," he answered, eager to help if he could.

"I want you to track the stock of Cannon Brothers over the last, oh, I don't know, eighteen months. And do the same for news stories about them during that same time."

"I can do that," Jessica offered.

"Okay, Jess," Maddy said. "Let's see if there's been some type of media push, up or down on this. And, Eric, see if you can track any recent short selling of Cannon Brothers and by whom."

"Okay," Eric said. "I know a couple of guys at work who can probably tell me."

"We should go," Marc said while examining the bill.

"I have a party to go to this afternoon," Maddy told Eric and Jessica.

"Oh, a party. Can I…" Jessica started to say.

"No," her father emphatically said.

When they had left the restaurant and were walking toward the parking lot, Marc suddenly stopped. The others did as well and turned to look at him.

"When we were talking about making Cannon Brothers stock crash you asked who stood to gain," he said to Maddy.

"Yeah, I did that's…."

"And didn't your guys spot those two Cannon Brothers themselves pulling into Cal Simpson's place a while back?" Marc asked Carvelli.

"That's right," Carvelli replied. "I'd forgotten about that."

"And Zach told me Cal Simpson and his daughter, Samantha, both knew about the engineer's memo. Zach also believed they were looking for it. He told me he believed his office at home and the firm had been searched shortly before his arrest. Cal Simpson would certainly know how to manipulate stock prices and short selling."

"Yeah, but how did he get his hands on the memo?" Maddy asked.

"Marjorie Griebler could've been on his payroll. She may have sent everything Zach did to him," Carvelli said.

"Possible," Marc agreed.

"It sounds like a stretch, though," Carvelli added. "How much stuff, paperwork, mail, you name it, does a busy lawyer turn out?"

"Quite a bit," Marc said.

Marc looked at Eric and said, "What we're asking you to do just became a lot more important. Are you going to get in trouble snooping around trying to find this stuff out?"

Eric paused for a moment thinking then said, "I don't know. I don't see how. I'll claim its research for a paper I'm doing for school. They'll buy that."

"Okay," Marc said. "Be careful. You finally have a real job. I don't want you to lose it."

Marc turned to Carvelli and said, "We need to find this Marjorie whatever and find out what she did with the document Zach was mailing to me."

"I'll use my Italian charm on her," Carvelli said trying to look seductive by half closing his eyes.

"Oh, god," Maddy groaned. "Use sodium pentothal on her. We don't have months."

THIRTY-TWO

Dan Sorenson drove Maddy past the dozen or so parked cars lining the driveway of Cal Simpson's house. Since Dan was not going to park, he could drive her right up to the door.

"You okay?" Dan asked Maddy who was in the back.

"I'm fine, Dan," she replied. She then said, "Tony, call Dan and let us know if the new necklace is working."

The transmitter to Conrad's van was in the necklace she was wearing. They had used a different one for her previous 'dates' and decided it was time for a change.

Dan's phone rang, and he answered it. He exchanged a couple of words with Carvelli, hung up and told Maddy it was working loud and clear.

Dan stopped the Town Car at the front of the big house and before he could get out to open Maddy's door, Aidan Walsh was there.

"I'll call up when I'm ready to be picked up," Maddy said to Sorenson so Aidan could hear her.

"Very good, ma'am," Sorenson replied.

"Not staying long?" Aidan asked her as he escorted her to the front door.

"Where's the hired help?" Maddy asked ignoring the question.

"Small party," Aidan replied.

Aidan led her through the house and onto the patio area. They found Cal making his way through the small crowd. There were about twenty people in attendance. A very small group for a party of Cal's.

A few seconds after arriving on the patio, Cal noticed her. While he walked toward her, Maddy looked around and recognized several people in attendance. Most of them she knew from pictures she had recently seen.

From the recordings of Cal's phone calls they had acquired a few first names. These were people he either talked to or referred to during these recorded conversations. Carvelli's group then looked up first names with people who attended the Fourth of July party and made an educated guess as to who they were. Maddy, with the help of her transmitter necklace, was going to try to confirm this today.

"Hello," Cal said as he kissed her cheek and handed her a glass of a cheap chardonnay.

"Hi," Maddy replied. She took a sip of the wine and remarked, "You shouldn't be so cheap with your guests, especially me. At least it's cold."

Ignoring her remark even though it pricked his ego, Cal gently took her arm and said, "Let me show you off, I mean, around."

163

Maddy stopped, turned to him and firmly said, "I'm not a trophy, Cal and I won't be treated like one."

In the van with Marc, Carvelli and Conrad Hilton listening along, Paxton said, "Atta girl. Kick him right in his ego."

"I'm sorry. Of course, you're not. That was a slip of the tongue. I meant to say let me show you around."

Maddy gave him a skeptical look then looped her left arm through his right.

For the next thirty to forty minutes Cal introduced her to each of his guests. To be sure the recording equipment in the van picked up each person's name clearly, Maddy repeated it when Cal introduced her.

Toward the end of the introduction tour, they came up to two men standing a bit off by themselves. Cal had been delayed by a woman Maddy recognized as a U.S. Senator. While Maddy waited for Cal she could overhear the two men talking.

"Cal will take care of it. He hasn't let us down yet, has he?" Maddy heard the shorter man facing her say.

"Ssssh, keep your voice down," the second man said.

Ignoring the admonition, the first man said, "The funding Bill is a done deal. Hell, the stock is already up over twenty percent. Relax."

"Yeah, I know. When is the next test?"

"Next week," the shorter one said. "By then the stock should be up another ten to fifteen percent, easy. Probably more."

At that moment, Cal rejoined Maddy and the two of them stepped over to the men on whom Maddy had been eavesdropping. Cal introduced them and Maddy was a bit impressed. The first one, the taller of the two, was Senator Christian Howell. He had been standing with his back to her but when he turned around she recognized him instantly. A potential presidential candidate.

Howell was pleasant and polite. Maddy could tell he was used to drawing attention to himself and handled it smoothly. In fact, with his ego being what it is, Howell believed Maddy was more smitten with him than he could be with her.

The second man, the one with the louder, looser mouth was a congressman from Minnesota; Del Peterson. Conrad had recorded several calls between Cal and the congressman and Maddy recognized the name immediately. She could also tell he had been drinking a little too much. This likely accounted for his loquaciousness. It also caused him to be much too friendly toward Maddy.

Cal and Maddy chatted with the two men for a few minutes. All the while Del Peterson held onto her hand and stood a little too close. She finally broke away and they moved on.

"Is he always like that or is it because he had too much to drink?" Maddy quietly asked Cal.

"He's always like that because he drinks too much," Cal replied. "He's actually not a bad guy. He's useful but a little weak. I don't know how his wife puts up with him."

Maddy laughed, then said, "You're a fine one to talk about what wives put up with."

Cal smiled and said, "I guess that was a little hypocritical."

Aidan Walsh was walking toward them obviously to talk to his boss. Cal excused himself and stepped away from Maddy to listen to Aidan. While he did this, Maddy took her phone from her purse, looked at it then put it to her ear.

As Cal and Aidan conversed Maddy turned so the camera lens on the phone was pointed at them. She took almost ten shots of what she hoped were pictures of Aidan. She replaced the phone and Cal rejoined her.

"What was the call about?" he asked.

"I have a date tonight," Maddy breezily told him as if it was no big deal.

"Oh?" Cal asked. "With whom?"

"Oh, what?" Maddy replied. "Relax. He's an old friend. He's married, I know his wife. He's in town and we're getting together for a very casual dinner."

"I'm very jealous," Cal lightly said.

"No, you're not," Maddy replied. "I need a bathroom. I'll be right back."

Maddy locked the bathroom door, put the lid down on the toilet, sat down and took out her phone. She scrolled through the photos, pleased she had several good quality shots of Aidan. A minute later she had finished emailing the photos to Paxton.

"So, this the mysterious Aidan Walsh," Paxton quietly said.

Marc and Carvelli were looking over her shoulder as she opened each photo on her phone.

"I'm pretty sure that's the guy who was out in Simpson's yard with the Doberman the night we..."

"Paxton doesn't need the details," Marc quickly said cutting him off.

"Do I want to know what night this was and what you were up to?" Paxton asked turning her head to look up at an embarrassed Carvelli.

"Um, ah, nothing," he quickly said.

Paxton scrolled her directory, pressed on a number and put the phone to her ear.

"Hi, Sean," she said when the call was answered. She looked at Carvelli and said, "I mean, Uncle Sean, former FBI agent and all-around badass."

This caused Carvelli to sit up straight with his eyes and mouth open.

"Who are you talking to?" Uncle Sean asked.

"This ex-Minneapolis cop who's been coming on to me," she replied.

"Thank him," Sean said. "It's about time somebody did."

Paxton smiled, covered the phone and said to Carvelli, "He said I should thank you."

She removed her hand from the phone and Carvelli leaned forward and loudly said into it, "Sean, you're absolutely right."

Everyone including Sean got a good laugh from that. Then Sean said, "I'll bet he's a good man."

Paxton looked at Carvelli, slightly smiled and said, "You're right. He is. Anyway," she continued. "I have photos of that guy, Aidan Walsh. I'll send them to you. You and Les check them out and call me. Is he there?"

"He'll be here in a few minutes," Sean replied, then told her his email address.

"On the way," Paxton said. "Thanks, Sean. Call me back."

"Send them to my hacker guy," Carvelli said as he held his phone. "I'll call him and let him know." He read off Paul Baker's email then called the hacker to let him know what was coming. He also told him to run facial recognition on Walsh.

"He has facial recognition software?" Paxton said.

"Um, well, he, ah, sort of does," Carvelli said.

"He hacks it," Paxton said.

"Don't ask questions you don't want answered," Carvelli said.

Paxton turned to Marc and asked, "Where did you find him?"

"Believe it or not, he comes in handy as long as you don't ask too many questions," Marc said.

All the while this was taking place, Conrad Hilton was sitting in the van's driver's seat with an expensive headset on his ears. He was still monitoring Maddy as she moved about the party.

Marc tapped him on the shoulder. When Conrad uncovered his right ear, Marc asked, "Anything interesting?"

"No, not really. Sounds like a bunch of rich assholes bragging about themselves. Small talk stuff."

"Let us know if you hear anything worthwhile," Marc said.

"Will do."

Lester Snelling was sitting on the couch in Sean's living room looking at the photos on Sean's phone. By the time he had seen the third or fourth one, he was ninety percent certain. When he finished, he was up to ninety-nine percent.

"That's him, that's Aidan O'Keefe. I'd swear to it. It's been what," he continued as he handed the phone to Sean, "at least thirty years, but it's him. And it makes sense that he'd be hooked up with Cal Simpson, aka Walter Kirk. I'll tell you something else, now that I know he's alive, he's the guy you're looking for, Sean. He's the guy who ratted us to your U.S. Attorney who gave you the tip."

"How do you know?"

"Because it was his brother who was our leader. His name was Timothy O'Keefe," Les said.

"Why would he rat on his brother?" Sean asked.

Les chuckled and said, "Because they hated each other's guts. And if that wasn't enough, Timmy put a bullet in Aidan because he caught Aidan in bed with Timmy's wife."

THIRTY-THREE

Congressman Del Peterson—definitely not working on behalf of his constituents—slipped onto the barstool. He held up a finger to get the bartender's attention and waited patiently for her. He was in an upscale restaurant called The Fireside Inn. It was located in a suburb of St. Paul—Eagan—outside of Peterson's Congressional District. He preferred places where he would not likely be recognized.

Congress was in its Labor Day recess for two weeks. Even though he was not at work in Washington, he still had work to do. Today, the Tuesday after Labor Day, he had spent the day at his local office in Maplewood, another suburb of St. Paul. It was a day to meet prominent constituents, donors and fundraisers. It was a type of day Peterson hated. Ass-kissing and sucking up to these people was a part of the job he hated. One more election, he kept telling himself, and his retirement plan would be fully funded. Even enough to unload the lovely Mrs. Peterson. That thought alone always brought a smile.

Two minutes after the congressman took his seat at the bar, a mildly swarthy-looking Italian gentleman walked in. Tony Carvelli also took a seat at the bar, two chairs down from Del Peterson. Carvelli ordered a scotch and ignored his target and the empty seat between them.

Barely three minutes after Carvelli sat down, a very attractive woman entered the bar. She was modestly but tastefully dressed and made up to look ten years older. She stood in the entryway looking at the crowd then headed toward Peterson and the empty seat next to him.

Carvelli could see her in the mirror behind the bar. When she was ten feet away, he looked at his watch, picked up his drink, stood and walked away from the chair he had saved for her.

The woman slid onto the chair and pushed the five-dollar bill Carvelli had left onto the bar rail. She ordered a white wine, glanced to her right and formed a polite smile with her mouth at Peterson.

Carvelli had gone to the men's room to get out of the way. When he came back he found an empty seat at the other end of the bar. His job was to simply keep an eye on things. After trailing Peterson for two days, Carvelli and his ex-cop pals could see an easy set-up.

Within a half an hour, the woman who had taken Carvelli's seat had moved into the empty one next to Peterson. A half-hour later they were in the dining room having dinner. By the end of the evening, Del Peterson was practically flapping his hands and barking like a seal for her.

Around the same time, Carvelli was sipping the scotch, Marc Kadella and his son parked his Buick SUV at Vivian Donahue's mansion. They exited Marc's car and as they walked toward the entrance, Eric stopped to look over the exterior and grounds.

"This is awesome," Eric said. "It's really awesome."

"God, I hate that word," Marc said to him. "The last really awesome event was the moon landing and that was before I was born. Come on, you," he said to his son.

A minute or so later they were escorted into the library where they found Vivian and Maddy waiting for them. Greetings were made including a hug for Eric from Maddy, which he held a little longer than necessary.

"You smell nice," Eric told her.

"Thank you, Eric," she said while giving Marc a strange look. "It's nice to have one of the Kadella men notice."

"You have a beautiful home, Mrs. Donahue," Eric told Vivian. "It's..."

"Awesome," Marc said.

"It's a museum," Vivian replied. "But it's also the family home. And please call me Vivian."

The four of them took chairs around a table and Maddy took out her phone.

"I'm going to call Paxton and put her on speaker," she said.

When Paxton was ready, Eric began.

"I spent a lot of today at work looking for short selling of Cannon Brothers stock. A couple of the analysts got involved and we found quite a bit of it. Much more than either of these guys would say was normal. Especially since they found the orders for the sales all being put into place within forty-eight hours of the day that memo hit the news," Eric said.

"That's no coincidence," Vivian said after Eric told them the number of shares that were shorted. "That must be a hundred fifty to two hundred million dollars' worth."

"The guys did some digging. That kind of traffic would have to be reported," Eric explained. "They came up with a list of fifty-two people and entities that held the short sale orders that were placed just before the crash."

"We spent the last hour before coming here comparing them to the guest list of Cal Simpson's friends that we have," Marc said. "You remember, he met with Cannon Brothers' executives a short while ago," Marc said.

"And you found what?" Maddy excitedly asked thinking they were on to something.

169

"Nothing," Marc answered. "Not a single match of anyone. But," he continued, "on the drive over here, I thought about Tony's guy, the computer…."

"Don't say hacker," Paxton said through the phone.

"Um, Tony's computer expert," Marc said. "Anyway, we should get the list to him and see what he can find out."

"I'll call Anthony now," Vivian said.

"Do you have your list of the short sellers with you, Marc?" Paxton asked.

"Sure," he replied.

"Photograph it and email it to me," Paxton told him.

"Um, sure, I'll ah…" Marc started to say.

"I'll do it," Maddy said. "Mr. Tech Savvy here will screw it up."

"Anything else?" Paxton asked.

"No, not really," Marc replied. "We need to figure out who these people are."

"If they're even real," Maddy said. "Why didn't this ring bells at the SEC?" Maddy said into the phone.

"Don't know," Paxton replied. "I know someone I can discreetly ask."

"Goodbye, Anthony," they heard Vivian say into her phone.

"He said to photograph the list and email it to his guy," Vivian said.

She handed Maddy a slip of paper and said, "Here's his email address. Anthony is calling him now to let him know what's coming and what we want."

"You know, folks," Marc said. "This could be a total waste of time."

"I don't think so," Maddy said. "Lynn and Zach's murders are tied to that engineer's memo. I'd bet on it. What other motive could there be? Having an affair, an affair that Samantha Simpson knew about? I don't buy it. No, something's going on and these politicians are in on it."

Vivian's phone rang, and she removed it from the pocket of her slacks and looked at the ID.

"Hello, Arthur," she said into the phone. "Have you found anything for me?"

"Yes, Vivian," the man replied. "There were several spending bills approved. Most of them were small appropriations for home district pork projects. Roads and bridges, a sewage plant in Kentucky, things like that. There were two bills that caught my attention that went to the President. Oddly they were both for the same company; Morton Aviation. They're developing a plane to replace the A-10 Thunderbolt also known as the Warthog. It's called the A-15 and they've appropriated fifteen plus billion to purchase seven hundred over the next six years.

"The other bill's for almost four billion to buy one-hundred executive type civilian jets for the government. Quite the coup for Morton Aviation."

"It certainly sounds like it, Arthur. Thank you and say hello to Edie for me."

"I will, Vivian. Call anytime."

Vivian had moved to a desk during the call and had written down the information. She returned to her seat at the table while everyone watched her with looks of anticipation.

"During all of the phone calls we have monitored and recorded, has anyone heard any mention of Morton Aviation?"

"Paxton," Marc said into the phone, "did you hear that?"

"I didn't hear the first part," she lied. "Something about a recording. The rest was garbled."

"Be careful what you say to her," Maddy admonished Marc.

"Okay, let me ask again. Do you know anything about a company called Morton Aviation?" Marc asked.

"No, never heard of them. I'll see what I can find out," she replied. "I have to go everyone. Talk to you later."

The very next day, in the middle of the afternoon, Conrad's van was parked in an apartment complex lot. It was the same lot—the exact same parking space—where Tony Carvelli had first found him. Conrad was again watching and recording the action in the same apartment in the complex down the hill from him. The action in the third-floor bedroom with the drapes left open featured a congressman friend of Cal Simpson's. Del Peterson, albeit unaware, was starring in a short porn movie with the woman who had picked him up two nights ago.

"You know, Conrad," Carvelli said from the back of the van, "you enjoy this a little too much."

"I do," Conrad laughed. "I just wish once I could be there when the sucker is shown the evidence. Oh, oh, here we go. I always like this shot."

"What?" a curious Carvelli asked as he duck-walked forward to take a look.

Conrad leaned to his left so Tony could look through the camera. "Oh yeah, that will endear him to the lucky Mrs. Peterson," Carvelli said watching the congressman with his face between Angela's legs.

Conrad lightly slapped Carvelli on the shoulder and said, "Hey, my turn."

Carvelli moved aside and a second after Conrad put his eye to the camera the van's side door opened. To their surprise, Maddy Rivers

171

unexpectedly climbed in. Before closing the door behind her, knowing what they were up to, she gave them both a 'disappointed-in-you' look.

"You two should be ashamed of yourselves. Ogling over a private, intimate moment between two people obviously in love," she said.

"What?" Carvelli said. "Obviously what?"

"Now get out of the way and let me take a look," she said as she crawled forward and pushed both men out of the way.

Maddy watched through the camera for at least thirty seconds then said, "I'll say this. By the way, she's moaning and groaning, you do have sound, right?" she said to Conrad while still watching.

"Yeah," he admitted.

"The old congressman is really good at what he's doing, or she's putting on a great act," Maddy said.

She turned away from the camera and asked Carvelli, "When are you going to have the chat with him?"

Carvelli didn't respond. Instead, he stared at her with the same disapproving look she had given him.

Maddy ignored him and said to Conrad, "Give me the headphones."

Conrad looked at Carvelli who simply shrugged as Conrad reluctantly handed her the headphones.

Maddy put them on, then returned to the camera to watch some more.

"Oh, wow. Oh yeah. Giddyup, ride 'em, cowboy," she said while watching and listening.

"Okay," Carvelli said. "That's enough. You've embarrassed us enough."

Maddy started laughing and handed the headphones to Conrad.

"It's a guy thing," Carvelli said. "Besides, it was Conrad, not me."

"Hey, you pushed me out of the way…"

"Shut up, Conrad," Carvelli sneered.

All the while Maddy was laughing hysterically. "That's why I stopped by. Just to catch you two."

She smiled at their discomfort then admitted she had done the same thing a few times working divorce cases.

"Let's get serious," Maddy said. "How are you going to go at him?"

"I'm going to go right at him and hit him like a freight train," Carvelli replied. "The whole nine yards. I'll lay a few pictures on him of him with Angela first. Then tell him we know it all. The insider trading, the money laundering, conspiracy to commit murder, you name it."

"When?" Maddy asked.

"Today," Carvelli said. "I'm going to follow him, and even if he goes home, I'll go after him. The idea is to hit him hard and scare him shitless."

"Give me a call later," Maddy told Carvelli as she started to leave.

"You want a copy of the tape?" Carvelli asked.

Maddy started laughing again then said, "Nice shot. I guess I deserved that."

Carvelli pushed open the glass door to the congressman's Woodbury office. He walked in and smiled at the teenage receptionist. He noticed two other staff members, one male and one female, concentrating on their work, ignoring him.

"May I help you?" the receptionist politely asked.

"Hello," Carvelli said. "Yes, I need to see Congressman Peterson."

"I'm sorry," she said. "The congressman isn't in. Can I take a…"

"Yes, he is," Carvelli said, still pleasantly smiling. "I followed him here and saw him come in."

"I, ah, I'm not sure…"

"Tell him I'm a friend of the friend of his he was with this afternoon and he really needs to see me."

Carvelli had said this much more forcefully and quietly as he leaned over the young girl's desk. Flustered she picked up her phone and punched in a two-digit number.

Within seconds of the receptionist's call, Peterson was scurrying out of his office door. Carvelli casually watched him approach, his right hand extended and a politician's smile on his face. Carvelli also noticed a thin bead of sweat forming along the congressman's hairline.

"I'm sorry, I didn't catch your name," Peterson said as they shook hands.

"Let's talk in your office," Carvelli said. Carvelli looked at the uncertain receptionist and said, "Hold the congressman's calls. He'll be busy for a while."

The door was barely closed behind them when Peterson turned to Carvelli and tried to take control.

"Who are you and what do you want?" he arrogantly asked as he heavily plopped down in his executive chair.

Carvelli, feeling a little sleazy, removed a half dozen still photos he brought along of Peterson in Angela's bedroom.

Peterson looked them over, then haughtily flicked his left hand over them, then said, "They don't even look like me. At best, that's a cheap double. Get the fuck out of here."

"You idiot," Carvelli said after sitting down in front of the desk. "I'm not trying to blackmail you. I'm here to keep you from spending the rest of your sorry life in prison. This," Carvelli continued, pointing at the photos, "is nothing. The girl works for us. We filmed with sound, the whole thing. This was just to get your attention."

Carvelli paused a moment to let that sink in. He stared at Peterson and noticed the arrogance was gone and there was fear in his eyes.

"Prison. I don't know what..." he tried to say.

"Be quiet, dummy," Carvelli said. "We know it all. Your relationship with Cal Simpson, the stock manipulation and insider trading. And, the conspiracy to commit murder."

"Murder! What the hell are you talking about?" Peterson almost shrieked but managed to keep his voice down. "Who, who are you and...?"

"I'm your new best friend," Carvelli said. "Here's what we're going to do. One, I'm going to set up a meeting with you and an assistant U.S. Attorney. Two, you will keep your mouth shut and not call a lawyer until I say so. You call a lawyer, we drop a net on you and Cal and the others..."

"I want to see your badge. Are you law enforcement?"

"No, I'm a private investigator. But we have recordings of phone calls between Cal Simpson, you and several others. How do you think we got your name and found out about this?"

"That sounds illegal," Peterson sounding a little less nervous.

"It is illegal," Carvelli admitted. "So, what? You think you'd survive the scandal? Tell me now and we'll release everything we know about you. Actually, it might not be totally illegal since we are not acting on behalf of the police or any other law enforcement entity. It would still destroy your life.

"Del, can I call you Del? We both know you're not that strong. You're not that tough. You simply don't have the balls to fight something like this. Besides, you did what you did, and you got caught. Be a man and do what you can to get out of it."

"I didn't have anything to do with any murders," Peterson said almost pleading.

"Doesn't matter. That's the beauty of a conspiracy charge. Even if you didn't know anything about it, if a murder is committed in furtherance of the conspiracy, all the assholes in the conspiracy are guilty. You're a lawyer. You should know this."

"Oh, god. Oh, shit. What the hell..." Peterson whined. "What do you want?"

"First, I am going to introduce you to some friends of mine, people who are now friends of yours. We're going to put you up in a motel tonight..."

"I'm not doing anything without a lawyer..." Peterson started to say.

"Yes, you are. You want to bring in a lawyer, we will simply turn over everything we have to the FBI and you can take your chances. Otherwise, we will help you. Your choice. What's it going to be?"

"All right," Peterson whined some more.

"Tomorrow you will meet with a legitimate U.S. Attorney who will outline your deal for immunity in exchange for your cooperation. We will then take a taped deposition from you and you will spill it all."

"I thought you knew everything," Peterson said.

"There are always holes that need to be filled in. Let's go," Carvelli said again.

"Wait, what am I going to tell my wife?"

"Give me a break," Carvelli laughed. "You can't think of a lie to tell the unfortunate Mrs. Peterson? By now you must be a master of it. Get your coat on. We're leaving."

THIRTY-FOUR

Marc was at his desk ploughing through the backlog still stacked up around him. His injuries were healing much more quickly than he had any right to expect. Gradually his memory of the events of that day was coming back. Some of it put him into a mild depression.

On the whole, Zach Evans had been a good guy and a better friend. He could be a bit of a knucklehead at times, especially when it came to women. But he did not deserve to be murdered. And Marc was convinced his father-in-law and possibly his wife had done it.

Marc was about half-way through the pile when the intercom on his phone buzzed. He was expecting a client with a check and hoped this was the call.

"Hey," he answered.

"Could you come in here for a minute please?" he heard Connie Michelson ask. "Bring a chair in."

"Sure," Marc replied.

Marc entered Connie's office, closed the door behind him and found an elderly couple seated in front of Connie's' desk. Connie introduced them as Benjamin and Sadie Halperin, a couple she knew from her synagogue.

"The Halperin's have been involved with an investment group. People they know who pooled their money to invest..."

"To get a higher return with lower fees," Benjamin interjected.

"Okay," Marc said.

"Mostly people from the synagogue. Not wealthy people but not poor people either," Connie continued. "Twenty-six total." Connie looked at the Halperins and asked, "All married couples?"

"Yes," Sadie replied.

"This group used a nephew..."

"Amoretz," Benjamin sneered.

"...of one of the men," Connie continued. She looked at her notes and read his name. "Eli Meier. He's a broker with a small firm in downtown Minneapolis."

"What did you call him?" Marc asked looking at Benjamin. "Amoretz," he said poorly.

"A knucklehead. An idiot," Benjamin said. "He was supposed to put our money in safe, low-risk things such as Triple A-Bonds, municipal bonds, things like that. Instead," he continued, his voice rising, "this schlemiel puts us in stocks, and we lose a fortune!"

"Benjamin," Sadie said placing a hand on his arm, "your blood pressure. Calm down. Connie will help us."

"And now this, this Eli, this putz, won't return our calls," Benjamin said.

"Cannon Brothers," Connie said to Marc.

"Oh, boy," Marc replied. "How much?"

"Three point two million," Connie said.

"And we do what about this?" Marc asked Connie.

"Have you ever been involved in a class action?" Connie asked.

Marc shrugged and said, "I had a couple of clients I referred to Spears, Kurtz about fifteen years ago. Tobacco litigation. That's it. They didn't make out very well. The lawyers and the state got most of the money.

"We could sue this guy's firm. They must have errors and omissions insurance," Marc said.

"Yes, sue them," Benjamin excitedly said. "Make them pay us our money back!"

Connie removed a form from a desk drawer and silently filled in the blanks. When she finished it, she showed it to Marc. He read it over, raised his eyebrows at Connie but said nothing as he handed it to Benjamin.

"Read it, please," Connie said.

Benjamin finished reading it and asked, "Where do I sign?"

"I want to make copies. You get as many of your friends involved in this as you can to sign one also. Then bring them in. I need you to bring me any paperwork you have from this firm about your accounts and your dealings with them," she added.

"I will make sure he gets them for you," Sadie answered.

The Halperins agreed to meet with their investment group and get them all to sign the retainer Connie had given them. Connie and Marc escorted them to the door and adjourned to her office.

"What the hell are we doing?" Marc asked. "I don't know anything about a stockbroker's liability. Do you?"

Connie opened the window behind her desk and lit a cigarette. She took a long drag, blew the smoke outside then said, "Nope, not a thing. But if he was instructed by this group to put their money into low-risk investments and he didn't, that's at least negligence. We may be able to drag Cal Simpson and his pals into it, too."

Marc sat silently for a minute while Connie worked on her cigarette.

"You know," he finally began, "we may be able to get it started, sign up a shitload of angry investors then ship the whole thing to Spears, Kurtz and let them do the heavy lifting."

"That's an option," Connie agreed.

"Why do I feel like I'm already over my head?" Marc asked.

"Because you are," Connie said.

"The first thing we need to do is find out who is with Cal Simpson. Then drop the suit on them, go immediately into court. Federal." Marc began.

"Slow down, big boy," Connie said. "Let's not get ahead of ourselves."

"...then ask that their assets be frozen. If we get Paxton and the feds involved, that would help get the judge to do it." Marc finished ignoring her.

"Maybe," Connie almost agreed. "We'll see."

"Wait a minute," Marc said. "How are you going to front expenses for this? I don't have that kind of money."

"I can, at least for a while. But I'm not going to let it bankrupt me, either," Connie replied as she tossed her cigarette butt out the window then closed it.

"Let's keep our eye on the ball," Connie continued. "So far we have two clients. It's their money we're trying to recover."

"We should bring in Barry and Chris. Chris probably knows more about the liability end of this than we do," Marc said referring to the other two lawyers in the firm. Chris was a business/corporate lawyer. Barry, another litigator.

"Good idea. I'll talk to them," Connie said.

Two hours later, having worked through lunch, the pile in Marc's office was almost under control. He was reviewing a divorce agreement for a client when his intercom buzzed.

"Hey," he said.

"Tony's on the phone," Carolyn told him. Without waiting for a response, she put him through.

"I heard from my guy about the names Eric came up with. The people and entities who sold short Cannon Brothers stock."

"What did he find?" Marc asked, holding back the excitement he felt.

"Nothing," Carvelli started to say.

"What?"

"You didn't let me finish. He checked everywhere for every name he had on the list. He found no connection to Cal or any of the people we suspect are in on this little scam," Carvelli said. "This morning he had an idea. He expanded his search to include distant relatives, employees, and things like that.

"The first name he widened his search for was Natalie Aldrich. They're in alphabetical order."

"I know," Marc impatiently said.

"Guess what he found?"

"Tony!"

"Okay. Well among other things, he found two busts for solicitation."

"She's a hooker?"

"Apparently was. I don't think she needs the money anymore. Her current job is as Mrs. Calvin Simpson."

"What! Are you kidding me? Is he sure? What?"

"Yeah, he's sure. He has a copy of the marriage certificate. And her birth certificate. Remember Maddy said Cal told her the little missus was visiting her sister? He even told Maddy the sister's name, Gayle."

"Yeah," Marc replied.

"She has a sister in Delaware named Gayle. She's the correct age, too. And Gayle's parents are the same names as Natalie's. It's her."

"I wonder if she knows he's using her maiden name. Using her as a cutout," Marc said.

"I doubt it. Too much money involved. Anyway," Carvelli continued, "my guy is…"

"Will you give this guy a name? Stop calling him 'my guy'," Marc said.

"Okay, Paul is going to keep at it. It's slow going but he's silly-smart, so I believe he'll crack more names. It'll just take some time.

"Paxton's in town. We're going to take the statement from our new friend," Carvelli said avoiding using Peterson's name.

"When?"

"We're setting up now. If you want to attend, we'll wait."

"Yeah," Marc said after thinking it over for a moment. "I need to get out of here. I was waiting for a client to bring a check in, but Carolyn can take care of it. Give me fifteen minutes."

"Okay."

THIRTY-FIVE

Before Marc could get his coat on and leave his office, he received another phone call. His office door was open and rather than use the intercom, Carolyn simply yelled through the door.

"Hey, Paxton's on line two for you," Marc heard her yell.

Marc was standing in his doorway and said, "What does she want? Tell her I'm on my way."

Carolyn passed that along then told Marc, "She says it's important. She needs to talk to you before you leave."

Marc shrugged and said, "Okay," then closed the door and sat down again.

"What's up?" he asked.

"I've been thinking," Paxton replied. "Are we going to have a 'fruit of the poisonous tree' problem here? Will we be able to use the information we get from this guy in court?"

Marc thought about what she had said for so long Paxton began to wonder if he was still on the phone. "You still there?" she asked.

"Yeah. I think if we get him to sign a waiver and repeat it into the camera, we should be okay. It's gotta be tight, though; that he freely came forward. No threats or coercion and no promises made. His conscience was bothering him and he, well, just gave it up."

"And waived an attorney," Paxton added. "Hey, you could act as his attorney."

"I have a rather obvious conflict," Marc drolly replied.

"So, it would cover my ass," Paxton laughed.

"We could just say Tony was legitimately investigating my accident. He got an opportunity to interview this guy and he spilled his guts. When Tony mentioned conspiracy and murder..."

"He folded," Paxton added. "Okay. That's our story and we're gonna stick with it. Wait a minute, how did I get involved?"

"I called you because you're a fed and he was blabbing about stock manipulation which is a federal crime. I knew you from Sammy Kamel's trial and..."

"This is getting a little thin," Paxton said.

"And we're getting ahead of ourselves. Most of this stuff we can deal with if and when the time comes," Marc told her.

"Is this how defense lawyers practice? Fly by the seat of your pants and just make up bullshit as you go along?"

"Pretty much," Marc admitted. "I'll see you in a little while."

"Before we get started, I want you to look this over and sign it," Paxton told Congressman Peterson.

Along with Paxton and Peterson, Marc, Carvelli, and Dan Sorenson were sitting around in the hotel room. Conrad Hilton was behind a video camera set on a tripod. Conrad would handle the recording.

"I don't think I want to sign this," the congressman said when he finished reading the waiver.

"Okay," Carvelli quickly replied. "Suit yourself. Let's go, everybody; he'd rather take his chances."

"Wait, wait, wait," a panicky Peterson said. "I didn't say I wouldn't sign. What about my immunity deal?"

"Here it is," Paxton said from her chair next to the camera. "You will tell us everything you know. Names, dates, places concerning the conspiracy to manipulate the stocks of Cannon Brothers Toys and any other company you know of. We, the federal government, are going to bust Cal Simpson and everyone involved. We know what he's been up to and we're going to get him."

When she used the name Cannon Brothers, Del Peterson realized she was not bluffing. None of these people had used that name with him before. Now, he knew for sure they had the information they needed.

"And we're going to tie the murders of Lynn McDaniel and Zachary Evans..."

"I don't know anything about that!"

"...to the conspiracy. We, the federal government, still have the death penalty. It doesn't matter if you knew or not. Everyone involved in the conspiracy goes down. Got it?"

"Yeah," Peterson muttered.

"What? I didn't hear you," Paxton seriously said.

"Yes, I got it," he said.

"I personally guarantee you will get a walk..." Paxton began.

"And maybe save your political career," Carvelli added knowing it was a lie.

"If you are totally candid," Paxton continued. "You leave anything out or lie about anything, the deal is off. Do you understand?"

"I want that in writing," he meekly said. "And why can't I have a lawyer look it over."

"Because you've agreed to waive your right to an attorney," Carvelli told him.

"You'll get it in writing after we tape your deposition. If I'm satisfied, I'll put your deal in writing."

Peterson looked at Marc and said, "I recognize you. You're a lawyer. Why can't you represent me?"

"I have a conflict," Marc tersely answered him.

"Sign," Paxton said pointing at the waiver in front of Peterson. He was seated at a small table, picked up a pen and scratched his signature on it.

"We'll take a break then get started," Paxton said. "There's water, soda, coffee," she added pointing at a credenza across the room. "No alcohol. We'll bring in food later. Use the bathroom if you need to."

Marc, Paxton, and Carvelli adjourned to a room across the hall. Dan stayed with Peterson to keep an eye on him. It was an identical suite also stocked with non-alcoholic beverages. Carvelli was reading the waiver while Marc and Paxton opened bottles of water.

"What do you think?" Paxton asked Marc.

"I think this guy is a total weenie. This is the caliber of people we send to Congress? No wonder Washington is a dysfunctional mess."

"That's not what I meant."

"He's a politician and a lawyer. He'll likely be very careful about what he says. But you can wear him down. I really don't think he does know anything about the deaths of Zach and Lynn McDaniel. If you were Cal Simpson, would you let this guy in on anything he doesn't have to know?"

"Ask him about the list of people who sold short Cannon Brother's stock. The list Eric gave us," Carvelli said as he handed the waiver back to Paxton. "See if he recognizes anyone."

"Will do," Paxton replied.

They finished their water then Marc said, "Go get him, tiger."

They started shortly after 4:00 P.M. and finished, with breaks, just before midnight. Peterson looked like he had taken a beating.

It had been decided that Carvelli would spend the night in the two-bedroom suite with Peterson. If they had to keep Peterson there longer, the other ex-cops would take their turns.

When they had finished they adjourned back in the room across the hall where they had a brief discussion.

"Some of the names he came up with as being involved. No wonder so many people try to get into Congress," Marc said.

"How do you think they can retire as multi-millionaires on a congressional salary? By being frugal?" Carvelli asked.

"You think we got it all?" Marc asked Paxton.

"Who knows? Like I told him, we'll review the video and if we think of more questions, we'll be back," Paxton said.

"He's gonna want his deal in writing. Can you do that?" Marc asked.

"I'm supposed to run it by my boss. Fortunately, she's in Washington at some big DOJ conference. So, I couldn't wait for her.

"Now, you two get out of here so I can get some sleep. I'll see you tomorrow."

The next morning, after they had met for breakfast, they were back in Paxton's room reviewing the video. Across the hall Del Peterson, still not getting it, was on the phone with his most recent paramour, the delicious Angela. Despite her setting him up to be photographed, he had not made the connection.

"Stop the tape," Carvelli said.

"There is no tape," Conrad replied.

"Conrad!" Carvelli said giving him a nasty look.

"What?" Marc asked.

Carvelli turned back to the TV screen and said, "This has been bothering me. This is the part where Paxton gives him the list of people who sold short Cannon Brothers stock. He said he didn't recognize anyone. I think he was lying. Watch."

Conrad started it up again and they all stared intensely at the screen. They watched while Peterson read the names and at one point, Carvelli pointed and said, "There. Did you see it? He read a name and his left eyebrow twitched. Back it up and run it again."

Conrad did this and the next time through, in slow motion, they all saw it. A slight twitch.

"He recognized a name," Paxton said. "I guess we better have a little chat with him."

They went back into the suite where Peterson was and Carvelli went right at him. "You were lying when you told us you didn't recognize any of the names on the list of people who sold short Cannon Brothers stock," Carvelli said.

"No, I ..."

"No deal if you lie to us," Paxton reminded him.

This obviously deflated him. He slumped down on the room's sofa, looked back and forth at everyone in the room who were all staring at him. "Okay," he said. "Yeah, I recognized one of the names. My wife's sister's maiden name is on the list. I don't know if it's her but..."

"What's the name?" Carvelli demanded.

"Betty Kemp."

"We'll check it out and do not withhold anything again. You got it?" Carvelli leaned down and snarled at Peterson.

"Yes," he meekly replied.

While this was taking place, in the early morning hours in the Nevada desert, Mike Nicoletti was finishing his pre-flight checklist. Some minor modifications had been made to the A-15 prototype. This was hardly unusual. The Air Force and their contractors were always tinkering with improvements. Not just during the production process. This would continue until the aircraft's service time was finished and it was dropped off in an airplane graveyard.

Ninety minutes later, Nicoletti was almost finished with this test flight and flying the A-15 toward the test grounds for his final run of the day. A simulated ground attack at 350 mph at 150 feet. The bird was handling as flawlessly as usual until he hit five thousand feet. Almost without any warning at all, the plane violently shuddered only once, and the right wing tore away putting the aircraft into a spiral of certain death.

The aircraft was diving at almost eight hundred feet per second. Nicoletti had barely four seconds to realize what had happened and jettison himself. As the A-15 passed one thousand feet, Nicoletti found and pulled the eject handle. He was almost at five hundred feet when he felt the jerk of the straps and saw the chute billow open above him.

Nicoletti looked down in time to see his ride explode on the ground. A wave of relief washed over him as the faces of his children went through his mind.

Five hundred feet is barely high enough for a jump. Mike Nicoletti was a terrific pilot. He was not a trained Airborne Ranger. Alive and grateful, he would spend a week in the hospital with a broken leg, fractured wrist, several ribs and multiple bruises. He also had a wife who insisted his test pilot days were over.

Fortunately for the Nicolettis, Mike's brain was not injured thanks to a state-of-the-art helmet. The first thing he told his wife, Jackie, was to sell all of their Morton Aviation stock.

Within days, the multi-billion-dollar government contracts awarded to Morton Aviation were withdrawn. Numerous other contracts Morton had were also either suspended or canceled. As a result, Morton Aviation stock went into a nose dive.

When Cal Simpson finished reading the reports in *The Wall Street Journal*, he lit a celebratory cigar.

THIRTY-SIX

"I see it, thanks," Carvelli said into his phone.

Carvelli slipped his phone back into the inside pocket of his tan, suede sports coat. He was standing on the corner of Third Ave and Seventh Street looking south. He had been waiting here for ten minutes trying to remember the last time he had ridden a public bus. It was probably high school and the fare, as he recalled, was around twenty-five cents. Now he needed two-fifty.

The bus he was waiting for pulled over and stopped for him. Carvelli got on, paid the fare and looked for his seat. It was almost 6:30 P.M. and rush hour was over. There were at least a dozen empty seats, but the one he wanted was occupied by a woman reading a romance novel.

Carvelli quietly sat down next to her. She turned her head to look at him, looked around at the empty seats and scowled. She silently slid over as close to the window and as far away from the intruder as she could. To ignore him, she went back to the paperback she was reading.

The bus had barely traveled another block when Carvelli whispered, "Hello, Marjorie. We need to talk."

Carvelli's crew, especially Franklin Washington and Tommy Craven, had been tailing her for almost two weeks. What they had learned was that Marjorie Griebler, Zach Evans' one-time assistant, had virtually no life. This actually made it more difficult to find a way to approach her. She arrived at the offices of Everson, Reed via this particular bus line by 7:00 A.M. every day. A normal day was finished at 6:00 P.M. Not once did she leave for lunch or to just get outside for a while.

At 6:10 she arrived at her bus stop and within a couple of minutes of 6:15 her bus picked her up for the ride to a block away from her small house. It was so routine, boring and lifeless, Tommy had started a pool to guess how many cats she had living in her house. It was Tommy who had called Carvelli while he waited on the corner to give him the heads-up which bus she was on. It was also Tommy who was following in his car to pick up Carvelli when he finished.

Marjorie, with a wide-eyed, shocked expression, looked at Carvelli and nervously whispered, "I don't know you. Now go away and leave me alone."

Ignoring her remark Carvelli said, "I'm a private investigator, Ms. Griebler. I'm investigating the murder—and that's what it was, a murder—of your former boss, Zachary Evans."

"I don't know anything about that. It was a terrible accident but…"

185

"It was not an accident," Carvelli whispered. "And I believe you are involved. Probably unwittingly, but you are involved."

"What are you talking about?" the fifty-something-year-old woman vehemently hissed.

By this point, there was fear coming off her that Carvelli could almost smell. Instead of looking at him, her eyes were shifting about the bus interior searching for help or an escape route. So far, the noise from the bus was covering their conversation. None of the other passengers was paying any attention to them.

"First of all," Carvelli continued, "calm down. I don't believe you're guilty of anything, yet," he added. "I have not given your name to the police and probably won't have to if you cooperate."

This last statement, regarding the police, made Marjorie's stress meter overload. She could barely breathe and Carvelli thought she was on the brink of crying. The word 'police' had never once in her life been used in the same sentence as her name. How could this be happening?

"I, I, didn't do anything!" she practically pleaded.

"Ssssh, relax," Carvelli said. "I think you did but without realizing it. Before Zach died, he gave you a document to mail. I know this because he told the person he was mailing it to what it was. Maybe it was in an envelope already addressed when he gave it to you. It was supposed to be mailed to a friend of his, a lawyer. His name is Marc Kadella."

The instant Carvelli mentioned Marc's name, the light of recognition flashed briefly in her eyes and on her face. It went away, but there was no mistaking it.

She started to say something but Carvelli abruptly cut her off by saying, "Don't lie to me. It will only get you in trouble. All I want to know is, instead of mailing it, who did you give it to?"

Marjorie lowered her head until her chin was touching her chest. She silently wept, believing her life as she knew it was over.

"Marjorie," Carvelli softly said, "tell me who it was. He'll never know it came from you. This conversation will stay strictly between the two of us."

"I'll lose my job," she sniffled. "I'm too young to retire and too old to start over."

"It won't happen. I'll protect you. The police won't know either. Zach was murdered because of what was in that envelope. The people who did this cannot get away with it," Carvelli assured her.

She took a deep breath to compose herself, sat up and looked at Carvelli. "Are you sure? I was told it was a hit and run accident."

"No, I'm sorry. It was a deliberate murder by the same people who killed Lynn McDaniel. It was about money and greed and what was in the envelope."

The bus pulled away from another stop while Marjorie stared out the window. Finally, after almost a minute, she turned back to Carvelli and nodded.

"Brody Knutson," she whispered.

"Who?" Carvelli asked, mildly shocked after expecting it to be Cal Simpson.

"Brody Knutson, the managing partner of Everson, Reed," she replied.

"You're sure?"

"Of course, I'm sure. He came to me a few days before and told me I was to give him all of Mr. Evans' correspondence," she said. "Why don't you believe me? If he finds out, I told you, I would be fired instantly."

"Sorry, it's just, I was expecting it to be someone else. Do you know if a man named Cal Simpson was a friend or client of Knutson?"

"I don't know," Marjorie said. "I don't know that name, but I did not work directly for him."

"Who does?" Carvelli quickly asked.

"I won't tell you that. I told you what I know, what I did, but I won't involve anyone else," she emphatically replied.

Carvelli looked at her for a moment then said, "Okay. I respect that. And, as I promised, this conversation will stay just between you and me. I promise."

With that, he reached up and pulled the cord to have the driver stop and let him off. While he watched the bus pull away, Tommy Craven stopped to pick him up.

"I'll find out who works for Knutson. Thanks, Marjorie," he quietly said to the back of the bus.

"What did you find out?" Tommy asked as he pulled away from the curb.

"Hang on," Carvelli replied. He retrieved his phone, found the number he wanted and dialed. It was answered on the first ring.

"Did you talk to her?" Marc asked without a greeting.

"Yeah, I did. I laid my Italian charm...."

"Stop. What did you threaten her with?"

"Jail. She folded like a cheap suit," Carvelli replied.

"And?"

"You're not going to believe this. She admitted intercepting the mail Zach was sending to you. Then she gave it to a guy by the name of Brody Knutson."

"What? You can't be serious."

"You know him?"

"I've met him," Marc admitted. "He's the managing partner at Everson, Reed. The same as if he was the CEO. Why would he want to sabotage a lawsuit his firm is defending?"

"You're the lawyer, not me," Carvelli said.

"I don't know. Unless he's in Cal Simpson's pocket," Marc replied.

"Or someone else's" Carvelli added.

"Why didn't Del Peterson tell us about this?" Marc asked.

"Likely didn't know. If you were Simpson would you tell him?"

"Maybe, maybe not. It's worth a conversation. Where are you?" Marc asked.

"Tommy's taking me to my car. We'll be there in five minutes."

"I'll call Maddy; you call Vivian. Let's meet at Vivian's if we can," Marc said.

"Where are you?" Carvelli asked.

"At my desk, but I was just about to leave. Connie is still here. I'll see if she wants to attend. Call me if we can't meet at Vivian's."

"Will do."

THIRTY-SEVEN

"Thanks, Tommy, I'll talk to you later. Be sure to keep track of your time, and I'll get you paid," Carvelli said.

They had arrived back at Carvelli's home in South Minneapolis. He closed the passenger side door of Tommy's car and waved as Tommy drove off. He felt his stomach growl and realized he had not eaten since breakfast. As he got in the Camaro, he thought about driving through Mac's. He pulled away from the curb and felt his phone vibrate.

"Yeah," Carvelli answered.

"It's Paul," he heard Paul Baker, his hacker say.

"What?"

"I got more names. In fact, in a couple more days, I should have them all cracked."

"Great, Paul. Did you get a written list for me? I'll swing by."

"Yeah, come by anytime."

"Ten minutes," Carvelli replied.

Marc and Connie were led to the library where they found Vivian on the phone and Maddy on a sofa. Vivian was seated at a table speaking to someone and taking notes. She wiggled her fingers in greeting while Marc sat next to Maddy. Connie took one of the matching chairs.

Marc was sitting on Maddy's right while she examined the seven-inch scar where his scalp had been ripped open. The stitches had been removed, and a nasty looking red line remained. It ran from two inches above his left ear diagonally toward the back of his head.

"What do you think?" Marc asked.

Maddy remained silent for a few seconds then took his left hand in both of hers. "I think how we almost lost you and how sad and scared I was," she quietly said. "And angry."

"I'm fine now, thanks. I meant the scar," Marc said.

"It's pretty bad right now. But it will lighten up, and your hair will cover it."

"Until you go bald," Connie said.

Maddy laughed and released his hand while Marc snarled at Connie, "That's not funny. Why do women think that's funny? If you woke up tomorrow going bald, there'd be panic in that house and you'd do something about it immediately."

"We're just teasing," Maddy said poking him in the ribs with an elbow.

"I almost died. You're supposed to be nice to me," Marc said sticking his lower lip out, feigning a pout.

189

"Poor baby," Maddy said.

"Who's Vivian talking to?" Marc asked, turning serious.

"I don't know," Maddy said. "I think someone from Washington. The cesspool, not the state."

"Thank you, Arthur. I appreciate the information," they heard Vivian say ending the call.

A moment later, Vivian joined them on a couch across from Maddy and Marc. She pleasantly greeted Marc and Connie then asked, "Should we wait for Anthony?"

"You found out something," Marc said. "What is it?"

"In today's paper," she began, "buried in the A section was a small article about a plane crash in Nevada. It was an Air Force test flight. The pilot was able to bail out and was not seriously injured. I assume that's why it wasn't a bigger story. The military has accidents, not frequently, but..."

"Often enough so that if no one is hurt it's not really a big deal," Marc interjected.

"Yes," Vivian agreed. "That's a good way of putting it.

"I noticed the story because the airplane was an A-15 prototype being tested for Morton Aviation. Sound familiar?"

"That's the company that Del Peterson told us about. He thought there was some insider trading being done by Cal for his little group," Marc excitedly said.

"Yes," Vivian agreed. "And I was told about a large contract being awarded to Morton Aviation by the government. Remember?"

"Yes," Maddy said.

"I checked," Vivian continued. "The contracts have been pulled pending an investigation. It seems the right wing ripped off during what should have been a routine test dive. The pilot was lucky to get out with his life."

"What's going on with Morton's stock?" Marc asked.

"It's crashing. If there has been short selling as there was with Cannon Brothers," Vivian said, "this could be worth a couple of billion dollars. Billion with a B."

There was a light knock on the door and Tony Carvelli came in. He greeted everyone and sat next to Vivian.

"My guy came up with a lot more names," he announced. He removed several folded pages of paper from his inside pocket. He gave it first to Vivian to look over then pass around.

While the review and discussion of the names was taking place, Marc moved to the table Vivian had used. He made a phone call and spent a few minutes on it.

"I just talked to the kid, Eric," Marc said when he returned to his seat. "He's going to do the same research into possible short selling of Morton Aviation that he did with Cannon Brothers."

"Do you recognize any of these?" Carvelli asked Marc.

"Tell us about Marjorie Griebler," Marc said as he took the list from Carvelli.

"Oh, yeah," Maddy said. "Did you finally get the chance to use that suave, debonair, Italian charm on her?" Maddy teased.

"His what?" Connie sarcastically asked.

"Actually, I did better than that. I cornered her and scared the hell out of her," Carvelli replied.

"Anthony, you didn't," Vivian said chastising him.

"She'll be all right. I got what I wanted. We were right. She specifically remembered being given an envelope to mail to you," Carvelli said looking at Marc. "She said Zach gave it to her a couple of days before he died. And guess who she gave it to?"

"Just tell them," Marc said referring to Maddy and Vivian. "I told Connie already."

"Brody Knutson," Carvelli said.

"Who is he?" Maddy asked.

"He's the managing partner of Everson, Reed," Vivian replied. "He's been trying to get me as a client for years."

"I don't get it," Marc said looking at Connie. "Why would he trash his firm's case? He had to know if that memo got out Cannon Brothers would crash and burn. It would open up a huge verdict for punitive damages. How could that be good for Everson, Reed?"

"They're big enough to take the loss," Connie said.

"But the newspapers reported the FBI found Zach and Lynn's fingerprints on it," Marc said.

"So? Makes it even better. If people think the firm put it out to the public but can't prove it, they look like ethical good guys to the public. Yet they can deny everything. They can deny violating a client's privilege," Connie replied.

"Which they've done," Marc said. "Wait a minute," Marc continued. "Everson, Reed is Cal's law firm. A bunch of them were at his Fourth of July party."

"True," Connie said. "So, do you think Brody slipped this to Cal and Cal leaked it to the media to crash Cannon Brothers?"

"They're about to file bankruptcy," Vivian said.

"Seven or eleven?" Marc asked referring to bankruptcy chapters. A seven would mean a liquidation and shut down. An eleven would mean an attempt to reorganize their debt and stay in business.

"I have heard it is a seven," Vivian said.

"They had over four hundred employees before this happened," Marc quietly said. "That's a lot of families hurt by what Cal and his pals are up to. Four hundred jobs lost, four hundred families now trying to pay their bills and feed their kids. And these people try to claim this type of crime is no big deal because it is victimless."

"And that doesn't take into account the pension plans, 401Ks, IRAs and other savings programs ordinary people have that take a hit because this stuff goes on all the time and the government does almost nothing about it," Maddy said. "I guess it should make us all feel better knowing that the politicians involved in this victimless crime have their salaries and pensions paid by the taxpayers," she added sarcastically.

The room went silent while everyone contemplated what Marc and Maddy just said. After a long minute, Carvelli broke the silence.

"Can we break Brody Knutson? We need corroboration for what Del Peterson has given us. This guy could be the ticket."

"Yes, we can break Brody Knutson," Marc replied.

"We need to go over the recordings again," Maddy said referring to the listening devices inside Cal's house. "I remember him referring to someone he called 'the lawyer' a few times. I don't think he ever mentioned a name. It could be this Knutson guy."

Marc turned to her and said, "Good catch. I heard it too. At the time it just seemed like an innocuous statement."

He looked at Carvelli and said, "Have a couple of your guys get together with Conrad and see if they can find this reference."

"And put some context to them," Carvelli added. "In the meantime, we'll start working on Brody Knutson. Find a way to go at him. Speaking of Conrad, has anyone heard from him lately? Has he been around?" Carvelli asked looking at Vivian.

She shook her head and said, "Not for a few days."

"I'll get a hold of him tomorrow and get him out here," Carvelli said.

"What can you share with us about the lawsuit?" Vivian asked Connie.

"We've hit a snag. We're getting more of this little investment group signed up. But every one of them signed an authorization that pretty much lets this broker they used do what he wanted. There's nothing in it about only investing in low-risk things. It gave him complete discretion."

"And," Marc said, "they received monthly, written statements spelling out exactly where their money was going. They also had online access to their accounts. Every one of them admitted they knew this."

"So, they're screwed," Carvelli abruptly pointed out.

192

"Not necessarily," Connie replied. "The stock was manipulated to cause it to crash. The broker should have placed a stop-loss on the accounts."

"What's that?" Carvelli asked.

"Basically, you put a flag on the stock. If it falls to a certain point the computers that run the markets automatically sell the stock. It's to reduce potential losses," Maddy told him.

"You can do that?" Carvelli asked, who then looked at Marc.

Marc shrugged and admitted, "I didn't know either before Connie explained it to me."

"We have a case for negligence," Connie said. "We'll see."

"I've been wondering," Maddy said changing the subject, "the memo that was sent to the media shows that the people who ran Cannon Brothers knew about the defect. How can they now just file bankruptcy and walk away? Children died. Some were crippled for life. This just isn't right. The people who put this product out on the market should be in jail."

"Negligent homicide," Marc said. "Why not? Maybe that's the way to go after them."

"Maybe," Carvelli agreed. "I could talk to Owen," he said referring to Owen Jefferson, the Minneapolis police lieutenant in charge of their homicide division and a friend. "He could go to the county attorney."

"Not a bad idea," Marc agreed. "If nothing else, it would be leverage to use on the people at Cannon Brothers to flip on Cal Simpson. I think that time we saw them meet with him was more than a social call."

"Let me and the guys find out what this lawyer, Brody what's-his-name…" Carvelli started to say.

"Knutson," Marc said.

"Yeah, him," Carvelli said. "Let me see what he has to say first. If we can crack him, that would be some corroboration of what the weenie congressman told us."

"Maybe I'll give Steve Gondeck a call," Marc said referring to a lawyer he knew in the Hennepin County Attorney's office.

THIRTY-EIGHT

"I thought we had guards at the doors? Who's in charge of security around here?" Carvelli heard a familiar voice say as he entered the MPD Homicide Division.

"Funny, Anderson," Carvelli replied to the man who had made the wisecrack.

"How are you, Tony?" the detective asked as the two of them shook hands.

"Where is everybody?" Carvelli asked as he looked around the mostly empty room. "Krispy Kreme come out with a new brand of doughnuts?"

"Would I be here if that was true?" Anderson asked. "We have to work for a living."

Bob Anderson was a friend of Carvelli's and a couple of years from retirement. He was also the best homicide detective with the MPD.

"Oh, is that what you call what you do? Working for a living."

"How's Jake?" Anderson asked referring to Jake Waschke, a mutual friend.

"He's good," Carvelli replied. "If you ever go outside again, you should stop by and see him."

"I know, I think about it, then get busy and forget. What are you up to?"

"Go see Jake," Carvelli said and poked a finger in his padded midsection. "I'm here to see your boss," he continued. Carvelli turned and looked at the office of Owen Jefferson. He was at his desk and waved to indicate Carvelli should come in.

"You go see Owen," Anderson said as he slipped on a sports coat. "I'm going to slide out of here and go see Jake right now while I'm thinking about it. I'll see you later."

"What's up, Mr. Carvelli?" Jefferson asked with emphasis on the word 'mister'. The two of them had known each other almost twenty years. During that time, while Carvelli was still on the job and after his retirement, their paths had crossed many times. Through mutual respect, they had become good friends. And even though Jefferson was now a lieutenant in charge of homicide and Carvelli worked for a well-known defense lawyer, they had remained good friends.

"Well, Lieutenant Jefferson," Carvelli said giving back a little unnecessary formality. "I would like to run something by you."

"All right, smartass," Jefferson said with a warm grin, "What?"

When Carvelli had finished telling Jefferson the story about Cannon Brothers Toys and the dead and injured children, he sat back and waited for a response.

"It's horrible, Tony," Jefferson said. "These assholes should be in jail. But you'll have to run this by Lydia Foster across the street."

Jefferson was referring to the new Hennepin County Attorney, Lydia Foster. She was barely six months into the job and not well known. Three years out of law school, she had been elected to the job, replacing a political appointee who had been a disaster. The new county attorney was still feeling her way around.

"How is she doing?"

"Too inexperienced," Jefferson shrugged. "Sure, I'm biased in favor of African-Americans, but she could have used more experience. But I hear she's calmed the waters over there after Penny Nugent just about chased everybody out the door. And she's smart enough to rely on her senior people. I think she'll probably be okay."

"What do you think? Could we make a case for some type of manslaughter? Kadella's going to check with Steve Gondeck," Carvelli said.

"You know, it would be nice to try. These corporate assholes pull this shit, then end up walking away rich. It would be nice to make them pay.

"When's Kadella seeing Steve?" Jefferson asked.

"Today or tomorrow."

"How is he doing?" Jefferson asked.

"Good. He was damn lucky."

"For a defense lawyer, he's not a bad guy. Tell him to have Steve call me after they meet," Jefferson said.

"Will do," Carvelli replied.

Carvelli went out the Fifth Street side of the Old City Hall Building. It was a beautiful late-summer day. Temps were in the upper seventies and there was plenty of sunshine. He checked his watch again thinking he had about a half-hour to wait.

He turned to his right to go down to the corner to go across Fifth. As he did a Light-Rail train pulled up and stopped. Before he got to the corner, the train was starting up to make its run to Target Field where the Twins were finishing another disappointing season.

After crossing Fifth, he found an empty bench with a view of the fountain in front of the government center. As nice as it was today autumn was in the air in the evenings. This, of course, would be followed by winter. Real winter that would be classified as Armageddon if it ever hit the East Coast.

While watching the lightly-clad younger women strolling by, Carvelli became lost in his thoughts. He did not see her coming until she plopped down on the bench next to him.

"Hey, Studley," Gabriella Shriqui startled him by saying. "Want to buy a girl lunch?"

"Jesus, Gabriella! You just took five years off of my life. Five years I can't afford."

"Well?" she asked.

"What are you doing here? Are you back to being a lowly reporter?"

"Checking on a trial; that councilman who got busted on a cocaine and bribery sting," she replied. "Don't you watch my show?"

"Oh, um, yeah, religiously," Carvelli stammered.

"What are you doing here, besides girl watching?" she asked.

"Business," he replied. "I'm meeting someone in about twenty minutes. Although she doesn't know it."

"What have you guys been up to? I haven't seen or talked to Maddy or Marc since the hospital. Are they mad at me for filming the accident?"

"No, of course not," Carvelli said then paused for a moment. "You know, we do need to talk to you. We..."

"You have a story," she said enthusiastically.

"Maybe," he agreed. "Look, sweetheart. You need to get out of here. I need to be alone. I'll make sure Maddy calls you. I promise."

"Okay," Gabriella said. "If she doesn't, I'll call her. We need to go out anyway. I'll see you later."

Gabriella was barely out of sight when Carvelli saw who he was waiting for. Coming across Third Avenue, earlier than usual, was a slender, attractive woman in her late twenties. She was dressed tastefully in a navy-blue skirt and white blouse. Very business-like. And her name was Brooke Hartley.

Carvelli watched as she quickly walked to the granite bench surrounding the fountain in front of the building. Dan Sorenson had been watching her for several days and, weather permitting, she came here every day to eat lunch. She took a place on the bench facing the building and removed a sandwich and yogurt from her purse. As she started to eat Carvelli stood up and walked toward her. As he did so, he realized Brody Knutson liked his assistants young and pretty. Carvelli took a seat a couple of feet from her, not too close to make her wary or uncomfortable. His approach with her was going to be very different than Marjorie Griebler.

"Please don't be upset, Ms. Hartley," Carvelli said. When he said this, her back straightened and her right hand went into her purse. Seeing her reach into her purse—he hoped for a can of mace and not a gun—Carvelli held up his hands in a gesture of friendliness.

"My name is Tony Carvelli. I'm a former Minneapolis police detective and now a private investigator."

He still had his hands in the air as he continued. "I'm investigating the deaths of Lynn McDaniel and Zach Evans. I'll show you my credentials if you promise not to shoot me," he said with a smile.

She smiled slightly at his discomfort and removed her hand from her purse. In it, she held a shiny, chrome whistle.

"Oh, god," Carvelli said. "Don't blow that thing. Half the cops across the street would come running and would love to arrest me just for the fun of it. I'd never hear the end of it."

He showed her his license and a picture ID. She looked them over, handed them back and said, "I don't know why you want to talk to me. I barely knew Zach Evans and had only met Lynn McDaniel once. It's terrible what happened, but I don't know anything about it."

"Okay," Carvelli replied. "Let me ask you a couple of questions. If you want to tell me it's none of my business, I won't be offended.

"How much money did you invest in Cannon Brothers stock?"

She looked at him with a puzzled expression and said, "None. I've never bought any of their stock. Thank God. The company's in bankruptcy. Why?"

"One more," Carvelli said. "How much did you invest in Morton Aviation?"

"What? Where is this coming from? None. I've never heard of Morton Aviation," she answered.

"I didn't think so," Carvelli said. He took a small piece of paper from his shirt pocket and read off a social security number.

"How did you get my social security number?" she asked, now becoming visibly angry.

"It's not an identity theft thing," Carvelli assured her. "It's possibly worse. Your name is on a list, with many other people, and was used to buy and sell stock. Specifically, for you, many thousands of shares of both Cannon Brothers and Morton Aviation. The shares were purchased in your name and under your social security number and sold when the price was high. Then you borrowed and sold short shares of these companies. You made a fortune doing this, and it was illegal."

"I did not!" she practically screamed. "How did you…"

"Sssh, Brooke, please. I know you didn't. Your information was used by someone on behalf of a lot of other people, including some crooked politicians.

197

"Trust me. I have an assistant U.S. attorney involved who knows you were used as a cutout. Please," Carvelli said, "you're going to be all right."

"Who? Goddamnit!" she said barely containing her fury.

"I'm sorry I upset you so much," Carvelli sincerely said.

"Are you sure about this? Wait, what does this have to do with the deaths of Zach Evans and Lynn McDaniel?"

Carvelli leaned closer and quietly said, "We believe the people who did this stock scheme are the ones who murdered Evans and McDaniel. They did it to help them manipulate the stock. Evans and McDaniel knew some things that could have caused these people some problems."

"Am I in danger?"

"No, not all. Do you know who Calvin Simpson is? Is he a client of ..."?

"Yes, he's a client of the firm and a friend of Mr. Knutson. Is he involved? Is Knutson? How much money is involved? What the hell is going on?"

"A lot of money. Under your name alone, they made over fifty million."

"What! How much? Am I going to prison? I didn't get a dime!"

"Brooke, relax, please. You're not going to prison. We know you were used. The U.S. attorney we are working with knows you were used. You are not in any trouble. We're pretty sure Simpson is involved and probably Knutson."

"That's something that arrogant little shit would do," she said.

"You don't like him much," Carvelli said.

"No, not really. I mean, he's not a bad boss. I've had worse. And I get paid well. He just creeps me out. He's always looking at my legs, and whenever I walk away from him, I can feel his eyes on my ass," she said.

"File a harassment claim."

"He's never done anything," she said. "Lucy, his other assistant feels the same thing. He's just a little creepy."

"Lucy Gibson?"

"Yeah, how did you know?"

"She's on the list, too. It seems pretty certain Knutson gave your information to Simpson. But we have no proof," Carvelli said.

"How else would he have..."

"Any number of ways," Carvelli said. "I need to have a chat with Knutson. What can you tell me about his habits; his routines."

"You want me to be a snitch for you?" she asked.

"Yeah, a little," Carvelli admitted.

"Do you have a card? I'll do it. I'll find a time and place for you to sit down with him in private."

"That's what I need."

"You keep saying, 'We'. Who are 'we'? I want to meet them. I want to be sure this isn't some scam."

"You want to call back to the office and tell them you're going home? That you feel sick? I'll take you now," Carvelli said.

"Okay," she said. "Let's go. I'll call on the way."

Fifteen minutes later they were at Marc's office. Maddy came by, Connie joined in and by the end of the day, Brooke Hartley was satisfied they were legitimate, and she agreed to keep an eye on Brody Knutson.

THIRTY-NINE

"Do I have a case with you?" Marc heard the man he called ask without even saying hello.

"No, I mean, I have a couple of cases pending with you guys but not with you personally," Marc replied.

Marc had called a lawyer with the Hennepin County attorney's office. His name was Steve Gondeck. Steve was the chief litigator in the felony division. He and Marc had several cases against each other over the years and were well acquainted. At least respectfully friendly, if not friends.

Marc had called and asked the receptionist for Steve and identified himself. This was why Gondeck answered the phone the way he did.

"I have a problem, and I'd like to run it past you, get your opinion on it," Marc said.

"On a case we…"

"No, there is no case, no client even. It's something you might want to look at. I wouldn't be involved at all," Marc said.

"Okay, now you have my curiosity piqued," Gondeck said.

"Piqued? That's a pretty big word for a prosecutor," Marc said.

Gondeck laughed and said, "Coming from a defense lawyer, I'll take that as a compliment."

"Hey, you're the one that's on the dark side. We're on the side of the angels."

"Nice try. When was the last time one of you even had a dog that still liked you once he found out what you do for a living?" Gondeck asked.

Marc paused for a moment before saying, "That's a good point. I always wondered why every dog I see growls at me."

"Now you know," Gondeck said. "Tell you what. It's a nice day and I need an excuse to get out of the office. You can buy me lunch. I'll meet you at that place across the street from your office in a half hour."

"That will work. See you then."

The two men had a booth in the back by themselves where they could talk. After ordering their lunch, Gondeck looked at Marc to start.

For the next half-hour, Marc told Gondeck what he knew about Cannon Brothers. He left out the part about stock market manipulation at first and stayed with just the engineer's memo, its contents, and the number of children killed and injured as a result of the cover-up. When he finished, he waited for Gondeck to reply.

Gondeck pushed his empty plate aside, wiped his mouth with a napkin, and thought quietly for a moment.

"These cases are difficult to bring and win," he began. "At best you're looking at second-degree manslaughter."

"I know," Marc replied.

"We have to show that the executives at Cannon Brothers exhibited culpable negligence that created an unreasonable risk to these kids."

"I know," Marc agreed again.

"We would have to prove that, at least, they read the engineer's report and went ahead anyway. I don't think constructive knowledge would be enough in a criminal case. We would have to show actual knowledge. Even then, was the risk unreasonable?" Gondeck said. "Do you know for a fact that they read the memo, ignored it and put a product on the market that was likely to cause death or great bodily harm? Will the guy who wrote it, the chief engineer, testify that..."

"He's dead," Marc said. "Some kind of gay pickup murder. Unsolved. I haven't seen the memo myself. Maybe it has a list of addressees on it with initials."

"That would at least show they read it. Then there's still the part about was the release of the product unreasonable? Did they know, or should they have known that these accidents were likely?"

"Don't know. I don't even know what happened to it. Maybe you can find out..."

"The feds have it," Gondeck said.

"How do you know that?"

"We're not complete idiots. We do pay attention to what's going on around town. We even read the newspapers," Gondeck said.

"What if I can give you a huge motive? Something that will help overcome the unreasonable risk part of the statute?"

"What?" Gondeck asked. He leaned forward halfway across the table and asked, "What are you up to? You looking for a conviction to help you win a civil suit? What's going on?"

"We're, ah, looking into, ah, I'm sorry, Steve, I can't tell you that yet. It's not about a civil suit. But I can tell you the motive is insider trading, stock fraud, stock manipulation, stuff like that. We don't have proof yet. In fact, if you could indict a couple of the Cannon Brothers executives, I think they'd flip on some people. These aren't guys who will look lightly at possible prison time."

Gondeck sat back in his booth seat and looked at Marc for a moment. "I could track down a copy of the memo. Take a look at it and see exactly what's in it," he said.

A look appeared on Marc's face like the light of remembrance just came on in his head. He snapped his fingers and pointed an index finger at Gondeck.

"Maddy's involved," he said.

201

"She is? Why didn't you say so?" Gondeck replied. "Now I'm in for sure," he laughed.

Steve Gondeck had always been a bit smitten with the lovely Ms. Rivers. He was three inches shorter than her, pudgy around the midsection, at least fifteen years older than Maddy and totally devoted to his wife and family. Marc liked to tease him about it and between them it was a running joke.

"I'm calling your wife," Marc said.

"Who? My what?" Gondeck said with a mock-confused look. "Anyway, I'll see what I can do about getting a copy of the memo. Soon, before I do anything with this, I'll need to see something solid about the stock manipulation motive."

"We have it," Marc replied. "I can't tell you what just yet, but we do have it."

"We found a total of five references on the recordings to someone Cal refers to as 'the lawyer'. Not once does he mention a name," Conrad said.

"But three days before the memo was in the Star Tribune, Cal was talking to Albert—the guy we think is Senator Albert Fisher—and he mentioned the package he got from the lawyer. He said he was going to have it sent the next day," Tommy Craven said.

The entire group, including all of the ex-cops, were meeting in Vivian's library. It was time for a complete review of everything they knew and Carvelli had everyone attend. It was also time for a discussion, a brainstorming session.

Conrad and Tommy had been the last ones to arrive. The others had been at it for over an hour by the time they did. The two of them had been in Vivian's boathouse listening to every recording and it had taken them almost two days.

"That's no coincidence," Jake Waschke said when Tommy finished.

A murmur of agreement went through the small crowd. Carvelli said, "Okay, I'm going to have a go at Brody Knutson tomorrow. I got a tip he is having lunch by himself at the Minneapolis Club at 1:00 P.M."

"Nice digs," Marc said. "How are you going to get in?"

The Minneapolis Club was as close to an "old money" place as there was in Minnesota. An exclusive, private club where old money met new money and politicians to avoid the riff-raff.

"What? I won't fit in with the upper crust?" Carvelli asked feigning being offended.

"Does anybody else want to hit that softball he just tossed up in the air?" Marc asked.

"Too easy," Dan Sorenson said among the laughter.

"All right, very funny. Vivian's nephew, David Corwin, is going to get me in as a guest. Once inside, I'll do the rest. Here's what I have in mind."

With that, Carvelli quickly explained how he planned to go after Brody Knutson.

"And here comes our pigeon," Carvelli said to his passenger. "Right on schedule."

Carvelli and David Corwin were parked on Second Avenue across the street from the vine-covered Minneapolis Club building and its Second Avenue entrance. Having never met Knutson, Carvelli had printed his picture from the law firm's website. That was how he recognized the lawyer.

"He's shorter than I thought he would be," David said.

"And balder than his picture," Carvelli added. "Haven't you ever met him?"

"Yeah, I think so," David said. "Many years ago. I know who is. The word is, he's a conniving, backstabbing S.O.B. who would run over his own mother for power and money."

"That hardly makes him unique for the people in that club," Carvelli said.

"Hey! I'm one of those people," David said then laughed. "But you're right. Give him a minute to get to his table then we'll go in."

The waiter appeared at their table almost immediately. David ordered coffee and Carvelli did also. As the waiter walked off, Carvelli took a casual look around the dining room. He spotted Knutson at a table for two off by himself across the room in front of a window.

"I'm glad I wore my best suit," Carvelli said.

"You look fine. Right at home," David replied.

"I'm not sure that's a compliment," Carvelli said. "I'd rather be in jeans and a sweatshirt."

"Me, too," David said. "But it's a good place to do business. And the food's good. Are you going to eat? It's on me."

"No, I'm going after him right away," Carvelli said.

Their coffee arrived, and David gave the waiter his lunch order.

"I'm starving," David said. "I'll eat while you go do your thing. Good luck."

Carvelli watched while a man stopped, shook hands with Knutson and spoke to him. Fortunately, Knutson did not offer the man the other chair at his table. As soon as he walked off, Carvelli decided to go.

"Hi, Brody, how's lunch?" Carvelli asked as he pulled out the chair at the table for two and quickly sat down.

"Who are you? What do you want and get lost before I call the maître d'," Knutson said.

"Just so you know who you're dealing with, I'll throw that gay little maître d' through a window if he comes over here," Carvelli said with a sinister smile. "Did you drink any of this?" he asked referring to the glass of water.

"Ah, um, no," Knutson stammered.

"Thanks," Carvelli said. He picked up the glass, took a large swallow and continued. "Here's the deal, Brody. I represent some people who will, for now, remain anonymous. Suffice it to say, they are all Italian gentlemen."

Carvelli placed his forearms on the table and leaned forward as close to Knutson as possible. Knutson, his eyes wide open, said nothing.

"We know everything. We know about the murders, the conspiracy, the stock manipulation, the money laundering, everything."

"I don't know what you're talking about," Knutson defiantly said.

"Shut up. We don't care about any of it. We also know, within say forty or fifty million, how much you, Cal Simpson and his crooked politicians plan to make off of this. Don't try arguing with me or denying it."

Carvelli paused for a moment then continued. "You're listening. That's good. Now, here's the good news. As I said, we don't give a damn about how crooked you are. In fact, the more, the better. And despite what you may believe from the TV and movies, we're not greedy people. What they want is one-third. For that, you and Cal and his pals get to keep the rest. And, again, despite what you may believe, we're not really prone to violence. It's usually a big expense. To be used only when necessary."

Carvelli leaned forward a little more and said, "One last thing. We know who Cal Simpson really is. I'll be in touch. Enjoy the rest of your lunch."

Knutson put on his best lawyer face, casually wiped his mouth with a linen napkin and calmly, quietly said, "Can I say something now?"

"I suppose," Carvelli replied.

"If I knew this Cal Simpson, attorney/client privilege would preclude me from even admitting it. As far as the rest of this nonsense, I have no idea what you are talking about. Now, may I finish my lunch?"

"We'll be in touch," Carvelli said.

By prearrangement, Carvelli left the building by himself. He walked past David Corwin who was eating by now and did not look up.

Carvelli hurried across the street to his car to wait for Brody to leave and David to finish his lunch and join him. Within thirty seconds after he entered the Camaro, Brody Knutson came out of the building. Before he passed through the brick, ivy-covered entryway, Knutson was on his cell phone.

"Say hi to Cal Simpson for me," Carvelli quietly said. Carvelli then made a call on his cell to let his guys know what happened and to make sure the tail on Knutson was all set up and ready to go.

FORTY

Brody Knutson was sweating like a marathon runner in ninety-degree heat. As nerve-wracking as the confrontation with the Mafia guy had been, what awaited him was going to be worse. He had placed a quick call to Cal Simpson as soon as he left the club. All he told Cal was he needed to see him right away. Brody could only hope Cal would not blame the messenger.

While hurrying up Second Avenue dodging through the lunchtime crowd, he called his office. Brooke answered and took the message that he would not be back. Of course, Brooke knew Carvelli was meeting him. When she finished the call, she almost laughed.

Knutson drove his new Lexus up the ramp of the underground parking garage. The Everson, Reed offices were on Third Avenue and Sixth Street across from the big granite government center. He exited onto Fifth Street and turned left to go west to Minnetonka. Waiting across the street on the sidewalk was Franklin Washington. He watched Knutson turn left onto Second, then called Dan Sorenson. Sorenson knew the route and was waiting for him. Thirty minutes later, Knutson took the left-hand turn for the driveway to Cal's house. When he did, Tommy Craven drove past then called Conrad Hilton who was standing by the recording equipment.

"All right, calm down, slow down, and tell me everything he said, again," Cal told an overwrought Brody Knutson.

They were in the office in Cal's house. With them was Aidan Walsh. Cal was seated in his executive chair behind the desk. Knutson was in a chair facing Cal and Aidan, his arms crossed over his chest, was calmly leaning against a window frame to Cal's right.

Knutson wiped his forehead with a handkerchief, took a deep breath and began again.

"He sat down without saying a word. I told him to get lost, but he wasn't the least bit scared. He told me he represented a group of men with Italian names. He obviously meant the Mafia.

"He said they knew everything; the murders, the stock manipulation, the conspiracy, the names of everyone involved including the politicians. Everything and everyone."

"Did he name them? Did he drop any names of politicians or…"?

"You," Knutson almost yelled. "He knew your name. Oh, yeah, I almost forgot. He said to tell you they know who you really are. I don't know what he meant by that."

"What did he look like?" Cal asked trying not to show the shock he was feeling.

"I don't know. Scary. He looked like someone who you don't mess with. I was scared shitless," Knutson replied.

"What did he look like?" Cal asked again only more slowly this time. "Take a breath, close your eyes and picture him in your mind. Then describe him to us."

Knutson took a breath, closed his eyes and sat quietly for a moment.

"Okay. He's definitely an Italian looking guy. I don't know, maybe mid-forties. Good looking in a bad boy sort of way I think women would like. Dressed well in an Italian wool, dark suit with pinstriping."

"Any scars, tattoos, any visible marks that were noticeable?" Aidan asked.

"No," Knutson said, his eyes opened and moving back and forth between Cal and Aidan. "Nothing visible. No facial hair. If you saw him on the street, you probably wouldn't notice him."

"Scary looking?" Aidan asked.

"Yeah, well, at least to me. Or, maybe it was what he said. How much he knew," Knutson replied. He looked at Cal and said, "Murder? What murders? I don't know anything about any…"

"Stop it!" Cal ordered. "Grow up! Do you think we could pull off something like this without anyone getting hurt?"

"Don't tell me, I don't want to know," Knutson wailed.

"What else did he say?" Cal patiently asked.

"Just that they want thirty percent. And they believe they know how much," Knutson said.

"But he didn't give you an exact figure," Cal said.

"No. Just that they know within forty or fifty million."

"Did he tell you when?" Cal asked.

"No. Just to pass it on to you."

Cal looked at Aidan and asked, "Why didn't he try coming to me?"

"Probably because you're not so easy to approach. You have security. Mr. Knutson here was easier. They could watch him and catch him out of the office."

"How did he get into this fancy club of yours?" Cal suddenly asked Knutson. "Don't they have security?"

"Yes, but it wouldn't be hard to get passed it. He could've strolled right in if there was no one at the front desk."

"Okay," Cal said. "You take off and keep quiet about this. If he contacts you again, be cooperative. Tell him you told me. Tell him it's not your decision to make. Tell him whatever he wants to hear. We'll look into this. Aidan will show you out. Oh, Brody, you did good," Cal continued as he came around the desk. He shook hands with Knutson, pleasantly smiled and said, "Call anytime. Especially if you hear from him. While the weather is still nice, I'm thinking about another party at the lake place. You'll be sure to come."

"Thanks, Cal. I feel better already," Knutson said.

A few minutes later Aidan was seated where Knutson had been.

"What do you want to do with him?" Aidan asked.

"Who? Knutson or the Italian gentlemen?" Cal asked.

"Both," Aidan said.

"Knutson," Cal began, "Nothing right now. We'll stay as planned. The other guy, I'll call D.C. and see what I can find out. You check with any sources you have. We need to find out where this is coming from."

"You still want to get rid of that other problem we talked about?" Aidan asked.

Cal went silent for a moment thinking about the question. "Yes," he finally said. "But like I said, let's make it look natural."

"You got it," Aidan said.

Barely a quarter of a mile down the shoreline on Lake Minnetonka, a small crowd was listening in. Inside Vivian's boathouse, Carvelli, Dan Sorenson, Tommy Craven, and Franklin Washington were all standing staring at a speaker. Conrad, Maddy and even Vivian were in chairs doing the same thing.

"Come on, give us a name," Carvelli said.

They were listening to Cal. He had made a phone call, apparently with a new cell phone, and was obviously leaving a message. So far, he had not used the name of the person he was calling. Conrad had recorded the beeps of the number being dialed. He would forward that to Carvelli's guy, Paul Baker, who would have the number itself in a few minutes. This might give them the name, but not necessarily.

When Cal finished leaving the message, they heard the sounds of him getting out of his chair. A moment later, from a bug in the living room, they heard Cal say to someone, probably Aidan, to follow him outside.

"They're going to kill Brody Knutson," Carvelli said.

"Sounds like it," Sorenson agreed.

"That's horrible!" Vivian exclaimed. "We must do something to stop it."

"Or use it to warn him and put him in our pocket," Maddy said.

"Exactly what I was thinking," Carvelli agreed.

"You two have devious minds," Vivian said. "But clever."

"Who or what is the other problem they talked about?" Sorenson asked.

"Who," Maddy said. "Somebody else they're going to kill, but this is supposed to look natural."

"I'm guessing someone's about to have a heart attack," Carvelli said.

"What can we do?" Vivian asked.

"Unless we can come up with some idea who it is, not much," Carvelli replied.

"Cal's thug mentioned they talked about it before," Tommy said. "How about me and Conrad go through the recordings for the past few days and see what we can find. Maybe now that we know what to look for, we might find something."

"Conrad?" Carvelli asked looking at the electronics man.

"Sounds like a plan," Conrad agreed.

"Get that call Cal made sent..." Carvelli started to tell Conrad.

"Done," he replied.

Cal left a short, cryptic message on the voice mail of a contact in D.C. He ended the call, then sat silently for a moment thinking through a thought that had occurred to him.

Cal got out of his chair and quickly walked out into the dining room. He found Aidan sitting on a couch in the living room with his phone to his ear. Before Aidan had a chance to speak Cal put an index finger to his lips. He nodded his head toward a door leading to the backyard and the two men went outside. When they had gone about fifty feet from the house, Cal turned to Aidan.

"Think. How the hell does this guy who talked to Knutson know so much?" Cal asked.

"Somebody can't keep his mouth shut," Aidan said.

"Maybe," Cal agreed, "Or this house has been bugged. When was the last time you had it swept?"

"It's been three or four weeks," Aidan admitted. "But we've been here the entire time. No one's been in here by themselves. Someone has always been around."

"Get it done," an obviously annoyed Cal sharply said.

"Okay, boss," Aidan replied.

"Wait a second," Cal said. "On second thought, do it very quietly. Just have a guy come by to do it. And have him come in a car, not a company van."

"We may be under surveillance," Aidan said.

"Maybe. Do the sweep very discreetly and if he finds something, leave it in place," Cal said. "We may be able to mess with them."

FORTY-ONE

Cal Simpson was at his desk concentrating on the information displayed on the computer screen. Despite the fact that he had warned them it would be months before their ill-gotten money could be distributed, his investors/co-conspirators were starting to pester him. What these people could not or would not grasp was that laundering almost three billion dollars was not easy or quickly done.

Samantha had been traveling between Europe and the Caribbean for almost two weeks. She was meeting with bankers, setting up various accounts and shuffling money through fifteen different countries. But it still had to be done carefully. Fortunately, Cal's Washington connection was in a position to make sure none of this made it onto the Feds' radar.

One of Cal's burner phones rang. He looked at the number and quickly answered it. Because his mind was previously occupied, he made a little mistake.

"Mason," he said, "thanks for calling."

As soon as he said the man's name, he realized what he had done. Before his caller could reply, Cal said, "Wait a minute. Don't say anything."

To the people recording his calls, this was another mistake.

Cal went outside to the backyard. He walked down to the lakeshore and put the phone to his ear. He explained to his caller what had happened regarding the visit by Tony Carvelli with Brody Knutson.

"So, you think this was an emissary from a certain group of Italian businessmen?" Mason asked.

"I don't know, but we have to find out. We're checking our own contacts, but you have your own sources. Can you check into it?"

"Yeah, I can. It will need to be done discreetly. They are not my focus and I don't want to wave any flags around," Mason replied.

Cal turned toward the house and saw Aidan waiting for him with two other men. He waved and held up an index finger indicating they should stay where they were.

"Do what you can. I'd appreciate it," Cal said into his phone.

He ended the call and joined Aidan and the two men with him each of whom was holding a small bag of equipment. He shook hands with the men.

"Check the house. Every square inch of it. As quietly as possible. If you find anything, don't touch it, don't say a word about it. Just make sure you mark it. You go with them," Cal told Aidan. "Every inch, guys," he repeated.

"Yes, sir. We'll cover it," the older of the two said.

"How long will it take?" Cal asked.

"Big house," the older man said. "It normally takes us an hour or so. We'll go slower and be extra careful. It could take a while; two to three hours."

"The house is empty. The staff is off for today. Do what you have to do," Cal said.

Less than a minute after the three of them went inside, Cal's phone rang again. He looked at the caller ID and frowned. As he walked back toward the lake, he answered the call.

"Albert," Cal said to Senator Albert Fisher. "What can I do for you?"

"I have people riding my ass, Cal. I tell them what you said about being patient but..."

"These are not people who are used to being patient," Cal said. "Who's bothering you?"

"The old socialist is the worst one," Fisher replied. "This morning I told him I would take him out and get him laid just so he'd calm down."

"What did he say to that?" Cal laughed.

"He cussed at me and stomped off. I think he's getting impatient to start the revolution," Fisher said. "That reminds me, how are things progressing with that long-legged Maddy?"

"I don't know," Cal said. "The girl's like steel. No married men. She told me she had that happen to her once and she wasn't going to do it again. Still, I like her company."

"Good luck," Fisher said. "Back to my problem. Can you give some of these guys a little taste at least?"

"No," Cal emphatically replied. "We're sticking to the plan. Anything else is too risky. Tell them you talked to me and the way we are doing the laundry takes time."

"Okay I told the old fool I would talk to you and I did. Take care."

"You too, Al," Cal said.

Almost three hours later, Conrad Hilton took off the headset and placed it on the table. With no other client to work for today, he was spending the day in Vivian's boathouse monitoring the listening devices at Cal's. The only thing he had picked up was the very brief phone call Cal had received. Conrad had listened to it three times to be certain of what he heard.

"Come on, come on, Carvelli," he impatiently muttered to himself, "Answer your damn phone."

After writing down the pertinent information from the recording, Conrad decided he should run this past Carvelli. The phone started to ring for the fifth time when he heard Carvelli answer it.

"Yeah, what do you have, Conrad?"

"Hey, I'm in the boathouse and…"

"I know. You told me you were going to be there."

"Oh, yeah, right. Got an odd recording a while ago. Simpson got a phone call, said hello and the guy's name then told him not to say anything. Cal got up and that's all I heard."

"What exactly did he say?"

"Okay, he answered the call and said, 'Mason, thanks for calling back.' Then he quickly said, 'Wait a minute. Don't say anything.' That was it. I heard his chair move and he must have gone outside."

"They found the bugs," Carvelli said.

"Sounds like it," Conrad replied.

"Who's this Mason guy?" Carvelli asked.

"Don't know. I think this is the first time we've heard that name," Conrad answered. "I'll check our list, but I'm pretty sure."

"I think you're right. The name Mason would ring a bell."

"What do you want to do about the bugs?" Conrad asked.

"Let me think about it," Carvelli said.

"What about Maddy? She's supposed to go to dinner with him tonight," Conrad said.

"I know. I don't want her in that house until we're sure she is not suspected of planting the bugs. I'll call her and have her call Simpson. She can tell him to meet her in a public place that we can monitor. She'll be safe there. Check for this Mason guy and I'll get back to you."

When the two tech guys were finished and had located all four listening devices, they reported back to Cal. They told him what they had found then Aidan escorted them to their car and paid them in cash. While Aidan did this, Cal, in a state of fury, stomped around the backyard.

Aidan returned to the back of the house and waited patiently for his boss. He also knew he had an ass-chewing coming.

"Who the hell did this?" Cal practically screamed in Aidan's face.

"I don't know," Aidan quietly admitted.

"It's your goddamn job to know!" Cal yelled. "What the hell am I paying you for?"

Aidan stood still, hands held loosely together at his waist. Cal was normally very good at keeping his cool, but once in a while, something would set him off. Cal turned, took several steps away and took a deep breath. A sure sign that the worst was over.

Cal turned back to Aidan and asked, "Someone on the staff?"

"Maybe," Aidan replied. "I kind of doubt it though. I doubt any of them would have the balls to pull a stunt like this."

"Fire them all. Have the agency send over new ones," Cal said.

212

"Should we keep an eye on them? Try to find out if one of them did it?" Aidan asked. "Now that we know where the bugs are, can we use that to send disinformation to whoever it is that is listening in?"

"Maybe," a much calmer Cal agreed. "Is it the mob guys? Could they have done this?"

"Sure," Aidan replied. "That's who I was thinking. If it's the Feds, Mason will find out for us. What about your girlfriend, Maddy? What exactly do we know about her?"

Cal thought about the question for a moment before answering. "I don't know. It's possible I suppose. But she's never been alone in the house long enough, has she?"

"I remember once I caught her alone in the kitchen. There's a bug in there, but she was just getting a glass of water. Still, she's a pretty clever girl. Could be," Aidan replied.

"I guess it's time we did a thorough check of the lovely Maddy Shore. We're having dinner tonight. Put a tail on her," Cal said.

"Will do, boss," Aidan replied.

"I think you and Conrad are right," Maddy told Carvelli. "At least we better assume they found the bugs."

"Hang on a second," Carvelli said. "Conrad's trying to call me."

Carvelli put Maddy on hold while he took Conrad's call. A minute later, he was back.

"Conrad says he got over to Cal's just in time to see two tech guys he knows leaving."

"That confirms it," Maddy said. "Now what?"

"We'll see. At this point, they don't know it was you, but we have to assume you're on the list of suspects. You want to pull out and stop seeing him?"

Maddy went silent thinking it over. "Not yet. Let's play it out for a bit."

"Sweetheart, Aidan is a very bad guy. I know you can handle yourself, but…"

"We'll be careful. I think they'll put a tail on me to try to find out more about me. Probably starting tonight. He doesn't even know where I live…"

"You don't know that," Carvelli said. "Call him," Carvelli continued. "Tell him you don't want to drive out to his place. Tell him to meet you downtown at Ruth's Chris on Ninth and Second. We can cover you better there."

"Sounds like a plan. I'll call you back after I set it up."

FORTY–TWO

Over the years of practicing law, Marc had learned the best way to ignore an annoying client. When one of them is sitting across the desk from him, venting about idiotic nonsense and unrealistic expectations, look them right in the eyes. Put an expression on your face that what he or she is prattling on about is as captivating as the Gettysburg Address and pay no attention to it. They will believe you are a great listener and truly out to take care of them. In fact, what Marc is really thinking about is how much longer he has to endure this torture. Of course, it helps to nod your head from time-to-time.

Seated across the desk this morning was the self-absorbed, albeit spectacularly good-looking daughter of a client. More precisely, she was the daughter of a client of an officemate, Chris Grafton. The original client, Gerald Middleton, was a minor real estate mogul in the Twin Cities. Chris had been his lawyer for almost fifteen years and the father was a terrific guy. Jerry Middleton was an up-by-his-bootstraps entrepreneur and as likable as anyone you could meet. This, of course, was a huge asset in the real estate business.

His daughter, Kelly was, and Jerry would admit this, a spoiled ball-busting man-eater. Now thirty-eight years old, with two kids after eight years of a third marriage, Marc had let Chris and Jerry Middleton convince him to do her divorce. Connie had done the first two. When Chris hinted that a third one was coming, Connie had conveniently gone to Europe for a month.

"Marc?" Kelly sharply said bringing him out of his semi-trance. "What do you think? I'm getting screwed, aren't I?"

"No, Kelly. You're not getting screwed," Marc told her again. You are going to get physical custody..."

"Yeah but that sonofabitch is going to get visitation. My kids shouldn't have to be around that tramp he's sleeping with," she almost yelled.

"Kelly," Marc softly, "they are not your kids," he said making air quotes when he said your kids. "You don't own them. They are children, not property. He is their father."

"Yeah, but..." she started to say.

Taking her father's advice about being tough with her, Marc leaned forward and with a stern look, interrupted her by saying, "Stop it! Here we go again. You leave your husband for a twenty-three-year-old golf instructor with whom you have been having an affair for over a year; a fact you threw in Sam's face. After six months, you realize the kid is a twenty-three-year-old golf instructor. You come to your senses and tell him, what was his name?"

"Chip," Kelly said trying not to smile.

"Of course," Marc snidely said.

"Chip, what else would you name a twenty-three-year-old golf pro. You leave Chippy and decide you want to reconcile with Sam. He now has a new girlfriend and..."

"Don't call her that," Kelly said.

"That's what she is and I'm sorry, but I've met her, and she seems like a nice person. Anyway, Sam has met someone else and is no longer interested.

"You then accuse him of molesting the girls. Sam and the girls get dragged into that swamp until you finally admit you lied. You should be thankful Sam is grownup enough to admit you're a good mother..."

"I am."

"...and knows the girls need you or you could have lost custody completely. Now, put a stop to this constant whining about Sam and Barbara. You're getting custody, child support and an even split of the assets. I'll help you through this."

Kelly sat silently staring at the top of Marc's desk for fifteen to twenty seconds. Without lifting her head, she looked at Marc. The corners of her mouth curled into a smile and she said, "Well if you're going to put it that way," and she started to laugh.

Marc chuckled a little too then said, "I haven't told you this, but I think you need to hear it. Don't get mad, but you did something stupid; this dalliance with Chip, the child. Now you're mad at yourself. It's not helping you or the girls and it's not fair to Sam, and you know it."

"Yeah, you're right," she agreed.

"What do you say we get this done so everyone can get on with their lives? You're still a very attractive woman, Kelly. You'll meet someone else, trust me," Marc said then thought, *and you can try to neuter him.*

Marc knocked on Connie's locked office door and yelled, "She's gone. You can come out now."

A few seconds later, Connie's door slowly opened, and she stuck her head out and looked around.

"You coward," Marc said to her.

"She's gone?" Connie asked.

"Yeah, you can come out," Marc said.

"We could hear through your door," Connie said while coming out into the reception area.

"Really? Was I that loud?" Marc asked looking at Carolyn and Sandy.

"No," Carolyn said, "she was. Didn't you notice?"

"Not really," Marc said as he took a phone message from Sandy.

"How can you ignore that?" Carolyn asked.

"It's a skill you develop doing divorce work," Connie replied. "Especially if you represent a woman scorned."

"Hey," Marc said turning to Connie holding the message slip in his hand. "I guess I'm meeting Maddy and Tony for lunch. You want to tag along?"

"Sure," Connie replied. "Where?"

"Artie's," Marc said.

"Just a moment, he's standing right here," Marc heard Sandy say into her phone.

Sandy held her phone out to him and said, "Steve Gondeck."

"I'll take it in my office."

Maddy and Carvelli were at a booth toward the back of the restaurant when Marc and Connie arrived. Carvelli leaned out and waved to them. Marc slid into the booth next to Maddy and Connie did the same on Carvelli's side.

"I have some good news, maybe," Marc said. "I got a call from Steve Gondeck just before we left to come here." Marc paused while the waitress took their orders and bantered a bit with Carvelli.

"He told me he's taking the Cannon Brothers' case to a grand jury in a couple of days. He's going to try to get some type of manslaughter indictment against the three top executives. The CEO, Dane Cannon, the COO, Greg Cannon, Dane's brother and the Executive Vice President, Marissa Duggins.

"He put one of their investigators on it and those were the people they came up with. They are the ones most likely to have seen the engineer's memo. He is also having letters served on each one today, advising them that they are the subjects of a grand jury investigation."

"They'll run to lawyers," Carvelli said.

"Sure," Marc agreed. "The lawyer will call Steve and try to stop him. He'll tell them to take a hike and go to the grand jury. He has three former Cannon Brothers employees who will testify that those three made the decision to put the skateboards on the market. They will also testify that the guy who wrote the memo would have shown it to them. We're looking for an indictment, not a conviction."

"How did you get Steve Gondeck to go along with this?" Maddy asked.

"Well, ah, um, I, ah, promised I would get you to sleep with him," Marc said.

Even Maddy burst into laughter at that statement. She half-heartedly threw an elbow into Marc for it, then, when the laughter died down, Marc turned serious.

"It was Paxton. She was very persuasive. Plus, if we do expose this conspiracy, the Hennepin County Attorney's office will get its share of kudos for it."

"We have another problem," Carvelli said.

"How did your date go last night?" Marc asked Maddy thinking that might be what Tony was referring to.

"Fine," she said. "Cal's guys are following me."

"We spotted them, Maddy drove around for a while, and we only saw one car. We boxed them in and made them stop at a red light. She drove off. It looked perfectly natural," Carvelli said.

"But they'll keep trying," Marc said.

"That's not the problem I was going to tell you about," Carvelli continued. "We'll figure out how much we want Cal to find out about her.

"The problem is, we know Cal found the bugs in his house. He left them in place and is trying to feed us bullshit. He doesn't talk on the phone to anyone, so we're not getting anything of substance."

"What do you want to do?" Marc asked.

"I think it's time I had another chat with Brody Knutson," Carvelli said. "And this time I'll tell him who I really am. Tell him I'm working with a U.S. attorney he needs to meet. I'll bring him out to the hotel and we'll hold him there until Paxton gets in."

"I called Paxton and she can fly in tomorrow morning. Maybe we have Tony bring Brody to the hotel and meet her, show him the video of Del Peterson and see if we can scare him into cooperating," Maddy said.

"Corroborate what the good congressman told us," Carvelli said.

"You guys need to shake the tree and shake it hard," Connie said. "You don't have enough with just Del Peterson."

"That's why we're going to indict the Cannon Brothers executives," Marc said.

"That case is really weak, Marc," Connie said. "And you know it. What if their lawyers are smart enough to see that? Indicting them was always a long shot."

"If we can get one or more of them to flip, that would help. But Knutson, as Cal's lawyer, knows where the worst of it is," Maddy said.

"Good point. Okay, you take another shot at Knutson," Marc agreed. "How and when?" he asked.

"Tomorrow morning, early. I'll catch him in the parking ramp. He has a reserved parking space. I talked to my snitch in his office and she told me he'll be in by seven."

"You're going to be up at seven to meet him?" Marc asked. "I'm glad I won't be there. Make sure you have plenty of coffee before you get there."

"Very funny, smartass. I'm finding I do my best work early in the morning," Carvelli said.

Maddy leaned across the table looked him directly in the eyes and asked, "What have you been smoking?"

Shortly before 2:00 P.M. one of Cal's phones rang. He looked at the caller ID, answered it and quickly said, "Hang on. I'll be right with you."

He was at his desk using his computer when the call came in. A minute later, he was walking down the backyard toward the lake.

"Okay, what's up?" he asked into his phone.

"We just got a notice from the Hennepin County Attorney," Dane Cannon almost breathlessly said. "We're the subject of a grand jury investigation."

This news stopped Cal dead in his tracks. For several seconds, he stood silently staring at the lake without breathing.

"Are you there?" Dane asked.

"Yes, I'm here," Cal calmly replied. "First of all, who are the 'we' that you're talking about?"

"Me, Greg and Marissa. We all got a letter identifying us as the targets of a grand jury investigation."

Relieved that it was likely limited to a fishing expedition by the county attorney into Cannon Brothers and the skateboards, Cal continued to walk toward the lake.

"Have you talked to a lawyer?"

"Of course. We called Parker Stanton immediately," Dave said.

"He's a corporate guy. You need a criminal defense lawyer. I'll call one I know," Cal said.

"The letter says we can testify before the…"

"No, absolutely not. You don't talk to anyone let alone the grand jury. Trust me. You cannot help yourselves by testifying before the grand jury under oath. For now, just keep your mouths shut. My guy's name is Thaddeus Cheney; Thad. He's the best. Just sit by your phone and keep your mouths shut. I'll make sure he calls you today. Do nothing until then."

"Yeah, okay. I've heard of this guy. He's good. I feel better already," Dane said.

"Relax, he'll get you through this," Cal said.

FORTY-THREE

Tony Carvelli and Dan Sorenson were in Carvelli's Camaro on station waiting for their subject. They were parked back-end-in, so the two men could look through the front in the parking garage of the U.S. Bank building in downtown Minneapolis. Brooke Hartley had given Carvelli the time they needed to be here, which did not please Carvelli.

Carvelli sipped his five-dollar cup of Starbucks and looked at the dashboard clock; 6:52 A.M. *Any time now*, he thought.

"Pretty talkative this morning," Sorenson said intentionally poking Carvelli.

"Shut up," Carvelli growled. "I have a gun you know."

Sorenson had all he could do not to choke on the coffee he swallowed. He got his breathing under control and laughed at Carvelli's discomfort.

"Anybody who is up this early every day needs to re-examine their life. It's not natural," Carvelli said.

"Okay, sunshine," Sorenson chuckled. "Here's our guy," he added as a new Lexus pulled into a reserved spot directly in front of them.

"Good," Carvelli said. "Let's go."

The two men got out of Carvelli's Camaro and got to the Lexus as its owner was exiting. As soon as he saw Carvelli, he froze stiff.

"Morning, Brody," Carvelli said. "Nice to see you again."

"What, what, um, ah, do you want?" Knutson stammered. "I did what you wanted. I passed the…"

"It's not what we want, Brody," Carvelli said. "It's what we are here to do for you."

"What?" Knutson tentatively asked.

"Save your life," Carvelli said. "Listen, we have something you need to hear. Come over to my car," he continued pointing at the Camaro. "Give us a few minutes to explain. Then I promise you, if you want to go upstairs, you can. Fifteen minutes," Carvelli said. "Then you can go."

"You're not going to hurt me or kidnap me?"

"No, that's not who we are. Please," Carvelli said.

Sorenson was in the backseat, Carvelli behind the wheel and Knutson, clinging to his briefcase against his chest, was in the passenger seat.

"First of all, my name is Tony Carvelli. I'm a licensed private investigator and a retired Minneapolis police detective. This guy is Dan Sorenson and he is also a retired MPD detective," he said as he handed Knutson his PI credentials.

"What the hell is going on?" Knutson angrily asked.

219

"I apologize for shaking you up the other day. It was necessary to get your attention. There's no Mafia involved. That reference to working for Italians was a cover. I'm not going to tell you who we work for at this point. But we do know everything I said to you; the stock manipulation, insider trading and conspiracy to commit murder."

"I don't know anything about any murder," Knutson pleaded.

"You're a lawyer. You know, legally, if you're in on the conspiracy, you're guilty of all of it," Sorenson chimed in.

"You've committed enough crimes to spend the rest of your life in prison anyway even without that." Carvelli then leaned toward him and said, "So don't try to act like a babe in the woods. Play it for him."

Sorenson held his phone out and put it right in front of Knutson. He turned on the recording.

"What do you want to do with him?" Knutson heard the voice of Aidan Walsh ask.

"Who? Knutson or the Italian gentleman?" he heard Cal Simpson reply.

"Both," Aidan said.

"Knutson, nothing right now. We'll stay as planned. The other guy. I'll call D.C. and see what I can find out. You check with any sources you have. We need to find out where this is coming from."

Sorenson shut off his phone and returned it to his coat pocket.

Knutson looked nervously back and forth at Carvelli and Sorenson three or four times. His tongue flicked out and he wet his lips. A drop of sweat trickled down the left side of his face.

"That, ah, that doesn't mean anything," he said.

Carvelli looked back at Sorenson who smiled and quietly laughed. He then looked at Knutson and asked, "What do you think they're talking about? They have already murdered two people, Zach Evans and Lynn McDaniel..."

"Can you prove that?" Knutson said.

"Is that what you need?" Sorenson asked. "Proof beyond a reasonable doubt? This isn't a courtroom and these two are not your friends. Aidan Walsh was asking his boss, Cal Simpson, if Cal wanted him to kill you."

"They wouldn't dare, I'm the managing partner of a very important and politically connected law firm. I'm not some street punk," Knutson arrogantly said.

"Really?" Carvelli said. "Play the second part," he told Sorenson.

Using his phone again Sorenson played more of the recording. It was the part where Aidan asked Cal if he wanted him to take care of another problem. Cal affirmed it and told him to make it look natural.

"Someone in your gang of crooks is going to turn up dead in the next few days. An accident or a heart attack," Carvelli said.

"Let me tell you who Cal Simpson and Aidan Walsh really are," Carvelli added.

For the next few minutes, Carvelli told the lawyer a brief history of Cal and Aidan starting with their real names. When he finished, Knutson could barely breathe.

"Yeah," Sorenson said from the backseat. "Your good buddies, your pals that you think are going to take care of you, are long-time gangsters. Between them, they have left a trail of crime and bodies stretching back forty years to Boston and New York."

"You want to wait a few days and see which one of your conspirators turns up dead?" Carvelli asked.

"Could be you," Sorenson said.

Knutson sat silently for a full two minutes. He was trying to think through this situation for some thread he could grasp and cling to. Anything to convince him that what he was just told had nothing to do with him. When the two minutes were up, and nothing occurred to him, he finally, calmly looked at Carvelli.

"What do you want? Can you help me?"

"Atta boy, Brody," Carvelli said as he started the car. "We're going to take a little drive, meet some people and watch a video your pal Del Peterson made for us. Then we'll talk about saving your ass."

Unseen by the three men in Carvelli's car was a woman who was watching them. She had first seen the three of them by Knutson's car. She slipped behind a concrete support pole in the ramp and watched them get in Carvelli's car. She stayed there until Carvelli drove past then continued to her job. The first thing she did was make a phone call about what she had witnessed.

On the way to the hotel, Sorenson made two phone calls; one to Marc and one to Conrad. They went to the same hotel they had used to make the video of Del Peterson's confession, a Hilton on the 494 Strip.

When they arrived, Carvelli obtained adjacent rooms on the tenth floor. Fifteen minutes later, Marc joined them.

As soon as Marc arrived Knutson recognized him and said, "You're a defense lawyer. I want to retain you to represent me. Money is no object."

Knutson was sitting in a chair by the window. Sorenson was on one of the two beds and Carvelli was on the couch. Marc looked down at an obviously stressed out Brody Knutson, smiled and shook his head. He sat down in a chair that matched the one Knutson was in with a small table between them.

"Sorry," Marc replied looking at the scared lawyer. "I have a conflict."

"Which is?" Knutson asked.

"I know you were involved in the murder of my friend and I want you to spend the rest of your life in prison."

"I was not!" Knutson tried to protest. "I want to call a lawyer. I have a right to an attorney."

"You're not under arrest," Marc said. "You have no such right."

"I can leave?" Knutson asked.

"That would be a very bad idea. You're better off staying and hearing what we have to say," Carvelli said.

There was a knock on the door. Dan Sorenson got up and let Conrad in. At that point, Carvelli's phone rang.

"Your plane is on the ground?" he asked. He listened for a moment then said, "Great. I'll meet you out front."

"She's here," Carvelli announced as he headed toward the door.

The airport being less than ten minutes away, Carvelli was back with Paxton in less than half an hour. When they arrived, the others were all watching the T.V. Conrad had hooked up his computer to it and they were watching the interview of Del Peterson. They stopped for a moment, so Paxton could introduce herself to Knutson.

When it was over, Knutson, having regained a bit of confidence, almost scoffed at it. "That proves nothing. Uncorroborated testimony of a co-conspirator."

"The people he named, do you really believe they will all hold up under questioning?" Carvelli asked.

"Rest assured, Mr. Knutson," Paxton said, "we will get corroboration."

She stood up, found the remote for the T.V. and before changing the channel she looked at Knutson and said, "There's news I picked up right after I landed, and I think it's something you should see."

Paxton pointed the remote at the TV and scrolled through the channels until she found CNN. On the screen, next to the female anchor, was a photo of Senator Roger Manion, the self-proclaimed socialist from Maine.

"...was found dead, slumped over his desk this morning. Authorities believe it was caused by natural causes, probably a heart attack that killed him. The senator, a potential candidate for president, was believed to be in good health. This according to staff members who spoke to us this morning. His sudden and untimely death will have a ripple effect through the politics of the U.S. Senate. Again, the big story of the day…"

Paxton shut off the TV and looked at an obviously shaken Brody Knutson.

"I can't tell you how, but we knew somebody, we didn't know who, was on Cal Simpson's short list for an accidental death. Manion was seventy years old and in good health. You think this is a coincidence?" she asked.

"We let him hear the recording before we came here," Carvelli said. "He looked at Knutson and asked, do you believe us now?"

Knutson, a frightened look in his eyes, abruptly stood up and announced, "I'm leaving. You can't hold me here and…"

"We know you intercepted the Cannon Brothers engineer's memo that Zach Evans tried to mail to Mr. Kadella. That got Zach and Lynn McDaniel killed. You are in this up to your ass. And Cal knows you talked to me. If you go running to him now, how long before he decides you're a liability?" Carvelli asked. "You're better off with us."

"I won't go to Cal. I need to talk to a lawyer. I just need some advice. Here," he continued while fumbling around with his wallet. He pulled out a business card and handed it to Paxton. "Here's my card. Call me tomorrow. I swear, I won't go to Cal."

Paxton looked around the room, flicked the card between her fingers shrugged her shoulders and said, "We're not kidnappers." She looked at Knutson and said, "Okay, twenty-four hours. If you're not on board by then, we'll go in a different direction. One way or another, this thing is coming down. Decide which side you want to be on."

When Knutson reached the lobby, he made two calls. The first to Uber for a ride. The second to a well-known criminal defense lawyer he knew; Thad Cheney.

Cheney took his call and told Knutson to come right to his office. After the call, Cheney decided it would be best not to tell Knutson about his representation of the Cannon Brothers and their executive vice president. He then placed a call to his best client, Cal Simpson.

FORTY-FOUR

Brooke Hartley used her pass card to enter the office building's parking ramp. She flipped off the Camry's windshield wipers and a minute later pulled into her reserved spot. One of the perks of putting up with Brody Knutson was free parking in a reserved place in the building. On a day like today, early-autumn, rainy, cool and windy, she especially appreciated it.

As Brooke walked up the concrete ramp, the only sound she heard was the clicking of her heels. She checked her watch, 6:05 A.M., then picked up the pace because she was already late. It was Brooke's day to go into the office early and if Knutson was there, depending on his mood, he could be a jerk about it.

When she arrived at Knutson's private office Brooke was relieved to find the outer door locked. This meant Knutson was not in yet. She entered into the reception area where her and Lucy's desks were located. Brooke hung her trench coat style raincoat on the coat tree, dropped her purse on her desk and headed toward the breakroom. Having set the coffee maker's timer before she left last night she knew there would be a fresh pot waiting for her.

"I need this," she quietly said while pouring herself a cup.

Brooke went back to her desk, put her purse in a drawer and turned her PC on. She began going through the files on her desk and the work she needed to start on. The coffee was perfect, and the cup was three-fourths empty when she started to feel it. At first, she was just a little light headed and a bit woozy. She tried blinking her eyes several times to clear it up which helped a little.

Another thirty to forty seconds went by and the room began to spin. Believing she needed to stand up and try walking, she got out of her chair, took two short steps then collapsed to the floor.

Lucy Gibson arrived at work at 7:30, a half-hour early. She immediately noticed Brooke's raincoat hanging on the coat rack. Listening to the silence in the office, she wondered where Brooke could have gone. Lucy hung up her coat next to Brooke's, dropped her purse on her desk and went into the breakroom. In need of a shot of caffeine, she was disappointed to find the empty pot placed on the counter. Thinking this was a bit odd since she knew Brooke set it up the night before, a tiny warning bell sounded in the back of her head.

Believing she had heard a noise, Lucy went to check on Knutson. She put her ear to the door to listen for a moment. There was no sound coming from his office, which was a bit unusual. As the managing partner of a large law firm, Knutson spent a lot of time on the phone. Even this early he would normally be at it.

She opened his door, took a small step inside the large office and fought back a scream. Lying on the floor were the bodies of Brody Knutson and Brooke Hartley.

Lucy put a hand to her mouth and bit down on the knuckle. She looked at Brody who was obviously dead. He was white as a sheet and the ivory-handled letter opener that he kept on his desk was sticking out of his chest, his white dress shirt half-covered with blood.

A terrified Lucy then looked at Brooke again and stared at her. It took a few seconds before she realized Brooke was still breathing. She took the two steps toward her, dropped to her knees and felt Brooke's neck. She not only had a pulse, but it was steady and regular.

"Brooke, Brooke, come on, wake up," Lucy desperately said as she shook her and rolled her onto her back.

Brooke's head rolled a bit, her eyelids fluttered, and she made a groaning sound.

Lucy quickly jumped up and dashed back out to her desk. Using her office phone, she dialed 911. As calmly as she could, Lucy told the operator who she was and what she had found.

Lt. Owen Jefferson forced his way through the mob in the hall outside Knutson's office. Several Everson, Reed lawyers tried to get a little cocky with him until he shoved his lieutenant's shield in their faces. Without another word, the crowd parted, and he strolled past them. When he reached the entryway door to Knutson's office, he stopped and turned to face them. Holding up both hands, his shield in his left hand, he demanded and got silence.

"This is a crime scene and I am the officer in charge. I want this hallway cleared, now! There's nothing for you to see or do. Go back to where you belong."

"We have a right to know..." an older, female lawyer standing directly in front of Jefferson started to demand.

"You have a right to know nothing at this point," Jefferson calmly replied.

"I am the vice managing partner of this law firm..." she tried to say.

"And if you interfere again, I'll have you arrested," Jefferson said staring down at her.

He looked at the mob who were still milling about like sheep, uncertain what to do. "Go back to where you belong, or I will have some officers get out their handcuffs." That did it. In less than a minute, the hallway was empty except for the uniformed cops.

Jefferson went through the open, exterior, double doors and into the work area.

"That must have been fun," Marcie Sterling, a female detective and his former partner said, "Telling a bunch of lawyers you were going to arrest them. That had to feel good."

"It does give me a warm, fuzzy glow," Jefferson admitted. "What are you doing here?"

"Helping out," Marcie replied.

"And Hunt is okay with this?" Jefferson asked. He was referring to Gabe Hunt, the homicide detective who had caught the case. Hunt was not known as someone who got along well with people, especially other cops.

"I'm keeping my distance. It's his case. I won't get in the way," Marcie answered her boss, friend and one-time mentor.

Gabe Hunt had been inside the inner office where Knutson's body was still lying on the floor. Two crime scene techs were also in there taking pictures and looking for evidence. Hunt turned his head, saw Jefferson and joined him and Marcie. A young, newly minted detective, Darian Clark, also stepped over to them. He had been keeping an eye on Brooke who was at her desk. Lucy Gibson was sitting in one of the client chairs away from Brooke. Jefferson led them all into the hallway where they could have some privacy.

"The one secretary, the brunette, Brooke Hartley, did it," Hunt said. "She came in early, found the victim in his office and stuck a letter opener in his chest. Looks like he tried to fight her off. There's a bruise on the left side of her face where he punched her. The only thing we don't know is why."

"Well, that wraps that up," Marcie said.

"Hey, screw you, Sterling," Hunt snarled. "The evidence is pretty obvious."

"Have you talked to her? Brooke Hartley?" Jefferson asked.

"I was about to, the other one, the blonde in the other chair, her name is Lucy..." he paused to check his notes when Darian said, "Gibson."

"Yeah, Gibson," Hunt agreed. "Go back in there and keep an eye on them," he ordered Darian, annoyed at being corrected.

"Anyway, she's the one that found them. She came in and found them around seven thirty," Hunt said.

Jefferson motioned to a young man in a tweed sports coat standing around with his hands in his pockets. He quickly joined the conversation.

"Morning, Doctor," Jefferson said to the assistant medical examiner. "Can you give us a time of death?"

"Between five-thirty and six-thirty," the doctor replied.

"So, let's say it was closer to six-thirty," Jefferson said. "The victim punches her in the side of the face while she's stabbing him. He knocks her out cold until she's found an hour later," Jefferson said.

"There's no evidence of anything else. No evidence anyone else was here," Hunt said defensively. "She's not a big girl. Guys fighting for his life, yeah, he could hit her that hard."

"I'll admit, it's at least a good theory," Marcie said. "Unless he finds something else."

"Wow, thanks," Hunt said mocking her.

"Must you always be an asshole?" Marcie asked.

Before Hunt could reply Jefferson put up a hand to stop him.

A minute later, back in the office, Brooke said to Hunt, "I want to make a phone call." Hunt, Jefferson and Marcie were all standing in front of Brooke's desk.

"You can make a call from our office," Hunt said.

"Am I under arrest?" Brooke asked.

"Ah, no, not yet," Hunt replied.

"Then I'm going to make a phone call now and I'm going to use my phone," Brooke said.

"I said, you can make it…" Hunt started to say.

"Where's your phone?" Jefferson asked.

"In my desk drawer in my purse," she replied.

"Find it for her," Jefferson told Marcie.

Marcie quickly found the purse and phone and gave it to Brooke. As she scrolled through its directory, Brooke said to Jefferson, "I would like some privacy please."

"Of course," Jefferson replied.

"What else can we do for you," an obviously steaming Gabe Hunt said as he walked away.

Brooke found the number, dialed it, and waited. It was answered on the sixth ring.

"Hullo," she heard a man groggily say. He cleared his throat, then more clearly said, "Hello, Brooke. What's up?" Tony Carvelli said.

"Were you asleep?" Brooke asked.

"Well, ah, yeah," Carvelli replied. "What time is it?"

"Almost nine. I'm sorry I woke you, but I think I'm in a lot of trouble. I think I need a lawyer and I don't have your friend's number."

"Tell me what's going on?" Carvelli asked as he slipped on a pair of sweatpants.

As quietly as she could, she quickly told him what she knew and what was happening.

"Jesus, what the hell happened?" Carvelli asked when she finished.

"Tony, I don't know," she whispered. "I don't remember anything. The cops are going to take me in for questioning. I'm really scared. Please…"

"Who's in charge there? Who's the cop that's in charge?" Carvelli asked.

"There's a tall, black man who seems to be in charge," Brooke replied.

"Ask him if his name is Owen?"

Brooke did that and on the phone told Carvelli it was.

"Give him your phone. It's okay. Let me talk to him," Carvelli said.

"He wants to talk to you," Brooke said holding the phone out to him.

"Lt. Jefferson," he said into the phone. "Who am I…?"

"It's Tony Carvelli, Owen," Carvelli said.

"What the hell…?"

"It's a long story. Listen, she is going to retain counsel, Marc Kadella. I'm calling him as soon as we're done talking. You know him. He will tell you no one talks to her without him being present. We'll both be there in a half-hour. Are we good?"

"Yeah, that's fine. We'll wait with her here at the crime scene. I assume she told you what happened."

"Yeah, she did. Thanks, Owen. I owe you one."

"You owe me more than one, you reprobate," Jefferson said.

"Let me talk to her again," Carvelli said. "I'll see you in a little bit."

Jefferson handed the phone back to Brooke.

"Okay, I'll call Marc, and we'll be there as soon as possible. Until then, talk to no one and I do mean no one. We'll be along. You'll be all right."

"Okay, please hurry and thanks," she said.

FORTY-FIVE

Marc and Carvelli stepped off the elevator and looked both ways down the hall. Seeing the uniformed officers, they turned left and walked down to Knutson's large, corner office. They were stopped at the exterior double doors by one of the cops. While Carvelli stuck his head inside to get Jefferson, Marc looked back toward the elevators. There were a half a dozen older lawyers, probably Everson, Reed senior partners with offices on this floor, standing in the hallway. Marc waved at them as Carvelli took his arm to bring him inside.

While shaking hands with Jefferson, Marc looked over at the other plainclothes officers.

"We could form a band," Marc said, "The Trench Coats."

"That kind of weather," Jefferson said.

"It'll be snowing soon," Marc replied.

"Shut up," Marcie facetiously said. "We don't need to talk like that yet."

"Sorry, you're right," Marc smiled. "Is my client under arrest?" he asked Jefferson.

"Not yet," Gabe Hunt answered.

Marc looked at Hunt then said, "That means no. Then we're leaving."

Marc had come across Hunt a couple of times before when Hunt was in Burglary. They were not pleasant experiences.

"Maybe I will arrest her," Hunt said.

"I'm not going to play your childish game of 'mine's bigger than yours', Detective," Marc said. He turned to Jefferson and calmly asked again, "Is she under arrest?"

"No," Jefferson admitted. "Please keep her available."

"Get out of there, Carvelli," Hunt loudly said.

Carvelli was standing in the doorway of Knutson's inner office watching the crime scene techs work. Knutson's body was still lying there and one of the techs was taking blood samples from the carpet.

Carvelli turned his head to Hunt and said, "I'm not in there, dipshit."

"I'm confiscating your client's phone," Hunt angrily said.

"No, you're not," Marc calmly replied. "We'll preserve it and if it becomes evidence, we'll surrender it when appropriate.

"Tony, help Ms. Hartley, please. We're leaving," Marc said. He handed two of his business cards to Owen Jefferson then said, "Marcie, nice to see you again. Owen, call anytime. If you decide to serve an arrest warrant on my client, I would appreciate a call. I'll surrender her myself.

That way Gestapo Gabe here won't have to kick in someone's door at four o'clock in the morning."

Marc looked at Hunt, who was starting to protest, then Marc said, "You're getting too old for that kind of behavior anyway."

"Tony's working for me on your case," Marc said to Brooke. "Because of that, he is covered by attorney-client privilege exactly the same as I am. You can speak freely with him in the room."

The three of them were at Marc's office in the conference room. They had all driven there separately, so there had been no conversation between them.

"I know and thanks," Brooke said.

"How are you feeling?" Carvelli asked.

"My headache's gone. I took some ibuprofen and that cleared it up," Brooke replied.

"How's your cheek and jaw?" Marc asked.

"Hurts like hell. It feels like somebody punched me. How does the bruise look?"

"Not bad, but don't worry, give it a day or two, and it will look a lot worse," Carvelli said.

"Great, thanks," Brooke replied.

"What happened?" Marc asked. "Start at the beginning when you first arrived at work."

"I don't remember!" she said almost pleading. "If I did it, I don't remember how or why…"

"Stop," Marc quietly said. "Start at the beginning. Tell us what you do remember."

Brooke took a deep breath, calmed herself and started over.

"Okay, I remember driving into the ramp and parking. It was raining real hard. I took the elevator up just like every day. I hung up my coat and put my purse on the desk. I set the timer on the coffeemaker the night before…"

"Are you sure?" Carvelli asked.

"I think so, yes. Actually, now that I think about it I definitely remember it because Lucy reminded me before we left. And I stopped and listened at Mr. Knutson's door for any noise that he might be in."

"Did you hear anything?" Marc asked.

"No, it was very quiet. Okay, so, I went into the breakroom and poured myself a cup of coffee. I remember it because I woke up a little late and had to hurry. I didn't have time for any at home."

"Okay," Marc said to encourage her to continue.

"And," she said and paused. "And that's it. That's all I remember. Except when I was sitting at my desk while the police were there, I

230

noticed a cup on my desk with about an inch of coffee still in it. I remember it because I remember thinking I must have drunk some."

"How many cups did you have?" Carvelli asked.

"I don't remember, why? Why is that important? I might have killed Brody Knutson..." she said becoming visibly upset. There were genuine tears in her eyes, and her lips trembled.

"I think it is important," Tony said. He looked at Marc and said, "I stuck my head in the breakroom. One of the things I noticed was the coffee pot on the counter. It was empty and looked like someone had rinsed it out. And I remember seeing the cup on your desk. There was coffee in it. But there was no ring around the inside of the cup. If you leave a cup with coffee in it all night, there will be a ring around the inside the next day. The coffee in your cup was fresh."

"How did you notice that?" Brooke asked.

"I noticed a lot of things when I looked around," Carvelli said. "Based on your memory loss, you might have been drugged. If that's true, someone else was in that office, drained the pot and cleaned it out."

"We need to get her blood and urine tested right away," Marc said. "Let me call Nate Lockhart and see if he's available."

A couple of minutes later Marc ended the call. He looked at Carvelli and said, "Okay, why don't you get her to him now. Then come back, and we'll finish up. Don't worry about the bill, he'll bill me."

"What about your bill? I have some money but..."

"Look, I feel like we got you into this and..."

"I'm a big girl. I knew what I was doing," she said.

"Don't worry about my bill. Just go with Tony. We'll take this one step at a time."

Less than an hour later they were back. During the time they were gone, Marc had received a phone call from Owen Jefferson.

"How did you come to be fingerprinted?" Marc asked when they were again seated in the conference room.

"What? I don't know," Brooke said.

"You've never been fingerprinted? They have your prints in the system."

"Oh! That's right. I was once, I'd forgotten. Back when I was in college a bunch of us were protesting about something, I don't even remember what. About a dozen of us were arrested and taken to the police department. We were fingerprinted, photographed and put in cells. I think they did it just to scare us. It worked, too. They didn't even charge us. They let us go after a few hours with just a warning."

Marc looked at Carvelli and said, "I didn't think prints were supposed to go into the system if charges aren't made."

"Yeah, I've heard that, too," Carvelli said. "I think there are cops that abide by it. Technically, they arrested her. That's probably enough, why?"

"Jefferson called while you were gone," Marc started to say.

"They found her prints on the knife sticking out of Knutson's chest," Carvelli said.

"It's a letter opener," Marc replied.

"You mean I did it?"

"No," Marc and Tony said together.

"That does not mean you did it," Marc said. "Your memory loss needs to be accounted for. If you were drugged then ..."

"We'll see," Carvelli said. "Does Owen want you to surrender her?"

"Yeah, he does," Marc replied.

"Oh, my god," Brooke said. "What did I do?"

"I want to hear the rest of your story," Marc said.

"I don't think you did anything. I think there was someone else in that office waiting for you. Brody Knutson, the little twerp that he was, couldn't knock out a four-year-old. I'm not buying that for a minute," Carvelli said.

"Good point," Marc agreed. "Now, let's hear the rest."

"And that's it. I don't remember anything until I found myself sitting at my desk. Lucy said she found me on the floor in Knutson's office. She woke me up, got me on my feet and helped me out to sit down. It was Lucy who called the police. The next thing I know there was this mean detective in my face trying to get me to tell him why I killed my boss. I've been around lawyers long enough to know not to say anything even though I wasn't thinking too clearly."

"Do you know where the letter opener came from?" Marc asked.

"Was it an ivory-handled expensive thing?" Brooke asked.

"Yeah," Carvelli replied. "Could be. I saw it and it had a white handle. Could've been ivory."

"Then it came from Knutson's desk. He had it on his desk. He fiddled around with it while he was on the phone all the time. He liked to brag about. He said it was an antique that a U.S. Senator gave him as a gift," Brooke said.

"Did you ever have occasion to handle it?" Marc asked.

"All the time. Lucy, too. If we straightened out his office, we handled a lot of things on his desk. I never thought anything of it."

There was a knock on the door and Carolyn stuck her head in. "Owen Jefferson is on the phone, again."

"I'll take it in here," Marc said. He picked up the phone on the credenza in the conference room and answered the call.

"We're on the way," Marc said.

"Gabe Hunt is outside my office pacing like a madman."

"Too bad," Marc said. "We'll be there in twenty minutes." He hung up the phone and turned to his client.

"Do I have to go to jail?" Brooke asked a look of fear in her eyes.

"Yes," Marc quietly said. "You'll be arraigned tomorrow. We'll try to get bail set."

"You mean they won't give me bail? I won't be out before trial?"

"Let's take it one step at a time. You'll be okay. They'll put you in segregation for tonight," Marc said.

"Oh god, what a nightmare," she said.

"The cops might put someone in your cell to try to get you to talk. Speak to no one," Carvelli said.

Brooke took a deep breath, exhaled and said, "Okay, let's go."

"Give me your keys. I'll go to your apartment with Maddy and get some things for you for tomorrow including a change of clothes and I'll take care of your car," Carvelli said as they started to leave.

FORTY-SIX

Maddy Rivers drove out of the underground ramp of her building and onto LaSalle. She turned right toward downtown and stopped at the red light barely fifty feet from the ramp's exit. Early morning rush hour traffic was just reaching its peak as she waited for the light on Twelfth. A car pulled up behind her but not the one she expected. Maddy looked in her side view mirror and smiled. She could see the car third in line behind her and its driver. He was the same man who had followed her home from Cal's the night before.

"Long night for you," she quietly said to herself.

It had been decided that she could not keep losing the tail Cal put on her forever. Last night she allowed Cal's thug to stay with her and led him to her condo building. Two retired MPD cops had followed Maddy's tail and had taken turns keeping an eye on him. So far, nothing had happened. She was easily able to slip out for a while and meet up with Carvelli. They went to Brooke's apartment then Marc's office.

It was also decided that Maddy should take him to her office job. Or at least one that had been set up for her. Marc knew a small firm of lawyers in a downtown building. They agreed to provide Maddy with a cover by letting her show up and pretend she worked there. Now all she had to do was let Cal's thug follow her there. The ruse would likely hold up, at least for a while.

While Maddy was being followed to 'work', Cal was enjoying a light breakfast at home. Aidan entered the dining room area and before he could sit down, Cal silently handed him a page of notepaper. Cal had written a brief note telling Aidan to gather the listening devices and destroy them. Fifteen minutes later Aidan was back with the news the 'bugs' were in Lake Minnetonka.

"Good, I was tired of working around them. Whoever's listening probably knows by now we found them anyway," Cal replied. "We need to find out who the hell this is."

"Sooner or later, this guy will show his hand," Aidan said. "That chick's arraignment for Knutson is this morning. I got Phil going to sit in and watch."

"Nothing will happen," Cal said placing his coffee cup on the saucer. "She'll plead not guilty and they'll argue about bail. We'll see if she gets it."

Aidan's phone rang, and he took the call. He listened to a brief report then said, "Okay, get out of there. Go home. I'll call you later."

Aidan ended the call and said, "They found the lesbian."

"Already? That was quick," Cal replied.

Aidan shrugged, sipped his coffee and said, "Some woman, probably another lesbian friend, stopped by. She had a key and let herself in. Ten minutes later the place was crawling with EMT's and cops."

Aidan's phone went off again. He answered it and listened to the caller, again. This time Aidan picked up the pad of notepaper and a pen from next to Cal. While he listened, he jotted down several notes.

"You checked that already?" Cal heard him ask the caller.

"All right, get some sleep." He turned to Cal and said, "That was Dooley. He followed Maddy to the Grain Exchange Building. It's on Fourth Street a couple of blocks from the government center. He followed her up to the sixth floor and saw her go in a law office.

"He then casually walked by like he was looking for an office and saw her taking her coat off at the receptionist's desk. He said there were about a dozen names listed on the door as lawyers. She was not one of them. He even called the attorney registration place for the state. They don't have her as a lawyer."

"She's a receptionist? She's better than that," Cal said.

"A receptionist for a firm that size would do a lot more than just answer phones," Aidan replied.

"Yes, that's true. Plus, she'd make a damn good first impression on clients," Cal agreed. "So, she's legit or at least it appears she is."

"You want to keep following her? Now that we know where she lives and works, she's not with the cops or the feds," Aidan asked.

Cal thought it over for a moment then said, "Yeah, stay on it for another couple of days."

"Okay, boss," Aidan answered.

"Good morning," the two of them heard a familiar voice say from the room's entryway.

"Good morning, Thad, how are you?" Cal replied.

"Good, Cal," the lawyer replied. "And you?"

"Never better," Cal said as he poured coffee for his guest.

"Here, Mr. Cheney, take my chair," Aidan said. He then walked around the table to the opposite side.

"Thanks, Cal," Cheney said. He took a swallow of the coffee then the ever paranoid and careful lawyer asked Aidan, "Has this room been swept for bugs?"

"Yesterday," Aidan answered.

Cheney looked at Cal and said, "Good news. It seems the sudden demise of Brody Knutson has rattled my clients. For some reason, and I did not disavow them of this notion, all three of them think you had something to do with it. At any rate, I have convinced them that their best legal strategy is to keep their mouths shut. Obviously, this indictment is a sham. It is precisely what I told you. The prosecution is trying to get one or all of them to cooperate."

Cal was looking at the lawyer's neck when he said, "Who wears a three-piece suit with a purple bowtie?"

Cheney laughed and said, "It sets me apart from the rest of the legal herd."

"So, you're sure they'll keep their mouths shut?" Cal asked.

"Yes. The prosecution has no case. We'll ride this out. No problem. Except…" he said and paused.

"Except?" Cal asked.

"Well, the woman, Marissa Duggins, I'm not totally positive about her."

"She'll no longer be needing your services," Cal informed him.

"How do you…"

"It seems she committed suicide last night. A tragic death by an overdose of barbiturates and vodka," Aidan replied. "Sleeping pills. The cops will find an empty pill bottle on her nightstand for a legitimate prescription. The vodka was her drink of choice."

"Cal, I didn't sign on…"

"Relax, Thad. I like you. I know what a crook you are," Cal said. He tossed a thick envelope in front of the lawyer. "Here's a little tip: make sure you get legitimate money from Dane Cannon," Cal said.

Cheney picked up the envelope and looked inside. There was twenty-thousand dollars in used one-hundred-dollar bills in it. The portly lawyer stuffed the envelope in his inside suit coat pocket and said, "Always nice to do business with you. I'm also sure the sudden tragedy of Ms. Duggins' death will also motivate my clients to maintain their silence."

Cal picked up the page of notepaper Aidan had written on and looked at it.

"What do you know about these lawyers, Godfrey and Stanton?" he asked Cheney.

"They're an insurance defense firm. They do exclusively work comp insurance defense. Why?" Cheney replied.

"Just wondering," Cal said. "Would they have any reason to be interested in me?"

A puzzled Cheney said, "I can't see what interest they might have in you. I know one of the partners. I went to law school with him. Unless you have a work comp case, I don't see any connection."

Cal looked at Aidan and said, "Sounds legit. What do you think?"

"Probably okay. So, she has a job. So what?" Aidan replied.

"How much would a legal secretary-receptionist make?" Cal asked Cheney.

"Depends on the firm. A good one could easily make seventy, eighty grand. Why?"

"Just checking on somebody," Cal replied. He said to Aidan, "Sharp girl. I'll bet she is good."

"Probably," Aidan agreed. "We'll give it another couple days."

The object of their attention, Maddy Rivers, knocked on the office door of Marc's friend. She heard him say, "Come in" and went inside.

"Hi, Rob," she said. "I'm taking off now. You guys will cover for me if someone comes looking for me or calls?"

"Sure, everyone knows. Hell, this is the most excitement we've had around here since, I don't know, probably ever," Rob replied. "Are you okay?"

"I'm good. I think only a couple more days should do it," Maddy said.

"Stay as long as you want," she heard a voice from behind said.

Maddy turned and saw the senior partner, Mike Stanton in the doorway. An older distinguished looking, silver-haired man was smiling at her.

"Rob's right, this mystery is the most interesting thing we've had around here. Which tells you how boring we are."

"Do criminal defense work," Maddy said. "You'll meet some interesting clients then."

"We're not that desperate," Rob said.

"Or bored," Stanton added.

Maddy flashed them both a smile and politely exited.

"We got a problem," Maddy heard Carvelli say through her phone.

While she was pretending to be a secretary, Maddy got a call from Carvelli. She let it go to voicemail and returned the call when she got to her car.

"What?"

"Conrad went to Vivian's this morning to check the recordings. While he was there, all four bugs went dead. He thinks they tossed them into the lake."

"We knew they probably found them. We weren't getting anything anyway," Maddy said.

"I know. I called Paxton and told her. We're kind of stuck on stupid right now. We need more evidence. With Knutson dead, I'm not sure where we go."

"We need to flip the Cannon Brothers," Maddy said.

"That's another thing," Carvelli said. He quickly told her about the news of Marissa Duggins' suicide.

"How did you find that out?"

"Steve Gondeck saw Marc in court this morning with Brooke. He told Marc, Marc called me. Gondeck says it looks like a legitimate suicide."

"What happened with Brooke?"

"I don't know," Carvelli said. "The court had not called them when Marc called me. I'm heading out to Vivian's now."

"I'll meet you there," Maddy said.

"Oh, sorry, I almost forgot. One more bit of bad news. Brooke's drug tests came back negative. They didn't find anything."

"Oh, boy," Maddy quietly said. "That's not good. Now what?"

"No, it's not good," Carvelli agreed. "I don't know what now. We'll see. I'll meet you at Vivian's."

FORTY-SEVEN

The murder of a prominent attorney—especially by his secretary—drew a lot of media attention. The local TV talking heads were already speculating that there must be a sex angle in this somewhere.

Normally the felony arraignment courtroom gallery had a few lawyers looking for clients and anxious relatives ready to make bail. This morning, there were also a dozen media members in attendance. There were no cameras, microphones or recording equipment which actually made it better. What all any of them really wanted was a salacious tidbit to embellish into a sex scandal. They were going to leave disappointed. More than a few of them were undeterred. Since there was no recording allowed they could let loose their inner fiction writer and simply make up whatever they wanted.

Judge Martin Eason, a judge Marc knew fairly well, was handling arraignments. His clerk had warned him about the crowd in his courtroom and why the media was in attendance. Wanting to get rid of them as quickly as possible, the judge told her to call Brooke's case first.

Brooke was led in and stood to Marc's left directly in front of the judge. Judge Eason looked at Marc's head and the walking boot on his still-healing leg. Knowing about the hit and run Eason quietly asked, "How are you doing, Marc?"

"Fine, your Honor. Thanks for asking," Marc replied.

Marc waived reading of the charges, which at this point, was second-degree murder. The prosecutor, a young lawyer who Marc had just met and could not remember his name, informed the court that certain discovery formalities had been done. He also told Eason that the case was going to be presented to a grand jury for a first-degree indictment.

"That isn't going to happen, your Honor," Marc interjected. He said this as a preemptive strike to get bail. "They have nothing to present to make a case that this was premeditated. In fact, they have no evidence that my client did this at all. I am going to bring a motion for an evidentiary hearing at the omnibus hearing. I firmly believe this case will never make it to trial."

"Apparently, Mr. Kadella is starting his bail argument," the wily-old judge said. "What about that, Mr. Clark? Are you going to prove premeditation?"

"Well, um, your Honor," the prosecutor said, "I was told to argue against bail. She clearly stabbed the victim with malice aforethought and…"

"I don't think I've heard that phrase since law school," Eason said. "I've read the complaint and am setting bail at one-million dollars. You tell Steve Gondeck… wait, never mind, I see him hiding out in back. Mr. Gondeck, please join us."

All eyes in the courtroom turned toward the back as the head of the prosecution's felony division came forward.

"As I was about to tell your young associate here, I'm setting bail at…"

"Your honor, this is very serious…" Gondeck started to say.

"Be quiet and don't interrupt," Eason sternly said.

An embarrassed Gondeck clamped his lips together while Marc suppressed a smile.

"I'm setting bail at one-million dollars, cash or bond. The defendant will surrender her passport."

"Your Honor, if I may?" Gondeck said. "An ankle bracelet to monitor her movements?"

"Denied," Eason said. "If you get a first-degree indictment, we'll reconsider bail then. Anything else?"

"No, your Honor," both Marc and the young prosecutor said.

Eason covered his microphone, leaned forward and said, "Steve," and indicated Gondeck should get right up to the bench. Marc did the same.

"What were you thinking about sending this kid to argue bail in a homicide case?"

"He has to learn sometime," Gondeck replied.

"Don't do it again. You embarrassed him," Eason said with a little smile.

Before leaving and while waiting for the media to trample out and chase down Gondeck, Marc took a moment with Brooke.

"I don't have a million dollars," she said almost pleading.

"Ssssh, let me see what I can do. I know someone. Go on back and I'll be back before noon to see you. Trust me, okay?"

"Do I have a choice?"

"Good point. No, not really. Go on, I'll be back later this morning," Marc said. He squeezed her hand and she slightly smiled. Marc watched the guards take her away while the next case was called.

As he turned to leave Marc saw a female reporter with Channel 8 waiting for him at the exit doors. As he walked down the room's center aisle toward her, knowing what she wanted he thought, *this might be a good idea.*

"Hi, Marc," she said when he got to her.

"Let's go in the hall, Terry," Marc said.

240

When they were outside the courtroom, Marc said, "Tell Gabriella to call me. I'll find time to come on the show."

"Really? How did you know…?"

"I know you're one of the reporters who works with her. Tell her to give me a call. We'll set it up."

"Thanks, Marc. That was easy," the reporter said.

On the elevator ride down to the government center's second floor, Marc checked his phone for messages. There was a text from Maddy telling him that she and Carvelli were at Vivian's and he should join them. At the end was a one-word question: Bail? Believing this was probably an inquiry from Vivian, he hurried to his car to see her.

One of the household staff opened the door for Marc and offered to escort him to the library. Being a semi-regular guest, he knew where it was and let the young woman go.

"How did it go?" Maddy asked when Marc entered the room.

Inside he found Vivian, Maddy, Carvelli, and Conrad waiting for him.

"Okay, Eason set bail at a million dollars. I had the pleasure of seeing Steve Gondeck get his butt bitten by a judge. That's always fun when it's someone else."

"Will they need some form of certified funds?" Vivian asked.

"It can be wired in and thank you, Vivian," Marc answered.

"From what Anthony told me, we, meaning he, got this young woman into this. We're going to help her get out of it," Vivian said.

Marc pulled a sheet of paper from his leather-satchel briefcase and gave it to her.

"The wiring instructions are on this," he said. He handed her another sheet of paper and continued as he pointed at a number on the second sheet.

"This is the court case number. Your bank will need to put that and the case name, the State of Minnesota versus Brooke Hartley, on it."

"I'll take care of it," Vivian said then went to a desk across the room.

"Did you tell her about the negative drug test?" Carvelli asked.

"Yeah, she has no idea. She still claims a complete blackout during the time of death," Marc said.

"Her fingerprints are on the murder weapon?" Maddy asked.

"Yeah, but I think that actually helps us. They found no other prints on the handle and an almost perfect set of fingerprints. What are the odds?"

"Zero," Carvelli said. "Unless they get evidence that Knutson's office and the letter opener were cleaned the night before."

Marc thought about this for a moment, then said, "Thanks for killing that idea. I'll talk to Brooke about it."

"Thank you very much and please hurry," they heard Vivian say.

"Done," she said to the others.

"Tell him, Conrad," Carvelli said.

"The bugs are gone," Conrad said.

"Yeah, I know. Maddy told me in her text. Any ideas what we do now?" Marc asked.

The room went silent for a moment then Marc asked Maddy, "Did they follow you this morning?"

"Yeah, they did. Right to the door. I waited until I got the call from Tony's guys that the tail had left before I did. I called Rob a little while ago. No one has called or come looking for me," Maddy said.

"You think they bought it?" Marc asked Carvelli.

"We'll see," Carvelli said. "My guys have her covered."

"Good," Marc said. He then asked again, "So, now, what do we do? How do we corroborate what Del Peterson told us?"

"His videotaped confession isn't enough to take to a grand jury?" Vivian asked.

"Paxton doesn't even have permission to work on this, let alone take it to a grand jury. She says her boss is adamant about not pursuing Cal Simpson. With only Peterson's video..." Marc stopped and sat silently for a moment thinking about something, staring at nothing.

"Which begs the question: Why? Why doesn't her boss want her pursuing Simpson?" Marc quietly said as if talking to himself.

"Paxton says it's because it is not in their jurisdiction and she has plenty of other cases to work," Maddy said.

Marc looked at Maddy, nodded his head and said, "Yeah, maybe that's all there is to it. Something's been bugging me, though. Remember when Tony first approached Knutson at the Minneapolis Club? Brody ran right to Cal. Then we picked up from the bugs Cal and Aidan talking. Aidan was going to check with people he knew, probably crooks and gangsters. Cal said he was going to call D.C. —that's Washington—and check with someone. Remember? They thought Tony was Mafia. They were trying to find out if the Mafia was on to them. Who in the government might know?"

"Justice and the FBI," Maddy answered him.

"Right. Then a while later, someone named Mason called him back. Remember? Didn't he specifically say, 'Thanks for calling back,' when this guy Mason called him."

"So, you think Mason is someone in the government and is a friend of Cal's?" Carvelli asked.

"I think we need to find out who this Mason guy is. It's not a very common name. We should be able to find him," Marc said. "Tony, have Paul start a search for a Mason in the government. Start with the DOJ and FBI.

"Maddy, give Paxton a call, and see if she knows anyone."

Marc looked at his watch and said, "I should go. I'll see if the bail money is in. Thanks again for that, Vivian."

"I'm not worried about it. I'll get it back," she replied..

FORTY-EIGHT

Tony Carvelli took the back stairs to Marc's office two at a time. For a man in his fifties—even compared to most American men in their twenties—Carvelli was in excellent shape. The impressive fact regarding his physical condition was that he did next to nothing for it. He ignored his bad diet and spent zero time in the gym. Yet his waist size was the same as when he was in his twenties and running up the back stairs had no effect on his breathing. Likely due to his one concession to healthy living having given up smoking many years ago.

Once inside the law offices, he greeted everyone, especially the secretaries, with his usual banter. Happy to see him, as always, they gave it right back to him. He nodded toward Marc's closed office door and looked at Carolyn who told him Marc was on a phone call.

"Take your chances," Carolyn said when Carvelli silently pointed at Connie's door.

He knocked on Connie's door and without waiting for a response, opened it just wide enough to stick his head in.

"Hello, beautiful," he smiled and said.

"Well, hello, Mr. Charm," Connie replied. "To what do we owe the pleasure?"

Carvelli stepped inside, closed the door and took one of the client chairs, then said, "I need to see Marc."

"Have you found this Mason person?" Connie asked.

"Person? When did you become so PC?" he asked.

"Screw you; I'm not. Mason is also a girl's name, dummy," she replied.

"It is? Damn, I hadn't thought of that," he said, a thoughtful look on his face. "Although, I'm not sure it matters. But to answer your question, no, not yet. I've been meaning to ask you, if you don't mind..."

"And if I do mind, you'll ask anyway," Connie said.

"True, but you might not tell me. How's the stockholder's suit going?"

"Oh, I don't know," Connie sighed. She reached into her middle desk drawer and removed a cigarette and a lighter. She pushed her chair back to the window behind her desk, opened it and lit up. After blowing a stream of smoke through the window, Connie continued.

"We'll be able to get most of their initial investment back but none of the gains they should have received. I've been trying to get the feds involved, but they're not interested."

"Why? This should be their deal."

"I know. I've talked to Paxton about it and she's getting stonewalled on her end, too. Too many heavyweight politicians involved. A lot of small investors are getting hosed and they don't seem to care," Connie told him.

"This can't be an isolated thing. This kind of insider trading and stock manipulation..."

"Goes on all the time," Connie finished the thought for Carvelli. "Money, politicians, power, and more money. How do these people enter Congress penniless and leave multimillionaires? They get to make the rules."

"How many times do I have to tell you?" they heard Marc ask. "There's no smoking in Minnesota. Smoking in Minnesota is the only crime punishable by death," he said as he closed the door and sat down.

"Yeah, yeah, screw you, Mr. Health Nut," Connie said.

Ignoring Connie's comment, Marc asked Carvelli, "What did Paul find out about this Mason guy?"

"Could be a girl," Connie said.

"Okay, guy or girl," Marc replied.

"The name, Mason, is not as uncommon as we thought. There are almost a thousand of them working for the federal government," Carvelli answered. "He narrowed it down to the FBI and DOJ and even there, came up with a list of thirty-two just in the D.C. area."

"Okay, that's a workable number at least. Now what?" Marc asked.

"I saw my guy..."

"Paul," Marc said.

"... this morning. Barely an hour ago. He'd been up all night and needed some sleep. Later he'll start going through them individually to find any connection to Cal Simpson or Aidan Walsh or any of the aliases we've come up with. It will take some time, but if it's there, he'll find it."

"How's our girl?" Connie asked.

"Maddy's fine. They are still on her, but it's getting looser, I think they bought into the job cover," Carvelli said.

"I got a call from Rob this morning. My friend at the firm. They have a couple calls for her. No messages but they covered for her," Marc told them.

Carvelli handed Marc a small brown paper bag with two items in it. One was a small Tupperware-like container with a brown liquid in it. The other was an unwashed, empty coffee cup.

"What?" Marc asked holding the item up.

"The coffee cup and what was left in it on Brooke's desk the morning Knutson was murdered," Carvelli answered.

"You broke into a crime scene and stole this?" Marc asked.

"Well, um, that's a harsh way of looking at it," Carvelli replied feigning hurt feelings. "I would say we gathered evidence for analysis."

"That does sound better," Connie said.

"Thank you," Carvelli told her. "See," he continued, looking at Marc, "I have an experienced officer of the court who agrees with me."

"I didn't say I agreed with you," Connie replied.

"Minor detail," Carvelli replied waving his hand at her. Carvelli took a slip of paper out of a pocket and gave it to Marc.

"Chain of custody sheet," he said. "I signed and gave it to you. You sign and get it to a lab unless you want me to."

Marc put the two items back in the bag and handed it back to him. "Yeah, go ahead. We need to find out what she was drugged with."

"There are drugs, date rape drugs, derivatives of roofies and new things that are out there that the body would metabolize very quickly. But, if it came from the coffee she drank, and I think it did, it should still be in here. Coffee doesn't metabolize drugs the way the liver does," Carvelli said holding up the bag.

"Which brings me to another question," Carvelli said. "How did whoever did this know Brody Knutson would be in his office that early? Assuming it was Cal or somebody like Aidan, how did they know?"

"Somebody tipped them," Marc replied. "The problem is, in a firm that size it could be any number of people who know his work habits."

"It had to be a phone call and not from an office phone. I got a list of names of people who work on the same floor as Knutson. It's a place to start. I gave it to Paul this morning. He's going to search for phone numbers for them and see if he can track any calls to one of the phones for Cal and Aidan. How's Brooke doing?"

"She's fine. She's home," Marc said.

"God, I feel guilty about dragging her into this," Carvelli said.

"Don't. They would have done it anyway," Marc said.

"Probably, but still…"

Paxton O'Rourke walked quickly through the cubicle farm toward the big corner office. Her boss, Norah McCabe, had summoned her to a meeting and being a minute late was not acceptable.

At first, when she read the email with the summons from Her Majesty, Paxton felt a real shiver of concern. Then she talked to a couple of the other lawyers who said they were also scheduled. Every one of the lawyers was meeting with her for a case briefing. McCabe had spent very little time at the Chicago office over the past month. The rumor was, she was back from a career advancement round of ass-kissing the higher-ups in D.C. and she needed catchup briefings from everyone.

Paxton stopped at Norah's door and checked her watch. One minute early. Perfect. She rapped on the opaque door window, opened it and entered.

"My next meeting is here, Mason," Paxton heard her boss say into her phone. "I'll call you later."

When Paxton heard Norah call the person on the phone, Mason, a buzz started in her head. So much so that she did not hear Norah ask her to come in and take a seat.

Paxton placed the stack of case files she had brought with her on the chair next to her. She had typed up a two-page synopsis of each of them and handed a copy to Norah.

"Welcome back, Norah," Paxton said as she handed her the case synopsis.

"Thanks, Paxton," she pleasantly replied.

It took less than a half-hour to go through the briefing. Most of Paxton's caseload were relatively minor matters. Small time drug deals, gun crimes and a couple of interstate transportation of prostitutes. Paxton had three one or two-day trials coming up over the next two weeks. Even those would likely plead out. The rest of her cases were making their way up the food chain toward a resolution.

"Well, it sounds like you're on top of everything," Norah said when they finished. "Just between you and me, I wish everyone else in this office was as efficient."

"It's not that hard. I handled a lot of more complicated cases when I was with the JAG Corp," Paxton said.

"I know that," Norah said. "And you're on your way to getting better cases. Hang in there. Um, one more thing," Norah said.

Here it comes, Paxton thought.

"You're done with this Calvin Simpson business, aren't you?"

"Sure, yeah, why?"

"Just wanted to make sure. It's not even our jurisdiction. So, I just wanted to be sure you've let it go."

Back in her office, Paxton put the stack of files back in her credenza. When she finished that, she sat at her desk for several minutes contemplating Norah's use of the name Mason. The way she spoke it, Mason was obviously more than an acquaintance. In fact, it sounded more like a personal call than a business call.

Paxton searched her memory for the name of Norah's husband. She had only met him once and he was a very forgettable man. His name was Doyle or Dale. Something like that. Certainly not anything close to Mason.

A thought occurred to her. She opened a desk drawer to retrieve her personal phone from her purse. She found the number she wanted in her directory and almost dialed it. Instead, she decided to go outside for privacy to make the call.

On the ride down the elevator, Paxton found herself wondering why Norah was so concerned about Calvin Simpson. From what she had experienced, Norah had no problem with the lawyers and investigators going outside the box; pursuing matters that might not come into her office through normal channels. Why the obvious desire to squelch Paxton's interest in Cal Simpson?

"Hey, Uncle Sean," Paxton said when he answered her call. "I have a question for you."

"Why haven't you called lately?" Sean asked.

"No, that's not the question," Paxton replied smiling.

"Very funny, smartass. Why haven't you…?"

"I've been busy. Sorry. I've been in Minnesota quite a bit," Paxton answered.

"How's that going?"

"That's why I'm calling. Did you ever work with or know someone named Mason?" Paxton asked.

"Mason? Let me think. Yeah, I did. Probably three or four of them over the years. Why?"

"Any that might have known or worked with my boss, Norah McCabe? Either at the FBI or DOJ?"

"Let me think," Sean said again. "My memory isn't what it used to be."

A moment later he asked, "Was McCabe ever at the U.S. Attorney's office in Philly?" Sean asked.

"Philadelphia?"

"Yeah. Was she ever…"?

"Yes, I'm certain of it. I've even heard guys joke about it. It's a joke about her around the office. She's quick to say, 'the way we did things in Philadelphia' or 'the big busts we made in Philadelphia.' Things like that. Why?"

"Mason Hooper," Sean quietly said. Then the light went on. "It was Mason Hooper who gave me the tip that led to the arrest of Les Snelling and his guys. You remember when Les picked out that thug's picture and his name? What was it?"

"Aidan. It was Aidan, wasn't it?" Paxton asked excitedly.

"Yes, Aidan. He was the guy that Les believed gave Hooper the tip about Les' bank gang."

"And, he works for Calvin Simpson. Sonofabitch," Paxton quietly said.

"In fact, now that I think about it. I remember the rumor around the fed offices in Philly was that Hooper had a big-time gangster snitch feeding him cases. It has made his career. Is he in Chicago?"

248

"No, I'm not sure where he is," Paxton said. "If I make an inquiry about him it will set off alarm bells. Could you? Can you check…?"

"Sure. I know just who to call. If he's in, I can probably get back to you today."

"Thanks, Sean. Call me as soon as you know."

Before Paxton went to lunch, Sean O'Rourke called his favorite niece with the news. Mason Hooper was indeed in Washington. He was now the Assistant to the Deputy Attorney General of the United States. Mason Hooper's immediate superior was the number two man at the Department of Justice.

Additionally, Sean's source also told him that Hooper met regularly and personally with a U.S. Attorney by the name of Norah McCabe. In fact, the two of them had been very close for almost twenty years.

FORTY-NINE

Marc parked his car next to Carvelli's Camaro on Vivian's driveway. He got out, but before going inside, he took a minute to look around. He was holding a leather satchel briefcase in his left hand and turned up the collar of his trench coat with his right. It was another windy, cloudy, wet autumn day. Almost all of the leaves were off of the trees because of the windy weather. It was still early-October, normally one of the best months of the year. This one seemed to portend an early and difficult winter.

A minute later, Marc, sans trench coat, entered the mansion's library. Waiting for him were the usual suspects; Vivian, Maddy, and Carvelli. There was a real wood fire going in the fireplace and Marc took a seat next to Carvelli across from Vivian and Maddy.

"Thanks," Marc said as Vivian poured him a cup of coffee. He took a small sip then said, "We have another problem."

"What now?" Carvelli asked.

"The leaves are almost off of the trees. Conrad's directional booster you guys stuck up in the tree at Cal's is going to be spotted pretty soon."

"Yeah, I know," Carvelli said. "He reminded me about it a couple of days ago. I don't know what to do about it. Unless someone wants to try to sneak down there at night and get it."

"Bad idea," Marc said. "I'm not sure it's worth the bother. They know about the bugs. So what if they find it?"

"Good point," Maddy agreed. "I think Cal is losing interest in me," she continued. "He's getting a little bored because I won't sleep with him. I don't know how much longer…"

"So, sleep with him," Carvelli said.

"Anthony!" Vivian loudly admonished him, accompanied by a severe look.

"I'm kidding, I'm kidding," Carvelli protested.

When he said what he did, Marc slid over on the couch as far as he could and leaned away from him. He looked at the two women, both of whom were giving Carvelli death-ray eyes and Marc said, "She has a gun, you know. I'd appreciate it if you'd refrain from saying things like that with me sitting next to you."

"Sorry, sorry, sorry," Carvelli said. "It was a bad joke."

To change the subject Carvelli quickly said, "Paul found out some interesting things about Mason Hooper."

Paxton had called Maddy the previous evening with the news about Mason Hooper. Maddy then called Carvelli who took it to Paul Baker to run a background check on him. Maddy had also called Marc, but Vivian was in the dark about this. Carvelli, delighted to be on to a new subject, took a few minutes to explain it to her.

"I don't have a written report from Paul, but I got the gist of it over the phone before I came here. Paul followed him almost back to the cradle.

"Mason Hooper began life and grew up in a South Boston neighborhood. One of those tough, Irish-gang places where the kids grew up to be cops or crooks."

"Or both," Maddy said.

"That's probably truer than you know," Carvelli said. "He lived in the same house—the same house his mother still lives in—until he went away to college.

"He went to Fordham...."

"Good school," Marc said.

"...on a basketball scholarship. He graduated four years later with a B.A. in criminal justice studies.

"I forgot to mention," Carvelli said. "His dad was a cop. A captain with the Boston P.D. That probably didn't hurt his being accepted into the FBI after college. Five years later the taxpayers put him through law school at Georgetown. He graduated cum laude three years later and he's been with the DOJ ever since."

"So far, nothing remarkable," Marc said.

"Except," Carvelli replied, "that house his mom still lives in—dad died of cancer about ten years ago—is on West 4th Street and is directly across the street from the home of one Margaret Ann Kirk. Maggie, as she is known, just happens to be the mother of a certain Walter Kirk. More affectionately known to us as Calvin Simpson."

With that, Carvelli, who had been leaning forward, elbows on his knees, sat back on the couch and crossed his legs.

"Oh, yeah," Marc quietly said. "There it is."

"Do we know for sure..." Maddy started to say.

"Paul got into Hooper's juvenile record," Carvelli said. "Don't ask me how, I don't ask him a question like that. Anyway, what he found was a few minor scrapes with the law. Mostly knot head, teenage boy stuff. Joyriding in a stolen car once was the worst of it. But every time he got jammed up as a kid, the name Walter Kirk was involved. They grew up together. They were good friends."

"Except Mason joined the FBI and then the DOJ after law school," Marc said.

"And his good pal Wally chose a different path," Carvelli said.

"And they've been holding hands and helping each other since," Maddy said.

"Slow it down," Vivian chimed in. "That's a very serious allegation. Do you have any proof? Any evidence?"

"Paxton thinks she might," Maddy replied. For the next few minutes, Maddy told Vivian about Paxton's Uncle Sean and his friend Lester Snelling.

"So, this Lester Snelling believes it was Aidan who gave up Lester's bank robbery crew and Uncle Sean says it came from Mason Hooper to him," Marc said.

"Makes sense," Carvelli said.

"Yeah, it does," Marc agreed. "But what do we do with it?"

"Uncle Sean is going to try to quietly do some investigation into Mason Hooper and his cases. See if he can come up with more cases where a snitch miraculously appeared and dropped a case into Hooper's lap," Maddy said.

"And that's how Cal Simpson has been able to get away with what he has done over the years. He's had a pal at Justice covering for him," Carvelli added.

"Maybe," Marc said. "Would Mason Hooper risk everything to help Cal just for career enhancement?"

"Oh god," Vivian said. "Do you think he might have a retirement nest egg put away somewhere?"

"Possible," Marc said. "Could Paul check on that?"

"He can check," Carvelli said. "I don't know if he can find anything. These are smart, sophisticated people. If anything like that is going on, they would know how to cover their tracks."

Maddy sat forward, snapped her fingers, pointed at Carvelli and said, "Can Paul track Hooper's career path? Can he look at the offices he was assigned to and personnel who were with him? We know Paxton's boss has a relationship with Hooper—Paxton thinks they're having an affair. What about others. We might get lucky and find a weak link there."

"I'll talk to him about it," Carvelli said. "Any other ideas?" Carvelli asked as he looked at each one of them.

"Maybe Paul could pursue the affair angle between this Mason Hooper and Paxton's boss," Maddy said.

"There might be a trail," Carvelli replied. "Credit card receipts, airline tickets. I'll see what he can come up with. Paul is going to build a nice retirement plan from just us," Carvelli added looking at Vivian.

"Stop worrying about the money. I've told you a hundred times, this is the most fun I have."

The four of them went silent for a moment, then Vivian asked, "What's going on with Brooke's case?"

"We're having the evidentiary hearing on probable cause Monday morning. I'll try to pull a rabbit out of a hat and get the case dismissed. It's a little risky, but I think we have a good shot."

"Why is it risky?" Maddy asked.

"Because all the prosecution has to do is show probable cause that a crime was committed, and the evidence points to Brooke. It's a pretty low threshold for them.

"I just remembered," Marc continued. "I have an idea I want to run past all of you."

"You have an idea?" Carvelli sarcastically kidded him. "When did this miracle occur?"

"I get an idea about once a month or so. You should try it, Mr. Smartass," Marc replied.

"I've been thinking about going on Gabriella's show. Have you seen her lately?" Marc asked Maddy.

"We're going out to dinner this weekend. Friday night. I'm seeing Cal Saturday night," Maddy replied.

Marc looked at Carvelli and before Marc could ask, Carvelli said, "She's covered. Both nights. We're going to watch her Friday night as well."

"Why do you want to go on Gabriella's TV show?" Vivian asked.

"We have ideas, but not much else," Marc replied. "We know with certainty what these people have been up to at least as far as the stock manipulation, insider trading and probably money laundering. We can look into Paxton's boss and this Hooper guy. Things like that. We've been doing that for months. We even have a list of politicians we were told are involved with Cal. But so far, we have nothing to really go after them with. We don't have independent corroboration. I want them for Zach's murder and the other one, Lynn McDaniel."

"We need to crack someone to corroborate Congressman Peterson," Maddy said.

"And we're not getting it. We started down this path to solving Zach's murder. We know who did it, how was it done and why…"

"Or so we think," Carvelli said.

"Exactly," Marc agreed. "We need to do something to shake this up."

"You want to go on Gabriella's show and lay it all out?" Vivian asked.

"Maybe," Marc answered her. "At least enough to shake the tree. And maybe get the snakes attacking each other."

"When?" Maddy asked.

253

"After Brooke's hearing. I'm thinking toward the end of next week. Monday and Tuesday, I'll be in court. Maybe Wednesday, too. Thursday would be good."

"I'll talk to her about it. She'll be happy to get you on," Maddy said.

"You cannot name names," Vivian sternly told him.

"I know, and I won't. But I think I can talk about Cannon Brothers Toys and Morton Aviation. The public relations campaigns, the engineer's memo, the stock manipulation and insider trading. We need to do something to kick this loose."

FIFTY

"I am so nervous I can barely breathe," Brooke whispered in Marc's ear.

The two of them, along with Jeff Modell, the office paralegal, had just stepped off of the elevator from the parking ramp. They were walking through the second- floor atrium of the Hennepin County Government Center toward the courtside elevators. It was half-past eight o'clock and the second-floor was busy with people scrambling to their offices. Brooke was clinging to Marc's arm so hard that his left-hand was starting to tingle.

"Brooke, you're cutting off the blood flow in my arm," Marc quietly said.

"Oh god! I'm sorry," she replied and let go of his arm. "I'm just…"

"Nervous," Marc said.

After going through security, they stopped at the bank of elevators and while they waited, Marc took her aside.

"Relax. Nothing is going to happen today," Marc looked her in the eyes and reassuringly said.

At that moment, three elevator cars appeared at the same time. This allowed the three of them to have one all to themselves. They began to ascend to fifteen and Brooke took a deep breath.

"Okay," she said. "Tell me again what this is about."

"It's an evidentiary hearing to determine whether or not they have sufficient probable cause to go forward. They'll put on their witnesses to go over the evidence they have against you. Normally, the defense doesn't do much of anything with this. It's a way to get a look at their evidence, at least some of it, and their witnesses. I'm going to put on a case and try to stop this thing right now," Marc told her. "When both sides are done Judge Williams will decide if the case should proceed to trial."

"What do you think?" she asked.

"I don't know. Probable cause is a pretty low threshold to reach. We'll see," Marc shrugged.

"That's reassuring," Brooke said. Which elicited a laugh from Jeff Modell.

They exited the elevator and ran into several media people milling about in front of 1534, Judge Mitchell Williams' courtroom. Recognizing most of them, Marc looked them over and asked, "Slow news day?"

Marc turned to Jeff and whispered to him to get Brooke inside. While Jeff and Brooke hurried into the courtroom, Marc stood in front of the door to block it.

"Arnie, you know I'm not going to let you talk to her," Marc said to a reporter from the St. Paul paper. "Why are you even here? Not enough crime in St. Paul?"

"Not this week," Arnie replied.

Marc held up his right hand to quiet everyone. When they finally stopped throwing questions at him, he said, "I'll answer every question you have right now. No comment. Thank you."

Marc joined Jeff and Brooke at one of the tables then went to the judge's clerk to check in. There was already a dozen or so court watchers seated in the gallery. Apparently, word had gotten out that this might not be a routine hearing.

Marc returned to the table and asked Jeff if he was hooked up and ready. Receiving an affirmative reply, he turned again to his client.

"I wish Tony were here," she said.

"He'll be here later. He can't sit in. He's going to be called as a witness and he can't be in the courtroom," Marc reminded her.

"I know, it's just, well, it's comforting to have him around," Brooke said.

"You got a daddy thing or a bad boy thing?" Marc playfully asked.

Brooke suppressed a laugh and said, "Both. I got a bad boy, daddy thing. Most of us do."

Now it was Marc's turn to suppress a laugh.

"Well, he has kind of, you know, that hot, older man thing going," she smiled and said. "Don't you dare tell him I said that."

"I don't have to. He already believes it. Telling him would make it worse. Besides, he's got a kind of 'friends with benefits' thing going with Vivian Donahue."

"Really? Old people? Wow, who would've thought?" Brooke said.

The door next to the judge's bench opened and the prosecutors came in. There were two of them. The older one, a man in his late-fifties, was well-known to Marc. His name was Gerald Krain, and he was easily the prosecutor most despised by defense lawyers in Hennepin County. The other was a young black man whom Marc had just met, Joseph Mosely. Fresh out of law school, he had not yet received word if he had passed the July bar exam.

Jerry Krain was a thirty-year lifer with the county attorney's office. He had been a methodical, careful and competent trial lawyer throughout his career. The reason he had not risen through the ranks was the Gibraltar size chip on his shoulder. He seemed to be totally pissed off at the world, which made it easy for the world to be pissed off right back at him. It wasn't just defense lawyers who despised him. His comrades in the county attorney's office felt the same way. What amazed everyone was how well he came off to a jury.

"Morning, Jerry," Marc loudly said knowing a pleasant greeting would likely annoy the man known as the Nazi.

"If you say so," he grumbled back at Marc. Krain sat down and began arranging things on the table.

"Carla would like you to check in," Marc said referring to the judge's clerk.

Without looking up, Krain said, "I'm here."

"You're in a better mood than normal," Marc said. "Your favorite hooker make bail and take care of you last night?" Needling the Nazi was a favorite pastime of defense lawyers.

As soon as he said this, Marc noticed the rookie lawyer seated on the other side of Krain visibly cringe. He looked at Krain as if expecting an explosion. Marc felt a twinge of sympathy for the young man. Knowing Krain's feelings about black people, Marc wondered why Steve Gondeck had assigned him to the second chair with Krain.

"That rapier wit is still functioning as well as ever I see, Kadella," Krain replied.

Brooke grabbed Marc's arm while Marc was laughing and pulled him toward her. "Why are you trying to make him mad?" she anxiously asked.

Marc turned and whispered, "I can't make him angrier than he already is. I'm just having a little fun."

"The judge wants to see just the lawyers," Marc heard Carla say.

Judge Mitchell rose to greet them and reached across his desk to shake hands. Of course, he knew Jerry Krain well and had Marc before him many times. The judge took a little extra time with young Joseph Moseley to make him relax and feel welcome. When everyone was seated, he looked at Marc.

"You're going to make a big deal out of this?" he half-jokingly asked.

"Well, your Honor," Marc replied. "I don't think they have much of a case and I think I can end it here and now."

Krain derisively snorted and with a sarcastic attitude said, "It's probable cause, Judge, I'll..."

"Thank you for that reminder, Mr. Krain. I'll keep it in mind," Williams said. "You're planning on calling witnesses?"

"Yes, a few," Marc replied.

"How many?" Krain asked.

"I'm not sure. I'll have to see your evidence…"

"He knows our evidence, Judge," Krain said. "This is…"

"His client's right to do this and we're going to." He looked at Marc and asked, "Today and tomorrow enough?"

"That should be plenty, your Honor," Marc replied.

"Okay. You put your case on today and the defense tomorrow. Will that work for you, Mr. Krain?" the judge asked.

"Yes, your Honor."

"Marc?"

"Sounds good, Judge," Marc said.

"Okay. Let's get at it," Williams said.

A probable cause evidentiary hearing is basically a mini-trial. It is used to convince the judge that the prosecution has enough evidence to proceed to the real trial. Normally the defense does not put on any witnesses of their own. The defense uses this as an opportunity to get a good look at the prosecution's evidence, the witnesses and how the evidence will be presented. Since Marc was trying to stop the case from going forward, he planned to call his own witnesses. This was an opportunity to convince the judge there was insufficient probable cause and dismiss the case.

There are problems with this strategy. First, if the judge does dismiss at this point, the defendant is not covered by the constitutional protection of double jeopardy. Legally, jeopardy attaches when the jury is sworn in. Or, if the trial is to a judge only without a jury, jeopardy attaches when the first witness is sworn in. That means if Marc is successful and Judge Williams dismisses, the state is free to find additional evidence and charge the defendant again.

The second problem is, by putting on his own witnesses Marc could be giving away his trial strategy. The prosecution can use that to better prepare their case for trial.

FIFTY-ONE

Judge Williams took the bench and looked over the gallery. Normally, these hearings were conducted routinely prior to trial and attracted little or no attention. Even cases with some media interest rarely brought more than one or two reporters in to attend.

The judge read off the case title and court file number. Both the state's attorney and the defense noted their presence for the record along with the defendant. Williams then spent a few minutes reminding the media that recording devices and cameras would not be allowed.

"Do you wish to make an opening statement, Mr. Krain?" Williams asked.

"Yes, your Honor," the prosecutor replied after standing at his table.

"Bear in mind, Mr. Krain, I've read the case file, pleadings and supporting memorandums. Be brief," Williams said.

Without a jury to impress, Krain kept his beginning statement short and to the point. Judge Williams had just told Krain he was up to date on the case. Because of this, Krain barely spoke for ten minutes. Just enough to give the judge a quick look at what the prosecution's case was. When Krain finished, Judge Williams, who had pretended to take notes while Krain spoke, turned to Marc.

"Mr. Kadella, do you wish to make a statement now?"

Marc stood and politely replied, "I'll defer for now, your Honor."

Williams turned back to Krain and asked, "Are you calling witnesses, Mr. Krain?"

"Yes, your Honor."

"You may proceed."

Krain stood and called his first witness. A moment later, Lucy Gibson was led into the courtroom by a sheriff's deputy. She was sworn by the judge's clerk and took the stand.

Marc had guessed correctly that Lucy would be first up. Normally, the prosecution would start with a strong witness. This would have been the lead investigator, Gabe Hunt. With a judge as the fact finder and not a jury, first impressions were not nearly as important.

The county attorney's office had decided against a first-degree murder indictment. Marc believed this was because of the difficulty they would have proving premeditation. Brooke Hartley was charged with second-degree murder and first-degree manslaughter.

Every criminal act has specific elements that must be proven. And each of them, for a guilty verdict, must be proven beyond a reasonable doubt. For today's hearing, Krain need only show that there was probable cause to believe Brooke Hartley committed the act that caused the death of Brody Knutson.

For second-degree murder, the state must prove that the act committed was done with the intent to cause the victim's death. It need not be premeditated— thought out beforehand—but done to kill. Stabbing someone in the heart with a sharp object, a letter opener, is a fairly obvious indication that death was intended.

This does not preclude the defense from offering evidence that death was not intended. They could claim that the two people were engaged in a heated argument and in a moment of passion, the stabbing occurred. This was the reason for the manslaughter charge. Krain was using it to head off any claim the defense would bring along those lines. If the prosecution did not charge it and the jury concluded that is what happened, the jury could not impose it themselves.

Marc could still bring a claim of self-defense. Except, self-defense is what is called an affirmative defense. An affirmative defense is one the defendant must assert before trial and then prove during trial. Since Brooke had no memory of the event and there were no witnesses, self-defense was not a practical option. Plus, you cannot really argue that "my client did not do it, but if you think she did, she acted in self-defense." It has to be one or the other.

Lucy Gibson's testimony lasted about forty-five minutes. Krain quickly and efficiently walked her through her story. She arrived at work and found Brody Knutson dead with his own letter opener in his chest. Brooke was unconscious on the floor a few feet away from him.

Krain spent most of his time with her, drawing out the animosity Brooke felt toward Brody Knutson. Marc objected to it three times as hearsay, but Judge Williams allowed it as a statement against Brooke's interest. The fourth objection, repetitive testimony, finally put a stop to it. By then even Judge Williams had heard enough.

Krain used this opportunity to put a photo up on the TVs located throughout the courtroom. It was a photo of Knutson's body lying in a pool of blood with the letter opener still in his chest. Lucy agreed that was how she found him. She also pointed out where Brooke had been lying.

When Krain finished with Lucy's involvement that morning, he passed the witness to Marc.

"No questions at this time, your Honor. We reserve the right to recall Ms. Gibson during the case for the defense," Marc said.

"Very well. Ms. Gibson, keep yourself available and stay away from any news stories that may be published or shown on TV."

"Yes, your Honor," Lucy said. She stood, stepped down from the witness chair, looked at Brooke and loudly said, "I'm sorry."

"And refrain from speaking to the defendant," Judge Williams admonished.

As Lucy was walking down the center aisle toward the exit, Williams told Krain to call his next witness.

"The prosecution calls Detective Gabriel Hunt, your Honor."

As part of the prosecution team, Hunt was the only witness allowed to sit in the courtroom. He was in a chair behind the prosecution's table against the railing.

Jerry Krain again showed why he was an effective prosecutor. This was his main witness and Krain did not miss anything that could help his case and point at Brooke.

Krain started off with the detective giving Judge Williams a thorough history of his career in law enforcement. Being a judge with almost fifteen years on the bench, Williams was not the least bit impressed. The judge did manage to do an excellent job of not showing his boredom, but he had heard it from many witnesses many times before.

Having thoroughly prepared his witness, Krain smoothly transitioned into the investigation itself. Since there wasn't much of an investigation done, this part of the testimony did not last long. Hunt did manage to superficially go through the steps he took to rule out other suspects. At the end, Krain made a point of emphasizing this part of the investigation.

"When did you come to believe the defendant committed this crime?" Krain asked.

"Not immediately, if that's what you mean," Hunt replied. "She was certainly a suspect right away, I'll admit. It wasn't until after I got the fingerprint results off of the letter opener that I decided she must have done it."

Since Hunt did not do the fingerprint analysis himself, this answer was close to objectionable. Marc did not bother because the fingerprint tech was going to testify anyway, so he let it go.

"Did you find any evidence that anyone else was there in the deceased's office who could have done it?"

"No, none at all," Hunt emphatically said.

"Your witness," Krain told Marc.

Since there was no jury, who were always sympathetic to police, Marc had no need to approach Hunt with a soft attitude. Instead, he decided to go right at him.

"You found no evidence of anyone else being there in Brody Knutson's office that morning?" Marc asked from his seat at the table.

"No, no one."

"What would you say if I told you my investigator found such evidence?"

This caused a bit of a stir in the courtroom which Judge Williams silenced with a stern look.

"I'd say he was lying," Hunt replied.

"Because you were so thorough?"

"Yes."

"Because you didn't miss anything?"

"I don't believe so, no," Hunt answered but visibly shifted in his chair.

"And the police crime scene techs didn't miss anything?"

"Well, you'd have to ask them..."

"I'm asking you, Detective. Aren't you in charge of this case? Aren't you the one responsible for it? The one who is supposed to make sure every stone is looked under?"

"Well, yes," Hunt agreed.

"The time of death was put at between five-thirty and six-thirty by the medical examiner, was it not?" Marc asked abruptly shifting gears.

"Objection, that would be testimony for the medical examiner," Krain said.

"I have the medical examiner's report, the autopsy, right here, your Honor," Marc said.

"Have you read the medical examiner's report, Detective Hunt?" Judge Williams asked.

"Yes, your Honor," Hunt replied.

"Overruled," Judge Williams said. "He can answer."

"Yes, that is what the M.E. found," Hunt admitted.

"What time did Ms. Hartley arrive at the office that morning?" Marc asked.

"According to the witness, Lucy Gibson, it was Ms. Hartley's turn to come in early. She arrived before six," Hunt answered.

"This was according to Ms. Gibson. Was she there when Ms. Hartley arrived at the office?" Marc asked.

"Um, no but that's the time Ms. Hartley was supposed to be there. No later than six."

Marc looked at Jeff Modell and nodded. A moment later, a photo appeared on the TV monitors.

"On the television monitor is a photograph we obtained from the parking garage surveillance camera. It's a photo of someone entering the underground parking facility of the U.S. Bank building..."

"Objection," Krain said. "We have no one to authenticate this..."

"I have an affidavit," Marc said as he stood to address the court. He was holding a one-page document in his hand, "from the building's head of security. It attests to the authenticity of the photo and we are prepared to bring him in to testify if necessary unless the state will stipulate and allow it in."

Marc walked over to Krain and gave him a copy of the affidavit and took one up to Judge Williams. They both took a minute to read it then Judge Williams looked at Krain.

"Will you stipulate?"

"Yes, your Honor," he said and sat down.

"Objection overruled. Proceed, Mr. Kadella."

"There is a date and time stamp on the photo, Detective. Please read it."

Hunt read off the information then Marc asked, "That is the date of Mr. Knutson's death, is it not?"

"Yes."

Another photo appeared on the screens. It was a clear shot of Brooke Hartley's face. She was leaning out of the driver's window to use her pass card to raise the ramp's entry gate.

Marc described the photo for the stenographic court record then asked Hunt, "Do you recognize the woman in this photo?"

"It's the defendant," Hunt answered.

"Brooke Hartley?"

"Yes."

"And what is she doing?"

"She appears to be driving into the building's parking ramp?"

"What time is stamped on that photo?"

"Six oh four," Hunt replied. "But..."

"I'll ask the questions," Marc quickly said cutting him off.

"Would it be reasonable to say it took her another minute to park her car?"

"I guess," Hunt said.

"I did it myself," Marc said. "It is. So, she parked her car at six oh five. Walked to the elevators and went up to the thirty-third floor. Another five minutes. Would you agree, Detective?"

"I'm sure you timed it, so I would agree."

"Yes, I did. Didn't you?" Marc asked.

When Hunt failed to answer, Marc continued.

"She went into the office, hung up her coat; you found her coat hung up didn't you?"

"Yes, we did."

"Her purse in her desk?"

"Yes."

"She then went to the breakroom and poured herself a cup of coffee..."

"Objection, is there a point to this?" Krain knew there was but wanted to interrupt it.

"Timeline, your Honor," Marc said.

"Overruled."

"I don't know if she got a cup of coffee," Hunt interjected.

"We'll prove that she did," Marc said. "She got a cup of coffee and went back to her desk. By now, it must be getting very close to six-fifteen," Marc said.

"And then, even though your thorough investigation missed it, she drank more than a half cup of coffee, then went in and murdered her boss. Is that what happened?"

"Okay," Hunt shrugged. "She did it closer to six-thirty than five-thirty. So what? She still did it."

"Because your investigation was so thorough," Marc replied, "is it possible someone drugged her and that's why she was found unconscious?"

"There's no evidence..."

"That someone else was there waiting for her and Brody Knutson was already dead? That he was murdered closer to five-thirty than six-thirty?"

"There's no evidence..."

"Because your investigation was so thorough," Marc replied with a touch of sarcasm.

"Objection, argumentative," Krain said.

"Sustained. Scale it back, Mr. Kadella."

"Plus assumes facts not in evidence and goes beyond the scope of the direct examination," Krain added.

Williams quickly held up a hand, palm out, toward Marc to stop him from responding. The judge thought for a moment before ruling.

"I'll overrule both objections. This is within the scope of direct in that it pertains to the detective's investigation. But," he looked seriously at Marc and said, "I want something on this claim about her being drugged."

"Yes, your Honor," Marc replied.

This answer caused Hunt to glance back and forth between Krain and Marc. Clearly, he was looking for help.

With the pause that this exchange caused, Krain stood again and asked for a break. The judge looked at Marc and asked him if he had much more. Knowing Krain was trying to get his cop off of the stand to regroup, Marc told the judge he was almost done.

264

Marc whispered to Jeff and a new photo appeared on the TV sets. It was a photo of a cup of coffee with two inches of coffee in it. It had a small ruler in it to show the exact depth.

"Your Honor," Krain stood and wearily said, "his obsession with coffee is growing tiresome. Somewhere along the line, there needs to be some relevance to this."

"Mr. Kadella?" Judge Williams said.

Marc stood and said, "I think he knows exactly where I'm going, and he doesn't want me to get there. Before I'm done, I'll connect to the relevance, your Honor."

"I'm going to hold you to that. You may continue."

Marc asked for and received permission to stand next to the TV closest to the witness. He held a collapsible, aluminum pointer in his hand. He used it to point at the cup in the photo. For the record, he verbally explained what was on the TV and what he was doing.

"One of my office assistants, at my request, conducted a little experiment for me. She is also the one who took the photos and will testify if necessary."

"In this photo, Detective Hunt, is a cup of fresh coffee. The cup is marked with the letter A and also has a ruler in it. You can see the depth is two inches. Would you agree?"

"Yes," Hunt said.

A new photo appeared side-by-side with the previous one. It was the same cup with the same ruler in it.

"This is the same cup twelve hours later. You'll notice the depth of the coffee is more than a quarter of an inch lower. Would you agree, Detective Hunt?"

"I guess," he replied.

Using the pointer, Marc pointed out a ring around the inside of the cup. It was a ring of coffee where the depth had been when it was first filled. The difference was overnight evaporation. A couple of quick questions for the record verified this.

Marc then went through the same procedure twice more with cups marked B and C. The results were the same; a drop in the level of liquid leaving a ring around the cup where the level had originally been when the cup was filled with fresh coffee.

Another photo appeared. It was Brooke Hartley's desk. On it was a coffee cup with some coffee in it.

"Do you recognize this photo?"

"Um, I'm not sure," Hunt meekly replied.

The photo changed, but now Gabe Hunt was standing next to Brooke's desk. He appeared to be staring down at it.

"Recognize it now?" Marc asked.

"Sure, it's her desk at work," Hunt answered.

A new photo appeared. This was the same photo only it was a blown-up close-up of the coffee cup on the blotter on the desktop.

"These last three photos are ones taken by the police crime scene techs. They were provided to the defense through discovery. This one," Marc said tapping the TV screen, "is a close-up of the coffee cup that was on Brooke Hartley's desk while you were doing your thorough investigation on the morning of the murder. Tell the court, Detective, if there is a ring around the inside of this cup from overnight evaporation?"

"No, there is not," he answered.

"Would you conclude from that the coffee in this cup was poured into it that same morning?"

"Yes, I suppose," Hunt hesitantly said.

The last photo in this sequence appeared. It was a shot of the break room taken from its doorway.

"Do you recognize this photo?"

"Looks like the breakroom," Hunt answered.

"It's a photo of the break room in Brody Knutson office suite, you're correct. What is this?" Marc asked pointing at an object in the photo.

"A coffee pot," Hunt said.

"An empty coffee pot," Marc corrected him.

"Yes, it's empty."

"It's not only empty, but it is obvious someone rinsed it out, isn't it?" Marc asked.

"Probably Lucy Gibson rinsed it out," Hunt blurted out without thinking.

"Did Ms. Hartley tell you she had no memory of that morning?"

"Yes, she did."

"But you believed she was lying, didn't you?"

"Yes, I did," Hunt admitted.

"And your thorough investigation gave you no reason to believe differently, didn't it?"

"Objection!"

"Sustained."

"I have nothing further, your Honor," Marc said.

"Your Honor, he was supposed to connect this to some relevance…" Krain jumped up and shouted out.

"Oh, I suspect he will," Williams said. "At least he is entitled to try. We'll take a break for lunch."

Two minutes after the break was ordered, Aidan Walsh received a phone call from a spectator. He listened to a report of the morning's

266

testimony then went to tell Cal Simpson. Brooke's lawyer was scoring points.

FIFTY-TWO

Marc re-entered the courtroom through the door behind the bench. He was followed by Gerald Krain wearing his normal scowl and the young man doing second chair duty for Krain. Marc took his seat next to Brooke and fiddled with the items on the table in front of him.

"What do you guys talk about back there?" Brooke asked, referring to the conferences lawyers have in the judge's chambers.

"Who's going to win and who's going to lose," Marc replied.

"Really? Are we going to win? Has he decided?" Brooke excitedly asked.

Marc laughed then said, "I'm kidding. The judge wanted to make sure they were going to finish up this afternoon. He doesn't want to drag this out for a third day."

"Are they going to finish?"

"Yeah, they only have three more witnesses," Marc said.

There was a moment of silence between them until Marc said, "Now that I think about it, sometimes we *do* decide who's going to win and who's going to lose. A lot of the time it will depend on what the judge will allow into evidence."

"That doesn't seem fair," Brooke said.

"Fair? What's fair got to do with it? I'm not even sure what that word really means. Usually, it means if something is good for me it's fair. But if it is good for you and bad for me, then it's unfair. It's a silly word for politicians to use to sucker idiots into voting for them.

"Here we go," Marc said as the judge and his clerk came out.

When everyone was settled back in their seats, Krain called his next witness. One of the two crime scene techs, John Barnes, was led into the courtroom.

"State your name and current occupation for the record," the judge's clerk said.

Krain started out by eliciting information from the witness about his expertise as a crime scene technician. Halfway through it, Judge Williams interrupted Krain.

"Mr. Krain, I am very familiar with Mr. Barnes' qualifications. Mr. Kadella," he continued, looking at Marc, "would you be willing to stipulate to the witness's expertise, in the interest of moving things along?"

"Certainly, your Honor," Marc agreed although he did not really want to. He was hoping the judge would become bored and not pay close attention.

Annoyed by the interruption, Krain skipped over the rest of his prepared questioning about his witness's qualifications. Instead, he went right into the process and details the crime scene techs used to process Knutson's office. Being a veteran with over ten years of experience, and having been thoroughly prepped by Krain, Barnes handled it with skill and aplomb. The man knew exactly what was expected and he did not miss a beat.

"When you finished your exam of the victim's office and your analysis of the samples you took from it, were you able to reach a definite conclusion as to a third person being in Brody Knutson's office that morning?"

"Yes, I did."

"And what was your conclusion?"

"We found evidence of only two people. The deceased and the defendant," Barnes replied.

"What about the other areas of the victim's office? The break room and the work area where his assistants were located?"

"We found a lot of evidence of a number of people in both areas. Hair and fiber samples, fingerprints..."

"Objection, the witness has not been qualified as a fingerprint expert."

"Are you a fingerprint expert?" Judge Williams asked Barnes.

"It is not my particular area of expertise, your Honor," Barnes admitted.

"The objection is sustained. Don't try testifying about fingerprints."

"Were you able to identify the people whose samples, hair and fiber samples were found in the outer offices?"

"Yes, we were. They mostly belonged to Lucy Gibson and the defendant, Brooke Hartley. There were also several from other employees of the law firm, staff, and lawyers."

"But none inside the victim's private office?"

"No, only the victim and defendant," Barnes agreed.

"Tell me about the blood spatter."

"There wasn't much. Just a short burst of blood from the one stab wound. Mr. Knutson was stabbed once directly in the heart and went down. It caused the one short burst of blood before he hit the floor," Barnes said.

At that point, a photograph appeared on the TV monitors. It was a picture of Knutson's feet and blood on the carpeting just a few inches from his feet.

"There is a photograph on the TV monitor. Do you recognize it?"

269

"Yes, it is a photo I took of the blood spatter from the single wound."

"Was the victim's blood on the defendant?"

"No, it was not. We obtained the clothing she was wearing, analyzed all of it and found no blood on her."

"Isn't this odd?"

"It's not typical, but it is not unusual either. As I said, the victim had only one stab wound directly into his heart. He went down and was dead within seconds."

Marc considered objecting since this witness was not qualified to testify as to how long Knutson lived. Having read the autopsy report, Marc knew the medical examiner was going to say this anyway, so he let it go.

"Plus, she was punched by the..."

"Objection, your Honor," Marc said only this time he was out of his chair. "This witness has no knowledge about any punch being thrown at Ms. Hartley if, in fact, it happened at all or by whom."

"How do you know she was punched?" Judge Williams asked.

"Well, um, Detective Hunt told me," Barnes muttered.

"Sustained," Williams ruled. "Come up here," he told the lawyers.

When they arrived at the bench, he hit the white noise machine to cover their discussion.

"Do you have any evidence that she was in fact punched and by whom?" Williams asked Jerry Krain.

"She was found unconscious with a bruise on the side of her face, Judge. It was obvious..."

"Who did it?"

"Since there is no evidence anyone else was in that room, a jury can infer that Knutson must have done it when she stabbed him," Krain said.

Williams thought this over for a moment then said, "I'll take it under advisement for now. Let's go."

"I have no further questions for this witness, your Honor," Krain announced when he got back to his table.

"Very well. Mr. Kadella?" Williams said.

Before Marc could begin questioning the witness, Brooke leaned over and whispered, "He didn't deal with the coffee on my desk."

"I know," Marc whispered back.

"Mr. Barnes, was there any sign of a struggle in the inner office of Brody Knutson?" Marc started his cross-examination by asking.

"Well, yes. There was a dead body lying on the floor with a letter opener sticking out of his chest and he was covered in blood."

When the laughter died down, Marc smiled, nodded his head and said, "I asked for that. I'll try it again. Other than the body of Brody Knutson, were there signs of a struggle such as you would find if two people were fighting?"

"No, not really."

"In fact, the room was neat and clean, was it not?"

"Yes, it was," Barnes admitted.

Marc whispered the words 'coffee cup' to Jeff before the next question. Jeff clicked his laptop and the picture of the coffee cup on Brooke's desk went up on the monitors.

"On the television monitor is a photo you took of my client's desk. Do you recognize it?"

"Yes, certainly."

"You did not send the coffee in the cup to a lab for analysis, did you?"

"No, we did not."

"Wouldn't it be standard procedure to do that?"

"Well, um, normally, I suppose," Barnes answered while nervously looking at Detective Hunt, still seated behind the prosecutor's table.

Noticing this, Marc decided to take a chance.

"Isn't it true you didn't bother to do this because Detective Hunt had told you that Ms. Hartley was guilty?"

"Objection, hearsay," Krain quickly said.

"Overruled, I'll allow it."

"Um, I, ah," Barnes stuttered.

"You're under oath, Mr. Barnes."

"Answer the question," Judge Williams told him.

"Yes, he had told us that it was obvious she was the only one who could have done it."

Marc glanced over at Hunt who was staring straight ahead trying to look impassive. As if this was the most normal thing to have done.

Marc stopped at this point and paused. He was going to ask another question about what other things the techs failed to do because of what Hunt said. Instead, he decided he got what he wanted; time to move on.

"Were you aware that Ms. Hartley had no memory of the events of that morning?"

"Yes, Detective Hunt told us that, but..." Barnes answered then stopped himself.

"But he said she was lying, didn't he?"

"Yes," Barnes reluctantly replied.

"Your testimony was that only Brody Knutson and Brooke Hartley had been in Knutson's office where his body was found, is that correct?"

"Yes."

"Because you found no evidence of anyone else being in there that morning, true?"

"Yes, that was our conclusion based on the evidence we obtained."

"Lucy Gibson was in there that same morning. She was the one who discovered Brody Knutson dead and Brooke Hartley unconscious. Isn't it true that someone else could have been there and left no evidence as Lucy Gibson did?"

Barnes sat silently for a full thirty seconds. What could he say? Of course, it was possible since Lucy Gibson had done it.

"Yes, I suppose so," Barnes quietly said.

Marc looked over the notes in his trial book for a moment. He looked up at Judge Williams and said, "I have nothing further, your Honor."

"Redirect, Mr. Krain?"

"Yes, your Honor. Is it unusual to find a dead body at a crime scene with no other significant signs of a struggle?"

"No, it's not unusual," Barnes gladly answered. "In fact, it happens frequently."

"How long was Lucy Gibson in the inner office where the body was found?" Krain continued.

"Objection. Lacks foundation and this witness was not there to time her. He couldn't possibly know."

"Sustained," Judge Williams ruled.

"How long could someone be in a room and leave no evidence behind?"

"Objection, speculation," Marc said.

"Do you have a scientific basis on which to answer that question as an expert?" Judge Williams asked Barnes.

"Um, no, not really."

"Sustained. Move along, Mr. Krain."

Krain, obviously frustrated, thought it over for a moment, then ended his re-direct exam.

Marc passed on any re-cross, and the judge called for a short break.

FIFTY-THREE

"Okay, Richie," Aidan said into his phone. "Get back inside and call me later."

Aidan was in Cal's backyard smoking when he received the call from his guy in court. The news was not good. He chain-lit another cigarette and paced around the pool area thinking of a way to tell his boss about the screw-up. A few minutes into it he realized there was no good way to soft-pedal the news.

Aidan found Cal at his desk in the office working from his P.C. Cal glanced up when the door opened and asked, "Are the guys done yet?" He was referring to the two men electronically sweeping the house for listening devices.

"Pretty soon," Aidan replied.

Knowing the techs had swept Cal's office for bugs already and they could talk freely, Aidan sat down in front of the desk and said, "We've got a problem."

"Oh?" Cal replied. It was one of Cal Simpson's absolutes. He wanted bad news right away. Problems needed to be dealt with as soon as possible. Good news could wait.

"The lawyer, this Kadella guy, seems to know about the Mickey Finn his client was hit with when Knutson was popped," Aidan said.

Cal leaned back in his chair, folded his arms across his chest and asked, "How? Tell me what you know."

"Richie called during a break a few minutes ago," Aidan said then paused.

"And?"

"And the secretary drank the coffee but didn't finish it all. They found some in her cup on her desk. He hasn't said so yet, this Kadella, but according to Richie, he's making a big deal about the cops not analyzing what was in it."

"And you guys missed it," Cal said.

"Yeah, there's no excuse for it. We cleaned out the coffee pot but missed the cup on her desk. He's gonna show she was drugged."

"Any way they can trace it back to us?" Cal asked.

Aidan shrugged, relieved that Cal did not seem too upset, and said, "I don't see how."

Cal visibly sighed and said, "Anything else? Is he going to get her off? Get the case dismissed?"

"Richie's not sure. He doesn't know, but he says Kadella is scoring points."

There was a soft knock on the door. Cal flicked a finger at it to indicate Aidan should answer it. When he did, he found the two techs standing there.

"Anything?" Aidan asked them.

"No, sir. Nothing and we were very careful. Very thorough," the senior of the two answered.

"Good," Cal said who had joined them. "I want you back next week. Same time."

"Yes, sir," the same man replied.

As Aidan peeled off two one-hundred-dollar bills as a gratuity, the younger man asked Cal, "I'm curious, Mr. Simpson, are you still seeing Maddy Rivers?"

"Who?"

"Maddy Rivers," he repeated. "That tall, gorgeous, hot chick I've seen here a couple of times."

Aidan gave Cal a quizzical look and Cal, grasping the situation, said, "Oh, yeah, Maddy. Sure. She's great. How do you know her?"

"A friend of mine went out with her a couple of times. It didn't amount to much. He pointed her out to me in a restaurant once. She's easy to remember," the man said.

"Yes, yes, she certainly is," Cal agreed. "Aidan, will you escort these two gentlemen out, please. Thanks again," he said to the techs as Aidan started to guide them out.

Less than a minute later, Aidan was back and confronted by an obviously irate boss. Cal was pacing about the living room, his head down thinking about what he had just learned. He stopped and looked directly at Aidan.

"Maddy Rivers? Madeline Rivers? Who the hell is…"

"I'll get right on it, boss."

A short while later, Aidan was back in Cal's office. Cal was still at his computer, but his mind was on the tall, auburn-haired beauty he knew as Maddy Shore.

"Pull her up on Google," Aidan said. "Madeline Rivers, private investigator."

"What?" a distraught Cal Simpson practically yelled. "She's a what?"

Instead of ripping into Aidan he did the search and found her information. It was a website for her business complete with a photo of her. Cal read over her bio and references, then sat back with his eyes closed, his face pointed at the ceiling. He took a deep breath, exhaled and then leaned forward to look at Aidan.

"Jesus H. Christ," Cal said. "How the hell did we miss this?"

"My fault, totally," Aidan said.

Cal dismissively waved his left hand and said, "It's all of our faults. We followed her for days. How could we…"

"She's obviously very good and was ready for us," Aidan said.

"And she works with this lawyer, Marc Kadella. Who, as you should recall, was brought in to represent Zach. He was hit by the van; I guess we know now where the surveillance came from," Cal said.

"What do you want done?" Aidan asked.

Cal sat silently for a moment contemplating Aidan's question. He slapped a hand on top of the desk, angrily stood up and walked out of the room. Aidan followed him waiting for a response to his question.

"I don't think there's anything we can do right now," Cal finally said. "We have to assume they—whoever else is involved—are watching us. And this lawyer, this Kadella guy is all over the TV and in the newspapers right now. No, we have to sit tight for a while.

"But," he continued, pointing a finger at Aidan, "it moves our timetable up. We are going to have to move things along faster than we had planned."

"Should I put a tail on her again?" Aidan asked.

"Yes, but find somebody good. Somebody she won't spot in ten minutes."

"I know somebody I can bring in from Chicago," Aidan told him.

"Good idea. Bring in someone from outside. She's obviously not acting alone. Whoever else is involved, this Kadella guy for sure, they're on a mission to solve Zach's death. And if they planted the bugs—and I'll bet she did it—they have help."

Richie, Cal's personal spectator, made it to his seat in the back of the courtroom as Krain was calling his next witness. The fingerprint technician from the state's Bureau of Criminal Apprehension was led in, given the oath, and took the stand.

"Please state your name and current occupation," the court clerk said.

A twenty-something man of Asian descent, Hmong to be precise, replied in perfect English, "Donald Vang. I am currently employed by the Bureau of Criminal Apprehension in the Forensic Science Division."

Krain carefully went through Vang's education and experience to satisfy the requirement that the witness was a fingerprint expert. Although Vang was in his mid-twenties, he had testified enough times to be comfortable with it. In fact, he secretly loved the spotlight. Having prepared him, Krain was able to let him loose and nail down the fingerprints on the letter opener. Through a series of photos that Krain's assistant put up on the monitors, Vang had almost everyone in the room bored to death by the time he was done. No doubt about it, the fingerprints on the letter opener found sticking out of Brody Knutson's chest belonged to no one except Brooke Hartley.

"Help me to be certain I understand you correctly, Mr. Vang," Marc said to begin his cross-examination. "On the handle of the letter opener, State's Exhibit A, you found a clear set of fingerprints that could only match those of Brooke Hartley. Is that right?"

"Yes, that's correct."

"It was her right hand?"

"Yes, it was her right hand."

"And every finger except the thumb, correct?"

"Yes, again."

Jeff put a close up of the letter opener with the fingerprint dust showing the prints up on the TVs.

"Now, I'm a layman and not a fingerprint expert," Marc began, "so help me out. To my eye, the fingerprints on the letter opener handle up on the TV, is this Exhibit A? The letter opener you examined?"

"Yes."

"Again, to my untrained eye, these fingerprints look really good. Very clear and well defined, would you agree?"

"Yes, they are."

"Are fingerprints normally this clean? This clear?"

"More often than you would think," Vang said, having been prepped for this question.

"Nonresponsive, your Honor," Marc said. "I didn't ask what I might think. I asked if this is normal."

"Answer just the question," Judge Williams said.

"Perhaps before you do," Marc interrupted. "I should tell you I have an independent fingerprint expert with far more experience than you, who has reviewed your work and is willing to testify."

Vang hesitated then said, "Well, no, this is actually quite unusual to get a set this clear."

"And, isn't it true, you found no other fingerprints from anyone else on the letter opener?"

"That is true, yes."

"Would it be possible, Mr. Vang, in your expert opinion, for someone to take the hand of an unconscious person and place each finger on an object like this letter opener and plant these fingerprints?"

"Of course," Vang admitted.

"And would your analysis of the fingerprints reveal that, if this person was wearing gloves?"

"No, it would not," Vang answered.

"You may call your next witness, Mr. Krain," Judge Williams said while a dejected Donald Vang was walking out.

Dr. Farida Najafi was sworn in, took the stand, and gave her name and occupation for the court record. This was the doctor from the medical examiner's office who had conducted the autopsy.

An hour and a half later, the doctor was finally finished making it absolutely clear how Brody Knutson died. She also left no doubt, if there ever was any, that the single stab wound, which was consistent with the letter opener, caused his death.

"And did the tissue analysis show any drugs in the deceased's system?" Krain asked.

Marc could have objected to this since Dr. Najafi herself did not perform the tissue analysis. Instead, he stood to address the court.

"Your Honor, as it was not Dr. Najafi who conducted the tissue analysis, I will forego an objection but reserve my right to do so at trial. If the need arises."

"Very well," Williams said. "You may answer, Doctor."

"No, there were no drugs of any kind found in the deceased."

"Doctor Najafi," Marc began, "You testified that the stab wound that killed Brody Knutson was done by a person between five-feet-six and five-feet-eight-inches tall, is that your testimony?"

"Yes, it is."

"And you base this upon the angle of descent of the wound, correct?"

"Yes,"

"A taller person would have stabbed in a more downward manner?"

"Yes, that's true," she answered.

"Would it be possible for a taller person to bend his knees a bit?"

"Objection. Assumes facts not in evidence. There is no evidence that a man did this," Krain said.

"Overruled," Williams quickly said. "You may finish, Mr. Kadella."

"Would it be possible for a taller person to bend their knees," Marc turned, looked at Krain and smiled, "and thrust the letter opener straight into the deceased's heart to make it look like someone shorter did it?"

"Sure, that's possible but I…"

"Thank you, Doctor," Marc said cutting her off.

"I have nothing further, your Honor."

Krain had her complete her answer on re-direct, that there was no evidence of a taller person stabbing Knutson. It was a little weak and Judge Williams was clearly unimpressed.

The prosecution rested, believing they had submitted enough evidence to reach probable cause. Even Krain knew they had more work to do to reach beyond a reasonable doubt.

Judge Williams adjourned for the day. The defense would go tomorrow.

FIFTY-FOUR

"Are you ready to proceed, Mr. Kadella?" Judge Williams asked.

It was Tuesday morning a few minutes past 9:00 A.M. Judge Williams had made it clear they were going to finish today. Since there was no jury involved, only Williams himself, he told the lawyers they would go late, however long it took to finish.

Marc stood and made a brief opening statement. Judge Williams knew what was coming so Marc kept it short and to the point. He spelled out the basics of what his witnesses would say, then wrapped it up.

"The defense calls Sondra Neil," Marc announced.

Since she was first up, there was no need to sequester her from the other witnesses. Because of this, she was seated in the front row behind the defense table.

Sondra Neil was a fifty-two-year-old professional and looked the part. Well-groomed and professionally dressed, Sondra always made a good impression on the witness stand.

She was sworn, took the stand then clearly gave her name and occupation for the record. Sondra Neil, with over twenty years at the FBI forensics lab, was one of the foremost experts in the country, if not the world, on fingerprint analysis. It took over twenty minutes for her to recite her qualifications for the record. She not only had a Ph.D. but had written three books on the science of forensic analysis. She was also quite expensive.

Judge Williams readily agreed, and Krain did not object, to qualifying her as an expert. This would allow her to give her opinion about matters within her area of expertise.

Jeff Modell hit a couple keys on his laptop and a photo of the letter opener appeared on the monitors.

"On the TV screen is a photo of State's Exhibit A, do you recognize this?" Marc asked.

"Yes, I do. It is a photo of the letter opener that allegedly caused the death of Brody Knutson."

"Have you had an opportunity to examine and analyze State's Exhibit A for fingerprints?" Marc asked.

"Yes, I did."

"And what, if anything did you find, Ms. Neil?"

"Mrs. Neil," she said with a smile. "I don't mind being identified with my husband."

"My apologies," Marc replied.

"First of all, I found a clean set of fingerprints from the right hand of a person. All four fingers except the thumb.

"I then compared them to a set of prints I had obtained from Brooke Hartley, the defendant."

"And what did you conclude?"

"Well, without going into too much detail about whorls, grooves, and ridges…" she began looking up at Judge Williams.

"Thank you," Williams quietly replied. He shook his head at his court reporter, so he would not take down that comment.

"…the prints on the handle of the letter opener, State's Exhibit A, are an absolute match with the defendant's fingers of her right hand. No doubt about it.

"In fact," she continued, "they may be the best set of prints I've ever seen. They're too good. Too clean. No one holds a knife or letter opener with the tips of their fingers. If you are going to stab someone…"

"Objection. The witness has not been qualified as a medical expert or technician…" Krain stood and said.

"Overruled," Judge Williams said with a touch of annoyance in his voice. "I want to hear what she has to say."

"As I started to say, your Honor, if you are stabbing someone, you don't hold a knife—or in this case a letter opener—with the tips of your fingers. It would be more in the palm of the hand."

"Did you find any evidence of this on the letter opener?" Marc asked.

"No, none."

"What, if anything, did you conclude from this, in your expert opinion?"

"The defendant's fingerprints were somehow planted on the handle of the letter opener by someone else."

"One last question, Mrs. Neil. Were you aware that Brooke Hartley was discovered unconscious lying on the floor a few feet away from the dead body of Brody Knutson?"

"What? No…what? I had no idea. I was not told that. That explains how her prints were found on…"

"Objection, foundation, speculation," Krain practically jumped up while saying.

"Sustained," Judge Williams said. "Don't go where I think you're going, Mrs. Neil."

"Yes, your Honor."

Krain spent a half an hour with his cross-examination. He did his best to discredit her qualifications and findings but came up empty. The best he could do was get her to admit it was possible that Brooke stabbed Knutson and left her prints on the letter opener as they were found.

On re-direct, Marc had her tell the court that the likelihood of that happening was close to zero. A much more rational explanation for prints being that perfect was they were planted.

While the courtroom emptied for the morning break, Marc wheeled his chair around Brooke to talk discreetly to Jeff Modell.

"There's a guy sitting in the back row on the left side in the seat next to the door. He was here all day yesterday and he definitely looks out of place," Marc quietly said.

"I noticed him, too," Brooke said. "You're right, he doesn't look like the rest of the crowd. Too serious."

"Okay," Jeff said.

"After the break is over I want you to use your laptop to get a photo of him. I'll look for him and let you know if he is in the same seat."

Jeff positioned his laptop on the table to have a clear shot of that seat. The photo was going to be difficult to get through the crowd.

"You better look for him as he comes in and I'll try to get him before he sits down. I might not have an open line of sight once everyone is back," Jeff told him.

Brooke took the time to head for the ladies' room. She came in while Jeff was making a video of everyone coming back from the break. This way, he got a very clear picture of Aidan's man, Richie.

The rest of the morning was taken up with the testimony of Tony Carvelli and Jordan Fisk. Fisk was the lab technician who had done the analysis of the coffee found in Brooke's coffee cup. First to go was Tony Carvelli.

Carvelli's testimony was not long at all. He identified himself as a private investigator working for the defense. Marc walked him through the process of identifying the coffee cup itself and the small Tupperware container he had poured the coffee into. The Tupperware was something he found in Brooke's desk. He cleaned it out, marked it with his initials and poured what was left of Brooke's coffee into it.

Carvelli then testified that he was the one that took the items to a local laboratory for analysis. This was all done to establish a secure chain of evidence to preclude the prosecution from claiming it was tampered with.

Krain almost lost it during his cross-examination. He raised hell about Carvelli crossing a crime scene tape and gathering evidence. Using this, he tried to have Carvelli's testimony thrown out.

Judge Williams almost casually overruled him. The judge made the obvious point that the police had every opportunity to do the same thing.

He also ruled the defense has a right to examine the crime scene for exculpatory evidence.

When the judge finally excused him, Carvelli wasted no time in beating a hasty retreat. Judge Williams looked at the clock then motioned for the lawyers to come up to the bench. He turned on the white noise when they arrived.

"How much time will you need for your next witness?" the judge asked Marc.

Marc looked at the clock and said, "I can finish before lunch, your Honor."

"Who are you putting on the stand?" Krain arrogantly asked.

"You'll see," Marc replied.

"Your Honor," Krain said to Judge Williams, "I saw a man in the hall before court. His name is Jordan Fisk. He's a chemist at the U. I believe he's going to testify about the coffee that was taken from the crime scene and…"

"Is that correct?" Williams asked Marc.

"Yes, your Honor," Marc answered.

"Good. Let's get him in here. I want to hear what he found," Williams said.

"Your Honor!" Krain burst out.

"Relax, Jerry. Let's see what he has to say, then we'll deal with your objection."

Dr. Jordan Fisk was a very highly respected chemist who was a professor at the University of Minnesota. He was also a partner in an independent research lab. He had been given the sample of Brooke's coffee to analyze. Dr. Fisk and his partner were both almost professional witnesses.

He took the stand and gave his name and profession. Jordan Fisk made a very different impression than the stereotype of a chemistry professor. He was a tall, dignified man who had that handsome older man look about him. It did not hurt the image that he favored expensive, Brooks Brother's suits.

Marc started out by going over Fisk's curriculum vitae to establish him as an expert. Ten minutes in, Krain stood and stipulated to the witness's qualifications. Ignoring him, Marc finished going through them anyway for the record.

Following a few preliminary questions about how the coffee to be analyzed was sent to him, and the process he used, Marc moved into his findings.

"There was a significant dosage of a street derivative of Flunitrazepam in the coffee provided to me for analysis, Defense Exhibit One," he testified.

"What is Flunitrazepam, Doctor?"

"It is more commonly known as roofies. It's also called the date rape drug. It will cause a person to lose control of themselves and will put them into a state of unconsciousness. This particular batch is a compound we are seeing more of colloquially called Roofie Express. It works very fast and is also metabolized very fast by the liver."

"Was there enough in the coffee sample to work on an adult?" Marc asked.

"Extrapolating the amount in the sample to what was in the cup that was consumed, whoever drank it would have been knocked out in one to two minutes," Fisk answered.

"How long would she have been out?" Marc asked.

"At least an hour, maybe two."

"Would she have a…"

"Objection to counsel's use of the pronoun 'she'," Krain said.

"Overruled," Williams quickly said.

"Would she have a memory loss, a blackout during that time?"

"Absolutely," Fisk answered.

"How long would it take for the body to metabolize the drug so there would be no trace of it in the blood or urine?"

"Hard to say positively. It depends on the person. With this amount, it could be as little as three hours but at most, five. Probably around four hours."

"Doctor, if someone was given this amount of the drug, would she have been able to go into another room, stab someone…"

"Objection. Goes beyond his expertise. Speculative," Krain said.

"Sustained," Williams ruled.

"May I approach the witness?" Marc asked.

"Yes."

Marc stood and handed a three-page document to Krain. He walked up to the witness box to Dr. Fisk. He had Fisk identify the document, marked Defense Exhibit Four, as his report. Marc moved to have it admitted and gave a copy to Judge Williams.

"I have nothing further," Marc declared.

Before asking any questions, Krain stood and said, "Your Honor, we ask the witnesses testimony to be stricken, and Defense Four be set aside. We have had no notice of any of this nor have we had an opportunity to question the witness or have lab tests done ourselves."

Marc, who was still on his feet, said, "Your Honor, they had every opportunity to do these things while they conducted their thorough investigation."

"He has a point, Mr. Krain," Judge Williams said, "Doctor Fisk, how long would it take a qualified lab to test what remains of the coffee and get results?"

"A few hours, your Honor, if they prioritize it," Fisk replied.

Judge Williams looked at Krain and said, "I'll give you forty-eight hours. Until noon on Thursday. I'm not going to let you drag this out. Do you have questions for this witness?"

"Not at this time," Krain said. "But if our lab results are different, I will ask the court to reconvene to admit testimony about it and we may want to put Dr. Fisk back on the stand at that time."

"Mr. Kadella?" Williams asked.

"The defense has no objection, your Honor. We are confident of the analysis as long as the prosecution uses an unbiased lab," Marc said.

"Your Honor!" Krain yelled.

"Stop," Williams said. He excused Dr. Fisk, looked at the clock and broke for lunch.

FIFTY-FIVE

While the gallery was emptying for the lunch break, Tony Carvelli re-entered the courtroom and walked up the center aisle against the stream. He passed through the gate and went to the defense table.

"Hi, Tony," Brooke said with a big smile.

"Hey, kid," Carvelli replied. "How are you holding up?"

"Okay. I think it's going pretty well," she replied.

"Look at this," Marc told Carvelli. He was referring to a photo displayed on Jeff Modell's laptop. It was a good picture of the man in the back of the room.

"You know him?" Marc asked.

Carvelli stared at the screen for several seconds then said, "He looks familiar, but I can't place him. Why?"

"He's been sitting in back by the door. He doesn't look like the usual court watcher crowd and he's certainly not media."

"Jeff, email that photo to me," Carvelli said. To Marc, he said, "I'll send it to Paul and I think I'll send it to an MPD detective I know in their Intelligence Unit. Maybe he'll know him."

Aidan answered the phone call he had been expecting by asking, "What do you have?"

"They found the drug we used on the girl. There was enough left over in her cup on her desk. They got some doctor guy to test it, and he testified about it. So, what do you want me to do?" Richie asked him.

Despite the cool weather, Richie was outside in front of the government center. He was a little shook up about Dr. Fisk's testimony and desperately needed a cigarette. There was silence from Aidan for several seconds while Richie walked around smoking.

"You still there?" he asked Aidan.

"Do nothing. Go back in and just do what you've been doing. Watch the trial. I'll talk to the boss."

At the same time, Gerald Krain and Gabe Hunt had retreated upstairs to Krain's office. Hunt had followed him in and barely closed the door when the volcano went off.

"Jesus H. goddamn Christ!" Krain bellowed. "How could you miss the coffee sitting on her desk? What kind of clusterfuck investigation..."

"It was the crime scene guys who..."

"Shut up! I don't want to hear any excuses," Krain yelled.

Krain turned away from the detective, stepped up to the window and stared at U.S. Bank stadium a half mile to the East. While he did this, Hunt stood silently waiting for another ass-chewing. With twenty-seven years on the job, Hunt was calculating his pension trying to decide if he should tell Krain where he could shove it.

Hunt heard the prosecutor deeply inhale then, while still looking out the window, calmly say, "It's a probable cause hearing." Krain turned around to face Hunt and continued, "I still think we'll survive that."

Krain took the chair behind his desk. Hunt sat down in one of the client chairs. "But we have a lot of work to do before trial. Fortunately, we'll know what they will be counting on to create reasonable doubt at trial. Before then, we'll have to be able to refute every bit of it."

"You think the judge will find probable cause?" a relieved Hunt asked.

"Yeah, it's a pretty low bar. But you're going to have to tighten up your investigation. The good news is, I think, they didn't find any of this drug in her system."

"How do you know?"

"Because if they had her tested, whoever did the testing would have been first on the witness stand. That's why they had their expert make a big deal about how long this stuff stays in the body."

"Makes sense," Hunt agreed.

There was a knock on the door, and Krain's secretary came in. She was carrying two box lunches and two bottles of water.

Although the door to Cal's home office was open, Aidan lightly rapped on the door's trim anyway. Cal looked up from the papers he was going through and said, "Must be bad news. That's the only time you knock. What is it?"

Aidan had entered the office and was taking a seat in front of the desk. "It's like we thought. They found roofies in the coffee that we missed on the girl's desk."

"Shit," Cal quietly said leaning back in his chair.

"But they got no way to tie it to us," Aidan said.

"The other secretary, Lucy," Cal said.

"She doesn't know dick," Aidan said.

"See to it," Cal said.

"That's not gonna look good, boss," Aidan said.

Cal thought about it for a moment, then said, "You're right. It would be as bad as popping the lawyer. Goddamnit!"

"Before the trial, we can arrange an accident. Once the publicity dies down," Aidan replied.

"Yeah," Cal agreed. "That's probably the thing to do."

"You decided what to do with Maddy?" Aidan asked.

"Nothing, right now. We'll string her along for a while. Besides, you read the stuff on the internet about her. She's not to be taken lightly," Cal said.

Aidan smiled a sinister smile and said, "I can handle a girl."

"The defense calls Lucy Gibson, your Honor," Marc said to start the afternoon session.

The exit doors opened and Carvelli escorted Lucy Gibson up the aisle and through the gate. Tony took one of the chairs in front of the bar behind the defense table. Lucy was reminded by Judge Williams she was still under oath and took the stand again.

"During your testimony for the prosecution," Marc said starting out very friendly, mildly, to put her at ease, "Mr. Krain made a big deal about how Brooke Hartley felt about Brody Knutson."

"Objection to the characterization of a big deal," Krain stood and said.

"Overruled," Judge Williams quickly said.

"Isn't it true that you felt the same way about your former boss?" Marc asked.

"Um, yeah, I guess," Lucy said very quietly.

"I'm sorry, was that a 'yes'?" Marc asked. "I didn't hear your answer."

"Yes," she said loud and clear.

"He made the same kind of comments toward you that you told the court he did at Brooke Hartley about how you dressed, how you looked, your perfume, things like that did he not?"

"Yes, he did."

"Did it make you uncomfortable?"

"A lot, yes."

"Did you ever think about murdering him?"

"Objection!" Krain bellowed.

Williams thought about it for a couple of seconds then said, "No, I'll allow it. Overruled. You may answer, Ms. Gibson."

"Of course not!"

"Did you ever hear Brooke say, 'I'd like to kill that old so and so'?"

"Objection, hearsay," Krain said.

"If Ms. Hartley ever said such a thing, it would certainly be a statement against interest hearsay exception," Marc said.

"Overruled."

"No, no, of course not. She didn't like it, but she never said anything like that."

"Why didn't you go to the H.R. people and file a complaint for sexual harassment?"

"Mr. Knutson was very powerful at the firm. Other girls had complained, and they were moved. I liked the job and the pay was good. Besides, it wasn't that bad. Mostly just comments he made. Things like that."

"Do you know if Brooke felt the same way?"

"Objection."

"Overruled."

"Sure, we talked about it a lot. Mr. Knutson was, well, a harmless maybe even lonely man. We put up with it."

"In fact, virtually every woman at Everson, Reed felt the same way, didn't they?"

"The ones that I knew, yes."

"The morning you arrived at the office, the day Mr. Knutson was killed, your testimony was: you hung up your coat, placed your purse on your desk and immediately went into the break room. Is that correct?"

"Yes, it is."

"You were going to get a cup of coffee, weren't you?"

"Yes, I was but..."

"Let me ask the questions, please," Marc politely said. "We'll get there."

"Okay," Lucy said, a touch embarrassed.

"Instead, you found the coffee pot sitting on the counter empty and rinsed out, correct?"

"Yes," Lucy agreed.

"And this surprised you didn't it, because you knew Brooke had set up the timer on the coffee maker to brew a fresh pot in the morning, didn't you?"

"Yes, she did."

"Did you look in the container on the coffee maker where the coffee grounds are put, and the water runs through to make coffee?"

Lucy visibly sat up and had a look of fresh remembrance on her face. "Yes, I did, and it was empty. And the wastebasket was empty. What happened to..."

"The used coffee grounds that you saw Brooke set up the night before," Marc said completing her thought.

"Objection," Krain weakly said.

"Sustained. Let the witness answer," Judge Williams said.

"Ms. Gibson, did Mr. Knutson have a cleaning service to clean his personal office?"

"No, he did not."

"Who cleaned it?"

288

"That was part of our duties, mine and Brooke, Ms. Hartley. Mr. Knutson did not want any strangers in his office snooping around. He was a pretty neat person, so it wasn't a big deal."

"Did you ever handle the letter opener, State's Exhibit A?" Marc asked.

"When we were cleaning up, sure. It was on his desk and we normally picked it up and moved it. He loved that letter opener," she answered.

"Did you ever see Mr. Knutson handling the letter opener?"

"He was always playing with it especially when he was on the phone."

"Did you clean up Mr. Knutson's office the night before his death?"

"Yes, we vacuumed and dusted and straightened everything up for him."

"Do you recall if either of you wiped the handle of the letter opener clean?"

"No, I don't think we ever did that."

At that moment, a court deputy came in through the door behind the bench. She silently handed Judge Williams a folded piece of paper. The judge opened it, read the note, frowned and nodded to the woman who gave it to him.

"Something's come up," Williams said looking at Marc. "Let's take a fifteen-minute break. Off the record," he said to the court reporter.

"A phone call on another case I need to take," he said to Marc and Krain.

"How did you know about the coffee grounds?" Carvelli quietly asked Marc while the courtroom emptied. "Even I didn't notice that."

"I didn't know," Marc answered. "In fact, I hadn't even thought of it until right now. I just took a chance and asked her about it. It seemed like a sensible thing. Besides, if she said, 'no, I didn't check for the coffee grounds'; I would have just let it go and moved on."

FIFTY-SIX

It was closer to a half hour before Judge Williams was back on the bench. He told Marc to proceed and Marc nodded at Jeff. Jeff clicked a couple of keys on the laptop and a photo of a serious looking man appeared on the TV screens. When the man's picture appeared, Marc noticed Lucy's eyes widen and a worried look came over her.

"Ms. Gibson," Marc began, "on the courtroom monitors is a picture of a man. Reminding you that you are under oath, I ask you, do you recognize this man?"

Hesitantly, Lucy nervously said, "Yes."

"And what is his name?"

"Um, Bret Holston," Lucy answered.

"And who is he to you?"

"He's a man I've been seeing socially."

"You're dating him?" Marc asked.

"Well, sort of, a little, I guess," she said.

Marc held up a sheet of paper with several columns of print on it. "I have here your phone records for the past two months. What would you say if I told you it shows you called him seventy-two times, and he called you over fifty times during that period?"

"Objection, relevance," Krain said. "They were dating so they called each other. So, what?"

"Mr. Kadella?" Williams asked.

"A little leeway, your Honor, and we'll get there," Marc said.

"Overruled, for now."

"Ms. Gibson? Would you agree with those number of phone calls?"

"How do you know his phone number?" Lucy asked.

"Is it 672-878-4366?" Marc asked.

"Um, yes, it is," she agreed.

"Answer the question, please," Marc said.

"Yes, I guess that number of calls would be right. So what?" she said becoming defensive and a touch hostile.

"During the forty-eight hours leading up to the time when Mr. Knutson was killed, there are nineteen calls between the two of you. Did you tell this man you know as Bret Holston, when Brody Knutson would come in early to the office?"

"I, ah, I don't recall…"

"You're under oath, Ms. Gibson," Marc reminded her.

"I may have. We talked about a lot of things…"

"Isn't it true he asked you specifically what time Brody Knutson would be in on the morning of his death?"

"I, ah, am not, ah…"

"Yes or no," Ms. Gibson.

"I think, I think, he, um, he did, yes."

"In fact, during the two months you were seeing him, the two of you talked a lot about your job and the office routines, didn't you?"

Marc was totally fishing, but knowing who the man really was, he believed he was on solid ground.

While Marc was going at her during this sequence, Carvelli's phone vibrated. He sneaked a quick peek at it, then headed for the hall.

"I don't think I would say we talked about it a lot, but he always seemed so interested in what I do for a living."

"So, the answer to my question is yes, you told him about the office routines, didn't you?"

"Yes," she reluctantly agreed.

"And at some point, you told him it was Brooke's turn to come in early on the day Brody Knutson was murdered, didn't you?"

"I, ah, don't recall…"

"You're under oath," Marc said.

"Objection, she already answered him," Krain said in an attempt to stop the bleeding.

"Overruled," Judge Williams said.

"I may have," she almost whispered.

"I'm sorry, what was that?" Marc asked.

By this point, Brooke was ready to cry. She genuinely liked Lucy and was starting to feel terrible at the hammering she was taking. But there was something about the photo on the TV, the man in it that made her realize her lawyer knew exactly what he was doing.

"I may have," she repeated clearly.

"On the morning of Brody Knutson's death, you arrived at work early, at seven-thirty, correct?"

"Yes."

"You found Mr. Knutson dead in his office and Brooke on the floor unconscious a few minutes later, isn't that true?" Marc continued much more lightly.

"Yes," Lucy agreed.

"And you helped Brooke up and out to her desk. You must have asked something similar to 'what happened', didn't you?"

"Yes, of course."

"And she told you she had no memory of what happened, didn't she?"

"Yes, that's what she said."

"Did you believe her?"

"Yes, I did. She was very out of it, you know? Very confused."

"According to the 911 operator record that I have," Marc said holding up a report from the 911 dispatch department that he had been given by Krain, "you called 9-1-1 to report the death of your boss at seven-forty-eight. Does that sound right?"

"Yes," she agreed.

"The call lasted a little over four minutes. Does that sound right?"

"Yes."

Marc held up the record of her calls made from her phone and continued. "According to your phone record, you received a call from the man you know as Bret Holston at eight-twelve and talked to him for three minutes."

"Yes, that's true. I thought he just called to say hello. He did that sometimes," she blurted out.

"And you told him what you found when you came into the office that morning, didn't you?"

"Well, yes. It seemed like a normal thing to do."

Carvelli slipped quietly back into the courtroom and took a seat in the back row, the second one in from the door. The man next to him, recognizing Carvelli being with the defense, looked nervously about. He was trying to decide if he should get up and leave.

"Hi, Richie," Carvelli whispered almost directly into his ear. "You and me need to have a little chat."

"I don't think so," he replied.

"Shouldn't you give Aidan a call?"

"I don't know what you're talking about," he replied. Without waiting for Carvelli to say anything else, he stood and fled out the door.

"I have nothing further, your Honor," Marc said, much to Lucy's relief.

"Mr. Krain, your witness."

Gerald Krain sat silently for a full minute trying to think of something he could ask to fix this. Not digging into Lucy Gibson's life and phone records was another screw up by Hunt. Unable to think of anything, Krain passed on any questions.

"Any more witnesses, Mr. Kadella?"

"One, your Honor," Marc said after standing. "The defense calls Sean O'Rourke."

Carvelli was already in the hall to fetch Paxton's uncle. He had flown in the night before and Marc had spent a couple of hours preparing his testimony.

Sean took the stand and gave his occupation as a retired FBI agent. In order to bolster his credibility, Marc had decided to do a very thorough presentation of Sean's career. By the time they were finished, there was not anyone in the courtroom who was not impressed. Sean O'Rourke had a long and very distinguished career with the Bureau.

"I'm going to cut to the chase here, Mr. O'Rourke and get right to why you were brought here. The photograph of the man on the TV screen, do you recognize him?"

"Yes, I do."

"And is his name, to your knowledge, Bret Holston."

"Well, I've never heard of him using that name, but he could be using it."

"Do you know what his name is?"

"He was born in Boston and his birth name is Aidan O'Keefe. He has a long criminal record including three prison terms. He was even an enforcer, in his youth, for Whitey Bulger's Winter Hill Gang."

The mention of the infamous and well-known Whitey Bulger brought a stir through the courtroom.

"He has been suspected of several murders and been convicted of armed robbery, serious aggravated assaults, and racketeering."

"To your knowledge is he still using the name, Aidan O'Keefe?'"

"Over the years we, meaning the FBI and law enforcement, have known him by at least eight aliases. He is currently using the name, Aidan Walsh."

"How do you know this, Mr. O'Rourke? Since you're retired, how do you know these things?"

"I've known of this man for at least twenty to twenty-five years. At your request, I checked with contacts I have in the Bureau and received an update on him. They know he's here in the Twin Cities and who he is working for."

"And who might that be?"

"Objection, hearsay. He admitted he does not have personal, law-enforcement knowledge of that?"

"Do you?" Judge Williams asked.

"I haven't been working a case on him if that's what you mean."

"Sustained," the judge said. "Do you have anything more, Mr. Kadella?"

"No, your Honor," Marc replied.

"Mr. Krain?"

"Do you have any personal knowledge concerning the death of Brody Knutson, Mr. O'Rourke?" Krain asked.

"No, I do not."

"Do you know if this person you claim to be Aidan Walsh or O'Keefe or whatever, do you know if he is involved in the death of Brody Knutson?"

"No, I do not," Sean admitted.

"Your Honor," Marc stood and said. "We made it clear that this witness was called for the sole purpose of accurately identifying the witness Ms. Gibson claimed was Bret Holston. He has done that positively. Mr. Krain's questions are clearly outside the scope of the direct exam."

"Good point. Mr. Krain, do you have anything to cast doubt on the credibility of the witness's identification?"

"No, your Honor," Krain said.

"Then maybe you should wrap this up."

"I have nothing further," Krain said.

Judge Williams called the lawyers up to the bench and first asked Marc if he had more witnesses. Receiving a negative reply, he told them to make their closing brief. Despite that admonition, Krain spoke for almost thirty minutes. When he was done, he had managed to make a good case for probable cause.

Marc quickly went through the same evidence and pointed out, probably unnecessarily, the weakness in the state's case.

"Your Honor," Marc began his conclusion, "it's important to look at the broad picture here. The prosecution is asking you to find probable cause to give them an opportunity to do the investigation they should have done in the first place.

"I absolutely contend that they did not reach the burden of a finding of probable cause. And, your Honor, they are miles away from guilt beyond a reasonable doubt. It would be unethical to continue this travesty. They cannot possibly believe there is evidence to prove guilt beyond a reasonable doubt. And, they are not going to find any more.

"This young woman, Brooke Hartley, has been through enough. Stop this now, your Honor. For the sake of justice, put an end to this farce. Thank you."

Marc took his seat and Judge Williams turned to Krain. He reminded him that he had until Thursday, a day and a half or so from now, to submit a report on his own lab test of the coffee. With that, the hearing was adjourned.

FIFTY-SEVEN

Aidan ended the call he had taken from Richie and tossed the phone on the passenger seat. He was in his year-old Cadillac on his way back to Cal's when the call came in. Because of what he had been told, Aidan's attention to his driving was definitely distracted. He was sitting at a red light that had turned green several seconds ago. Being Minnesota, the driver behind him gave him a polite beep of his horn to wake him up. He pulled over and parked as soon as he got through the intersection.

While Aidan sat in the car he thought about what Richie had told him. His picture had been displayed during Lucy's testimony. How did the defense come up with that? How did they find all the phone calls between him and Lucy? How did they get his unlisted number to know who she was calling?

According to Richie, he had been identified only as Bret Holston. But Richie left because of the defense team guy that confronted him. He did not see the rest of the day's testimony. Did the defense know who he was? Now what? He had to tell Cal and then what? Aidan put the car in drive and was at Cal's home fifteen minutes later.

"There's that soft knock again. The one you use when you have bad news to tell me," Cal said looking up from his desk at Aidan.

Aidan took his usual chair at Cal's desk, took a deep breath and told him about Richie's phone call.

Cal looked at his watch and without a word picked up the remote on his desk and turned on the TV. He quickly found a local channel that was just starting its five o'clock news show. The story came up after the first commercial break. On the screen, over the left shoulder of the female anchor, was the photo of Aidan that was displayed in court. Cal increased the volume to be sure to hear it all. When the woman was done reading the story Cal shut off the TV.

"Okay, they identified you as Aidan O'Keefe but apparently have nothing about who you work for," Cal said. "This means we're definitely going to move up the timetable. It won't be long before they put us together."

"How soon?" Aidan asked.

Cal thought about the question for a moment, then said, "I think we need to wrap this up and get out of here as soon as possible. Next week at the latest. Samantha is still in Europe moving money. If we walk now we may lose some but that can't be helped."

"What about your friends in D.C.? The ones that are getting really impatient."

Cal smiled and said, "We're done setting them up. Samantha's done a great job."

"The apple doesn't fall far from the tree," Aidan said.

"I wish that were the case," Cal laughed. "Anyway, the politicians and military people think their accounts are all set up. By the time they figure out they've been scammed, we'll be on the beach and untouchable. In the meantime, get rid of that phone."

"I already have. It's in pieces in the lake," Aidan replied. "Have you decided it's time to get rid of me?" Aidan asked.

"No, not going to happen. You're too valuable and loyal. You'll have to trust me. I won't do that," Cal said. Cal was also thinking that Aidan could just as easily dispatch him. Better they stick together.

"What about Lucy?" Aidan asked.

"I don't know, what do you think?"

"I think she's untouchable now. Besides, she's already spilled everything she knows. It would only lend credibility to her if she were dealt with."

"Agreed. Probably best to leave her alone."

"What about this P.I. chick? Your girlfriend, Maddy?" Aidan asked.

"Without the bugs, they don't know that we know who she is. Is your guy in place? The one from Chicago you were going to put on her?"

"Yeah, he got in last night. I took him around to her place myself. He was gonna set up on her."

While Cal and Aidan were discussing Aidan's awkward court appearance, Marc, Brooke, Carvelli, Jeff and Sean O'Rourke were leaving court together. They had waited a half-hour for the media to leave and the crowd to thin out. Marc had gone out into the hallway to make a few comments to the press. Satisfied, they began to melt away to file their stories.

"Tell me the truth," Brooke said to Marc. The four of them were waiting for an elevator. It was quitting time in the large building and the elevators were busy.

Before Marc could answer, Carvelli's phone rang. He looked at the ID and walked off a few steps to take it.

"My honest opinion," Marc replied, "is I don't know. Having said that, I feel pretty good. I think Judge Williams is going to dismiss it. Unless there is a big difference in their lab test results."

"Can they appeal it if he does dismiss it?" Sean asked.

"Yeah, they could," Marc said. "I doubt they will. The judge has broad discretion in these things."

"We definitely showed reasonable doubt," Jeff added.

"True," Marc agreed. "But that's not the standard. We'll see."

An elevator car arrived. When the doors opened, they looked into it and a sardine could not have slipped in. Marc smiled at the sullen crowd and the doors closed.

"Thanks, Paul. I'll get back to you," they heard Carvelli say.

"What?" Marc asked when Carvelli rejoined them.

"Ready for this? He didn't find any unusual bank accounts in the names of Mason Hooper or Norah McCabe."

"That's a little disappointing," Sean replied.

"But," Carvelli continued with a sly smile, "he dug a little deeper and found two accounts under the names of Norah's children. And combined they have a little over three point six-million in them."

"Where?" Marc asked.

"The Caymans," Carvelli replied. "What do you think, Sean?"

"I know some people who will be very interested to find this out," the ex-Feeb answered.

"He's emailing the report to me in an hour or so. He wasn't done with it," Carvelli told Sean. "When I get it, I'll forward it to you."

"Great," Sean replied. "I'll bet they have more than that. Cal Simpson is rich and if Mason Hooper has been covering for him all these years…"

"I'll talk to my guy," Carvelli replied. "I'll have him keep digging."

"Have him check out Hooper's parents. Hooper would have access to their social security numbers and any other information he might need."

The man that Aidan had brought in to follow Maddy was watching her move around her apartment. His name was Harry Semple and he was a forty-eight-year-old retired British SAS soldier. Ten years ago, he left the British Army under a cloud. The rumors about his association with the London underworld had proven to be true. Nothing had been proven about any criminal activities that he might have been involved in, so no charges were brought. He was given a "notice to leave" type discharge. Essentially, he had been fired.

SAS soldiers are among the most rigorously trained and toughest in the world. None of his comrades were sorry to see Semple go. Among his many postings, he had spent several tours in Ireland and was an expert in urban surveillance. He was also a little too enthusiastic about enhanced interrogation.

Semple had essentially been run out of the U.K. and made his way to Boston. From there, he went to Chicago where he earned a good living as a mob enforcer and collections expert. His skill at urban surveillance served him well.

This evening he was standing at the window of a darkened living room. It was an eighth-floor apartment directly across LaSalle from Maddy's condo. The occupants of the apartment, a very well-to-do elderly couple, had left for Arizona in early October. The sub-lessee would be moving in next week. A bribe to building security had gotten him the use of it until then.

Semple sat down in a chair facing the window. Unconcerned about being seen in the dark room, he lit a cigarette and sipped his glass of Guinness Draught. He stared admiringly through his field glasses at Maddy and quietly said, "Well, lassie, what are you up to tonight? It's a shame a beauty such as yourself doesn't have more of a social life."

Semple stayed on watch until midnight. Maddy watched television, made or received three phone calls and fiddled around on a laptop until 10:00. She watched the ten o'clock local newscast then made a call when it was over. Whoever it was she called, she spoke to for about fifteen minutes, then went to bed.

While his surveillance target was on the phone after the news was over, Semple's phone rang. He checked the caller ID, did not recognize it, but decided to take the call anyway.

"Did you get a new phone?" Semple asked when the caller identified himself.

"Yeah," Aidan replied. "Checking in. Anything?"

"No, sir," Semple answered. "The lass is on the phone and likely heading to bed."

"Do you need relief?"

"No, I'm fine."

FIFTY-EIGHT

On Thursday morning Marc was the first to arrive at their offices. It was a few minutes after 7:00 and he was getting ready for a full day. He had three appointments with prospective clients and from all of them he was expecting to receive a nice retainer. The business of a lawyer goes on regardless of what else he was doing.

The day before, Wednesday, the day after the in-court revelation about Aidan Walsh nee' O'Keefe, there had been a mild media storm of speculation concerning who and what he was. It was becoming generally conceded, at least in the news, that Brooke Hartley appeared to have been set up. But who was this man and more importantly, where was he?

The object of this attention was holed up in the home of Calvin Simpson. While Cal and Samantha continued their money laundering scheme—turning large deposits into smaller deposits and then back into larger deposits in untouchable banks—Aidan cooled his heels.

On the other hand, Carolyn Lucas and Sandy Compton, the office legal assistants, were ready to quit their jobs. Thanks to Marc's courtroom surprise, the phone rang constantly from various media outlets. At first, Marc refused to take the calls. By lunchtime, Carolyn and Sandy were threatening to turn him into a soprano if he didn't.

Marc had spent most of Wednesday afternoon answering the phones himself, so the assistants could get some work done. While doing so, he decided to have a little fun jerking around the reporters and adding fuel to the media speculation fire.

"Are we going to go through another day like yesterday?" Marc heard Carolyn ask from his office doorway. He looked up at her as she asked, "Want some?" indicating the coffee pot she was holding.

"Sure," Marc replied. "I don't know. Probably not, but tomorrow we should shut off the phones."

Carolyn re-filled his cup and said, "You're going to do this? Go on with Gabriella this afternoon?"

"Yes, I am," Marc answered.

The office phone rang, and Marc said, "I'll get it." He answered the call, looked at Carolyn and said, "Speak of the devil. Yes, darling, what can I do for you?" Marc said into the phone as Carolyn turned to leave.

"Are we still on?" Gabriella said.

"It's not even eight o'clock and you're already worried."

"The station wants to run promos all day. After the shitstorm you created the past two days, we could get quite an audience," Gabriella said.

"Great, my mother will probably watch."

299

"I thought she watched every day?"

"Today, if her little darling son is going to be on, she'll have half the geezers in town tuned in," Marc said.

Gabriella laughed. She had a laugh that could actually make men weak and said, "We'll be sure to be extra careful when we comb your hair. We want mom to be proud. Try not to spill too much lunch on your tie."

"Have you heard from the judge? Has he made a decision?" Gabriella asked.

"Not yet," Marc answered. "Probably this morning, maybe."

"What does that mean, probably maybe?"

"It means we'll see. I'll see you at one," Marc said.

"Call me if you get a decision so I can scoop it," Gabriella said. "Please," she added.

"We'll see."

"Marc..."

"Bye, bye, nosey. I'll see you at one," he said and hung up.

At 10:30 Carolyn answered a phone call. "He's with a client, but he's been in there long enough. I'll interrupt him. Hang on."

Carolyn lightly tapped on Marc's door and opened it. "Carla, Judge Williams's clerk, is on the phone."

Marc looked at the young man, his new client, and his father, the source of attorney fees, and asked, "Do you have any questions?"

"No," the father said. "If you need to talk to a judge..."

"I really do. You could wait if you need to talk some more. I don't mean to hustle you out," Marc said.

"No, we're good," the father said again. "Do you want me to give you the check or..."

"Carolyn can take care of that. I really should take this call," Marc said as he stood up. He handed the signed retainer agreement to Carolyn. He shook hands with both and waited until his door was closed to answer the phone.

Twenty minutes later, the conference call between Judge Williams, Marc and Gerald Krain ended.

"YES!" Marc yelled after hanging up the phone.

Immediately his door opened, and the entire office was standing there. They had been waiting, listening for a reaction.

"He dismissed it," Marc said. "Krain's pretty mad. Making noises about an appeal but I doubt they'll do it."

"They don't have the evidence to win at trial," Barry Cline, Marc's friend and colleague said. "Cooler heads than the Nazi will prevail at the county attorney's office," he continued using Krain's defense lawyer nickname. Barry had his share of run-ins with Krain also.

"Now what?" Carolyn asked.

"Now I call Brooke and let her know. Judge Williams said he would email an order out yet this morning. That reminds me," Marc said. He turned to his computer screen and opened his email. He found the one he wanted, opened it and printed the attachment. The printer on his credenza spit out a document and Marc held it up.

"The test results from the lab at the BCA," he said. "Their test was virtually identical to ours, finding the drugs in Brooke's coffee. Obviously, she was drugged, and Williams tossed out the case."

"Good afternoon and welcome to the Court Reporter. My name is Gabriella Shriqui and I'm your host.

"We're fortunate today to have with us in the studio, prominent local criminal defense attorney, Marc Kadella. Marc has been a frequent guest and always has something very interesting to discuss with us," Gabriella read off of the teleprompter.

She continued with, "In the cause of full disclosure, I must admit that Marc has become a good friend of mine. We've never dated or anything like that, but I do consider him a friend."

Finished with the introduction, the camera moved back to get a shot of both of them as Gabriella turned to Marc. They were using an anchor desk and seated right next to each other.

"Hello, Marc, it's good to see you again," Gabriella said flashing a big smile.

Marc returned the greeting, then Gabriella spent a couple of minutes asking him about Brooke Hartley's case. The news had leaked out even before Judge Williams wrote his formal order. When Marc finished explaining his side of that case, Gabriella asked, "I understand you're here to discuss something very serious that you believe is related to the murder of Brody Knutson. Would you care to share that?"

"I sure do," Marc said. "As you probably remember Gabriella, since you were there and filmed it, a client of mine was deliberately run over during a hit and run and died. I was also a victim of that hit and run...."

"Would you mind if we showed it to our audience?"

"No, go ahead," Marc said.

Of course, this was set up before they began taping earlier in the day. For the next minute, the death of Zach Evans was shown twice. Once at normal speed, once in slow motion.

"Ever since then, myself and some others have been trying to solve this; find out who is responsible for it. There were two men involved, two brothers. Ryan and Michael Tierney. Michael was the driver and positively identified. They are well known to the Boston police as vicious gangsters. They have also disappeared. The Boston police believe they were murdered. Probably because of an unrelated matter.

"During the course of our investigation, we have uncovered a massive criminal conspiracy. It involves stock fraud, insider trading, money laundering and murder. We have a videotaped confession from one of the conspirators, a congressman from Minnesota."

"Good god," Gabriella said sincerely shocked. Up to this moment, she had not been told any of this. "That's quite an accusation. Do you have any proof of this?"

"As I said, we have a videotaped confession from one of the conspirators," Marc said again. "One of the politicians involved with it. He's a congressman from Minnesota. That's all I can say about him at this time.

"Legally, uncorroborated co-conspirator testimony is not sufficient to establish guilt," Marc told her. "We have been trying to get further corroboration of what he gave us. Brody Knutson was on the verge of giving us that when he was murdered."

"Do you think Knutson was killed to shut him up?" Gabriella asked.

"I can't say that for sure, so I won't," Marc replied. "This conspiracy used inside information on at least two companies to enrich themselves. Doing this, they drove the price of the stock up and cashed in. Then they manipulated information about the stock and through short selling drove the stock price down and made another fortune. Because of this they are responsible for the bankruptcy of Cannon Brothers Toys and almost put Morton Aviation out of business. Between these two companies, the conspirators' stock manipulation, fraud and insider trading made themselves a fabulous amount of money and put over a thousand people out of work.

"And based on what we have on our video, I don't believe the death of Senator Roger Manion was a natural heart attack. His doctor was on TV and said he was surprised because the senator's heart was fine. They need to take a closer look at the toxicology and check for heart attack inducing drugs."

"Are you saying he was murdered by the people involved in this conspiracy to keep him quiet? That he was a part of it and could corroborate what you have filmed from the congressman?"

"I'll say this: first of all, I know Brooke Hartley did not murder Brody Knutson. As to who did, I cannot make that accusation. Knutson was talking to us. We almost filmed him once. Then he got scared and a couple of days later, he was murdered."

Marc was looking at Gabriella when he said this. He turned to look directly into the camera and said, "Soon, either the Justice Department or the media is going to get that video. Even if it isn't enough to convict, it will bring out the truth about what we have found."

With a couple of breaks in the taping for commercials, Marc took up almost twenty of the twenty-four minutes of airtime laying it all out. The only thing he did not do was use the names he had.

Marc was leaning against Carolyn's desk watching the show on the office TV. Everyone in the office, including Maddy and Carvelli, were watching as well.

When it was over, Carvelli looked at Marc and said, "You need protection, my friend. Cal Simpson is not going to take that lightly."

"He's right," Connie agreed.

"I disagree," Marc said. "I don't think he'd dare, now that we've gone public. But at least for a few days, I'll hide out at home."

While this was being discussed, Sandy, Carolyn and Jeff Modell were answering the constantly ringing phones. Every reporter in the Twin Cities was trying to get through to Marc. Every call was given a terse "no comment" and a hang-up.

"You, young lady," Carvelli said looking at Maddy, "are done with Cal Simpson."

"I can get in there and find out some things. Is he running? What's he up to? He doesn't know I'm involved," Maddy protested.

"Don't be so sure of that," Marc said. "He's going to figure out this whole thing started about the time you showed up. Tony's right, you're done with him. We're not taking any chances."

"I can take care of myself," she said fighting back.

"Aidan is an animal with friends. He wouldn't hesitate to kill you," Carvelli vehemently told her.

"They're right," Connie quietly said. "The guys are right about this. If anything happened to you, think about how that would make us all feel."

"Thanks, Mom. Lay the guilt on me," Maddy told her. "But, okay. You're right, I'll be a good girl," she sullenly added.

"That's it," Cal said to Aidan. The two of them were in Cal's office watching the Channel 8 newscast. It is the same station Gabriella works for and they made good use of the interview. "We're out of here this weekend," Cal continued.

"They haven't mentioned our names," Aidan said.

"What do you think is on that video he has?" Cal asked.

"If he has it. It could be a bluff to get us to overreact," Aidan said.

Cal thought about this for a moment, then said, "True, but it did look like Knutson was going to talk to someone. And this thing is going to unravel in the next few days. No, I'm gone Saturday. The little woman can have the house and the mortgage along with the lake place. Are you ready?"

"Yeah, I can go anytime. I've got a cold car in a garage, a bag packed and enough cash to get me where we're going. I'm just sorry I won't be able to get my hands on Maddy. She's the cause of this, I can feel it in my bones."

Congressman Del Peterson was at his home in Minnesota watching the 10:00 P.M. local newscast. His wife Rita was with him in the living room. When the news was over, and they went to commercial, she looked at Del and said, "Boy, that's really something. Do you have any idea who he's talking about?"

"Uh, no," Del said to the clueless woman. "Not a clue."

"Well," she stood and said, "I'm off to bed. Don't be up too late and don't drink anymore. Goodnight," she added then headed toward the stairs and her separate bedroom.

Peterson finished his third scotch and went to the bar. He dropped another ice cube in the glass, re-filled it, took the bottle and returned to his chair.

The reality of what he was involved with and the confession he had made was finally sinking in. By the time he shakily stood up and headed for the detached garage, he was drinking straight out of the bottle.

The next day Rita was up and about at her usual time, 7:00. It was almost 8:30 before she realized Del was not moving about upstairs. Believing she should check on him, she went up to his room, opened the door and found his bed unused.

It took her another half-hour to get around to checking the garage for his car. When she did, she almost gagged from the fumes. It was there she found him. He was sitting in the driver's seat, the car still running and Del in the driver's seat, an odd-looking shade of blue with an empty bottle of scotch between his legs.

FIFTY-NINE

Harry Semple, the SAS urban tracker, was back in the apartment on LaSalle. It was Friday evening; the sun was down, and he had a clear view of Maddy Rivers. He had watched her return to her apartment and put groceries away about a half-hour ago. She stood over the sink eating what looked to be a chicken breast she brought home with her groceries.

Semple smiled while watching her eat, and thought, *some supper*. By now he had been watching her for several days and was developing feelings about her that he could not explain. There was something about her that stirred him from within. Yes, she was a beautiful woman, but he had watched beautiful women before. There was a feline sensuousness about her. It was like watching a predatory big cat. A leopard or jaguar. Semple, being a predator himself, could sense it about this long, cool woman, even if he could not articulate it. If he could explain it to another person, he would be told he was falling in love. Or at least as much as he was capable of falling in love.

Maddy finished her 'meal' and tossed the remnants in the garbage. After washing her hands and face she took her phone, dialed a number and walked into the living room.

"Hey, Dan," she said to Dan Sorensen. "I'm in for the night, you can take off if you want to."

"Are you sure? It's still early. I can stay for a while," Sorenson replied. He was in his car, parked a half-block away from Maddy's building.

"Dan, I'm in," she repeated. "I literally have a double-barreled shotgun on my coffee table that Tony let me have. I'll be okay. Go home and spend some time with your wife."

"Do I have to? I don't want to interrupt her or catch her doing something I don't want to know about."

"Why are all men disgusting?" Maddy laughed.

"We have meetings to come up with stuff," Sorenson said.

"I believe it. Good night, Dan."

"Good night, sweetheart. Stay home," Sorensen replied.

"I will."

Semple kept up his vigil as he normally did. He would wait for her to go to bed then give it another hour. He saw her finish the call to Sorenson then turn on the TV.

While he continued to watch, he thought about the call from Aidan earlier in the day. Aidan's boss—using his own sources Semple found out it was Cal Simpson—wanted Maddy snatched up. There was a ten-grand bonus in it if he could pull it off. Of course, this set off mixed feelings in Semple. He did not want her hurt, but money is money.

A few minutes before 9:30 he saw her shut off the television. Maddy went to the closet and put on a leather coat. She picked up her purse and keys and went out the door.

While Maddy was preparing to leave, Semple was making a phone call. Aidan's man, Richie, had bribed the security guard at Maddy's building. Richie told the young man he was looking for his cheating wife and her lover lived in this building. He wanted to park in the building's private lot and look for her. Richie was in the parking lot fifty feet from the underground garage exit.

A couple minutes after Semple's warning call, Richie watched Maddy drive out to LaSalle. He pulled out to follow and called one of the men in a dark, Ford van a block away. Keeping their distance, they followed her a few blocks to a local convenience store.

Maddy parked in the small, dark lot alongside the building. She went inside and went right to the freezer in back. She found what she wanted, a half-gallon of chocolate almond, then stood in line for three minutes. She paid for the ice cream and walked out and back to her car. Maddy noticed a dark, Ford van now parked next to her and an alarm buzzed in her head. When she arrived at the driver's door, she reached into her purse and felt the comfortable grip of her Lady Smith nine mm handgun.

"Careful," Semple snarled at the two thugs from the van. "Be very careful with her," he demanded.

While Maddy was in the store, the van parked next to her car. Harry Semple arrived and watched the takedown from his car across the parking lot aisle. Semple saw Maddy's hand go into her purse and immediately sensed it would come out holding a gun. Aidan's men in the van beat her to it by barely a second. The one in back hit her on the left side with a high voltage taser and she dropped like a rock.

By this time, Richie had joined them to help lift her into the van. Richie knew there was something scary about the Brit, the guy Aidan had brought in. When he said to do something, Richie and his guys did not argue.

"Be careful," Richie repeated while Semple kept watch.

They got into the back of the van and laid her on a blanket. One of the men crawled up and got in the driver's seat. While he did this, Richie pulled a syringe from his coat pocket and removed the stopper on the needle. He used his left hand to sweep Maddy's hair out of the way and carefully shoved the needle into her neck.

"She'll be out for at least four or five hours. It's only a two-hour drive, so she'll be fine," Richie said to Semple.

"You stay in back with her," Semple said. "You," he continued looking at the man with the Taser, "take his car," he said referring to Richie. "I'll follow. Don't speed. Drive carefully."

The two vehicles made one stop to pick up Aidan at his apartment. He got in the car Semple was driving and for the rest of the trip, the van followed them.

"Can you guys find your way back all right?" Aidan asked Richie and the van's driver.

They were standing in a guest bedroom of Cal's lake place outside Foster, Minnesota. Maddy was lying peacefully on the bed and Harry Semple was watching over her. It was almost midnight and she would be out for another two or three hours.

"Yeah, no problem," Richie said. "We just go out the driveway and take a left. Follow that back to the stop sign and take another left. That takes us into town and the main street. I got Google on my phone. We'll be fine."

"Okay, take off. I'll see you in a day or two," Aidan lied.

Semple took a chair in Maddy's room and kept vigil over her all night. Every half-hour or so Aidan would check in on them to see if she was awake.

"She's awake," Semple told Aidan waking him at three o'clock. Aidan was asleep on a couch downstairs, and the two of them went back to the bedroom. A still very groggy Maddy was lying on the bed. Her arms were extended by the ropes that were tied to the headboard. The two men stood at the foot of the bed watching her, waiting for her to come around.

"Does Cal know what you did?" Maddy said when the cobwebs cleared.

"Of course, he knows, Madeline Rivers," Aidan said.

Maddy was able to suppress it so it did not show, but the use of her real name sent a shock wave through her. She immediately knew she was in very real, probably mortal, danger.

"How are you feeling?" Semple asked.

"Who are you?" Maddy asked the man with a British accent.

Ignoring the question, Semple asked, "Would you like something to drink? Are you thirsty? Do you need to use the loo?"

"Yes and yes," Maddy answered.

"Get her a bottle of water," Semple told Aidan.

"Who put you in charge?" Aidan asked.

Semple had started untying the ropes, then said, "Just be a gentleman and get her some water, please."

"Be careful with her," Aidan said, as he pulled a pistol from behind.

"You won't cause us any trouble, now will you, lass?"

"Just give me a chance and we'll see," Maddy replied.

Aidan leaned down in front of Maddy, so his face was barely six inches from hers. They were in the basement of Cal's lake place. Maddy was seated in the middle of the room in a simple wooden armchair. Her arms and legs had been secured with duct tape.

Aidan smiled and while he did, Maddy was thinking about how easy it would be to break his nose with her forehead.

"You going to torture me now, moron?" she asked.

"I wouldn't be so sassy if I were you," Aidan said.

"Why? What are you going to do to me? You brought me here to torture and kill me. Well, you dickless wonder, get on with it. I just hope I live long enough to see what Cal has in mind for you. Do you really believe he's going to let you live? That's laughable. That guy behind you," she continued referring to Semple, "is here to put a bullet in your head when this is over."

"Not true," Semple said.

A furious Aidan reached back with his right hand and back-handed Maddy across the face so hard it knocked her over.

"How's that for a start, you bitch?" Aidan said standing over her and snarling down.

Aidan did not see it coming and had no idea what hit him. The next thing he knew he was lying on the floor staring at the ceiling in a lot of pain. And he could not breathe. Kneeling next to him with his right hand firmly gripping Aidan's throat was Harry Semple.

He leaned his head down next to Aidan's ear and whispered, "I know what you have to do to her. But until then, don't you lay another hand on her or I'll snap your neck like a twig."

Semple lifted his head looked Aidan in the eyes and asked, "Am I clear?"

"Yes," Aidan croaked.

Semple helped Maddy up while Aidan found a chair. He asked her, "Are you okay, lass?"

"What? You think that pussy can hurt me? Cut me loose and he'll see what an ass kicking is all about," Maddy replied looking at Aidan.

Semple heartily laughed and said, "I believe you could do it."

Semple went into the downstairs bathroom and came out with a wet washcloth and towel. Despite the bravado, Aidan had hurt her badly.

Another shot like that and she would be missing four or five teeth. Semple cleaned up the blood on her face and in her mouth.

"If you expect me to thank you, forget it," Maddy told Semple.

"No, I don't expect you would," he replied. He turned to Aidan and said, "Now, we'll just wait for Mr. Simpson."

"How do you know his name?" Aidan asked.

Semple sat down across from Aidan and ignored the question.

SIXTY

"Come on, come on, answer your damn phone," Carvelli said impatiently.

It was already late Saturday afternoon and Carvelli was trying Maddy for at least the tenth time. So far all he got was five rings, then voice mail. He had left a message the first few times, but none since.

Becoming more and more worried, he called Dan Sorenson, his guy who was to have been watching her last night. It was a brief conversation. Dan told him about Maddy calling last night and letting him go. Carvelli blew a gasket, screamed at Sorenson and told him to get over to her apartment and use the key he had to check on her.

Carvelli paced around his living room for a couple of minutes cooling down. He made a mental note to call Sorenson later and apologize. He picked up his phone to call Marc when an incoming call came through. It was an MPD caller ID number. Almost in a panic, he answered the call.

"Tony," he heard a man say, "It's Bob Fields." Fields was a friend and patrol sergeant with the police.

Almost too scared to ask, Carvelli said, "What's up, Bob?"

"I don't know what's going on, but we found Maddy Rivers' car. It's parked at a convenience store on Grant and LaSalle."

"Any sign of violence? Any blood?"

"No, not that we can see. There's a half-gallon of melted ice cream in a bag next to her car. Nothing else. I have the night manager coming in to see if he can ID her and if he knows anything."

"Who caught the case?" Carvelli asked wondering who the detective was.

"Owen Jefferson is on his way," Fields said. "In fact, he just pulled up. I called him at home, he gave me your number then I called you. I mean, you know, everybody loves Maddy. I figured he'd want to know."

"You did great, Bob. Tell Owen I'm on the way."

Driving over fifty on streets with 30 mph speed signs, Carvelli was there in under ten minutes. Somehow, he managed to call Marc and tell him without killing anyone while he did it.

Carvelli arrived at the scene the same time that Marcie Sterling did. Marcie was an MPD detective and former partner of Owen Jefferson.

"Owen called you at home?" Carvelli asked her as the two of them quickly walked together toward the crime scene.

"Yeah. Hey, even I like Maddy. Sure, I hate her because of the way she looks, but I still like her a lot," Marcie replied.

Jefferson saw them coming and stepped away from the crime scene tape. He greeted them and said to Carvelli, "That's the night manager over there," Jefferson said, referring to a black kid that looked no older than eighteen.

"We showed him a picture of her and he remembered her right away," Jefferson continued. "Says she came in around nine thirty last night."

"He remembers it that clearly?" Carvelli asked.

"He's a male," Marcie said. "Of course, he remembers her."

"He said she bought some ice cream, paid cash and left. That's all he knows. The ice cream was found on the ground next to the driver's side door."

Carvelli turned his head toward the street and saw Marc running toward them. Trying to keep up with Marc were Tommy Craven and Franklin Washington. They were babysitting Marc and had been in his kitchen when Carvelli called.

He breathlessly asked, "Where is she? What happened? Is there any blood?"

"Calm down," Carvelli said.

"Fuck calm!" Marc yelled using the F word which was very unusual. "This is Cal Simpson and his pitbull, Aidan Walsh. We need to go out to his place, kick the door in and beat the shit out of both of them!"

"Sounds like a plan," Washington said.

"We can't just…" Carvelli started to say.

"I'm going right now. You coming?" Marc said.

Carvelli looked at Jefferson who held up his hands and said, "I haven't heard any of this. Did you?" he asked Marcie.

"Any of what?" she replied.

While Marc and the crew were on their way to Simpson's house, Cal was packing his Mercedes to leave. Driving out he took a left-hand turn on the road at the end of the driveway to go to his lake place. When he made the turn, Marc and his friends were less than thirty seconds away.

"What do you think?" Tommy asked Carvelli.

The four of them had made a thorough examination of the house's exterior. From what they could see there was no sign of life anywhere to be found.

Carvelli, Tommy and Franklin were standing together by the pool. All three of the ex-cops were holding semi-auto handguns at their side. Marc was peering into a window next to the back door.

"No one's here," Carvelli replied. "I think someone would have come out by now."

They heard a loud crash and looked at the house and saw Marc entering a back door. Apparently, he had kicked it open.

The three of them took off running after him, and Franklin said, "This place is gonna have an alarm."

They found Marc stomping around the first floor, not quite sure what to do next. The ex-cops did.

They caught up to Marc in the living room. Carvelli said, "There's bound to be an alarm."

"Tough shit," Marc said.

"You wait here," Carvelli told him. "Just wait here and we'll clear the place."

"Okay," Marc calmly agreed.

Franklin and Tommy had already split up. Tommy took the upstairs, Franklin the basement, and Carvelli the main level. In barely two minutes, they verified the house was empty.

"Let's get out of here," Carvelli said. "Minnetonka is probably on the way," he continued, referring to the local police.

They had arrived in two cars and pulled out of Simpson's driveway barely ahead of the local cops. Carvelli was leading the way and he pulled onto Vivian's driveway a quarter of a mile down the road.

While walking toward the house Marc asked Carvelli if he had called Vivian.

"No," Carvelli quietly said. "You know how she feels about Maddy. This is news I have to deliver in person."

Two minutes later the four men were standing in Vivian's library. Carvelli had told her. Being a paragon of decorum, Vivian took the news without comment. For a full minute, there was silence in the room, while the men waited for a reaction. Finally, a single tear trickled down each side of her face.

"My god, what have we done?" she quietly said.

Carvelli led her to a couch by the fireplace. He sat down next to her and held her hand while she quietly cried. The others, all three of them, wiped tears from their eyes while they watched.

Marc sat down on the opposite couch and said, "They must be at his lake place. The one outside Foster."

"You're right," Carvelli said. "But how do we get..."

He stopped himself, retrieved his wallet from his coat and looked through the contents, "Got it," he said holding up a business card.

Carvelli took out his phone, dialed the number and when it was answered, identified himself. The conversation lasted less than three minutes. He thanked the man profusely at the end of the call.

"I got it," Carvelli said. He stood and said, "Let's go."

Before he could walk away, Vivian stood, grabbed his arm and said, "Anthony, find her. Bring her back."

Carvelli lightly kissed her, gave her a brief hug and said they would.

Outside, as they scurried to the cars, Marc asked, "Who did you talk to?"

"You remember the Foster County sheriff? I called his lead investigator, Chris Newkirk, at home. He told me he'd be at the sheriff's office with the cavalry."

While Marc and company were driving to Foster, less than an hour ahead of them was Cal Simpson. When he arrived at the lake house, he was greeted by both Aidan and Harry Semple in his driveway.

"Where is she?" Cal asked. "Is she secured?"

"Of course," Aidan answered.

Cal followed Aidan downstairs with Harry Semple silently bringing up the rear. When Cal saw Maddy strapped to the chair, an odd sadness fell over him. He pulled up a chair and sat facing her about five feet away.

"You probably won't believe this, but it makes me sad to see you like this," Cal said.

"So, cut me loose," Maddy said. "Then I'll show you what feeling sad is really like."

"I've read your bio, Ms. Rivers, and I know you're very capable. But I doubt you could handle all three of us," Cal replied.

Maddy leaned forward as much as she could, looked Cal directly in the eyes and said, "Why don't you see if you can find the balls to give it a try. What do you say, Cal? Once around the dance floor?"

"You know, hearing you like this, I think I like you even more. What a shame. What a waste," Cal said. "The little woman has filed for divorce. We could've had a great life together."

"Except the first time I found you asleep, I would have slit your goddamn throat," Maddy said.

Cal laughed and said, "You know, I believe you would."

Cal stood and motioned for the other two men to follow him out through the patio door. When they got outside he said, "Wait until it's good and dark. It won't be long. Then take care of her."

"Don't worry," Aidan said. "We've already loaded enough chain and cinder blocks in the boat to keep her under until the fish are done with her. We'll go out to that deep spot."

Cal reached into his coat pocket and came out with a thick envelope. He handed it to Harry Semple and said, "A bonus. You've earned it."

"Thanks, Mr. Simpson," Semple said. Without looking into the envelope, he stuffed it in a back pocket of his pants.

Cal read his watch by the light through the door and said, "I'm on a tight schedule. I have to go. I'll see you in a few days," he told Aidan.

"All set," Aidan said.

They went back inside, and Cal said to Maddy, "Sorry, darling, but I have to run."

"Don't have the balls to do it yourself, you dickless coward?" Maddy asked. As terrified as she was and hurting knowing she was about to die, she was determined not to show it. She was not going to give them the satisfaction.

"You are fabulous," Cal said sadly shaking his head. "Such a waste."

While Aidan stood back with a gun in his hands, Semple tied Maddy's hands and feet together, kneeling in front of her, with his back to Aidan to block his view while he did it. When he finished, Aidan tossed him a hand towel which he used to gag her. Satisfied she was secured, the two men carried her down to the dock and into a speedboat. Despite what was in store for her, both men very gently placed her on a bench seat along the right-hand side.

"We can't get a search warrant for this," Sheriff Goode told the four men. "What you have isn't enough."

They were in the sheriff's office in Foster discussing how to go about searching Simpson's place. After Sheriff Goode's statement, there was silence in the room. Along with Marc and company, Sheriff Goode and Newkirk, there were four deputies in the room, including Newkirk's partner, Abby Bliss.

Finally, Newkirk spoke up. "How about this? Let's say, hypothetically, me and Abby were just out driving around. And we went past Simpson's and noticed some odd things going on, hypothetically. And it looked like a burglary in process, so we called for backup. And you guys just happened to be close by and came running."

"And hypothetically," Sheriff Goode continued, "I just happened to be out and about and decided to drop by and check it out for myself."

"Sounds like a plan," Franklin Washington said. "Hypothetically."

Aidan throttled down the boat's motor but did not shut it off. The boat drifted several feet on the calm lake before coming to a complete stop. Having used the boat's depth finder, Aidan knew they were stopped over forty feet of water.

314

"You hold her still while I chain the bricks to her," Aidan told Semple.

There was a three-quarter moon in the partly cloudy sky, plenty of light to do their dirty work. As Semple knelt in the bottom of the boat, he looked at Maddy's eyes. No longer able to contain it, she was making muffled sounds pleading for her life. Her eyes showed the terror she was feeling, and a weird pain of sympathy came over Semple.

"No," he said to Aidan as he stood up. "I'm not gonna let you do this."

Aidan jerked his .40 caliber semi-auto handgun from his hip holster. He pointed it at Semple's chest and said, "Then you'll go first. I'm tired of you anyway."

Harry Semple, the SAS counter-terrorist soldier, stared back calculating the odds. Unfortunately, like everyone, father time was working on Semple as well. He was in his late forties and no longer as quick as his mind told him he was. His left hand shot out toward the gun but was the blink of an eye too slow. He grabbed it as Aidan squeezed the trigger.

In the quiet on the water, the gun roared like a cannon shot. The bullet entered Semple's throat and severed his spinal column as it exited, killing him instantly.

When Semple tied Maddy's hands and feet, he had done so as loosely as possible. Before Semple's body dropped to the floor, quick as a cat, Maddy was up and at Aidan.

He tried to swing the gun around toward her, but he had slowed down over the years as well. With both hands, Maddy hit him hard in the chest. He would not have gone down but for one of the cinder blocks. As he stumbled backward, he tripped and started to go over the rail.

As Aidan started to go overboard, Maddy grabbed the gun and snatched it out of his hand. For good measure she was able to give him another push to put him in the water. The momentum of Aidan going overboard pushed the boat away from him. When Aidan came to the surface, the boat was almost ten feet from him.

"I can't swim, I can't swim!" he yelled as he kept bobbing up and back under, flailing his arms about.

His thrashing about gave Maddy the few seconds she needed to free her hands and feet and remove the gag. She stood in the boat aiming the pistol directly at the floundering thug. Three or four more seconds passed while she thought it over. Shoot him in the head or let him drown? And then she realized the man slapping his arms about had a lot of information they needed.

Maddy reached down and found the anchor rope. She pulled on it until she had about fifteen feet of it loose.

"Here, catch this," she yelled at Aidan as she tossed him the line. Her aim was excellent, it hit him on the head. As Aidan struggled to get a hold of it Maddy tied it off on a cleat on the gunwale.

By now, Aidan had the rope and was about to pull himself to the boat.

"Not a chance, asshole," Maddy said aiming the gun at him. "You stay right where you are. I'll go slow and pull you in but you're not getting back in this boat."

"I'll drown or freeze," Aidan pitifully whined.

"Good luck," Maddy replied. "Do your best. Keep your head up."

At three knots per hour—a bit slower than walking speed—it took over half an hour to get back to shore. Instead of trying to tie the boat to the dock, Maddy ran it up on the ground. By this point, having almost drowned several times, Aidan was barely able to crawl out of the cold water.

Maddy jumped ashore and waited for Aidan to crawl up to it. "Get up or I'll change my mind and put one in your forehead, you scum."

"Okay, okay, let me get my breath," Aidan pleaded as he struggled to his knees.

As Aidan stood up, Maddy took a couple of steps back. There was a floodlight on the dock that clearly illuminated both of them. By now Aidan was on his feet, bent over, hands on his knees still recovering from being dragged through the lake.

Marc stepped through the patio door and looked down toward the dock. Surprised, he saw her but was not sure if it was real. Carvelli came out and joined him.

"Maddy!" she heard Marc's voice yell through the darkness. It was coming from the house and for an instant it distracted her. Just enough. She turned her head for a moment toward Marc. When she looked back at Aidan she saw the revolver he had pulled from an ankle holster in his hand.

The bullet hit her in the upper chest just as she squeezed off two quick shots at Aidan. Both shots hit him in the lower abdomen and dropped him. Maddy went down flat on her back. Aidan went down on his butt and was in a sitting position.

Marc and Carvelli both witnessed the shootings. As soon as they saw Maddy go down both of them yelled her name and took off running toward her.

As they ran, Carvelli pulled his gun and when he saw Aidan sitting up trying to raise his hand with the gun it, Carvelli stopped and very coolly, from almost fifty yards, emptied his ten-shot magazine at the gangster.

Marc slid through the grass on his knees the last five feet to her. When he got to her, he knelt over her as she stared upward, unblinking with a shocked look in her eyes. Marc put his left arm under her head while the blood poured out of the wound. He took his handkerchief and pressed it on the bullet hole and put his face an inch from her nose.

"No, no, you can't do this. Please, don't leave me. Not now, please," he pleaded and begged. He placed his mouth next to her left ear and whispered. "I love you, Maddy. You have to know that. I love you and you can't leave me now."

"Get a car down here, right now," Marc heard someone yell from behind him. While he held her, and continued to whisper to her, the sheriff's deputies went into action. Barely thirty seconds passed before Newkirk's SUV pulled up. By now they were all down at the dock, helping with her while everyone ignored Aidan Walsh. Everyone except Carvelli.

They slid Maddy into the back of the SUV and Marc and Abby climbed in with her. Newkirk took the wheel and went barreling off of the property and down the driveway to get her to the hospital.

Carvelli looked down at Aidan and noticed air bubbles in the blood seeping out of his mouth. He would find out later that only three of the ten shots he had taken had found their mark. It would turn out to be enough. Realizing Aidan was still alive but dying, he knelt down next to him.

"Where's Cal Simpson?" Carvelli asked.

Aidan was looking up at him, still alive but fading. The corners of Aidan's mouth moved slightly upward in a smile. He stayed this way but did not answer the question.

Carvelli grabbed him by his shirt at the throat, lifted his head off the ground and looked him in the eye. "You're dying. You're not letting him get off that way. Where is he?"

Aidan's lips parted. His lips, mouth and teeth were red from the blood, and he tried smiling again. He looked back at Carvelli and uttered one word: "Gone."

The deputies did their best to get him to Foster and the hospital. Aidan Walsh was pronounced dead on arrival.

SIXTY-ONE

Marc rolled over on his side, pulled the blanket up to his chin and ignored the pounding on the door. Halfway between still asleep and awake, his conscious mind hoped the noise would go away. Instead, after a short pause, it started up again.

"Dad!" Marc heard someone yell then pound on the door. "Wake up!"

His conscious mind registered the word "Dad" and his eyes snapped open. He heard his son yell it again and pound on the door. Marc threw the bed covers back, got up and half-stumbled to the door.

"Hey," he groggily said to his son and daughter.

"How is she?" Jessica asked as Marc stepped aside to let them in his motel room.

Marc yawned and said, "She's going to be fine. You," he continued looking at Eric, "find me some coffee."

"Thank God," Jessica replied to the news.

"Here," Eric said to his dad, as he handed a small suitcase to him. "Clothes, underwear, socks, shaving stuff and toothpaste and a toothbrush which you need to try out."

"Thanks. Coffee," he repeated pointing to the door.

"I'll be back," Eric said.

While Marc was digging through the suitcase for the items he needed, Jessica checked out the room.

"Plush," she said with a touch of sarcasm.

"Yeah, well, at four o'clock in the morning you can't be too fussy," Marc replied.

"Are you okay?" Jessica asked.

"Now she asks," Marc replied. "Yes, baby. I'm fine."

While Marc shaved and showered in the tiny bathroom, he let his mind drift back to the previous night's events.

On the drive into Foster, Chris Newkirk called ahead to have a surgical team ready. In the back, Marc kept pressure on Maddy's wound while Abby checked for an exit hole. She did not find one which meant the bullet was still in her.

"Is that good or bad?" Marc asked.

"It would be better if it had passed through," Abby replied. "It is what it is, they'll deal with it."

Newkirk screeched to a halt at the emergency entrance to the Foster County Medical Center, the same place Marc was taken to in July. Within seconds, Maddy was on a gurney and being rushed into surgery. Marc tried to go with her but was stopped at the door. After washing her blood off of his hands, he took a seat in the hall to await the outcome. A few minutes later, Newkirk and Abby joined him.

"Don't worry," Abby patted his knee and said, "they're great with GSW, gunshot wounds. We get more than our share of them."

A short while later, they were joined by Carvelli, Tommy Craven and Franklin Washington. An hour after that, Sheriff Goode arrived.

"I forgot to tell you," Carvelli said to Sheriff Goode, "the feds are going to be all over this. You might want to just seal off Simpson's place for now."

"Why do the feds care?" Goode asked.

Marc looked at him and answered, "Because we have a videotape of Del Peterson, the congressman who committed suicide, confessing to a massive criminal conspiracy. Cal Simpson is the ringleader. We're going to release it to the media and let the chips fall where they may. That reminds me," he continued. Marc stood up, pulled out his phone, looked at Carvelli and said, "I'll wake up Gabriella. She's going to want to come down."

"I thought I'd wait until we know more to call Vivian," Carvelli said.

"Call her now," Marc told him. "She's probably worried sick. At least let her know we found Maddy."

"I suppose," Carvelli said.

They made the calls and promised to wait at the hospital for them. For the next half-hour, everyone milled about the hallway. Standing up, walking around, then sitting back down trying to do something while waiting.

While they waited Goode took a call from a deputy still at Simpson's.

"Really? Well, count it, mark it as evidence and lock it up. And keep your sticky fingers to yourself," Goode said.

"They found an envelope on the dead guy in the boat stuffed with cash. Forty or fifty grand," Goode said to Carvelli.

"What dead guy in the boat?" Marc asked.

"There was a dead guy in the boat," Carvelli said. "Probably one of Cal's guys although I didn't recognize him. Looks like he took a bullet in the throat."

Carvelli looked at the sheriff and said, "You know, if nobody claims the money, it's yours. Or, your department's."

"I know," Goode smiled. "I'm already thinking about what I want to spend it on."

Finally, an older man in a blood-splattered surgical gown appeared. The small crowd surrounded him, allowing Marc to be closest to him.

319

"Okay, she's out of surgery. We found the bullet, removing it was the hard part that took so long," he said. "She's lost a lot of blood but her vital signs are good. Give it a few days and she'll be fine unless complications arise."

"So, she's going to be okay?" Marc asked.

"Yeah, she'll be fine," the doctor replied. "In fact, the bullet didn't hit any vital organs at all."

Marc and Carvelli called Gabriella and Vivian back. Neither had left yet and both decided to wait until morning.

A few minutes after receiving the news, Marc and Carvelli were alone in the hall. They were sitting on chairs against the wall silently staring at the floor. Neither said a word or looked at each other as they dealt with their tears.

On the drive to the Medical Center, Jessica said to her dad, "Tony told us you told Maddy you loved her."

"Yeah," Marc admitted. "I guess I wanted her to know."

"It's about time," Eric said from the back seat.

"What does that mean?" Marc replied giving his son a quizzical look.

Jessica laughed and said, "Come on, Dad. It's been obvious for quite a while. Trust me, she's in."

"Really?" Marc asked a little surprised.

"Really," Jessica laughed. "Men are so clueless."

The elevator doors opened on the third-floor and Marc, Eric and Jessica stepped off. They looked ahead and saw Vivian, Tony and Gabriella.

"That's the same room you were in," Jessica said to Marc.

Also waiting were Newkirk and Abby Bliss.

At the room's door, there was a round of hugs, then Marc and Carvelli stepped away to talk to the detectives.

"We need to get a statement from her," Newkirk said.

"If she's up to it," Abby added.

Marc asked Carvelli, "Have you been in to see her?"

"Yeah, for a couple minutes then the nurse kicked us out," he answered.

"Have Vivian and Gabriella..."

"They were in with me."

"We were waiting for you," Newkirk said. "Tony says you're her lawyer."

"I am," Marc agreed. "Let me go in and check with her and I'll let you know."

Marc went to the door and motioned for Eric and Jessica to come in with him. They went inside and found Maddy half asleep. When she heard the door close she came to.

"Hey," Marc softly said.

"Hi," she smiled back. She looked at Jessica, held her arms out and said, "Come here."

When she finished hugging his sister, Eric took his turn. They finished, then Marc told them he needed to talk to her alone.

Marc sat on the edge of the bed, took her right hand, softly brushed the hair off her forehead and asked, "Are you up to seeing the cops?"

"I don't want to talk about that. Come here and hug me. Hold me and tell me you love me, again," she said.

When he finished doing as she asked and was looking down at her, she pulled his head down, kissed him and said, "I love you, too. When you were in this hospital..."

"Same room," Marc said.

"...I thought I was going to lose you. Then when the helicopter took you away, my heart broke into a dozen pieces. Why did we wait until we almost lost each other before we realized how we felt?"

"Because men are clueless about these things," Marc said.

"And women are probably worse," Maddy said with a weak smile.

"I'm glad you said that. If I had said it, there would be a line of angry women picketing my office on Monday. Are you up to talking to the cops? If not, they can come back," Marc said.

"No, I'm okay. Let's do it now. But I want you here and if I get tired we'll stop."

"Deal."

It took a while and Marc almost stopped it a couple of times. Newkirk and Abby were as soft and considerate as they could possibly be. Maddy's memory was a little fuzzy at times, but she clearly remembered the fight on the boat.

"Oh, God," Maddy said. "That guy who got shot on the boat. He saved my life. He sacrificed himself to stop Aidan from killing me." Her eyes were filling with tears as she said this.

The cops had put Semple's fingerprints through the AFIS program and found him. Newkirk explained to Maddy and Marc who he was. When he finished there was silence in the room.

"I wonder why he did it?" Marc finally asked.

"I guess we'll never know," Abby replied.

When they finished Marc went out into the hall with the investigators.

"She is one tough chick," Abby said. "It's an amazing story."

Carvelli joined them as Newkirk asked, "Where is Cal Simpson?"

"All I could get out of Aidan was the word gone," Carvelli answered. "You can bet he's out of the country by now. I'm sure he planned his escape down to every detail. You're probably going to have to leave him to the feds."

While they were talking, the others went back in to see Maddy. Newkirk and Abby left after another minute.

"So, how did things go between you? She admitted it, too, didn't she?" Carvelli asked.

"Yeah, she did," Marc answered. "Thing is, I've just become involved with a woman that can kick my ass without breaking a sweat."

"And don't look to me for any help," Carvelli replied.

SIXTY-TWO

After a brief discussion in Maddy's hospital room, it had been decided that she was fine right where she was. The discussion had centered on moving her mostly for security purposes. Cal Simpson had plenty of contacts he could reach out to and take another shot at her. Sheriff Goode had offered protection, but his department was a little small for it. Instead, Vivian had hired a highly reputable security firm she knew. They would provide two armed guards for her around the clock. Maddy being Maddy got a little angry about it, but when Marc persisted she acquiesced. At least until she got home.

Monday turned out to be disclosure day. Marc and Carvelli both appeared on Gabriella's show. The station had agreed to a live, hour-long show leading into the early-evening news. The video of the deceased Congressman Del Peterson's confession was shown in its entirety without comment. The rest of the show was taken up with a Q & A between Gabriella, Marc and Carvelli.

Ten minutes after the show was over the FBI were in the building demanding the video. News people being who they are would only agree to give them a copy within twenty-four hours. Channel 8 was a Fox News affiliate and Fox wanted a twenty-four-hour jump on the competition.

The FBI did not wait twenty-four hours to jump-start their investigation. That evening they obtained federal search warrants for Cal Simpson's Lake Minnetonka home, his place in Foster County, and an office he kept in downtown Minneapolis.

They hit every one of them that night and came up with absolutely nothing. There wasn't a computer, bank record or even a scrap of paper remaining in all three places. In fact, the downtown office never did have anything in it. Cal would go there from time to time for show, but that was all. The building management and occupants had never seen a single employee in the office space.

Everything else, anything that could even remotely give the Feds information, had gone up in smoke. Literally. Aidan had bribed a couple of employees of the Hennepin County downtown incinerator. Aidan oversaw the work, just to be sure, when several boxes of computers and records were fed to the flames.

By the end of that week, there was a howl inside the D.C. beltway. A couple of dozen members of Congress and senators did damage control televised denials. Even though Peterson had specifically named them, none of them ever met anyone named Calvin Simpson. As for Del

Peterson, a couple of house members admitted casually knowing him, the rest swore they had never spoken to him. Besides, as tragic as his death was—they all uttered the usual pious palaver about their thoughts and prayers going out to his family—obviously he had serious, unresolved problems. Quite deluded and mentally ill.

Eventually, of course, a special prosecutor with the usual impeccable reputation, a D.C. lawyer and total insider, was appointed. His staff would eventually grow to twenty lawyers and another two dozen investigators. They would take eighteen months, spend seventy-five million dollars—mostly on first-class airfare, five-star hotel suites, lavish expense accounts and salaries—then come up with three unrelated, minor convictions of congressional staffers.

Since Cal's pals came from both sides of the aisle, neither party was in a big hurry to cooperate. The special prosecutor found no records of money being transferred to any members. Of course, he did find records of a significant number of them, including over thirty, who were not named in the video, receiving unusual stock windfalls. It seemed quite a number of them made out by buying Cannon Brothers and Morton Aviation stock. They sold it off at the shares' peak then made another nice piece of change on short sales. Since Congressional members and staff are not subject to inside trading laws, nothing could come of this curious coincidence.

The Cannon Brothers executives, Dane Cannon and his brother, Greg Cannon, ended up walking away unscathed. Without Cal Simpson, there was nothing to tie them to the conspiracy. They did use their position inside the company to enrich themselves at the expense of their shareholders which is the classic definition of insider trading. Except the government obviously cares little about this since it goes on daily and virtually no one is ever pursued for it.

"Norah, I told you I would take care of this," Mason Hooper quietly said into his personal cell phone.

"The OPR called me again ten minutes ago," Norah McCabe screamed loud enough to be heard outside her office.

"Calm down," Hooper said. "I'm seeing him in ten minutes. I have the photos. Don't worry."

"They asked me about the bank accounts. What the hell am I supposed to tell them?"

"Nothing," Hooper said. "Just sit tight and keep your mouth shut. I'll see him and get back to you. We have to let the dust settle."

It had been three weeks since Sean O'Rourke had passed on the bank account information to his FBI pals. They had verified the information and taken it to the Department of Justice's Office of

Professional Responsibility. The OPR had assigned an investigator and Norah McCabe had some serious explaining to do.

Hooper entered the Assistant A.G.'s outer office and one of his assistants told him to go right in. He was having a meeting with his boss who was expecting him.

The Assistant Attorney General, H. Kimball Abbott of Connecticut was a powerful lawyer and party elite. POTUS could barely stand being in the same room with him. Since their first meeting, POTUS had a bad feeling there was something amiss about him. Being a good and faithful party hack, Abbott had assured the then President-elect he would be as loyal as a dog and protect him from any scandal. Of course, this was a blatant lie and both of them, professional political liars each, knew it.

"Come in," Mason's boss said to his number one deputy. He walked around his massive desk to greet Hooper with a handshake.

Hooper was carrying a thin, manila file folder in his left hand. The two men sat down at a table and Hooper said, "Thanks for seeing me on short notice, Kim."

"What's up, Mason?" Abbott smiled.

Hooper took a couple of minutes explaining about Norah McCabe's predicament. When he finished, Abbott had a serious, somewhat puzzled expression.

"I don't know what I can do about it. If the OPR has it, I can't interfere," Abbott said.

"Okay," Hooper replied. "That's what I'll tell her. Like I said, I knew her when I was in Philadelphia and I said I'd look into it."

"It's damned inappropriate for you to even bring this to me," Abbott finally said.

"True," Hooper said, "But in a minute, you'll see why I don't care. Now, let's talk about me. I'm going to retire, effective immediately. Norah McCabe, and maybe some others, could make some allegations about me. I'd appreciate it if you'd cover them up and make sure nothing comes of any of it."

"What the hell are you talking about?"

It was at that point Hooper opened the manila folder. In it were a half-dozen photos lying face down. Taking his time, Hooper turned each one of them over so Abbott could see them. In each one, Abbott was naked and there was at least one very young boy or girl, or both, also naked in each photo. POTUS was right, H. Kimball Abbott, from old-money wealth, was one sick puppy.

"You can keep these. If you lie or don't provide cover for me, I have more."

Part of Mason Hooper's plan all along was to retire, get divorced and dump Norah McCabe. Unknown to Norah, Hooper had over twenty-million stashed overseas from Cal Simpson's friendship.

It would take another eight months to resolve Norah McCabe's case. It ended with her surrendering the money in the bank accounts in her children's names. She was allowed to resign and keep her pension and the rest was quietly covered up.

A few months later, based on information McCabe had given her about the money Hooper had stashed that he didn't think McCabe knew about, Hooper was dragged back to the U.S. He would eventually make the same deal as McCabe. His bribery attempt of Abbott came to naught when Abbott got drunk and put his car over a cliff.

The old man, the one the locals knew as a Canadian expatriate, carried his gear onto the beach. As usual, he went down to the water's edge and set up. With him he brought a small cooler with two bottles of a Costa Rican beer he favored and two bottles of water. He also had his fishing equipment and a beach chair.

Cal Simpson, according to his impeccable Canadian passport, was now Burt Labrosse, a retired, well-to-do Canadian. He was also almost unrecognizable. Cal/Burt had grown a beard and stopped coloring his hair. Both were eighty-percent gray. Despite being in his mid-fifties, he looked at least seventy. If an FBI agent with his previous picture in hand saw him, the agent would walk passed without a second look. His only connection to his old life was the battered Boston Red Sox ball cap he wore on the beach.

When Cal drove away from his lake place that night, he felt an odd, deep regret about Maddy. But the practical Cal knew it had to be done. He drove into Foster to get to the highway to Duluth. As he drove by the sheriff's office he saw the cars pulling out of the driveway and turn toward the lake. Somehow, he knew they were headed toward his place. He hoped Aidan would get away but if he did not, Cal knew he would keep his mouth shut. It didn't really matter though since Cal had lied to Aidan about his escape plan.

A couple of hours later he was on a private airplane lifting off from the Duluth airport. Three and a half hours after that he was in Toronto. From there, with the Canadian passport under his new name, Cal flew to Amsterdam. A day later, using a British passport, he was in Lisbon. He then went back to the Canadian passport and flew to Bogota, Columbia. From there Cal hired a private plane which got him to Costa Rica.

The entire trip had taken almost a week, but the cover it provided was worth it. He had settled in a villa he had purchased through a cut out in Samara on the Nicoya Peninsula. The nightlife was enough—he was already entertaining a married woman with an indifferent husband—and his days were quite sedentary. He was even learning to enjoy quiet time fishing on the beach.

Cal had read about Aidan and Maddy on the internet. Aidan's death oddly made him a little sad. He actually liked him and had come to trust and rely on him. Even more oddly, he was not at all upset that Maddy had escaped his wrath. She amazed him. Without a doubt an impressive combination of intelligence, beauty and ability.

For a couple of days, fueled by anger at her escape and Aidan's death, Cal had considered going after her. Eventually, he gave up on the idea. They had their shot at her, Cal and Aidan, and had missed. Time to let it go and move on. There was nothing to be gained by it and as good as she was Cal could easily miss again.

After casting his line into the ocean, Cal settled back in his chair. It was not even 9:00 A.M., but a beer would not hurt. A short while later he put the empty bottle in the cooler and noticed some motion to his right. He looked around the beach and figured maybe twenty or so people were on it. Still a little early.

The motion he had seen was the honeymooners from France. They had been out on the beach about the same time as now for the past four days. A very nice, very attractive couple.

Standing behind Cal, the husband said in his French-accented English, "Good morning. Are they biting this morning?"

"Not so far," Cal answered in his English accented French. Continuing in English he said, "The Sea Bass and Red Snapper were abundant yesterday but not so today. How are the lovebirds this morning?"

"Exhausted," the husband replied. "She's wearing me out. I'll be your age in another week."

When the laughter died down, the wife handed her husband a metal object from her bag. The husband bent down behind Cal and whispered, "Au revoir, Cal Simpson."

Between the wind coming off the ocean and the waves on the beach, there was enough ambient noise. The husband—the French couple were lovers but not married—pulled the trigger of the silenced .22 revolver twice. The two shots were a barely audible pop, pop. The soft, hollow point bullets shattered as they passed through his skull and shredded his brain. Cal's head started forward, but the shooter caught him and gently laid him back in his chair. He handed the gun to the woman, she slipped it back into the bag she carried, and they continued their normal stroll.

327

By the time anyone on the beach noticed the old fisherman was not asleep, the assassins were boarding separate planes. They were a team of professional contract killers who worked out of Marseille. This was their first contract outside of Europe and the pay was double their normal rate. Before boarding his flight, the man had sent a short, three-word text in English to the person who hired them.

On a popular, clothing optional Mediterranean Sea beach in the south of France, eight hours ahead of Costa Rica, Samantha Simpson was resting under an umbrella. She had removed her bikini top to work on her tan. She looked at the young, Italian boy toy on the next lounge chair and made up her mind he had to go.

Samantha heard her phone buzz in the beach bag next to her lounge chair. She dug it out and looked at the text message she had been waiting for. It was a very brief, three-word text from Costa Rica: *It is done.*

Samantha deleted the text and decided to call it a day. As she was putting her top back on, the sleeping boy toy stirred. Samantha ignored him as he tried to reach for her. Instead, she finished packing up to go back to her small, rented villa above the beach. Before leaving, she looked at the young man and in flawless Italian said, "Go home, Carlo. I won't be needing you anymore."

"Stronza," he angrily muttered as she walked away.

Samantha showered then made a light supper salad for herself. While she ate, she thought about Cal. She had warned him all along that he was becoming too greedy. The politicians will let you steal a lot as long as they are in on it. But over three billion was entirely too much if you screwed them out of their share.

Being the far more intelligent and savvier of the two Simpsons, Samantha knew she had to make a deal. There was no way the feds would stop looking for them. Through an international lawyer she had come to know in Geneva, she had made a deal with the U.S. Government. Samantha would send the money into the U.S. Treasury and deal with her father in exchange for ironclad immunity.

It was now the next spring, five months after Cal had fled. A few days ago, the lawyer in Switzerland had received the grant of immunity. The government, the A.G.'s office, had readily agreed to it, but nothing moves quickly in Washington. The day before they sent the written grant of immunity, as a good faith gesture, Samantha had surrendered half of the funds.

With the fate of Cal now resolved she needed to finish her end of it. Samantha finished her salad then picked up her phone. Although it was almost ten o'clock in Geneva, she knew the lawyer would be expecting her call. Before she started dialing, Samantha quietly said, "Sorry, Daddy. I warned you not to be so greedy. You should have done what I did. Settle for a hundred million."

The rest of Cal's theft would be back in the U.S. the next day. Samantha Simpson would buy a presidential pardon two years later for a paltry five million. Two months after that she would move into her small mansion on Maui.

SIXTY-THREE

"Foster County Sheriff," Deputy Todd Lester said, answering the phone.

"Good morning," he heard an authoritative voice say. "My name is Dan Stone and I'm the Chief of Police in Michigan City, Indiana. I wonder if I might have a word with Sheriff Goode."

"Sure thing, Chief," Lester replied. "I know he's here, but I'm not sure he's in his office. Give me a minute and I'll track him down for you."

"You got it," Stone said.

Deputy Lester found Sheriff Goode in the breakroom chatting with two other deputies. He told the sheriff about the call from the chief of Michigan City.

"That's a little odd," Goode said as he got up to go to his office. "Did he say what it was about?"

"No, sir," Lester replied. "Just asked for you."

"This is Sheriff Goode," he said into the phone on his desk. "What can I do for you, Chief?" he asked. While he did this, he also pulled up the website for the Michigan City police. He found the chief's name and the phone number matched the caller ID.

"How's the fishing up there, Sheriff? Is the ice off the lakes?" Stone asked.

"Yeah, we're all set for the opener on Mother's Day," Goode answered wondering if this guy really called to ask about fishing.

"I've been up there a couple times. Beautiful country. But that's not why I called. I have some information for you on a hit and run homicide that happened in your town last July."

By the time Chief Stone finished telling the sheriff what he knew, Goode was scanning through an email attachment Stone had sent.

"You're sure about this?" Goode asked.

"Oh, yeah, no doubt about it. You'll see confessions in the report."

"I didn't mean to doubt you, Chief, but…"

"Don't give it another thought," Stone said. "I'd be surprised, too, if I were you. Here's my direct number," he continued as he read his phone number to Goode. "If you have any questions, feel free to give me a call."

"Well, yeah, I'll, ah, do that. And listen, thanks a lot. This answers some questions," Goode replied.

"No problem. You take care, Sheriff."

330

Goode spent the next forty minutes reading through the case file and reports Chief Stone had sent. During the course of this, he shook his head in wonder at least a dozen times. When he finished, he retrieved the copy from his printer and went to another office.

"You two don't seem too busy," Goode said to Chris Newkirk and Abby Bliss. "Are you getting itchy feet yet?" Goode said to Newkirk.

"Shut up, Sheriff. He doesn't need any ideas," Abby said.

During the winter, after having worked together for two years, the love bug had bitten both Newkirk and Abby. The wedding was set for mid-June.

"Who, me, nervous?" Newkirk said feigning a heart attack.

"Very funny, you too. I'm the one who should be nervous," Abby said. "You should thank your lucky stars."

"She has a point," Goode said sitting down next to their desks.

"She does indeed," Newkirk smiled.

Goode handed Abby the printed material, then told them both about the phone call. When he finished, the two investigators looked at each other with mildly surprised expressions.

"Isn't that interesting?" Abby asked.

"I've been at this long enough to not be too surprised about anything. But I'd have to say, after everything that happened, this will rank in my top ten," Newkirk replied.

"I was thinking," Goode said, "Since you're not doing much around here anyway, you want to go down to the Cities and deliver the news in person? This should be done with more than a phone call."

"Yeah, I agree," Newkirk said. "You want to run down there?"

"Yes, I do. There's this store at the Mall of America I want to check out," Abby replied.

"Thanks," Newkirk said to Goode. "Now I get to go mall shopping."

"Have fun," Goode laughed. "You should call ahead to make sure he'll be there."

"Please, dear God, let him be on vacation," Newkirk muttered.

He was not.

Thanks to the wonders of GPS technology, Newkirk had no trouble locating Marc's office. The two of them arrived fifteen minutes early, parked in the back lot and went up the back stairs.

Because of the interest and curiosity, they used the conference room for the meeting. Everyone in the office crowded in to hear what the investigators had to say. Newkirk's phone call to Marc had made it clear that they had important information about Zach Evans' death.

Newkirk and Abby were given seats at the head of the table while everyone else took the other chairs or brought their own. It was Abby, because she had read through the report on the drive down from Foster, who started off.

"We got a call from a Chief Stone with the Michigan City P.D. this morning. That's Indiana. He told us and sent us the case file, about who was behind the death of your friend, Zachary Evans," she began looking down the table at Marc, Maddy and Tony Carvelli.

"Do you remember a guy you defended a few years back for killing his wife?"

Marc took a little too long to remember so Abby filled in the blank. "A former judge by the name of…"

"Gordon Prentiss," Marc said. "What would Gordon Prentiss have to do with this? I didn't know he even knew Zach or why he would …"

It was then the light went on in Marc's head. Uncertain though, he kept quiet.

"Don't know if he did know Zach Evans. In fact, according to the confessions in the report," Abby continued. She held up two copies and slid them down the table to Marc, "it doesn't look like he did."

She paused, looked very seriously at Marc and said, "Evans was killed by mistake. You were the target," she said confirming what Marc had just realized.

The room almost exploded as everyone tried to ask questions.

"Stop!" Marc loudly said. "She'll get there. Go ahead, Abby."

"Apparently, he's a very bitter, angry guy. He maintains his innocence and blames you for losing his trial.

"While in prison—I guess he's doing his time at Indiana State Prison in Michigan City—he made friends with another inmate, a wiseguy wannabe who hung around bad asses in Boston. Prentiss, who still has access to money, had a hundred thousand dollars wired to an account this other guy, Jimmy Burke is his name, set up. Burke hired two guys he knew to do the job."

"The Tierneys," Carvelli said.

"Right," Newkirk replied.

"Anyway, they were following you for about a week. They were supposed to make it look like an accident but never got the chance. They followed you to Foster when you were representing Evans. The driver…"

"Little Mikey," Newkirk said.

"…isn't, or rather wasn't, the brightest bulb on the tree. He saw you guys and mistook Zach Evans for you."

"You're both about the same age, same size and hair color," Maddy said to Marc. "And, like she said, this guy wasn't the smart one. Sean O'Rourke told us that."

"That's right," Marc agreed.

"Prentiss and Burke have been on bad terms ever since. Prentiss wanted his money back and Burke had no way to do that. He had already paid the Tierney's."

"And they disappeared shortly after the hit and run," Carvelli said.

"Right," Newkirk replied. "The Michigan City police checked with the Boston P.D. Boston's snitches say the Tierneys are buried in the New Hampshire woods. They believe their demise is unrelated to your case. Ryan had been having a little fling with a mob boss's mistress. At least that's the rumor."

Abby said, "The acrimony between Prentiss and Burke came to a head a couple months ago. Burke stabbed Prentiss in the chest with a homemade knife, a shiv. Prentiss wasn't hurt too badly, but it caught the attention of the prison authorities and it all came out. Prentiss is going to be relocated and Burke got an extra thirteen years for conspiracy. Prentiss got another twenty for the death of Zach Evans," Abby concluded.

"To be served consecutively," Newkirk added.

"Do you understand what this means?" Connie asked Marc.

"Yeah, I do," Marc said, still a little shocked. "We set out to find out who killed Zach Evans. Instead, we unraveled a corruption scandal, insider trading crimes, money laundering, stock manipulation and murder conspiracy. And it wasn't Zach they were after at all. It was that arrogant, pompous ass Gordon Prentiss taking a shot at me. Unbelievable."

"What about the other victim. The female lawyer?" Carolyn asked.

"Lynn McDaniel," Carvelli said. "You didn't tell her?" he asked looking at Marc.

"I thought so," Marc said. "You know, I think you were out for some reason."

"Cal Simpson's thug, Aidan Walsh, admitted to me he killed her," Maddy said. "You guys got that, didn't you?" Maddy asked Abby.

"Yeah, we did," Abby agreed.

"Unbelievable," Marc said again.

Maddy leaned over, kissed him on the cheek then said, "It helped bring us together."

"Silver lining," Marc smiled.

"You two aren't going to be nauseating forever, are you?" Connie Mickelson asked.

Author's Note

There is no Foster County or Foster, Minnesota. I decided to use a fictitious setting for the lake home of Cal Simpson and subsequent events there. In fact, there are hundreds if not thousands of 'Foster, Minnesota' cities and counties. All of them containing resort areas with multiple lakes and recreation.

Since there is no Foster, Minnesota, there was no Jacob Foster holding the flag during the charge of the First Minnesota Volunteer Regiment. At least none that I know of. The story of Jacob is an accurate portrayal of flag bearers during the Civil War. It was an honor to be chosen to do so. In fact, soldiers of both sides fought for the right to carry the flag into battle. I must admit if I had been there I likely would have put some distance between the flag bearer and myself. These men, on both sides, were bullet magnets whose life expectancy, once the shooting started, could be measured in seconds.

The charge of the First Minnesota at Gettysburg is factual. Fewer than three hundred men, in a suicidal charge, threw themselves into a breach in the Union line and may have saved the nation. It was one of many instances during that battle and throughout the war of unfathomable courage. Men willing to sacrifice their lives for a cause greater than themselves. And we are raising a generation who need a puppy for comfort if they hear a bad word.

Finally, I must confess to entirely making up the street drug Roofie Express that I used to drug Brooke Hartley. Call it literary license.

Thank you for your patronage. I hope you enjoyed InsiderJustice.

Dennis Carstens

Email me at: dcarstens514@gmail.com

An excerpt from Exquisite Justice Marc Kadella Legal Mystery Courtroom Drama Series Book 8 is Below:

Exquisite Justice

ONE

Damone Watson, his ever-present Bible tucked securely under his left arm, stood in the doorway and surveilled the scene. Damone was in the entryway of the Minneapolis City Council meeting room. He was half an hour early for the meeting, and the room was already full. About two-thirds of the faces were black, and the rest were a combination of white and Hispanic. Almost every one of them was here to pay homage to Damone. He was here to receive a plaque of appreciation from the city council and a key to the city from the mayor.

Damone stood in the doorway for less than thirty seconds waiting for it to happen. Someone in the audience noticed him and a buzz went through the room. As it did, he went inside and began to humbly work the crowd. By this point, everyone was on their feet, applauding as he strolled around smiling, shaking hands, and acknowledging the adulation while making his way to the front row. Of course, three seats in the middle of the front row had been reserved for the evening's man of the hour and his two aides/bodyguards. Before taking his seat, Damone, holding the Bible in his left hand, pleasantly waved with his right.

Damone Watson was born forty-three years ago on the South side of Chicago. His father, Victor Watson, was a part-time construction worker and a full-time drunk. Victor's brother, Albert, was a business manager for a local union which allowed him to get no-show jobs for Victor which kept the family afloat. That is until Victor got into an argument with a man in a bar over some minor transgression. Within seconds, a push and a shove escalated into a one-sided gunfight that left Victor on the floor with a third eye in his forehead.

Damone, all of eleven-years-old at the time, was now the man of the house. His younger brother, Jeron, age nine, and two younger sisters, Jamella and Elesha, six-year-old twins, all looked up to their big-brother for support.

Their mother, Danielle, had barely an eighth-grade education. Minimal job skills and experience made her almost unemployable, except for the most menial of jobs; minimum wage in the hotels downtown doing maid and laundry service.

Uncle Albert did what he could until he was caught up in a union shakedown scam six months after Victor's death. Because all of his co-conspirators sang like canaries to the prosecution, Albert ended up the patsy. A ten-year sentence he would not survive in a federal prison ended his contributions to his nieces and nephews.

Before his twelfth birthday, Damone was a first-class dope slinger for a local street gang. The Parker Boy Crips, named for a local park, were a small collection of wannabe tough guys with a one-block turf to call their own. Little did they know that the young Damone was the best thing to happen to them.

By the time he was fourteen, helped by a borderline genius IQ, Damone had become the de facto gang leader. By the time he was twenty, his little gang had grown to over two hundred members and Damone Watson's income was in excess of a hundred thousand dollars a month. It would have been considerably more except Damone knew how to buy loyalty. He had also ruthlessly eliminated the real competition for the top spot. Damone had personally put seven people in the cemetery. It all changed shortly after his twenty-second birthday.

His eighth personal homicide became his undoing. The leader of a rival gang became a little too bold intruding on Damone's turf. Damone knew the young man, and he believed the two of them had a turf understanding. Instead, the rival decided to test Damone with a minor incursion across the border. Damone knew an example had to be made. Except, this time, there were witnesses including an undercover cop. To compound his carelessness—some would say arrogance—he failed to dispose of the gun. When he was arrested, the gun was found in the wall safe of Damone's luxury apartment.

During the trial, after pleading self-defense, his lawyer managed to convince the jury that his fear of the rival had some merit but not much. Instead of premeditated first-degree murder and a life sentence, Damone received a break. The jury came back with a second-degree verdict instead.

The judge, an older black man, thoroughly fed up with the South Chicago chaos, was clearly displeased with the verdict. During Damone's sentencing hearing, the judge spent a half-hour verbally hammering him. Unable to give Damone the life sentence the judge believed he so richly deserved, he gave him the maximum twenty years. The judge also put a lengthy letter in the file to let the parole board know how he felt. He wanted Damone to serve every minute of it. The letter worked. Despite the parole board having been convinced of Damone's conversion to Christianity while in prison, he did the full twenty.

Upon his release, he went back to Chicago for a short while before moving to Minneapolis. In the nine months Damone had lived there, the city had come to embrace him as a gifted community organizer and role model. Gang violence was down, two new first-class community centers were being built, school attendance in the black neighborhoods was up, and cocaine sales had practically dried up. Damone, while outwardly humble, inwardly was delighted to take full credit for all of it.

At precisely 7:00 P.M., the thirteen members of the city council and the mayor came into the room. As they filed in, every one of them looked at Damone, smiled and nodded their head at him. The thirteen city council members were made up of six whites; four women, two men and seven blacks; five women, two men. There were no Asians, Hispanics or Muslims. The council president was one of the white women, Patti Chenault. The mayor was a white man, Dexter Fogel.

For the next hour plus, each of the fourteen in turn, including the mayor who went last, took four to five minutes for a brief speech to lay accolades on the man of the hour. In reality, the show was for the cameras. There were local TV news cameras in back getting film for the 10:00 P.M. broadcasts. The politicians, being politicians, used the opportunity to make sure the city's residents knew they were all on the Damone Watson bank wagon.

And why not? Damone was their success story. A tall, attractive, intelligent, articulate black man, who was sacrificing his own life for social justice; a troubled young man from a broken home. A murdered father, a struggling mother trying her best to keep her family together on the mean streets of Chicago. What choice—the media loved to point out—did the young Damone have but to be drawn into a street gang?

Then, a near tragedy for him. A gunfight—many said it was self-defense—and another young black man was railroaded by the criminal justice system into an undeserved prison term. But instead of turning him even more bitter, angrier, more anti-social, Damone Watson found Jesus and has now dedicated himself to helping others. To lift children out of the grip of generational poverty was a wonderful story of redemption. The media and political class ate it up with a spoon.

There were only a few minor matters on the council's agenda following the paean to Damone. By 8:30, the assemblage was starting to thin out and by 9:15, the meeting was adjourned.

Damone and his bodyguards, along with a small group of admirers, took the tunnel under Fifth Street to go back to their car. They were parked in the ramp below the government center. Ever mindful of his image, Damone's transportation was a modest five-year-old Chevy Tahoe. Not the shiny, new Cadillac Escalade he would have preferred.

The two aides/bodyguards—Lewis Freeh and Monroe Ervin—were each six-foot-four and a solid two fifty to two sixty. And well-armed. When they reached the Tahoe, Lewis got in the driver's seat while Monroe opened the passenger side back door for Damone. Monroe quickly joined Lewis up front and a minute later they drove out onto Fourth Avenue. Monroe shifted around to look at his boss.

"I got a text during the meeting from one of Jalen's people," Monroe said. He was referring to Councilman Jalen Bryant. The text message came from his campaign manager, Kordell Glover.

"Now what?" an obviously irritated Damone replied.

"Same thing," Monroe said. "When can we meet?"

"You gonna endorse him?" Lewis asked while looking to Damone in the mirror.

"We'll see," Damone answered.

"You think he's serious about his big crusade?"

Damone heartily laughed and said, "Of course, he's a politician. They're all serious when running for office." Then Damone turned serious and said, "That's what I need to find out."

Damone had converted a small, run-down office building on Plymouth Avenue in North Minneapolis. It was a three story. On the first floor, it was converted into a place where neighborhood kids could hang out. There were two pool tables, three rooms with TV's and a hoops court next door.

The second floor was a set of offices for Damone's business. His office was twenty-feet deep and the entire width of the building. It was in the very back of the building with eight windows. The glass in all eight of them had been replaced with one-way glass. Damone could see out, but no one could see in. The office was paneled and furnished expensively enough to make most Fortune 500 CEOs envious.

To maintain his humble, modest image, he never met outsiders in his office. He had a conference room to use for that. It held an oval conference table with squared off ends on each end. There were eight comfortable yet relatively inexpensive leather and chrome armchairs around it. The only windows were the tinted exteriors and the interior walls were paneled with modest, walnut paneling. Nice, but hardly ostentatious. It served well his man of the people image.

The third-floor was his home. The entire five thousand square feet had been remodeled into one, two-bedroom, and three-bath luxury apartment, always secured by alarms and armed guards, mostly Lewis and Monroe.

For an hour and a half after arriving back at his office, Damone was on today's burner phone making calls. He never used a phone for more than one day. It was a touch inconvenient, but he was not paranoid; he was careful.

338

Shortly after 11:00 while he was sipping his Cognac, there was a knock on the door. Before he could respond, Lewis opened it and stepped aside for Damone's late-night guest.

Lewis closed the door behind her and took up his position guarding it again. Damone casually sipped his drink while the woman walked toward him. She reached the left-hand side of his huge, antique mahogany desk and stopped. So far, neither had spoken a word.

While he watched, the city council president, Mrs. Patti Chenault, pulled the zipper in the back of her dress down and let the dress fall to the floor. She stood before Damone dressed in a white lace, see-through bra, a white lace garter belt holding up mid-thigh, white silk stockings and high heeled spikes. For a woman pushing fifty, she pulled it off quite well. A twenty-year-old would get horned up as quickly as Damone did looking at her.

"Well, what do you think?" she asked with her best sultry voice.

"It's okay," Damone said with a shrug.

"Asshole," she said with a soft laugh.

She moved to him, and as he sat in the chair, she straddled his knees. While he ran his hands over her, she unbuckled his belt and opened his pants. She reached inside his underwear, smiled and said, "It's okay. Junior is ready to go."

"He's always like that," Damone bragged.

Patti stood up and pulled his pants and underwear down to his ankles. She moved up and this time, straddled his lap.

"Ahhh! Oh yeah," she purred. "That will do just fine."

TWO

"Are you sure you want to do this?" Maddy Rivers asked Marc Kadella.

They were in Marc's townhouse getting ready to start their day. Marc was becoming a successful criminal defense lawyer. He was in his early forties, a once divorced father of two young adult children. Eric, his twenty-year-old son, and Jessica, an eighteen-year-old daughter, were both in college.

Marc was also a solo practitioner and rented office space from another lawyer, Connie Mickelson. It was in the Reardon Building on Lake and Charles ten minutes from downtown Minneapolis. There was a total of four lawyers, including Connie, who shared the expense of three staff members. The third lawyer was Barry Cline, a litigator trying to do only business litigation. The fourth was another man several years older than Marc and Barry. He was Chris Grafton and had a thriving corporate practice primarily for small to mid-size businesses.

Their staff consisted of two legal assistants—Sandy Compton and Carolyn Lucas, whose husband was a St. Paul police detective, John. The final member of the merry little band was an outstanding paralegal, Jeff Modell.

Even though none of them were formally in business together, they were all good friends and helped each other without question. It was Carolyn, like a good top-sergeant, who ran the place and kept the wheels turning.

Maddy Rivers was a private investigator who originally came to work on cases for Marc with the recommendation of a PI friend of both of them, Tony Carvelli.

Before moving to Minnesota, Maddy had been a police officer with the Chicago P.D. A tall, statuesque beauty, on a foolish whim she had posed for Playboy magazine. The immaturity of most of the CPD had driven her out of Chicago.

Over the years, without even realizing it was happening, Marc and Maddy had grown close. Recently each of them had almost died. Marc was the target of a hit and run "accident." Maddy had been shot while they pursued that case and broke open a serious conspiracy involving stock manipulation, insider trading, political corruption, and murder.

Almost losing each other had caused the two of them to realize how much they meant to each other. Because of it, Marc and Maddy finally admitted how much they loved each other, and a deep romance had resulted.

"Yes," Marc replied to her question. "I need to do this," he continued while Maddy adjusted the knot in his tie.

"Why are you wearing a tie?" she asked.

"I don't know. A habit, I guess. Besides, it's always good to look like a lawyer if you're going to prison. I think it gives you a better chance to get out."

"Why? Because they don't want you contaminating the inmates?"

Marc paused then said, "That's a good point. I hadn't thought of that, but it could be the reason."

"Be careful," she said as she kissed him. Being almost as tall as Marc, she did not have to look up to him when she did this.

"Yes, Mom," he sullenly said.

"Hey, Bub," she said poking him in the chest with an index finger. "You started this…"

"Am I ever going to hear the end of that?"

"No! I'm going to enjoy holding it over your head. And, I'm going to worry about you. Get used to it. Don't you worry about me?"

Marc silently thought about the question. The honest answer was to say no because she was far more capable of taking care of herself than him. Plus, she carried a gun.

"Well?"

"Of course, I worry about you," he said.

"But you had to think about it?"

"No. But you can take care of… wait. I didn't mean…, oh god, I'm in trouble again."

"You're in a hole, babe. Stop digging," she laughed. "I have to go meet a new client. A business guy Tony tossed to me. And I need to stop at my place first."

She kissed him again and said, "I'll see you later. Give me a call and let me know how it went. This is a little weird."

Maddy turned to walk toward the front door. She looked back and said, "Love you. See you later."

Marc said, "Love you too. I'll call." Then under his breath, he said, "What did I get myself into?"

"I heard that!" she yelled as she opened the door.

When the door closed behind her, Marc quietly said to himself, "Great! That will give me something to look forward to tonight."

Marc turned onto the frontage road and drove past the sign that read Columbia Correctional Institution. He was arriving at a Wisconsin maximum-security prison in Portage, WI. Stopping for lunch at a Wendy's in Wisconsin Dells had pushed the drive time to a little more than four hours, perfectly timed for his one o'clock meeting.

He found a spot in the parking lot marked for visitors. As he walked toward the imposing structure, even though it was warm, early-summer weather, Marc felt a slight chill. Despite what certain big-mouth politicians liked to spread, even a so-called country club prison was still a prison. And a max-security was a scary place.

Marc was meeting a former client who had been transferred to this facility. He was here at the client's request, and Marc had made arrangements with the warden himself. Despite the presence of the warden to greet him—Marc had called ahead—he still had to go through the entire security screening process. At 1:10 the warden led Marc into the secured visitor's area.

As he entered, he immediately saw to his left, a row of booths. Each one was equipped with a telephone to talk to the inmate. There was bulletproof Plexiglas all the way to the ceiling. On the far end was an observation room with a corrections officer inside to observe and monitor, if allowed.

"Take whatever one you want," the warden said indicating the empty booths.

"How is he?" Marc asked.

"Health-wise he's fine. He's only been here a couple of months. According to the staff he seems to have settled right in. I let them know you're here. He'll be brought in any minute."

"Thanks, warden," Marc replied.

"You're a lawyer. Legally you can see him whenever you want," the warden shrugged. He pointed at the observation booth and continued. "Obviously we can't monitor your conversation. But he'll be watching. When you're done just wave to him to let him know, and someone will come and get you."

As the two men shook hands, the secured door in the inmates' area opened. A man Marc would not have recognized came in wearing blue prison dungarees. Despite the fact he was barely in his sixties, his hair and beard were snow white. He was sporting a full beard, and his hair was at least six inches longer, slicked back and three inches over his collar. He had also aged ten years, even though it was less than three years since Marc had last seen him.

Marc sat down in the booth he was standing next to and picked up the phone. The inmate did the same.

"Hello, Judge," Marc said. The gaunt, white-haired man he saw through the Plexiglas was former Hennepin County District Court Judge J. Gordon Prentiss III.

At one time Prentiss was an almost aristocratic member of Minnesota society. The son of an extremely well-connected lawyer, Gordon, the name he preferred, was the governor's selection to the U.S. Senate. A Minnesota senator had suddenly died, and Prentiss III was

342

headed toward the big time. Unfortunately, his wife was found lying on her bedroom floor with a knife in her chest. Almost on top of her, unconscious with his hand on the knife handle, was the would-be U.S. Senator. The cops took several photos before they brought him around. The photos, along with documented spousal abuse, cooked Prentiss' goose. Marc was his lawyer.

"I haven't heard anyone call me that for quite some time."

Marc and Judge Prentiss, while Prentiss was on the bench, had a long, acrimonious relationship. Most of the defense lawyers in Hennepin County also had a difficult time with then-Judge Prentiss. His attitude toward criminals was barely enough to let them have a trial before execution. At the time, to say Marc was stunned when Prentiss asked him to represent him would be putting it very mildly.

"What can I do for you, Gordon?"

"I just wanted to apologize to you, in person. And to tell you how terribly sorry I am about your friend," Prentiss said.

While doing his time in a prison in Indiana—it would be too risky to let a judge do prison time in his own state—Prentiss had become angry with Marc. After exhausting his state court appeals procedures, he hired a pair of thugs to murder Marc. This was done through a fellow inmate.

The two hitmen followed Marc to a small town in Minnesota. Marc and his friend, a client by the name of Zach Evans, were leaving the courthouse. The hit was attempted by running Marc down as he crossed the street. The driver of the van that tried it, no one's idea of a genius, hit and killed Zach instead. He did manage to hit Marc as well, but he survived.

A couple of months later, Prentiss and his inmate co-conspirator, had a falling out over the money Prentiss paid. The argument led to Prentiss being stabbed—a slight wound—that resulted in the entire story coming out. Additional time for Zach Evans' death was tacked onto both men's sentence. Enough extra time to ensure Gordon Prentiss was going to die in prison. They were also transferred to different prisons.

Marc sat silently for almost thirty seconds staring at the old man. Finally, he said, "What the hell got into you? Did you really think killing me would accomplish anything? And now my friend is dead..."

"I don't expect you to understand or forgive me. I was angry. I was innocent of my wife's death, and I needed to blame someone. I know it's not rational. I know it's not right, but these places can do things to you. That's not an excuse. It's just a fact.

"I admitted what I did, and I'll die in here. Or, maybe get out when I'm in my nineties. I just needed to say I'm sorry."

"Are you finding Jesus?" Marc asked.

Prentiss laughed a little and said, "You won't believe it, but I am. At least a little. It gives me a little solace. Not that it matters now, but I believe you know I was innocent of Catherine's death."

"You're right; it doesn't matter," Marc replied. "But you know what? I guess I do forgive you. Hanging onto that anger accomplishes nothing. And it won't bring my friend back."

"Thank you," Prentiss quietly said.

"You should know, I had occasion to meet one of the jurors. She told me it was the photo of you lying on the floor with the knife sticking out of Catherine's chest and your hand on it that did you end. She told me they couldn't get past it," Marc said.

"It was too prejudicial. It should have never been allowed into evidence," Prentiss said with obvious bitterness.

"Stop it. There isn't a judge out there, including you, that would not have allowed the jury to see it."

"Yes, I guess you're right," Prentiss agreed.

"Take care of yourself, Gordon."

While Marc was walking back toward his car, he thought about Catherine Prentiss' death. Gordon was absolutely, one hundred percent correct. He did not murder his wife. But he did drive her to suicide, and she brilliantly set him to take the fall for it.

THREE

Minnesota State Senator Jamal Halane, a very light-skinned, second-generation Somali, was having breakfast at his usual restaurant, the Guriga. Guriga in Somali means home. The Guriga is located on Washington Avenue near the Cedar/Riverside area of Minneapolis. It is in the heart of the largest Somali community and is a popular meeting place. This, of course, was very dear to the hearts of most Somalis. Being driven from their homeland by terrorists and landing in this country of promiscuity, drugs, and crime made many yearn for a return. The good senator was not one of them. He was quite at home with the American dream, especially the promiscuity part.

Halane had a reserved booth that he used daily whether or not the legislature was in session. Today, during the summer, it was not. He had been on the premises since 8:00 A.M., and it was now almost 10:00. Having finished his normal breakfast of Malawah—a sweet Somali pancake—he had stayed to greet constituents.

Every morning the restaurant would fill with those who would respectfully approach him. Halane had developed a politician's memory and amazed himself at the number of names he remembered. This would invariably impress the supplicants who would pass it on to friends and family. In the coming election, Halane would receive ninety percent of their votes. A solid constituency.

Halane looked toward the door and saw a small man come in. He was about Halane's age—fortyish—and dressed in traditional Muslim clerical garb. Halane checked his watch and smiled at the man's punctuality.

It took the man almost ten minutes to make his way to Halane's booth. The customers crowded around him to give and receive traditional Muslim greetings. His name was Imam Abdullah Sadia and he was the most respected Imam of the main Minneapolis Mosque.

"As-salamu alaykum," the Imam politely said to Halane as he sat down across from him. The standard 'peace be upon you' greeting among Muslims.

"Wa aykumn as-salam," Halane replied. 'And upon you, peace' was the reply.

A waiter appeared—no woman could wait on the Imam—with a cup of his favorite coffee. The Imam nodded and gave the man the same greeting then sipped the spiced French press brew.

While this took place, the booths in front and back of them emptied as did the nearby tables. It was well understood that these two community leaders demanded privacy.

"Are you meeting with our friend?" the Imam asked.

345

"Yes," Halane replied. "He will be here in about a half-hour."

"And?"

"All is proceeding on schedule."

"I have heard from our friends," the Imam said. "They are impatient. Grateful, but impatient."

Halane smiled and replied, "Allah's plans are long-range plans…"

"You are aware of how long Allah's plans are for?" the Imam chastised the senator. "Do not speak blasphemy."

"I meant no disrespect, Imam. I only meant these things will proceed as Allah wills them," Halane quickly, nervously replied.

"Of course."

"The young ones are doing their duty, even though they don't know it," Halane said.

"This accursed country fills the heads of our children with many temptations. Too many are lured by the trivialities of greed and luxury they believe they can have. They throw away Paradise for foolish pleasures here in the land of Satan."

Halane had no response to the Imams rant. If he said anything at all, he feared the Imam would throw it in his face. Halane had no idea how much this man, whom he considered a fanatic, knew about the senator's own wanderings from the path to Paradise.

Halane had heard this man's tirades about the land of Satan many times. The last thing he wanted was to trigger another one. Halane knew what really galled the Imam was a loss of control over people's lives. And their money. Fortunately, he saw the man he was meeting pull up at the curb in front of the restaurant early.

"He's here," Halane quietly said.

"Go and bring back good news."

"Insha Allah," Halane replied. God willing.

Senator Halane hurried out of the restaurant. He left no money for the bill, believing quite incorrectly the owner would be insulted. The owner of the Guriga Restaurant was not a particularly devout Muslim. He was simply adept at portraying himself as one. As to the good senator, he was glad he brought in customers willing to kiss the politician's ass, but despised Halane for being a cheap, petty phony.

When he reached the sidewalk, Halane ran, or at least moved with what passed for running for him, toward the vehicle. Years of soft living on other people's money had left the politician a chubby candidate for an early heart attack. He went around to the street-side backseat passenger door. His ego expected someone to open the door for him. Instead, when no one got out to open it, he opened it himself and climbed into the backseat of the Chevy Tahoe.

Halane closed the door behind himself and said, "As-salamu alaykum," while buckling his seatbelt.

"And peace be unto you, brother," Damone Watson replied in English. "How is the Imam this morning?"

"Impatient," Halane said as Lewis drove the Tahoe through the light traffic.

"Unfortunate, but that is your problem. These things take time," Damone said. "He will have his representative back in the state senate this fall," Damone confidentially said referring to Halane.

"Insha Allah," Halane said.

Damone laughed and said, "You can stop pretending you are a devout Muslim. We both know better."

"Are you sure we can speak freely in here?" Halane asked.

"Yes, it is checked for listening devices at least daily. And GPS location devices. Is your phone off?" Damone asked.

"I do not have it with me. I left it in my car."

For the next forty minutes, Lewis, with Monroe literally riding shotgun, drove around while the two men talked. The fall elections were only a few months off and campaigning was already in full swing. Halane was being challenged by a well-known black woman and his re-election was anything but certain. He was counting on Damone's support. Damone quietly put out the word through the black community. For solid business reasons and his attitude toward women, Damone was going to help the groveling fool sitting next to him.

"What do you think of Jalen Bryant? What do you think of the woman who is running, Carpenter?" Damone asked referring to the mayoral race in Minneapolis.

The fact that Damone was asking Halane his opinion about anything was a boost to Halane's ego. He threw his shoulders back, sat up straight and paused as if considering the question. After a few seconds, he said, "Jalen Bryant is a crusader, or at least claims to be. Carpenter is a lightweight fool. But she's a very appealing liberal which plays well with white, Minneapolis liberals."

"You don't think a black man such as Jalen would appeal to white liberals?" Damone asked.

"In Minneapolis, certainly. Jalen could defeat Carpenter," Halane replied.

"I agree," Damone said. "This will do, Lewis," Damone said to his driver.

Lewis pulled the Tahoe to the curb and stopped. Lewis watched the senator in his mirror, Monroe turned his head to look at him as did Damone.

"Thank you for your time, Senator. I will be in touch."

Halane nervously looked about the interior of the vehicle and said, "You want me to get out here? How will I get back?"

"I'm sure you'll find a way," Damone replied.

This time Lewis exited the car and opened Halane's door for him. Lewis stood patiently in the street waiting while the bought and paid for senator fumbled with his seatbelt before getting out. Lewis shut the door with a solid thump and without a word climbed back in, took his seat and drove off.

"I don't know which is worse," Halane muttered as he walked to the sidewalk. "Dealing with the fanatic Muslims or the arrogant blacks."

He reached inside his coat to retrieve his phone to call Uber. The empty pocket reminded him he had left it in his car. He cursed loudly drawing attention from a passerby, then started walking.

"He is an insufferable little man," Monroe said to Damone after Lewis started driving away.

'Yes," Damone said with a sigh, "but useful. I have it on good authority that his senate colleagues hold him in high regard. They're terrified of being labeled a racist, so he is eagerly accepted.

"Now," Damone continued, "Lewis, I want you to contact Jalen's campaign manager, Kordell Glover. Set up a meeting in our office for this evening. Helping elect a black mayor will offset our support of this dog, Halane."

"Yes, sir," Lewis replied.

"The more I think about it, the more ambivalent I become about getting his endorsement," Jalen Bryant said. He was in the passenger seat of his campaign manager's car on his way to meet Damone Watson. "What does he want, and can we really trust him?"

Kordell Glover was driving and laughed at his client's statement. "What, you mean that maybe all of this 'man of the people, rehabilitated gangbanger, drug dealing murderer' might not be as it seems?"

"I don't know," Jalen said. "I'm not sure what to make of him."

"We'll use him, get you in office and then we can decide whether or not to keep him around."

Jalen Bryant was a thirty-seven-year-old, married father of two children, an eight-year-old and a five-year-old, both boys. Unknown to everyone except his wife and Kordell was Jalen's true political philosophy. He was a closet law and order candidate who, unlike previous mayors and city council members leaned toward the police. Criminals needed to be taken off the streets and locked up. He was

348

secretly in favor of school choice. Children of all races, especially inner-city black children, deserved better schools and the opportunity to go to the same schools as the children of the white politicians. As bad as these beliefs were, his worst sin was the abortion statistics that showed the black community was being decimated by careless sexual behavior and irresponsibility.

"Come in," Damone said to his guests. Monroe had greeted Jalen and Kordell in the office parking lot and escorted them to Damone's second-floor conference room.

"Please," he continued after handshakes, "have a seat."

The three of them each took a chair at the table, and Damone started off.

"I'm sorry this took so long. I guess you're looking for an endorsement," he politely said with a pleasant smile while looking at Jalen.

"Well, yes," Jalen replied. "You seem to have a good deal of influence around the city. I believe your endorsement would be a big help."

"Absolutely! I'll do whatever I can to help you get elected. This city needs a strong, capable black man as its mayor."

The three of them continued for another hour. They discussed events Damone could help with and he promised fund-raising and other contributions he would make. When they finished, as Jalen and Kordell were leaving, Damone assured them his election was a foregone conclusion.

Kordell had driven less than a block from the meeting place when he said, "That was easy."

"A little too easy," Jalen replied. "We haven't received the real bill, yet."

"What, you mean you don't believe he is only interested in civic improvements?" Kordell asked with a touch of obvious sarcasm included.

"I don't know what to believe, but all this 'brother this and brother that' talk seems a little phony," Jalen said.

"It does, indeed," Kordell agreed.

18683308R00187

Printed in Great Britain
by Amazon